THE EXPATS

CHRIS PAVONE

THE EXPATS

A NOVEL

CROWN PUBLISHERS • NEW YORK

2012 Crown Publishers International Edition

Published by Crown Publishers, an imprint of the Crown Publishing Group, a division of Random House, Inc., New York.
www.crownpublishing.com

Simultaneously published in hardcover in the United States by Crown Publishers.

Library of Congress Cataloging-in-Publication Data
Pavone, Chris.
The expats : a novel / Chris Pavone.
p.   cm.
Summary: "An international spy thriller about a former CIA agent who moves with her family to Luxembourg where everything is suspicious and nothing is as it seems."—Provided by publisher.
1. Americans—Luxembourg—Fiction.   I. Title.
PS3616.A9566E97 2012
813'.6—dc23   2011046207

ISBN 978-0-307-98706-8

Printed in the United States of America

Book design by Elina D. Nudelman
Title page photography by Satoru Murata
Jacket design by Christopher Brand
Jacket photography: Kristina Hruska/Millennium Images, UK (woman); Walter Bibikow (Luxembourg); Jonathan Kantor (planes)

10 9 8 7 6 5 4 3 2 1

TO MY LITTLE EX-EXPATS, SAM AND ALEX

TRUTH IS BEAUTIFUL, WITHOUT DOUBT; BUT SO ARE LIES.

—Ralph Waldo Emerson

THE ONE CHARM OF MARRIAGE IS THAT IT MAKES A LIFE
OF DECEPTION ABSOLUTELY NECESSARY FOR BOTH PARTIES.

—Oscar Wilde

"Kate?"

Kate is staring through a plate-glass window filled with pillows and tablecloths and curtains, all in taupes and chocolates and moss greens, a palette that replaced the pastels of last week. The season changed, just like that.

She turns from the window, to this woman standing beside her on the narrow sliver of sidewalk in the rue Jacob. Who is this woman?

"Oh my God, Kate? Is that you?" The voice is familiar. But the voice is not enough.

Kate has forgotten what exactly she is halfheartedly looking for. It's something fabric. Curtains for the guest bath? Something frivolous.

She cinches the belt of her raincoat, a self-protective gesture. It rained earlier in the morning, on the way to school drop-off, mist snaking in from the Seine, the hard heels of her leather boots clicking on the wet cobblestones. She's still wearing her lightweight slicker, the folded *Herald-Tribune* poking out of her pocket, crossword puzzle completed at the café next to school where she eats breakfast most mornings, with other expat moms.

This woman is not one of them.

This woman is wearing sunglasses that cover half her forehead and most of her cheeks and the entire area of the eyes; there's no way to positively ID whoever is under all that black plastic and gold logos. Her short chestnut hair is pulled back severely against her scalp, pinned in place by a silk band. She is tall and fit, but full through the chest and hips; voluptuous. Her skin is glowing with a healthy, natural-looking tan, as if she spends a lot of time outdoors, playing tennis, or gardening. Not one of those extra-dark deep-fries that so many French women favor, tans generated by the ultraviolet radiation of fluorescent lamps in coffin-like booths.

This woman's clothes, while not actually jodhpurs and a show coat, are reminiscent of riding. Kate recognizes the plaid jacket from the window of a hideously expensive boutique nearby, a new shop that replaced a cherished bookstore, a swap that vocal locals claim signals the end of the Faubourg St-Germain they knew and loved. But the bookstore's esteem was mostly in the abstract and the shop usually empty, while the new boutique is habitually mobbed, not just with Texan housewives and Japanese businessmen and Russian thugs, paying in cash—neat, crisp piles of freshly laundered money—for stacks of shirts and scarves and handbags, but also with the rich local residents. There are no poor ones.

This woman? She is smiling, a mouth full of perfectly aligned, brilliantly white teeth. It's a familiar smile, paired with a familiar voice; but Kate still needs to see the eyes to confirm her worst suspicion.

There are brand-new cars from Southeast Asia that retail for less than this woman's plaid jacket. Kate herself is well-dressed, in the understated style preferred by women of her type. This woman is operating under a different set of principles.

This woman is American, but she speaks with no regional accent. She could be from anywhere. She could be anyone.

"It's me," this woman says, removing her sunglasses, finally.

Kate instinctively takes a step back, stumbling against the sooty gray stone at the base of the building. The hardware on her handbag clanks alarmingly against the window's glass.

Kate's mouth hangs open, soundless.

Her first thought is of the children, a full-fledged panic coming on quickly. The essence of parenthood: immediate panic on the children's behalf, always. This was the one part of the plan that Dexter never seriously considered: the compounded terror—the unconquerable anxiety—when there are children involved.

This woman was hiding behind sunglasses, and her hair is a new color in a new cut, and her skin tone is darker than it used to be, and she has put on ten pounds. She looks different. Even so, Kate is astounded that she didn't recognize her at first glance, from the first syllable. Kate knows it's because she didn't want to.

"Oh my God!" she manages to sputter out.

Kate's mind races, hurtling herself down the street and around a corner, through the heavy red door and the always-cool breezeway, under the portico that surrounds the courtyard and into the marble-floored lobby, up in the brass-caged elevator, into the cheery yellow foyer with the eighteenth-century drawing in the gilt frame.

This woman is holding her arms open, an invitation to a big American-style hug.

Rushing down the hallway to the far end, to the wood-paneled office with the rooftop-skimming views of the Eiffel Tower. Using the ornate brass key to open the bottom drawer of the antique desk.

And why not hug? They're old friends, after all. Sort of. If anyone is watching, it might look suspicious if these two people didn't hug. Or maybe it'd look suspicious if they did.

It hasn't taken long to find herself thinking that people are watching. And that they always have been, all the time. It was only a few months ago that Kate had finally been able to imagine she was living a totally surveillance-free life.

Then inside the desk drawer: the double-reinforced steel box.

"What a surprise," Kate says, which is both true and not.

Then inside the lockbox: the four passports with alternate identities for the family. And the thick bundle of cash doubled over with a rubber band, an assortment of large-denomination euros and British pounds and American dollars, new clean bills, her own version of laundered money.

"It's so nice to see you."

And wrapped in a light blue chamois cloth, the Beretta 92FS she bought from that Scottish pimp in Amsterdam.

PART I

1

TWO YEARS EARLIER, WASHINGTON, D.C.

"Luxembourg?"

"Yes."

*"Lux*embourg?"

"That's right."

Katherine didn't know how to react to this. So she decided on the default response, deflection via ignorance. "Where is Luxembourg?" Even as she was asking this disingenuous question, she regretted the decision.

"It's in Western Europe."

"I mean, is it in Germany?" She turned her eyes away from Dexter, from the shame at the hole she was digging for herself. "Switzerland?"

Dexter looked at her blankly, clearly trying—hard—to not say something wrong. "It's its own country," he said. "It's a grand duchy," he added, irrelevantly.

"A grand duchy."

He nodded.

"You're kidding."

"It's the only grand duchy in the world."

She didn't say anything.

"It's bordered by France, Belgium, and Germany," Dexter continued, unbidden. "They surround it."

"No." Shaking her head. "There's no such country. You're talking about—I don't know—*Al*sace. Or Lorraine. You're talking about Alsace-Lorraine."

"Those places are in France. Luxembourg is a different, um, nation."

"And what makes it a grand duchy?"

"It's ruled by a grand duke."

7

She redirected her attention to the cutting board, the onion in mid-mince, sitting atop the counter that was threatening to separate entirely from the warped cabinetry beneath it, pulled apart by some primordial force—water, or gravity, or both—and thereby pushing the kitchen over the brink from acceptably shabby to unacceptably crappy plus unhygienic and outright dangerous, finally forcing their hand on the full kitchen renovation that even after editing out every unnecessary upgrade and aesthetic indulgence would still cost forty thousand dollars that they didn't have.

As a stopgap, Dexter had secured C-clamps to the corners of the counter, to prevent the slab of wood from sliding off the cabinetry. That was two months ago. In the meantime, these clumsily positioned clamps had caused Katherine to shatter a wineglass and, a week later, while slicing a mango, to bang her hand into a clamp, causing her knife to slip, the blade sliding silently into the meat of her left palm, bathing the mango and cutting board in blood. She'd stood at the sink, a dishrag pressed to her wound, blood dripping onto the ratty floor mat, spreading through the cotton fibers in the same pattern as that day in the Waldorf, when she should've looked away, but didn't.

"And what's a grand duke?" She wiped the onion-tears from her eye.

"The guy in charge of a grand duchy."

"You're making this up."

"I'm not." Dexter was wearing a very small smile, as if he might indeed be pulling her leg. But no, this smile was too small for that; this was the smile of Dexter pretending to pull a leg, while being dead serious. A feint of a fake smile.

"Okay," she said, "I'll bite: *why* would we move to Luxembourg?"

"To make a lot of money, and travel around Europe all the time." And there it was, the full, unrestrained smile. "Just like we always dreamed." The open look of a man who harbored no secrets, and didn't admit the possibility that other people did. This was what Katherine valued above all else in her husband.

"You're going to make a lot of money? In Luxembourg?"

"Yes."

"How?"

"They have a shortage of great-looking men. So they're going to pay me a bucket-load for being incredibly handsome and staggeringly sexy."

This was their joke; had been their joke for a decade. Dexter was neither notably good-looking nor particularly sexy. He was a classic computer nerd, gangly and awkward. He was not in reality bad-looking; his features were plain, an unremarkable amalgam of sandy hair and pointy chin and apple cheeks and hazel eyes. With the aid of a decent haircut and media training and possibly psychotherapy, he could become downright handsome. But he projected earnestness and intelligence, not physicality or sexuality.

This was what had originally appealed to Katherine: a man who was completely un-ironic, un-arch, un-bored, un-cool, un-studied. Dexter was straightforward, readable, dependable, and nice. The men in her professional world were manipulative, vain, ruthless, and selfish. Dexter was her antidote. A steady, unself-assuming, unfailingly honest, and plain-looking man.

He had long ago resigned himself to his generic looks and paucity of cool. So he emphasized his nerdiness, in the standard fashion: plastic glasses, frumpy and seemingly unchosen rumpled clothes, bed-heady hair. And he joked about his looks. "I'll stand around in public places," he continued. "Sometimes, when I get tired, I think I might sit. And just, y'know, *be* handsome." He chortled, appreciating his own wit. "Luxembourg is the private-banking capital of the world."

"And?"

"I just got offered a lucrative contract from one of those private banks."

"How lucrative?"

"Three hundred thousand euros per year. Nearly a half-million dollars, at today's exchange. Plus living expenses. Plus bonuses. The total could end up as high as maybe three-quarters of a million dollars."

This was certainly a lot of money. More than she'd imagined Dexter would ever earn. Although he had been involved with the web since pretty much the beginning, he'd never had the drive or vision to get rich. He'd sat idly by, for the most part, while his friends and colleagues raised capital and took risks, went bankrupt or had IPOs, ended up flying around on private jets. But not Dexter.

"And down the line," he continued, "who knows? *Plus*"—holding out his hands, telegraphing his coup de grâce—"I won't even need to work that much." Both of them had at one time been ambitious. But after ten years together and five with children, only Dexter sustained any modicum of ambition. And most of what remained was to work less.

Or so she'd thought. Now apparently he also aspired to get rich. In Europe.

CHRIS PAVONE

"How do you know?" she asked.

"I know the size of the operation, its complexity, the type of trans-actions. Their security needs are not as intense as what I deal with now. Plus they're Europeans. Everyone knows Europeans don't work that hard."

Dexter had never gotten rich, but he made decent money. And Kather-ine herself had risen steadily up the pay grades. Together they'd earned a quarter-million dollars last year. But with the mortgage, and the never-ending large-scale repairs to the small old house on the so-called emerging fringes of the supposedly rejuvenated Columbia Heights, and the private school—downtown D.C. was dicey, public-school-wise—and the two cars, they never had any money. What they had were golden handcuffs. But no, not golden: their handcuffs were bronze, at best; maybe aluminum. And their kitchen was falling apart.

"So we'll be loaded," Katherine said, "and we'll be able to travel everywhere, and you'll be with me and the boys? Or will you be away all the time?"

Over the previous two months Dexter had done an abnormal amount of travel; he was missing a lot of the family's life. So at that moment, his business travel was a sore point. He'd just returned from a few days in Spain, a last-minute trip that had required her to cancel social plans, which were few and far between, not to be canceled trivially. She didn't have much of a social life, nor an abundance of friends. But it was more than none.

At one time, it had been Katherine's business travel that was a seri-ous issue. But soon after Jake was born, she had cut out her own travel almost entirely, and scaled back her hours drastically. Even under this newish regimen, she still rarely managed to get home before seven. The real time with her children was on weekends, wedged between food shopping and housecleaning and tumbling classes and everything else.

"Not much," he said, inconclusively, nonspecifically. The evasion wasn't lost on her.

"To where?"

"London. Zurich. Maybe the Balkans. Probably once a month. Twice."

"The Balkans?"

"Sarajevo, maybe. Belgrade."

Katherine knew that Serbia was one of the last places Dexter would want to visit.

10

"The bank has interests there." He produced a half-shrug. "Anyway, travel won't be a defining part of the job. But living in Europe will be."

"Do you *like* Luxembourg?" she asked.

"I've been there only a couple times. I don't have that great a sense of the place."

"Do you have *any* sense? Because I obviously could've been wrong about what continent it's on." Once Katherine had begun this lie, she knew she'd have to play along with it fully. That was the secret to maintaining lies: not trying to hide them. It had always been disturbingly easy to lie to her husband.

"I know it's rich," Dexter said. "The highest per capita GDP in the world, some years."

"That can't be true," she said, even though she knew it was. "That has to be an oil-producing country. Maybe the Emirates, or Qatar, or Kuwait. Not someplace that I thought, until five minutes ago, was a state in Germany."

He shrugged.

"Okay. What else?"

"It's . . . um . . . it's *small*."

"How small?"

"A half-million people live in the entire country. The size is Rhode Island—ish. But Rhode Island is, I think, bigger. A little."

"And the city? There's a city, isn't there?"

"There's a capital. It's also called Luxembourg. Eighty thousand people live there."

"Eighty thousand? That's not a city. That's—I don't know—that's a *college* town."

"But it's a beautiful college town. In the middle of Europe. Where someone will be paying me a lot of money. So it's not a normal Amherst-style college town. And it's a college town where you won't need to have a job."

Katherine froze mid-mince, at the twist in the road of this plan that she'd anticipated ten minutes ago, as soon as he'd uttered the question "What would you think of moving to Luxembourg?" The twist that meant she'd have to quit her job, permanently. In that first flash of recognition, deep relief had washed over her, the relief of an unexpected solution to an intractable problem. She would *have* to quit. It was not her decision; she had no choice.

She had never admitted to her husband—had barely admitted to herself—that she wanted to quit. And now she would never have to admit it.

"So what *would* I do?" she asked. "In Luxembourg? Which by the way I'm still not convinced is real."

He smiled.

"You have to admit," she said, "it sounds made-up."

"You'll live the life of leisure."

"Be serious."

"I *am* serious. You'll learn to play tennis. Plan our travels. Set up a new house. Study languages. Blog."

"And when I get bored?"

"*If* you get bored? You can get a job."

"Doing what?"

"Washington isn't the only place in the world where people write position papers."

Katherine returned her eyes to her mangled onion, and resumed chopping, trying to sublimate the elephant that had just wandered into the conversation. "Touché."

"In fact," Dexter continued, "Luxembourg is one of the three capitals of the European Union, along with Brussels and Strasbourg." He was now an infomercial for the goddamned place. "I imagine there are lots of NGOs that could use a savvy American on their well-funded payrolls." Combined with a recruiting agent. One of those unfailingly cheery HR types with creases down the front of his khakis, shiny pennies in his loafers.

"So when would this happen?" Katherine pushed the deliberations away from herself, her prospects, her future. Hiding herself.

"Well." He sighed, too heavily, a bad actor who overestimated his abilities. "There's the catch."

He didn't continue. This was one of Dexter's few awful habits: making her ask him questions, instead of just providing the answers he knew she wanted. "*Well?*"

"As soon as possible," he admitted, as if under duress, cementing the bad reviews, the rotten-fruit throwing.

"Meaning what?"

"We'd be living there by the end of the month. And I'd probably need to go there once or twice by myself, sooner. Like Monday."

Katherine's mouth fell open. Not only was this coming out of nowhere, it was coming at top speed. Her mind was racing, trying to gauge how she could possibly quit on such a short timetable. It would be difficult. It would arouse suspicion.

"I know," Dexter said, "it's awfully quick. But money like this? It comes with sacrifices. And this sacrifice? It's not such a bad one: it's that we need to move to Europe asap. And look." He reached into his jacket pocket and unfolded a sheet of legal-sized paper, flattening it onto the counter. It appeared to be a spreadsheet, the title LUXEMBOURG BUDGET across the top.

"And the timing is actually *good*," Dexter continued, defensively, still not explaining why there was such a big rush. Katherine wouldn't understand the rush until much, much later. "Because it'll still be summer break, and we can make it to Luxembourg in time for the kids to start a new school at the beginning of the term."

"And the school would be . . . ?"

"English-language private school." Dexter had a quick, ready answer to everything. He'd made a spreadsheet, for crying out loud. What a romantic. "Paid for by the client."

"It's a good school?"

"I have to assume that the private-banking capital of the world, with the highest income on the planet, is going to have a decent school. Or two."

"You don't have to be sarcastic about it. I'm just asking some marginal questions about the education of our children, and where we'd live. You know, *small* matters."

"Sorry."

Katherine let Dexter suffer her anger for a few seconds before picking up again. "We would live in Luxembourg for how long?"

"The contract would be for one year. Renewable for another, at an increase."

She scanned the spreadsheet, found the bottom line, a net savings of nearly two hundred thousand a year—euros? Dollars? Whatever. "Then what?" she asked, warming to that bottom line. She'd long ago reconciled herself to being broke, forever. But now it was looking like forever was, after all, finite.

"Who knows."

"That's a pretty lame answer."

He walked around the deteriorating kitchen counter and put his arms around her, from behind, changing the whole tenor of the conversation. "This is it, Kat," he said, his breath hot against her skin. "It's different from how we'd imagined it, but this is it."

This was, in fact, exactly what they'd dreamt: starting a new life abroad. They both felt like they'd missed out on important experiences, both encumbered by circumstances that were exclusive with carefree youth. Now in their late thirties, they still yearned for what they'd missed; still thought it was possible. Or never allowed that it was impossible.

"We can do this," he said softly, into her neck.

She lay down her knife. A farewell to arms. Not her first.

They'd discussed this seriously, late at night, after wine. Or as seriously as they could, late, tipsy. They'd agreed that although they had no idea if it would be difficult to arrive in another country, it would definitely be easy to leave Washington.

"But Luxembourg?" she asked. The foreign lands they'd imagined were places like Provence or Umbria, London or Paris, maybe Prague or Budapest or even Istanbul. Romantic places; places where they—places where everyone—wanted to go. Luxembourg was not on this list, not on anyone's list. Nobody dreams of living in Luxembourg.

"Do you happen to know," she asked, "what language they speak in Luxembourg?"

"It's called Luxembourgeois. It's a Germanic dialect, with French tossed in."

"That can't be true."

He kissed her neck. "It is. But they also speak regular German, plus French, and English. It's a very international place. No one's going to have to learn Luxembourgeois."

"Spanish is my language. I took one year of French. But I speak Spanish."

"Don't worry. Language won't be a problem."

He kissed her again, running his hand down her stomach, down below the waistline of her skirt, which he began to gather up in fistfuls. The children were on a play date.

"Trust me."

2

Katherine had seen them many times, at international airports, with their mountains of cheap luggage, their faces merging worry with bewilderment with exhaustion, their children slumped, fathers clutching handfuls of red or green passports that set them apart from blue-passported Americans.

They were immigrants, immigrating.

She'd seen them departing from the Mexico City airport after a bus from Morelia or Puebla, or air transfers from Quito or Guatemala City. She'd seen them in Paris, coming up from Dakar and Cairo and Kinshasa. She'd seen them in Managua and Port-au-Prince, Caracas and Bogotá. Everywhere in the world she'd gone, she'd seen them, departing.

And she'd seen them arriving, in New York and Los Angeles and Atlanta and Washington, at the other ends of their long-haul travels, exhausted, yet not even close to finished with their epic journeys.

Now she was one of them.

Now this was her, curbside at the airport in Frankfurt-am-Main. Behind her was a pile of eight oversized mismatched suitcases. She'd seen such gigantic suitcases before in her life, and had thought, Who in their right mind would ever buy such unmanageable, hideous luggage? Now she knows the answer: someone who needs to pack absolutely everything, all at once.

Strewn around her eight ugly person-sized suitcases were four carry-on bags and a purse and two computer bags and two little-child knapsacks, and, on low-lying outcroppings, jackets and teddy bears and a ziplock filled with granola bars and fruit, both fresh and dried, plus brown M&M's; all the more popular colors had been eaten before Nova Scotia.

This was her, clutching her family's blue passports, distinct from the Germans' burgundy, standing out not just because of the vinyl colors, but also because locals don't sit around on piles of hideous luggage, clutching passports.

This was her, not understanding what anyone was saying, the language incomprehensible. After a seven-hour flight that allowed two hours of sleep, baggy-eyed and spent and hungry and nauseated and excited and fearful.

This was her: an immigrant, immigrating.

◆ ◆ ◆

SHE'D BEGUN BY reconciling herself to taking Dexter's family name. She'd acknowledged that she no longer needed her maiden name, her professional name. So she'd marched over to the District of Columbia's municipal office and filled out the forms and handed over the money order. She'd ordered a new driver's license and rush-service passport.

She'd told herself that it would be easier to navigate bureaucracies, to live in a Catholic country, if the husband and wife shared the same name. She was already giving up the rest of her identity—the web of outward appearances that veiled the more complex truths beneath—and a name was, she reasoned, merely incremental.

So she was already someone she'd never before been: Katherine Moore. She would call herself Kate. Friendly, easygoing Kate. Instead of severe, serious Katherine. This name had a nice ring to it; Kate Moore was someone who knew how to have a good time in Europe.

For a few days she'd auditioned Katie Moore, in her mind, but concluded that Katie Moore sounded like a children's book character, or a cheerleader.

Kate Moore had orchestrated the move. She had frozen or canceled or address-changed dozens of accounts. She had bought the ugly luggage. She had sorted their belongings into the requisite three categories—checked baggage, air-freight, sea-freight. She had filled out shipping forms, insurance forms, formality forms.

And she had managed to extract herself from her job. It had not been easy, nor quick. But when the exit interviews and bureaucratic hurdles had finally been cleared, she'd endured a farewell round of drinks at her boss's house on Capitol Hill. Although she'd never quit a job in her adult life, she'd been to a few other send-offs over the years. At first, she'd been disappointed that it hadn't occurred at some Irish pub, with everyone drinking excessively around a bar-sized pool table, like in the movies. But of course the people from her office couldn't congregate in a bar, drinking. So they'd sipped bottles of beer on the ground floor of Joe's brick town house, which Kate was partially relieved and partially disappointed to discover was not noticeably larger, nor in much better condition, than her own.

She raised her glass with her colleagues, and two days later left the continent.

This, she told herself again, is my chance to reinvent myself. As someone who's not making a half-assed effort at an ill-considered career; not making an unenergetic, ad hoc stab at parenting; not living in an uncomfortably dilapidated house in a crappy, unneighborly neighborhood within a bitter, competitive city—a place she chose, for all intents and purposes, when she shipped off to her freshman year at college, and never left. She'd stayed in Washington, stayed in her career, because one thing led to another. She hadn't made her life happen; it had happened to her.

The German driver turned up the music, synthesizer-heavy pop from the eighties. "New Wave!" he exclaimed. "I love it!" He was drumming his fingers violently against the wheel, tapping his foot on the clutch, blinking madly, at nine A.M. Amphetamines?

Kate turned away from this maniac and watched the pastoral German countryside roll past, gentle hills and dense forests and tight little clusters of stone houses, huddled together, as if against the cold, arranged into tiny villages surrounded by vast cow fields.

She will reboot herself. Relaunch. She will become, at last, a woman who is not constantly lying to her husband about what she really does, and who she really is.

✦ ✦ ✦

"HI," KATE HAD said, walking into Joe's office first thing in the morning. This one syllable was the full extent of her preamble. "I'm sorry to have to tell you that I'm resigning."

Joe looked up from a report, grayish pages output from a dot-matrix printer that probably sat on a Soviet-made metal desk somewhere down in Central America.

"My husband got a job offer in Europe. In Luxembourg."

Joe raised an eyebrow.

"And I thought, we might as well." This explanation was a gross simplification, but it had the benefit of being honest. Kate was resolved to complete honesty, in this process. Except for one subject, should it arise. She was pretty sure it would, eventually.

Joe shut the folder, a heavy blue cover adorned with a variety of stamps and signatures and initials. There was a metal clasp at the side. He closed it. "What type of job?"

"Dexter does electronic security, for banks."

Joe nodded.

"There are a lot of banks in Luxembourg," she added.

Joe gave a half-smile.

"He's going to work for one." Kate was surprised at the amount of regret she was feeling. With each passing second she was becoming increasingly convinced that she'd made the wrong decision, but was now honor-bound to follow it through.

"It's my time, Joe. I've been doing this for . . . I don't know . . ."

"A long time."

The regret was accompanied by shame, a convoluted type of shame at her own pride, her inability to reconsider a bad decision, once made.

"Yes. A long time. And honestly I'm bored. I've been kind of bored, for a while. And this is a great opportunity for Dexter. For us. To have an adventure."

"You haven't had enough adventure in your life?"

"As a family. A family adventure."

He nodded curtly.

"But really, this isn't about me. Almost not at all. This is about Dexter. About his career, and maybe making a little money, finally. And about us living a different type of life."

Joe opened his mouth slightly, small grayish teeth peeking out from under a bushy gray mustache that looked like it had been pasted onto his ashen face. For consistency, Joe also tended to wear gray suits. "Can you be talked out of this?"

For the preceding few days, while Dexter had been gathering more practical details, the answer would probably have been yes. Or at least maybe, possibly. Then in the middle of last night Kate had committed herself to making a final decision, had sat in bed and wrung her hands, bolt-upright at four A.M., agonizing. Trying to figure out what she wanted. She'd spent so much of her life—all of it, really—considering another question: what was it that she needed? But figuring out what she wanted was an entirely different challenge.

She came to the conclusion that what she wanted, now, began with quitting. Walking out of this office forever. Abandoning this career permanently. Starting an entirely new chapter—a whole new book—of her life, in which she was a different character. She didn't necessarily want to be a woman without any job, without any professional purpose; but she no longer wanted to be a woman with this job, this purpose.

So in the overcast light of a muggy August morning, the answer was "No, Joe. I'm sorry."

Joe smiled again, smaller and tighter; less of a smile, more of a grimace. His whole demeanor shifted, away from the midlevel bureaucrat he usually appeared to be, toward the pitiless warrior she knew he was. "Well then." He moved aside the blue folder, and replaced it with his laptop. "You understand there will be a lot of interviews?"

She nodded. Although quitting wasn't something people discussed, she was vaguely aware that it wouldn't be fast or simple. And she knew she'd never again set foot in her eight-by-eight office, never again walk into this building. Her personal material would all be messengered to her.

"And they'll start right now." Joe opened his computer. "Please"—he gestured with a flick of his hand, demanding and dismissive at once, his jaw tensed and his brow furrowed—"shut the door."

✦ ✦ ✦

THEY SET OFF from the hotel through the warren of narrow cobblestoned streets of the central district, dipping up and down along the natural contours of the medieval fortress-city. They walked past the monarch's palace, cafés with outdoor tables, a broad square with a farmers' market overflowing with produce and flowers.

Through the thin rubber soles of her shoes, Kate felt all the ridges and valleys of the hard stones underfoot. She had once spent a lot of her life walking uneven streets in the rough neighborhoods of unfamiliar cities; she'd once had the footwear for it. She'd even spent time walking these very same cobblestones, more than fifteen years earlier. She recognized the arcade that connected the two main squares, at the southern end of which she'd once paused, wondering if what she was walking into could be a dangerous trap. She'd been trailing that Algerian kid who, as it turned out, was on his way to do nothing more nefarious than buy a crepe.

That had been long ago, when she'd had younger feet. Now she'd be needing an entirely new collection of shoes, to go with her new everything else.

The children were marching dutifully in front of their parents, engrossed in a typically esoteric little-boy conversation, about Lego hair. Dexter took Kate's hand, here in the middle of town, in the liveliness of a European main square, people drinking and smoking, laughing and flirting. He tickled her palm with the tip of his forefinger, a clandestine invitation—a surreptitious promise—to something later, alone. Kate felt herself blush.

They settled at a brasserie table. In the middle of the crowded leafy square, a ten-piece band—teenagers—had just struck up a cacophony. The scene was reminiscent of the many Mexican cities where Kate had once loitered: the plaza ringed with cafés and tourist shops, all the generations of residents—from gurgling newborns through gossiping old ladies, clutching each other's arms—gathered around a bandstand, the amateurs playing local favorites, badly.

The long, far reach of European colonialism.

Kate had spent the most time in Oaxaca's *zócalo,* which was a half-mile east of her one-room apartment, next to the language school where she was taking private half-day advanced lessons, mastering dialects. She dressed herself as other women like her, in long linen skirts and peasant blouses, bandannas to tie up her hair, revealing a small—fake—butterfly tattoo at the base of her neck. She was blending in, hanging around cafés, drinking Negra Modelos, using a string bag to tote produce from the 20th of November market.

One night, a few tables were pushed together, with a German couple and a few Americans plus the requisite young Mexican men who were always hitting on the women—they threw a lot of darts in the dark, these types, but every once in a while hit a bull's-eye—when a good-looking, self-assured character asked if he could join them. Kate had seen him before, many times. She knew who he was; everyone did. His name was Lorenzo Romero.

Up close, he was more handsome than she'd expected from his pictures. When it became clear that he was there to talk to Kate, she could barely contain her excitement. Her breath came short and shallow, her palms began to sweat. She had a hard time concentrating on the jokes and innuendo of his repartee, but it didn't matter. She understood what was going on. She allowed her blouse to fall open. She touched his arm, for too long.

She took a final sip of beer, steeling her nerves. Then she leaned toward him. *"Cinqo minutos,"* she said, and inclined her head toward the cathedral, at the north end of the square. He nodded his under-standing, licked his lips, his eyes eager.

The walk across the plaza lasted forever. All the little kids and their parents had gone home, leaving just the young adults and the old people and the tourists in the square, a mix of cigar smoke and marijuana, slangy drunken English, and the cackling of grandmothers. Under the trees, away from the streetlamps, couples were shamelessly groping.

Kate couldn't believe she was actually doing this. She waited impa-tiently on Independencia, alongside the cathedral, in the shadows. He arrived, and came in for a kiss.

"No." She shook her head. *"No aquí."*

They walked silently toward El Llano, the park where there used to be a zoo, now a derelict space, scary for Kate by herself. But she wasn't. She smiled at Lorenzo, and walked into the darkness. He followed, a predator coming in for the kill.

She took a deep, deep breath. This was it, finally. She turned around a thick tree trunk under a heavy canopy of leaves, and waited for him to follow, slipping her hand into the inside pocket of her loose-fitting canvas jacket.

When he came around the tree trunk in the dark, she nuzzled the nozzle into his stomach and pulled the trigger twice before he had any idea what was happening. He fell limp to the ground. She fired once more, to the head, to be sure.

Lorenzo Romero was the first man she'd ever killed.

3

"Have you seen her?" the Italian asked. "The new American?"

Kate took a sip of her latte, and considered adding some sort of sweetener.

She was having a hard time remembering if this Italian woman was named Sonia or Sophia or, in a one-of-these-things-does-not-belong type of way, Marcella. The only name she was confident in was the elegant British woman, Claire, who'd chatted for fifteen minutes but then disappeared.

Plus it didn't occur to Kate that this question could be directed at her, because she herself was the new American.

As a way of underscoring her not-answering, Kate studiously looked around the items on the table, for coffee-sweetener options. There was a small ceramic container of white sugar cubes. There was a large glass pourer of brown sugar—or, rather, brown*ish* sugar; this didn't look like the stuff you use for baking brownies, which Kate had done exactly twice in her life, for school fund-raisers. There was a little steel pitcher of steamed milk, and a glass carafe of unsteamed.

Kate had once been very good at remembering names; she'd once religiously employed mnemonic aids. But she'd now been out of practice for years.

If only everyone could wear name tags, all the time.

There was a squat hard-plastic container of cardboard coasters featuring a baroque coat-of-arms, with a lion and pennants and maybe snakes and a sun and a crescent moon, and stripes, and a castle turret, plus gothic lettering that she couldn't make out because from where she sat it was upside down, this highly stylized thick black lettering. So she didn't even know what language it was that she was unable to read.

There was a steel napkin dispenser, the napkins themselves those little tri-folds that manage to be both flimsy and sturdy at the same time, which seems impossible, but is not. She'd recently found herself repeatedly wiping snot from Ben's little nose with these tri-folds, which were everywhere; the kid had a cold. And she hadn't come across those handy pocket packets of tissues that you can buy at virtually any genre of retailer in the States, in gas stations and convenience stores and supermarkets, in candy shops and newsstands and drugstores. The drugstores in Luxembourg apparently sold only drugs. If you asked for tissues—if you *could* ask for tissues—the stern-looking woman behind the counter would probably laugh at you. Or worse. They were very stern-looking, all the women behind all the counters.

There was a white iPhone and a black iPhone and a blue BlackBerry. A Blueberry. Kate herself hadn't yet gotten around to procuring a local cell, and despite earlier assurances to the contrary from the Mumbai customer representative of her service provider based in Colorado, there was no dialing code, no combination of digits, no change to network settings, no anything she could do that would enable her French-designed Taiwan-produced Virginia-procured mobile telephone to make or receive calls here, in Europe.

It had been simpler when there had been other people to handle the tech aspects of her life.

But what was apparently not on this table was artificial sweetener; there was never any artificial sweetener on any table.

"Artificial sweetener" was not something she had learned how to say *en français*. In her mind, Kate formed a French sentence that was translated from "Is there a thing to put in coffee like sugar but different?" She was trying to remember if the word for *sugar* was masculine or feminine; the difference would change her pronunciation of the word for *different*. Or would it? With which noun should that adjective agree?

Is *different* even an adjective?

But "Is there a thing to put in coffee like sugar but different?" was, Kate feared, simply too retarded-sounding, so what the hell did it matter if she pronounced the final consonant sounds of *different/differente*? It didn't.

There was, of course, an ashtray on the table.

"Kate?" The Italian was looking directly at her. "Have you seen her? The new *Americana*?"

Kate was stunned to discover that she was the one being addressed. "No."

"I believe that the new American woman does not have children, or at least none who attend our school, or she is not the person who is bringing the children to school or collecting them," piped up the Indian.

"Correct," said the other American at the table. Amber, maybe? Kelly? Something like that. "But she has a *hot* husband. The whole tall-dark-handsome thing. Right, Devi?"

The Indian tittered, her hand covering her mouth, actually blushing. "Oh I do not know anything about his handsomeness or lack thereof, I can tell you that for certain." Kate was impressed with how many words this woman used to communicate her ideas.

She couldn't help but wonder what these women had said about her and Dexter, two weeks ago, when they'd arrived for the first day of school. She looked around the strange café-bar in the large low-ceilinged room in the basement of the sports center. Upstairs, the children were taking tennis lessons from English-speaking Swedish coaches named Nils and Magnus. One was very tall and the other medium-tall; both could be accurately described as tall blond Swedish tennis coaches. Apparently, all the tennis coaches here were Swedish. Sweden was six hundred miles away.

They did this every Wednesday. Or they will do this every Wednesday. Or this was the second Wednesday they were doing this, with the plan that this is what they will do, on Wednesdays.

Maybe there already was a routine, but she just didn't recognize it yet.

"Kate I apologize if I already asked this so please forgive me if it seems rude but I cannot remember if I asked: for how long are you planning to live in Luxembourg?"

Kate looked at her Indian interlocutor, then at the other American, then the Italian.

"How long?" Kate asked herself for the hundredth time. "I have no idea."

◆ ◆ ◆

"HOW LONG WILL you live in Luxembourg?" Adam had asked.

Kate had been staring at herself in the mirror that covered a full wall of the windowless interrogation room—officially called a conference room, but everyone knew better—up on the sixth floor. She tucked a strand of wayward auburn hair behind her ear. Kate had always worn her hair short, as a matter of practicality, in fact a necessity when she'd traveled regularly. Even when she'd stopped going abroad, she was still a harried working mother, and short hair made sense. But it was generally difficult to schedule haircuts, so her hair was often at least a bit too long, and strands were always escaping. Like now.

Her cheeks looked flabby. Kate was tall and slender—*angular,* is how someone once put it, not particularly generously but undeniably accurately—and she wasn't one of those insane types who thought she was fat, or pretended to think it. The flab was just in her cheeks, an extra sag that meant she hadn't been eating well or exercising enough, but probably didn't amount to anything more than an excess pound, maybe two.

Plus the bags under her gray-green eyes were more noticeable today, under these bright fluorescent lights. She'd been sleeping badly—awfully—and last night had been particularly disastrous. Kate looked like crap.

She sighed. "I explained this already, two hours ago."

"Not to me," Adam said. "So please, explain it again."

Kate crossed her long legs, ankles knocking against each other. Her legs had always been one of her best physical assets. She'd often wished for fuller breasts, or more of an hourglass figure. But in the end, she had to admit that shapely legs were probably the most practical choice among the bizarre body forms that men found attractive. Big boobs were clearly a pain in the ass, whereas the ass itself, if not small, had a tendency to droop into something absolutely dreadful in women her age who exercised as infrequently as she, and didn't categorically deny themselves ice cream.

Kate had never seen this Adam character before, a squared-off ex-military type. But that was no surprise. Her company employed tens of thousands of people over the globe, with thousands in the D.C. area, scattered among who knows how many buildings. There would be a lot of people she'd never seen.

"My husband's contract is for one year. As I understand it, that's pretty common."

"And after one year?"

"We'll hope he gets renewed. That too is a common expat circumstance."

"And what if his contract isn't renewed?"

She looked over Adam's shoulder into the large two-way mirror, behind which, she knew, was an array of her superiors, watching her. "I don't know."

✦ ✦ ✦

"BOYS."

"But it was Jake. He—"

"Boys."

"Mommy: Ben took my—"

"Boys! Stop it! Right this second!"

Then there was silence in the car, the stillness of the morning after a tornado has torn through, big old trees uprooted, branches down, roof shingles blown away. Kate took a deep, deep breath, trying to calm herself, relaxing her death grip on the steering wheel. It was the bickering that she really couldn't stand.

"Mommy, I have a new best friend," Ben said, apropos of nothing, his voice light-filled and carefree. He didn't care that he'd just been yelled at, fifteen seconds earlier. He didn't hold a grudge against his mother.

"That's great! What's his name?"

"I don't know."

Of course not: little children know that it doesn't matter what you call a rose.

"At the roundabout, take the. Second. Exit. And enter. The motorway." The GPS device spoke to Kate in an upper-class English accent. Telling her what to do.

"Enter. The motorway," mimicked Jake, in the backseat. *"En*ter. The motor*way,"* with a different inflection. "Enter. The *motor*way. Mommy, what's a *motorway?"*

There was a time when Kate had studied maps; she used to love maps. She could drive anywhere, her internal compass never wavering, her memory of the turns and directions impeccable. But with this Julie Andrews–esque GPS leading her by the hand through every swerve and dip in the road, she was freed from using her brain, from making her own effort. This thing was like a calculator: faster and easier, but debilitating.

Kate had halfheartedly suggested that they could live without a GPS, but Dexter had been adamant. His sense of direction had never been good.

"A motorway is a highway," Kate said, in an extra-patient voice, trying to bury her outburst, to atone. The niceness of her little boys melted

Kate's heart, which in comparison seemed inhumanly cold. Her children made her ashamed of herself.

The low-hanging sun momentarily blinded her as she glanced to the southwest, at the oncoming traffic in the roundabout.

"Mommy, is this the motorway?"

"No. We'll be entering it, after the roundabout."

"Oh. Mommy, what's a roundabout?"

"A roundabout," she said, "is a traffic circle."

She hated roundabouts, which seemed like an open invitation to sideways collisions. Plus they were semi-anarchic. Plus she felt like she was constantly swinging her children out of their car seats, as well as dumping over the grocery bags in the trunk. *Plunk,* and there went all the vegetables, the cherry tomatoes rolling around, the apples getting bruised.

In Latin America, the roads had been abysmal, the driving habits lethal. But she'd never had her children in the backseat.

"Mommy, what's a traffic circle?"

They were everywhere, traffic circles, a new universal. Along with the window levers that were exactly the same, wherever she went. And the toilet flushes that were all built into the walls above the toilets. And the broad light switches, and the wrought-iron banisters, and the highly polished stone-tile floors. . . . Every fixture and finish seemed to have been granted to builders on an exclusive basis, monopolies by fiat.

"This is," she said, trying not to become exasperated with all the boy's questions. "This is a traffic circle, sweetie. And here in Luxembourg they call it a roundabout."

What do you *do* with children, all the time? In Washington, she'd had charge of the kids on weekends; preschools and the nanny had borne the brunt of the day-to-day child-care responsibilities. She'd wanted more time with the kids, then.

But now? Now it was every day after school, every evening, every night, every morning, and all weekend long. How was anyone supposed to amuse them, without spending her life lying on the floor, playing with Lego? Without the kids killing each other, or making an unbearable mess, or driving her crazy?

Now that she had what she'd wanted, she was having her doubts. Which had been her worst fear about this whole thing.

"Mommy, is this the motorway?"

"Yes, sweetie. This is the motorway."

The dashboard began to blink. The onboard computer regularly sent her messages in German, tremendously long words, sometimes blinking, that she struggled to ignore. It was just a rental; they hadn't yet tackled the task of buying a car.

"Mommy?"

"Yes, sweetie?"

"I need to poop."

She glanced at the GPS: two kilometers more. "We'll be home in a few minutes."

The motorway ended and she was on a street beside the rail yard, side-by-side idle high-speed trains, then past the station's clock tower, in the heart of the Gare district. Now she knew where she was going. She turned off the GPS, kicking out the crutch. The only way to learn.

✦ ✦ ✦

"YOUR HUSBAND WORKED there for four years before he joined the bank?" Adam hadn't looked up from his notepad, his pen poised.

"That's correct."

"He left one year before the IPO."

"Yes."

"That doesn't seem to be particularly, um, intelligent timing."

"Dexter has never been much of a financial strategist."

"Apparently not. So then at this bank. He did what, exactly?"

"He worked in systems security. His job was to figure out how people might try to breach the system, and prevent it."

"What system?"

"The accounts. He was protecting the accounts."

"The money."

"That's correct."

Adam looked dubious. Kate knew that he was—they all were—suspicious of Dexter and this move to Luxembourg. But Kate wasn't. She'd done her homework long ago, and Dexter was above suspicion. That's why she'd let herself marry him.

But of course they wouldn't know that. Of course they should be suspicious. Maybe even she should be suspicious too. But long ago she'd promised herself that she wouldn't be.

"Do you know much about this type of work?" Adam asked.

"Practically nothing."

Adam stared at her, waiting for more of an explanation. But she didn't particularly want to give one, not aloud. She didn't even want to spell it out for herself, in her mind. The fundamental truth was that she didn't

29

want to understand Dexter's world, because she didn't want him to understand hers. Quid pro quo.

Adam wasn't willing to take silence for an answer. "Why not?"

"As long as we didn't talk about his work, we wouldn't have to talk about mine."

"And now?"

Kate stared across the table at this man, this stranger, asking her these intimate details, questions she didn't even ask herself, answers she didn't want. "Now what?"

"Now that you're leaving us, will you tell him about your work?"

Kate takes a step forward, and raises her arms to this woman. They embrace, but it's guarded, cautious; maybe because they don't want to crush each other's obligatory scarves or perfectly arranged hair. Maybe not.

"It's so good to see you," the woman says, quietly and earnestly, into Kate's hair. "So good."

"And you," Kate says, just as quiet, less earnest. "You too."

As they break away, the woman leaves one hand on Kate's upper arm. The touch feels like genuine warmth. But it could be that she's preventing Kate from moving, pinning her in place with a grip that's soft but unyielding.

Not only is Kate imagining that people are watching, she's also doubting everything. Absolutely everything.

"Do you live here? In Paris?"

"Most of the year," Kate says.

"In this neighborhood?"

Kate happens to be looking in the direction of their apartment, just a few blocks away. "Not far" is what she says.

"And the rest of the year?"

"We spent this summer down in Italy. A rented villa."

"Italy? How wonderful. What part?"

"Southern."

"Amalfi Coast?"

"Thereabouts." Kate doesn't elaborate. "And you? Where do you live now?"

"Oh . . ." A small shrug. "Still not completely settled. Here and there." She smiles. Smirks, really.

"So"—Kate waves her arm at the little street, which is not exactly the Champs-Elysées or the boulevard St-Germain—"what brings you to this corner of Paris?"

"Shopping." The woman hefts a small bag, and Kate notices that she's wearing an engagement ring, a modest diamond, but no longer the gold wedding band that she used to wear. The disappearance of the band makes sense. But the appearance of the diamond is bewildering.

If there was one thing this woman enjoyed, it was indeed shopping, of the rue Jacob ilk: antiques, fabrics, furniture. Coffee-table books about antiques and fabric and furniture. But Kate had thought that was just an act.

It's impossible to know which parts of the woman, if any, were real.

"Of course," Kate says.

They stare at each other, smiles plastered.

"Listen, I'd love to catch up, y'know, fully. Is Dexter in town?"

Kate nods.

"Would it be possible to grab a drink tonight? Or dinner?"

"That'd be good," Kate says. "I'll have to check when Dexter can make it." As she's speaking, Kate realizes that the woman is going to press for an immediate phone call, so Kate preempts: "I can't ring him right now."

She rummages around in her bag for her phone, buying time while she thinks of a rational reason. "He's at the gym" is what she comes up with. Good enough, and possibly even true. Dexter either goes to the gym or plays tennis every day. His full-time job of managing investments is, at most, a half-time job. "So give me your number."

"You know what?" This woman cocks her head. "Why don't you give me yours?" She reaches into her purse and removes a leather notebook and a matching pen. Precious little items, bought at the same boutique as the coat. This woman showed up in Paris and spent a fortune a couple blocks from Kate's home. Can this be a coincidence?

"I can't seem to find my charger," the woman continues, "and I wouldn't want a dead phone to cause us to miss each other."

This is utter bullshit, and Kate almost laughs. But it's fair turnabout. It's tough to be angry with someone for lying while you yourself are also lying, for the same exact reasons. Kate rattles off her number, and the woman dutifully scribbles it down. Even though Kate knows full well that this woman doesn't need to write down any phone number to remember it.

Kate marvels at how many layers of disingenuousness are passing between them.

"I'll call by five, okay?"

"Wonderful." They trade another embrace, another pair of fake smiles.

The woman begins to walk away. Kate finds herself watching her rear, larger than it used to be; this had once been a skinny woman. Not that long ago.

Kate turns and heads in the opposite direction, away from home, for no reason other than to put distance between herself and this woman. She struggles not to look back, not to follow her. She knows she shouldn't. She knows she couldn't.

"Oh, Kate?" The woman is walking back toward Kate, in no rush.

"Yes?"

"Could you give Dexter a message, from me?" Still walking slowly, nearing Kate.

"Of course."

"Tell him," she says, now upon Kate, one step away, "the Colonel is dead."

4

"So," Kate said, looking up from the coloring books she was arranging on the table in front of the boys. Another family dinner in another mid-price restaurant, the same three-week-old solution to the challenges of settling into a new life in a new home on a new continent. "You've already been working, quite a lot."

Dexter raised his eyebrows, taken by surprise by the criticism—the complaint—in his wife's comment. "There are a lot of things that I needed to take care of immediately."

"And that's going to quiet down, now." A statement that Kate suspected was contrary to fact. But she wanted to make him refute it. Although their relationship had been good since the move, he hadn't been as present as she'd hoped.

"Not really."

"I thought you were going to be able to ease into this job. That you'd have time to help us get settled."

After three hours' worth of tours with a real-estate agent, they'd chosen a sprawling apartment in the city's old center. Rental furniture had arrived within days of their signing the lease, and then they moved from the hotel. Kate started unpacking their ugly giant suitcases and their rented pots and pans, towels and sheets. Their shipping container of belongings was still at least a month away from arriving.

Kate had expected Dexter to join her in the unpacking, but he hadn't. "You promised that I wouldn't have to do all this alone, Dexter."

He threw a noticeable glance at the children. "I *want* to do it with you. But I also need to work."

"Why right now? Why right away?"

"Because I had to set up a secure office immediately. I needed to install security systems. I needed to buy devices and hire electricians and carpenters, to check their work. I needed to get all this done immediately, because I also needed to start working on something important that's happening now."

"What, exactly? What's happening?"

"It's hard to explain."

"Can you try?"

He sighed. "Yes, I can try. But please, not tonight. Okay?"

Kate stared at him, not immediately answering, even though they both knew what she was going to answer, and that this silent pause was nothing more than her registration of protest. The longer she paused, the stronger the protest. "Okay," she said, after a couple seconds. Not too long; not that strident a protest. "But I want you to tell me, at least, who your client is."

He sighed again. "Katherine, I——"

"I told you: please call me Kate."

He glowered. *"Kate.* I explained this already. Everyone in this city works in banking. It wouldn't be good—it would be *bad*—if my client's competitors knew that they'd hired a security expert from the States to analyze their procedures."

"Why?"

"It's a sign of weakness, of insecurity. It's information that the competition could use against us, to lure clients away, by claiming we're not secure enough. It would even be bad if people who worked *at* my client knew."

"Okay, I get that. But why can't you tell *me*?"

"Because there's no upside to it, Kat. *Kate.* These bank names don't mean anything to you now. But sooner or later, you'll find that maybe your best friend's husband works for my client. And she might press you, maybe after a few drinks. 'C'mon, Kat, you can tell *me.*' Then you'd be in an uncomfortable position. For what?" He shook his head. "It's pointless."

"It's pointless? To be honest with your spouse?"

"No, sweetheart. It's pointless to tell you something whose sole meaning will be that you have to keep it a secret. From everyone. That's a pretty big downside. With no upside."

Secrets. What did Dexter know about keeping secrets? "So what do I tell people?"

"You tell them the truth: that the terms of my contract prohibit me from disclosing the name of my client."

"From your *wife*?"

"Nobody's going to care. This whole economy is based on secrecy."

"Still," she said, "it sounds awfully—I don't know—unmatrimonial." She marveled at her inability to resist accusing Dexter of her own transgressions.

"It'll be okay," he said. "Trust me."

❖ ❖ ❖

DEXTER DROVE THE rented Volvo around the embassy in the gentle drizzle, circumscribing the compound in a wide and bumpy circle—not really a circle, but an uneven five-sided polygon, a misshaped pentagon—looking for a parking space. They finally found a tight spot under a heavy chestnut tree, the ground beneath littered with leaves and shells. The Brits called these conkers. When they fell, they conked you on the head.

There were a half-dozen people milling around the security hut, waiting for guards to beckon, dispatch their belongings through an X-ray machine, escort them across the garden to a tiny waiting room in the consular building, and wait five, ten, fifteen minutes.

Kate had visited this embassy once before, years ago, and hadn't needed to wait.

They were summoned. Kate and Dexter entered a tiny room. One wall was dominated by a bulletproof window, with a uniformed man on the other side.

"Good morning," he said. "Passports please?"

They slipped their passports through a slot. He examined the documents, then his computer. For a minute, maybe two, there was nearly complete silence. Kate could hear a clock ticking on the other side of the glass. The man clicked his mouse, moved his cursor, tapped his keyboard. A couple times, he glanced at Kate and Dexter through the thick glass.

Kate had no reason to be nervous, but she was.

"So how can I help you this morning, Mr. and Mrs. Moore?"

"We moved here," Dexter said. "We arrived a few weeks ago."

"I see." The officer held Dexter's gaze steady.

"Is there a problem?" Dexter was staring back through the glass, trying to smile, but managing only something that suggested he might need the toilet.

"Does one of you have a job here, Mr. Moore?"

"I do."

Kate could feel her heartbeat racing. It's very easy to get very nervous when you're far from home and someone in uniform is in possession of your passport, on the other side of bulletproof glass.

The official glanced at Kate, met her eye. She hadn't yet graduated from that phase of her life when as a rule she'd been worried about her own secrets. When it would never occur to her that someone would be suspicious of her husband, instead of herself.

He turned back to Dexter. "Do you have a work permit?"

"Yes," Dexter said. "Yes I do."

"We don't have any record of it. Your work permit. But the Luxembourg government sends us copies. Of work permits newly issued to Americans."

Dexter folded his arms across his chest, but didn't say anything.

"When was it issued?"

"Excuse me?"

"Your work permit, Mr. Moore. When was it issued?"

"Um, I'm not sure . . . It was . . . recently."

The men stared at each other through the thick glass.

"There must be some mix-up," Dexter alleged.

"There must."

"Do you need a copy of it? My work permit?"

"We do."

Kate could feel the tension coming off Dexter, an electrical field.

"Then I'll come back," Dexter said. "With a copy. Do we both need to return?"

"No, Mr. Moore. Just you."

✦ ✦ ✦

"ONE LAST SUBJECT, Katherine."

She'd been staring at the tabletop, unburdening herself of the proprietary information in her brain. There would be more of this tomorrow, and the day after, and for who knows how long, as someone ran through her files and projects and personnel, revisiting the same details again and again. Making sure she wasn't lying.

"Is there anything further you want to add now, about your decision five years ago, to leave the field?"

She'd looked up at Adam, a challenge in his eye. She stifled a panic. A vision that she'd been unable to quash the night before, of being escorted to the parking lot, a windowless van supposedly on its way to another office but really to an airfield, a small private jet, accompanied by two burly guys on a nine-hour flight, deposited at the prison entrance in North Africa where she'd be beaten daily for the next month, until she died of internal bleeding without ever having seen her family again.

"No," she said. "I don't think so."

Adam dropped both hands from the table down to his thighs, in exactly the type of pose he'd adopt if he were preparing himself to take physical action.

✦ ✦ ✦

KATE SHOOK OUT the umbrella, left it on the welcome mat to dry. The message light was blinking on the telephone. First the children needed to be settled in front of the television, after finding appropriate pro-gramming in French. Groceries needed to be unpacked. Dinner needed to be started in the kitchen with the German appliances—the dozen options on her oven's dial included the likes of *Ober-Unterhitze, Inten-sivbacken,* and *Schnellaufheizen.* She loved the sound of *Intensivbacken,* so she used that setting for everything.

Then she dropped a glass bottle of peach nectar. It shattered on the stone floor, sending not only chunks and shards and slivers of glass everywhere, but also sprays and drips and puddles and pools of thick, sticky juice. This took her fifteen minutes to clean up, on hands and knees, with paper towels and sponges and the cheap upright vacuum cleaner that had come with the rented furnishings.

It was impossible to overstate the extent to which she hated what she was doing.

A half-hour passed before Kate got around to pushing the message button.

"Hi, it's me." Dexter. "Sorry, but I'm not going to make it home for dinner tonight." Again. This was a tiresome new development. "I have a six o'clock call, then an eight. I'll be home about nine thirty. I hope. Tell the boys I love them."

Erase.

"Hello, Kate, this is Karen from the AWCL." What the hell is the AWCL? "Just wanted to touch base, and to let you know that another American couple just arrived in town." Who cares? "Thought you should meet."

✦ ✦ ✦

"YOU'RE SURE?" ADAM had asked.

Kate had struggled to keep her breathing even.

This could be about that thing that happened in Barbados, which hadn't been entirely authorized. Or it could be about the missing file on the Salvadoran goons, which she hadn't had anything to do with. Or it could be nothing more complicated than that Joe didn't trust her, pure and simple.

But most likely it was about Torres. For the past five years, Kate had been convinced that Torres would come back to haunt her. To take revenge upon her.

Or it could be about nothing other than protocol.

"Yes," she said. "I'm sure."

Adam stared at her. She summoned the courage to stare back. Chicken, across a conference table. Five seconds, ten. A half-minute of silence.

He could wait forever. This is what he did for a living.

But so could she.

It wasn't Torres himself who haunted Kate. It was the unexpected woman. That innocent woman.

"Okay then," Adam finally said. He glanced at his watch, scrawled a note on his pad. "ID on the table."

Kate removed the lanyard from her neck, hesitated, then set it down.

Adam tore the paper from his pad. He stood, walked around the table to Kate, his hand extended. "This is where you go tomorrow morning, nine A.M."

Kate looked at the paper, still not understanding that this phase was over. Things always end more suddenly than expected.

The confrontation was not going to happen. Not today, not here. And if not today, and not here, then when? Where?

"Ask for Evan," he said.

Kate looked up at Adam, trying to contain her amazement that the subject of Torres was not going to arise. "How long will this take?" she asked, in order to have something to say, to shift the subject away from her absolute relief. It was still not too late to screw this up. It would never be too late.

"At least a couple days. I don't know how much more. You should set aside two full weeks, which is the amount of time that you'll be continuing to draw a salary. It won't take that long, but it's a useful way to frame your schedule. It is, of course, the normal timetable."

"Of course."

"So that's it." Adam smiled, extended his hand again, this time for a shake. "You are no longer an employee of the Central Intelligence Agency. Good luck, Katherine."

5

"I'm Julia," the woman said. "Pleased to meet you."

"And I'm Katherine. Kate." She took her seat in the caned café chair, and looked across the table at the new American, foisted upon her by the AWCL, which she now knew was the American Women's Club of Luxembourg, which furthermore she'd joined. It was apparently what you did, if you were an American woman, in Luxembourg.

"So how are you getting settled?" Kate asked.

She felt like a fraud for asking this question, which other women were always asking her. The question implied that the asker was already settled, that maybe she could offer advice, or help. Kate wasn't, and couldn't.

"Okay, I guess," Julia said. "But I don't know how to do *anything* here."

Kate nodded.

"Do you know how to get done the things you need to get done?"

"No." Kate shook her head. "But what I'm an expert in—what I *really* know how to do—is assemble crap from Ikea. There are no closets here."

"None!" Julia said. "You're right. These old buildings were built before closets."

"So I've spent the past month putting together bureaus and wardrobes. And lamps, too. Why is the electricity different from America's? Does that make *any* sense?"

"None. Doesn't your husband do that type of thing? Assembling furniture?"

"Never. What my husband does is work. All the time."

"Mine too."

They both stared into their wineglasses. The waiter arrived, and took their orders.

"So," Julia started again, "how long have you been here?"

"Four weeks."

"That's not very long."

"No. It isn't."

This was sort of hellish. Kate wanted to excuse herself, get up and walk away, disappear. This was one of the many aspects of expat life that she found herself ill-equipped for: making pointless small talk with strangers.

"I hear," Julia said, "you're from Washington? That must be exciting!"

And this? How tedious.

But Kate was determined to try. She needed friends, and a life, and this is how you acquired those things: by talking to strangers. Everyone was a stranger, all on equal footing in strangerhood. The defining signifiers in the place you were from—family, school, experiences—those things didn't matter here. Everyone started from the same scratch, and this was it. Sitting with a stranger, making small talk.

"Actually, I'm not *from* D.C.," Kate said. "I lived there for fifteen years. Where I'm from is Bridgeport, Connecticut. And you? Where are you from?"

The waiter delivered their first-course salads.

"Chicago. Have you ever been?"

"No," Kate admitted, mildly ashamed. This was something that Dexter had teased her about, and she'd played along, and it had become one of their inside-marriage jokes: that Kate hated Chicago so much she wouldn't step foot there. She even refused to be friends with anyone from Chicago.

"Pity," Julia said, glancing up from the task of dividing her goat-cheese toast in half—in fact, portioning her whole *salade composée* in half. "It's a nice city."

The truth was that Kate didn't hate Chicago, not at all. She'd simply never had an opportunity to go there.

"Maybe you'll visit when you move back," Julia said. "When are you planning to go home?"

"We're here open-ended."

"Us too."

"What does your husband do?" Kate asked.

"Something in finance I don't understand." Julia was staring at Kate. "And yours?"

"Ditto."

"They all do something in finance we don't understand, don't they?"

"It certainly seems that way."

This was what Luxembourg was for: making money, avoiding taxes.

"I sort of vaguely know what mine does," Julia admitted. "He trades currencies. But what the hell that actually means, I couldn't tell you. What about yours?"

"He's a systems security expert, specializing in transactional software for financial institutions." This is the line she'd internalized.

"Wow! That's very, um, specific. What does that mean he actually *does*?"

Kate shook her head. "Honestly, I don't have much of an idea."

What she knew was the single broad stroke that Dexter's job was to make it impossible—or as impossible as possible—for hackers to steal money during electronic transfers. This is what had somehow become Dexter's specialty, over the past decade, moving from Internet service provider to a bank to another bank, until about a year ago he'd struck out on his own as an independent consultant. Then Luxembourg.

"Where does he work?" Julia asked.

"He has office space on the boulevard Royal, but he's freelance."

"Who are his clients?"

Kate blushed. "I have no clue."

Julia giggled. Then Kate returned the laugh, which became hilarious to both of them, until Julia suddenly grimaced. "Oh my God," Julia said, flapping her hands as if attempting flight. "I just laughed wine through my nose. *Ahhhhh!*"

When their laughter subsided, Julia picked up, "And you? Are you working here?"

"Not in a paying job, no. I'm taking care of the kids, and the house." This was another sentence that Kate had uttered dozens of times. It still wasn't sitting well; she averted her eyes as she said it. "What about you?"

"I'm an interior designer. I *was* an interior designer. I don't think I'll be doing much of that here. Any of it."

Kate had never imagined she'd be going on blind lunch dates with women with ex-careers like decorators. "Why not?"

"You need to know *lots* of society people—those are your clients. Plus you need to know *all* the tradespeople—everyone who would do the work you need done—and all the shops, all the resources. I don't know anyone here, or anything. I *can't* be an interior designer in Luxembourg."

Kate closely examined this new American. Shoulder-length blond hair—almost certainly dyed, but a high-quality job—curled and feathered, conditioned and blown-out; this woman made a big effort. Blue eyes, a touch of mascara and shadow, but subtle, not too much of it. Pretty but not beautiful; attractive in a non-intimidating way. A shade taller than Kate, maybe five-nine, and skinny, narrow everywhere, the type of body that comes with no children. She was thirty-five. At least.

"How long you been married, Julia?"

"Four years."

Kate nodded.

"I know what you're thinking," Julia continued. "Married four years, mid-thirties . . . where are the kids? So to get it out of the way, I'll tell you now: I can't."

"Oh." American women, Kate had come to realize, were awfully forthcoming about their reproductive health. "I'm sorry."

"Me too. But that's life, isn't it? Throwing lemons at your skull."

"I guess."

"Anyway, our lemonade is we're planning to adopt. Since the biological clock isn't an issue, we decided we'd wait until forty came and went. So we could devote this decade of our lives to having fun, while Bill makes a fortune. *Then* settle down, have kids."

Kate was taken aback by this excessive garrulousness. People who were too outgoing made her suspicious. She couldn't help but presume that all the loud noise was created to hide quiet lies. And the more distinct a surface personality appeared, the more Kate was convinced that it was a veneer.

This Julia was setting off all Kate's alarm bells. Nevertheless, Kate had to admit there was something likeable about her. "Sounds like a great plan."

"Doesn't it?" Julia took another sip of her wine. "So what did you do back home?"

"Research for the government. Position papers. On international trade, development, that type of thing."

"That must've been interesting."

"Sometimes," Kate said. "Sometimes it just *sucked.*"

They both laughed again, sipped again, realized their glasses were nearly empty.

"Monsieur," Julia called to a passing waiter. *"Encore du vin, s'il vous plaît?"* Her French accent was abysmal. It was questionable to even call it French.

The waiter looked confused. Kate could see he was trying to puzzle out Julia's sentence through her wildly misshapen vowels. Then he finally understood. *"Oui madame."*

He returned with the bottle of Riesling.

"And you?" Julia asked. "More for you?"

"I shouldn't. Our main courses haven't even arrived yet." Julia had eaten exactly half her salad, then put down her fork. Kate was impressed with the everyday discipline of it.

"Don't be ridiculous. *Pour elle aussi,*" Julia said to the waiter.

When he was safely out of earshot, Kate said, "Your French is great."

"Thank you for lying, but no," Julia said, "it's not. I have a horrible accent. The curse of the Midwesterner." She didn't sound particularly Midwestern. But then again, the whole of America was having its accents leveled. In twenty years, everyone, everywhere, would sound the same. "But I've studied up on my vocabulary." Julia picked up her glass, aimed it at Kate. *"A ta santé,"* Julia said, and they clinked glasses. "And *à nouvelles amies.*"

Kate looked at this woman, her eyes twinkling from the wine, her skin flushed.

"To new friends," Kate agreed.

✦ ✦ ✦

KATE SQUINTED THROUGH the bright low sunshine at the sight of her husband, shuffling up the gravel path.

"What are you doing here?" she asked.

The family hadn't seen much of Dexter over the past week. And what little they'd seen was a distracted, distant man. Kate was glad he was here now. Practically thrilled, at such an unthrilling event.

"It's a slow day," Dexter said, leaning down to peck her on the lips. Kate had long struggled with the pointlessness of the perfunctory peck, but she could never bring herself to tell Dexter to cut it out. She knew she'd have a hard time articulating her antipathy, and was afraid she'd come off as unloving, despite her admittedly contrarian opinion that it was the perfunctory peck itself that was unloving. So she didn't say anything, and pecked right back.

"I figured I'd see what you and the kids do, after school."

He looked around the playground, which was anchored by a large pirate ship and a tall enclosed slide, similar to a water slide, without the water. Jake was somewhere inside that structure; Ben was sneaking around the side of the pirate ship, almost completely unhidden, failing to control his giggles.

A half-hour earlier, the boys had culminated a few days' worth of relentless bickering with Jake punching Ben, followed by Ben pulling Jake's hair, causing both boys to scream and cry. They needed time-outs, here in public. Kate had banished them to sitting against tree trunks, cross-legged on fallen leaves, out of sight of each other. They looked terrified there in the woods, and Kate felt awful about it, but it had been a successful time-out. They emerged truly repentant.

"This is pretty typical," Kate said. She was sitting at a metal café table with a cup of coffee and a bottle of water for when the children inevitably arrived announcing "I'm thirsty." Her French grammar was open to a page humiliatingly near the front cover.

Dexter watched the children stealthily moving, silent. "What are they doing?"

Kate tried not to wince as she mumbled, "Playing spies." She didn't want to explain this game she'd invented.

"Excuse me?"

"Spies," she said, louder. "They're playing spies. It's a game I made up."

He seemed to tense up, oddly. Then he forced a smile and asked, "How does it work?"

"Do you see the napkins sticking out of their back pockets?" She'd found another use for the flimsy tri-folds. She was going to write a book, *101 Uses for Flimsy Napkins*. "You get a point by snatching the napkin out of the other's pocket, which you have to do by sneaking up behind your opponent. You have to be patient, and careful, and deliberate."

Dexter looked around, smiling. "This doesn't seem so bad."

The sun was low in the southern sky, in what seemed like a winter angle, even though it was still September. A relatively warm day, the children running around in shirtsleeves. But that low sun augured something different. By sunset, Kate knew, the weather would change for the worse; it always did.

Before school pickup, she'd spent the day alone, attending to chores: laundry and its hanging from the drying rack, food shopping, bathroom cleaning. The bathrooms and kitchen were thoroughly streaked from minerals in the heavy water, which made the place reminiscent of an abandoned Antarctic station. She needed decalcifying solution, or bleach, maybe both. So she'd gone to the *hypermarché*—a store so much larger than a regular supermarket that it was called a hypermarket—only to realize that all the labels were in French or German, and this was exactly the type of vocabulary she hadn't learned in her pre-move immersion lessons, and would never learn here at her twice-weekly Berlitz class.

Kate went home to collect her pocket dictionary, and returned to the market, via a traffic jam caused by a few dozen tractors parked in the middle of the street: milk farmers, protesting something or other. Mad at the cows; mad cows. Or mad at taxes; that was more likely. Everyone everywhere was mad at taxes. Taxes needed publicists.

Start to finish, it took her two hours to buy a four-euro cleaning product.

She couldn't explain all that; couldn't complain. She was not in a position to complain about this life, not yet. Probably not ever. She'd wanted this, had expressed to her husband every confidence that she'd enjoy this. She couldn't whine.

"Yes," she said, "it's not so bad."

✦ ✦ ✦

KATE HAD BEEN an obvious candidate: she'd chosen to go to a D.C. college, which correlated with an interest in public service. She was studying not only political science but also Spanish, at a time when the most significant foreign threats were in Latin America, and the most crucial intelligence was from south of the border. Both her parents were dead, and she maintained no close relationships with other family members, or indeed with anyone. She even knew how to handle a gun: her father had been a hunter, and she'd fired her first bolt-action Remington when she was eleven.

She fit the profile perfectly. Her only drawback was that she wasn't especially patriotic. She'd felt betrayed by her country's abandonment of her parents, who were essentially left to die because they were poor. Capitalism was heartless. America's social safety net was woefully insufficient, and the results were inhumane, barbaric. After a dozen years of Republican hegemony, society was becoming more stratified, not less. Bill Clinton hadn't accomplished anything yet beyond battering the world with the word *hope*.

But it was easy to keep her misgivings to herself, just as she'd always kept everything to herself. She'd never written an angry letter to her senator, nor a vitriolic term paper. She'd never carried a picket sign in solidarity with a striking union, never marched in any protest. It was the early nineties. There wasn't much political activism to get sucked into against better—or at least cooler—judgment.

The spring of her junior year, Kate was invited to sherry with a professor of international relations, a lifelong academic who Kate eventually learned was also a spotter—a side gig of identifying students who might make good officers. A week later they had coffee in a campus cafeteria, and the professor asked her to a meeting in his office. A governmental outfit was recruiting interns, he'd claimed. They preferred graduate students, but they sometimes considered well-qualified undergrads.

Kate appeared to be perfect material to these recruiters, because she was. And in turn the CIA was perfect for Kate. There had been nothing in her life except vast stretches of disappointment interspersed with brief glimmers of potential. She needed something large to fill her immense emptiness, to corral her potential and focus it, somehow, into something. She was seduced by the romance of it; she was energized by the possibilities.

So she swallowed—with fingers crossed behind her back, lightly—the indoctrination. She accepted that she was playing an important role in a crucial mission against mortal enemies. It was certainly true that America, imperfect as it was, didn't suffer by comparison to Cuba or Nicaragua or Chile, much less to the tattered remnants of the Soviet Union or the lumbering behemoth of China or even the stagnating, ineffectual social democracies of Western Europe. The United States was the sole remaining superpower, and everyone wants to play for the Yankees. Or nearly everyone.

Kate was welcomed into the new family of the Directorate of Operations, tightly bound and all-encompassing, populated with people like her, smart driven people with questionable capacities for intimacy. She enjoyed her work, even though some aspects woke her in a cold sweat in the middle of the night. She flourished in the Clandestine Service.

Then she somehow managed to make room for Dexter. And before long for children. As Kate's life filled with this new family—this real family—the secrets did become a problem, a nagging discomfort, an arthritis of the psyche. She had to push aside her old life, her manufactured one, the one bound by sentiments that were not love. She needed the Company less and less. She needed her husband and her children more and more.

She began to sacrifice that old identity to live in her new one. It was the new life, after all, that everyone wanted.

6

"It's like freshman year of college, isn't it?"

Dexter spit out a mouthful of toothpaste froth. "What do you mean?"

Kate looked at her husband in the three-paneled mirror, each panel angled in a different direction, collecting scattered reflections and creating a fractured composite. Bathroom Cubism.

"You're meeting all these new people, trying to figure out who's going to be your friend, who's going to be your enemy, who's going to be the loser you run away from at parties." The toothbrush was dangling from the side of her mouth, and she shifted it. "Imagining where you'll hang out, where you'll buy coffee, where you'll do whatever. And everybody's in the same situation, basically: we're all finding our separate ways, together."

"That does sound like college," Dexter said. "But that's not my life. I spend my days staring at a screen, alone." He cupped a handful of water to wash away his toothpaste-foam; he was a neat and clean man, a considerate roommate. "Not chatting up new friends."

Kate too spit, rinsed.

"Do you know that today," Dexter continued, "I literally did not talk to anyone? Except to order my sandwich at a bakery. *Un petit pain jambon-fromage, merci.* That's what I said." He repeated the sentence, ticking off with his fingers. "Ten syllables. To a stranger."

Kate too was still friendless. She knew the names of people, but she wouldn't call any of them a legitimate friend. Now that Dexter had laid his superior loneliness on the table, though, she'd feel ridiculous to do the same. "I had lunch with a woman today," she said. "Julia. We kind of got set up, on a blind date."

Kate returned the tube of under-eye moisturizer to the cabinet, next to a purely decorative crystal bottle of perfume. The last time she'd worn a scent had been in college, a tiny bottle given by an aspiring boyfriend as a Valentine's present. But perfumes were habitually eschewed in her line of work; they were noticeable, identifiable, memorable, traceable. All the things you didn't want to be.

"Get this: she's from Chicago."

Dexter caught Kate's eye in the mirror. "Are you sure you can be friends with her, Kat?" He never passed up an opportunity with this joke, though this time he didn't seem to be taking his customary glee in it. The joke, like most of his kisses, had become perfunctory.

"I'll give it my best." She sniffed the perfume bottle—this one a Valentine's Day present from a husband. Maybe she'd start wearing this, now that she could. "But Dexter?"

"Mmm?"

"Could you please stop calling me Kat? Or Katherine? I want to be Kate, here."

"Sorry, I keep forgetting." He kissed her lips, minty clean. "It's going to take me some time to get used to my new wife."

But this kiss was not perfunctory. He dropped his hand to her waist, the elastic band of her underpants. "Chicago, huh?" He chuckled, then moved his lips to her neck, and his hand to her thigh.

Much later, Kate realized that Chicago should have been her first clue.

◆ ◆ ◆

WHY HAD SHE never admitted the truth to Dexter?

At the beginning of their relationship, obviously, it would have been ridiculous to tell him anything. It wouldn't have made any sense at least until they were married. But then?

She looked over at him, a book in his lap, as ever. Dexter was a voracious reader—technical magazines and banking journals and serious nonfiction and, bewilderingly, a type of quiet English mystery novel that Kate thought of as women's fiction. There was always a tall pile at his bedside, his only mess in an otherwise neat, orderly existence.

What was the thing that made her maintain this secret? After they were married, after they had kids? Even after she stopped being an operations officer?

It couldn't have been solely protocol, although protocol wasn't completely dismissible. Could it have been as simple as not wanting to admit that she'd been a liar for so very long? The longer she'd gone without admitting the truth, the worse it became when she contemplated the conversation. "Dexter," she'd say, "I have something to tell you." God, it would be horrible.

Also, she didn't want to admit to Dexter the things she'd done, the types of acts she'd been—still was—capable of. If she couldn't tell him the whole truth, she was loath to tell any of it. That seemed worse. And since the worst of it was that morning in New York, which was also the reason for the end of it all, her story wouldn't be complete—it wouldn't make sense—without explaining that event. And her story wouldn't be defensible with it.

Plus she had to admit that a small part of her secrecy was that she was holding something back, for herself. If she never told Dexter the truth, she was still reserving the right to return to her old life. To one day be a covert operative again. To be a person who could keep the largest secrets from everyone, including her husband, forever.

◆ ◆ ◆

KATE HAD REPORTED to the hotel suite in Penn Quarter at nine A.M., as ordered. She'd taken a seat in front of a yellow legal pad, a Bic pen, and a sympathetic-looking middle-aged man named Evan, who for the next eight hours patiently quizzed her on every operation she'd ever participated in, every asset she'd ever run, every loose end she could've left untied.

She'd been doing this for nearly three full days when Evan asked, "What about Sarajevo?" They'd already talked through anything she may have failed to get into her mission notes—locations of offices, names of attachés, descriptions of girlfriends. Then they'd moved on to lesser events. Her earliest training missions in Europe: making a drop in a converted palazzo near the Piazza Navona; an overture to a Basque nationalist in Bilbao; following a cash-mule through the cobblestoned streets and private banks of Luxembourg.

And now apparently they'd be discussing nonevents. "I've never been to Sarajevo," she answered.

"Not once?"

"No."

"But your husband has. Recently." Evan looked up from his own yellow pad, filled with scribbles and underlines, big X's and arrows. "Why?"

Nobody wants to admit to being ignorant of a spouse's comings and goings, habits and proclivities. Kate didn't want to talk about Dexter's trips abroad. She couldn't see how they were at all relevant to her career.

"I don't know," she said, trying to sound—trying to be—dismissive. "Work."

✦✦✦

MAIL STARTED TO arrive; the address change and mail forwarding had kicked in. Kate opened an envelope from the U.S. government, a check to compensate her for unused vacation; she'd need to send this slip of paper back across the ocean to deposit the dollars. The fully executed lease for their D.C. house, finally, which they unfortunately were renting for slightly less than their mortgage payment. Some junk mail: a suburban Virginia health-club pitch, a solicitation for a book club—did book clubs really still exist?

There had still not been any mail from Dexter's bank, from which she was hoping to learn his employer. But there probably shouldn't be: he was an independent contractor, not an employee. He had an office address where he'd receive business-to-business correspondence. She was mildly suspicious—who wouldn't be?—but reminded herself, once again, of her own private clause in their wedding vows: to never investigate her husband.

Because of course she'd investigated Dexter, before they were married. Exhaustively, and more than once. The first time had been right after they'd met, at the Dupont Circle farmers' market, both reaching across a box of produce from opposite sides. It was a beautiful summer morning, a friendly time of day; both of them were on natural endorphin highs from early-morning exercise—this was back when Dexter was a runner, and Kate biked regularly, a short-lived passion—so they were both uncharacteristically outgoing. They went for coffee at the bookstore up the street, laden with bags of fruits and vegetables, on their way to their apartments, which turned out to be just a few blocks apart. It was a wholesome meeting; almost too wholesome.

Kate wondered if it was a setup. She sat at her computer in the bay window on the top floor of the yellow-brick house, amid the muffled sounds of the newborn crying in the apartment downstairs. She logged onto the secure server and perused the various Dexter Moores of America until she identified the one who interested her. She followed the trail of his Social Security number across one database after another, college and the District's DMV and the Arkansas Department of Education, his father's police record—aggravated assault in Memphis—and his older brother's military history, killed in Bosnia.

After an hour, she was satisfied: this Dexter Moore was an upstanding citizen. She picked up the telephone and dialed, and asked him to the movies. Later in the week, she'd be leaving town for a month—maybe more—in Guatemala, most of it up north in the jungle.

Two years later she delved even deeper, pulling phone records and bank statements, surreptitiously capturing a full set of fingerprints that she used to check against the CIA's database. She confirmed again that Dexter was who he claimed to be, perfectly straightforward and undeniably respectable.

She'd already said yes.

That was six years ago. That was when she'd been able to suspend her normal state of disbelief about people, to renew her faith in life's innocence. A faith she'd lost far earlier, in her teens, with the onset of her family's string of disasters.

So then she'd believed—she'd wanted to believe, she'd *needed* to believe—that she could put aside her cynicism to marry this man, to lead a semblance of a normal life. After she'd investigated him to her full satisfaction, she promised herself that she'd never do it again.

She realized, even at the time, that this may have been an act of willful ignorance; she may have conspired to deceive herself, all these years.

"Ben," she said, flagging down her youngest as he ran on his way to emergency-play.

"What?"

"Come here." She opened her arms, and the boy leaned in, wrapped his wiry arms around her thighs. "I love you," she said.

"Me too Mommy but I have to go now so bye-bye I love you bye-bye."

It may have been self-deception. But it was what she'd needed, to get this.

✦ ✦ ✦

KATE COULDN'T HELP herself. She rifled through the file cabinet, thumbing quickly through credit-card statements and insurance policies and old utility bills. Nothing. Then she took another pass, slower, removing one file at a time from the top drawer, paging through every piece of paper, fanning out the user's manuals to routers and external drives and a stereo system that she knew for certain had been left behind in Washington.

She poured herself a fresh cup of coffee, and returned to the bottom drawer, starting at the rear. She came across an old manila file with a creased and torn tab that read MORTGAGE REFINANCE. Inside, behind the uniform residential loan application and in front of the verification of assets, she finally found it: a bare-bones contract for services between Dexter Moore and the Continental European Bank.

Kate read through the two pages' worth of legalese, twice. There was absolutely nothing remarkable.

Briefly, she was angry with Dexter for hiding the contract from her. But of course this is what he would have to do, if he wanted to keep the bank's identity from her.

So she forgave him. And instead she berated herself for her suspicion, for her snooping. For the things she promised herself she wouldn't do, the feelings she wouldn't have.

Then she forgave herself also, and went to school, to pick up the children.

◆ ◆ ◆

"MY PARENTS," KATE said, "are both dead. We—my sister and I— buried them in back-to-back years."

"My God," Julia said. "Where's your sister now?"

"Hartford, I think. Maybe New London. We're not in touch."

"Big fight?"

"Not exactly," Kate said. "Emily is a drunk. Usually a junkie too."

"Yikes."

"When my parents were ill, there wasn't a lot of attention to go around. Or for that matter money. My parents were too young for Medicare, and my dad's plant had closed—an electronics manufacturer—so they both had part-time jobs, inadequate or nonexistent health insurance, when they got sick. They were screwed. It was inhumane, how they were treated."

"Is that why you've moved abroad?"

"No. We're here for the experience. But I guess I do carry some resentment. Or I don't know if *resentment* is right. Disappointment? Don't get me wrong: I love America. But not everything about it. So my sister, she slipped through the cracks of the disaster of our family. She became her own disaster."

While Emily lost herself in alcohol and drugs, Kate buried herself in a tomb of numbness, unattached and unattachable, a lonely workaholic. She also began to develop one of the roles that would define her adulthood: martyr. The primary caregiver *and* a crucial wage-earner *and* the person who did the housework. The sacrifices; the suffering. Kate had never realized, until its disappearance, that she'd relished that facet of herself.

"Eventually, I had to give up caring about Emily. She was beyond helping."

"How do you stop talking to your sister?"

"She was never good about staying in touch. So once both our parents had died, and we weren't close to any of the extended family, we didn't *need* to communicate about anything. It was easy for me to simply stop calling her."

This was not true. Kate had diligently stayed in touch with Emily for years after their parents were dead, all throughout Kate's college and Emily's slow descent into destitution. But when Kate joined the Company, maintaining a relationship with Emily became not just a personal trial but a professional handicap. A liability that could be used against her. Kate knew she had to rid herself of the compassion that she'd held on to, needed to strip it away, like ripped and soiled clothing, beyond cleaning or repair, directly into the trash.

She heard from Emily a few times over that first CIA year, messages that went unreturned. Then not again for a half-decade, when Emily needed to be bailed out of jail. But Kate, in El Salvador, couldn't help. When she returned to the States, she wouldn't.

"So then Dexter's family," Kate continued. "His mother, Louise, is dead, and his father has remarried a dreadful woman. His brother, also, is dead."

"His brother? How awful."

"His name was Daniel. He was a lot older than Dexter; he'd been born when Andre and Louise were just children, really. Daniel ended up joining the Marines, in the late eighties. A few years later, he found himself out of the Marines, officially, and in the Balkans, unofficially, as one of those so-called military advisers, who we've now renamed private contractors. But same as it ever was, Daniel was a mercenary."

"Wow."

"His body was found in an alley in Dubrovnik."

"My God," Julia said flatly. She seemed surprisingly unsurprised; or conversely she was so shocked she was stunned into numbness. Kate couldn't tell which.

"Yes. So anyway"—shifting gears—"that was probably much more of a long-winded answer than you bargained for to the question 'Do you miss your family?'"

✦ ✦ ✦

AFTER KATE UNBURDENED her family saga, Julia told Kate the story of her meeting Bill. She'd been donating her design services to the silent auction portion of a fund-raiser, trying to kill a whole flock of birds—charity, networking, client-attracting, socializing—with one stone. And Bill was doing what young finance guys habitually did, which was spending excessive amounts of money on trying to attract the right type of woman, aka an unmarried socialite, which was the breed of twenty-something female that tended to populate five-hundred-dollar-a-head cocktail parties that benefited prep-school scholarships for inner-city kids.

Bill assumed that Julia was one such woman. By the time she disabused him of his misconception, three hours later, they were naked. This was a state of affairs that Julia had expedited, because she couldn't believe her great good fortune at having this incredibly handsome man interested in her.

"And over the years," she said, "I've discovered that men find me *much* more interesting when I'm naked." Kate could tell that Julia wasn't joking.

They pulled into the packed parking lot in front of the gargantuan store Cactus. The women sprinted through the punishing rain, then caught their breath under the overhang.

"Darn." Julia was rummaging around in her purse. "I must've left my phone in your car," Julia said. "May I go get it?"

"I'll come with you," Kate said.

"Oh no. This rain is too horrible. You go inside. I'll run back."

Kate picked her car keys out of her bag. "Be my guest."

"Thanks."

Kate glanced out over the parking lot, the main road, the wet grimness of the suburb, the hulking mass of concrete filled with stores filled with shelves filled with crap that she shouldn't want, or buy. This outing was a mistake. They should have done something else. Coffee somewhere, or sightseeing in Germany, or lunch in France. Mini-travel.

Travel was becoming Kate's avocation. She had started researching the family's next trips as soon as they'd returned from Copenhagen, which had been their first long weekend away. This upcoming weekend would be a drive to Paris.

"Thanks," Julia said, shaking water from her umbrella. She handed over Kate's keys with a small inscrutable smile.

Kate makes it to the corner and around it, into the rue de Seine, out of sight from the rue Jacob and anyone there who might be watching her, before she allows herself to pause, to stop walking, to release the breath that she didn't realize she'd been holding, sinking deeper into thought, into contingencies. Into panic.

They'd been living in Paris for a year, unremarkably, unostentatiously, attracting no attention, no suspicion. They should be in the clear.

So why would this woman be here, now?

The mounting anxiety forces Kate to stop moving, distracted, in the archway of a pair of immense wooden doors. One of the doors creaks open, pushed by a tiny, decrepit woman wearing an impeccable bouclé suit and carrying a cane. She stares at Kate in that bold way that old French women seem to have invented.

"*Bonjour!*" the old broad suddenly screams, and Kate almost falls over.

"*Bonjour,*" Kate answers. She can see past the woman, to the bright, leafy courtyard at the other end of the dark breezeway whose walls are filled with mail-boxes and electrical junctions and rubbish bins and loose wires and chained-up bicycles. Her own building has a similar passage; there are thousands of them in Paris. All competing for the best-place-to-kill-someone award.

Kate resumes walking, lost in thought. She stops again at the large windows of an art gallery. Contemporary photography. She watches the reflections of the passersby in the windows, mostly women who are dressed like her, and the men who form matched sets. Also a gaggle of German tourists in their sandals and socks, a trio of American youth in their backpacks and tattoos.

There's one man walking on her side of the sidewalk too slowly, wearing an ill-fitting suit and the wrong shoes, rubber-soled lace-ups that are too casual, too ugly. She watches him pass, continue up the street, out of view.

Kate continues to stare through the windows, now looking inside, not at the reflections. A half-dozen people are milling around large, airy rooms that spill one into another. The front door is wedged open with a plastic shim, letting in the fresh autumn breeze. It will be loud in there. Loud enough for Kate to have an unremark-able phone conversation that won't be overly noted by anyone.

"*Bonjour,*" she says to the chic girl at the front desk, interchangeable with all the other pretty young things at the cash registers and hostess stands, installed to attract the money that's always roaming around the streets of the central *arrondisements.*

"*Bonjour, madame.*"

Kate can feel the young woman assessing, evaluating Kate's shoes and hand-bag and jewelry and haircut, sizing up the whole package in a glance. If there's one thing these Parisian shopgirls know how to do, it's to quickly figure out who's a legitimate customer versus who's just browsing, or at best walking out with the cheapest thing in the joint. Kate knows she passes the test.

Kate looks around the large-format prints in the front room, semi-abstract land-scapes: rigid rows of agricultural fields, repetitive facades of modernist office build-ings, undulating ripples in bodies of water. They could be anywhere in the world, these landscapes.

She dutifully looks at each photo for a few seconds before moving on, into the next room, this one filled with beaches. There's a young couple in here, talking at full volume in Spanish, with a Madrid accent.

Kate takes out her phone.

She had managed to pretend that she'd never see this woman again. But Kate was never really convinced. In fact, she has always known, in the back of her mind, the opposite: she'd see this woman again, exactly like she just did.

Is this Dexter's past, catching up with him?

She hits a speed-dial button.

Or her own?

7

Kate spent her Paris liberty in the Marais. Dexter agreed that she was entitled to see some of the cities on her own. Travel wasn't fun if you didn't get to see or do what you wanted; it was merely a different type of work, in a different place.

In Copenhagen two weekends ago, Kate had spent her allotted hours wandering through downtown boutiques. Now in the Village St-Paul she bought a set of old tea towels, an engraved silver ice bucket, and an enameled saltbox; housewifely, antique-y French things. She also purchased a pair of sturdy rubber-soled canvas shoes, to pad her soles against the stone streets of Luxembourg, of Paris. Of cobblestony old Europe.

The sky was bright blue overlaid with tall puffy clouds, Indian summer, seventy degrees. Or twenty-one degrees, is how she should be thinking of it.

Kate was still getting used to the idea of strolling around a foreign city with absolutely no concern that someone might, for any of a variety of reasons, want to kill her.

She zigzagged back toward the river, to rendezvous with her husband, her children, on the Ile St-Louis. After four hours without them, she missed them; she couldn't stop picturing their faces, their smiling eyes, their wiry little arms. She spent so much of her new life wanting to get a break from the kids, then the rest of her time impatient to get back to them.

She arrived at the brasserie, ducked inside, didn't see her family. She took a seat outside, squinted into the sun. She saw them coming over from the Ile de la Cité, with Notre Dame towering behind, gargoyles and flying buttresses, the boys running on the pedestrian-only bridge that separated one island from the other, weaving in and out of people and bicycles and leash-free Jack Russell terriers.

Kate stood, called out, waved. They ran to meet her, hug her, kiss her.

"Mommy, look!" Jake thrust out an action figure, a black-clad plastic Batman.

"Yah!" Ben yelled, too excited to contain himself. "Look!" He had a Spider-Man.

"We found a comics store," Dexter admitted. "We couldn't resist." He sounded apologetic, ashamed to have bought the children crappy plastic products licensed from American corporations and manufactured in Southeast Asia.

Kate shrugged; she was past criticizing how anyone got through a day with children.

"But we also went to a bookstore, right, boys?"

"Yeah," Jake agreed. "Daddy got us *The Small Prince*."

"*Little*."

"Right. It's quite a little book, Mommy." Quite the little authority.

"No. The book is called *The Little Prince*. At Shakespeare and Company."

"Yeah," Jake agreed, again. He was agreeable. "When can we read it? Now?"

"Not quite now, sweetie," she said. "Maybe later."

Jake sighed, the immense disappointment that a little boy can feel, hundreds of times a day, over anything, everything, nothing.

"*Monsieur?*" The waiter was beside Dexter, who ordered a beer. The waiter stepped aside to allow a middle-aged Russian couple to vacate their table, loudly and rudely. The woman was laden with shopping bags from the exorbitant boutiques on the rue St-Honoré, more than a mile away. These people had come too far, to the wrong place.

"*Et pour les enfants?*" the waiter asked, ignoring the Russians. "*Quelque chose à boire?*"

"*Oui. Deux Fanta, orange, s'il vous plaît. Et la carte.*"

"*Bien sûr, madame.*" The waiter picked up a pair of leather-bound menus, then shuffled aside again, as a different couple began to install themselves at the next table.

Even discounting last night's oyster appetizer—"a giant gray booger swimming in snot" is how Jake described it—the meal had not been a success with the children. So Kate was hoping—praying—that this brasserie would have something kid-friendly. She was scanning the menu, eyes darting frantically.

The man at the next table ordered a drink and the woman added, *"La même chose,"* the voice familiar. Kate looked up to see a devastatingly handsome man sitting across from her, while the woman was across from Dexter; both women were wearing sunglasses. Because of this configuration and the glasses, and Kate's preoccupation with the menu—she was leaning toward the braised pork knuckle, served with the always-welcome applesauce—it took a full minute before the two women, seated side by side, realized who each was sitting next to.

✦ ✦ ✦

"OH MY GOD!"

"Julia!" Kate said. "What a surprise."

"Ah," Dexter said, grinning at Kate. "You're the Chicago woman." Needling.

Kate kicked him under the table.

They all had a round of drinks, and the foursome decided to dine together, later. Bill suggested that the hotel probably offered babysitting, and it turned out he was correct. Kate was quickly learning that Bill was the type of guy who was always correct.

So they fed the children, and returned to the hotel. The concierge promised that the babysitter would arrive by 22:00. Kate and Dexter put the boys to bed, with hopefully the full understanding in their young brains that if they woke in the night for a drink of water, or a pee, or a nightmare, there'd be a stranger in the room, and she probably wouldn't speak any English.

The four tipsy adults spilled into the streets at ten thirty, headed for some fashionable new restaurant that Bill chose. It was on a quiet, seemingly deserted street, but inside was warm and lively and tight, knees bumping table edges, chairs wedged against walls, waiters a fluid jumble of soaring and falling arms and hands with plates and bowls, the clinking of glasses, the clanging of forks against knives.

Their waiter shoved his nose deep into the balloon glass, his brow furrowed, critically assessing the wine he was about to serve. He raised his eyebrows, a facial shrug. *"Pas mal,"* he said. "It is not bad." He had to slide and dance and spin to get around the table to pour the wine correctly, sidestepping other patrons and other staff, the wayward limbs of gesticulating guests.

Kate looked out the window, over the half-curtains—bistro curtains, she remembered they were called, and now she realized why—and across the avenue, to an ornate Art Nouveau railing on the shallow balcony in front of extraordinarily tall windows that were glowing with candlelight behind sheer billowing curtains, through which Kate could see the movements of a party in progress inside, shifting shapes and flickering lights, and a woman parted the drapes to blow cigarette smoke through the barely opened French doors—aha! French! doors!—out over the wide avenue.

The men fell into a conversation about skiing. Bill was regaling Dexter with tales of Zermatt, Courchevel, Kitzbühel. Bill was one of those experts in everything, a guy who had a favorite Alp resort and Caribbean island and Bordeaux vintage; he'd researched ski bindings and tennis strings, had a preferred British rugby team and cult sixties TV show.

Dexter was in awe of him.

Bill picked up the bottle and poured everyone an equal portion of the last drops. Then he shot his cuff to look at his watch, one of those big fat money-guy watches with a metal bracelet. Dexter wore a drugstore Timex.

"Nearly midnight," Bill announced.

"Should we have another bottle?" Julia asked, looking around for demurs, confirmations, noncommitments.

"Well, we could." Bill leaned in to the rest of his foursome, conspiratorially. "Or we could go to this place I know."

◆ ◆ ◆

"NOUS SOMMES DES amis de Pierre," Bill said to the doorman.

They were standing on the wide sidewalk of the broad, quiet boulevard, just the other side of the Pont d'Alma.

"Est-il chez lui ce soir?"

The man behind the velvet rope was big and black and bald. "Votre nom?"

"Bill Maclean. Je suis americain."

The man grinned at this piece of obviousness, and inclined his head at a willowy girl in a silver sheath dress who was standing a few yards away, smoking; she herself looked a bit like a cigarette. The girl flicked aside her butt and sauntered inside.

Kate and Dexter and Julia and Bill waited, amid a dozen people who were perhaps waiting for the same type of thing. Maybe the same exact thing, from the same person. Other supposed friends of Pierre.

This was not something Dexter and Kate had ever done in D.C. Or anywhere else. He took her hand, fingertips cold in the brisk autumn air, and tickled her palm with the tip of his forefinger. Kate stifled a giggle at the tingle, at her husband's secret signal for sex.

The cigarette-girl reappeared, nodded at the bouncer, then lit a new smoke, and resumed looking bored.

"Bienvenue, Beel," the bouncer said.

A different big and black man, this one with a short afro and beside the rope, not behind it, opened the brass hinge and held aside the thick, braided strand.

Bill ushered his wife forward, through the gap in the rope. Then he repeated the gesture for Kate, his fingers lightly pressing the fabric of her jacket, his fingertips barely but unmistakably felt through the silk and wool. Kate knew with a jolt that this touch was wrong. Bill hadn't touched Julia this way.

"Merci beaucoup." Bill shook the bouncer's hand.

The hallway was dim and red, low light reflected off walls that were both glossy and matte. Kate reached out her hand, and let her fingers trail across the fleur-de-lis flocked in plush velvet against a satin background. The hall widened, and opened, and they were beside a short bar, ordering a bottle of Champagne, Bill laying a credit card on the gleaming wood, swept up by the bartender and stowed next to the register, an open tab.

Beyond the bar, low tables and couches surrounded a diminutive dance floor. Two women were dancing playfully around one man, who was standing still, letting his head bounce from side to side. Minimalist dancing.

Bill leaned in to Kate's ear. "It's early," he explained. "There will be more people."

"Early? It's midnight."

"This place doesn't open until eleven. And nobody would show up at eleven."

They arrived at the table of a slender olive-skinned man, reeking of cigarettes, his ears littered with rings, his arms with tattoos, his shirt unbuttoned halfway down to his crotch. He and Bill exchanged cheek kisses. Bill introduced him as Pierre, first to Kate, then to Dexter, and finally to *"ma femme, Julia."* Pierre seemed surprised that Bill had a wife.

The Americans took a table beside Pierre's, populated by a similar-looking man and a pair of modely-looking young women in jeans and slinky blouses and not a single extra ounce of body fat.

Kate took another sip of wine.

✦ ✦ ✦

IT WAS DARK, and loud, and the dance floor and lights and music tugged at everyone's concentration, pulling toward this light and that body, this beat and that voice, and all these distractions, this sensory overload, created a sort of privacy, an energy shield behind which Kate felt like she could finally take a moment and study Bill, this husband of a woman who had quickly become her best friend on the continent.

Bill's arm was thrown over the back of the banquette, and his jacket was off, and his shirt was undone two buttons. His wavy dark hair had gone a bit wild, and he was sporting the easy smile of someone who'd been drinking for six hours. He looked completely in his element here, at this Right Bank *club privé*. He leaned his head back to listen to Pierre, then let out a full and loose laugh. He could be a fashion designer, or a filmmaker. But what he didn't look like was a currency trader.

The humor of Pierre's joke receded, taking with it the better part of Bill's smile. He turned back to his American companions, his table, and his eyes found Kate's, and rested there a few beats, saying nothing and asking nothing, just looking. She wondered what he was looking for, and who the hell he was.

Bill's being, his presence, dominated his surroundings. Making his wife seem small and quiet, even when she was standing tall, loudly. They were a strange match; Bill was kind of out of Julia's league.

"Hey guys," Kate said to her husband, and to Bill, pulling her phone out of her pocket. "How about a picture?" They both looked reticent, but not enough to argue.

Kate had come across a lot of Bills: alpha males, trying to out-alpha one another. It had been her job to deal with them. In private life, it had been her habit to avoid them.

"And Julia?" she asked. "Could you lean in also?"

The trio smiled, and Kate snapped the picture.

She looked at these men across the low littered table, her own man and this new one. One whose entire being was suffused with confidence, flowing up from some deep well that originated Lord knows where—maybe he'd been spectacularly good at some sport, or he had a photographic memory, or was impressively well-endowed—and oozing out into a sleekness, a fluidity, as if all his gears were well-oiled, perpetually lubricated and running efficiently, manifested in smooth physical movements and playful smiles and an undeniably animal sexuality.

This man didn't run his hand through his hair, or adjust his shirt collar, or dart his eyes around the room, or run his mouth meaninglessly; he didn't fidget in any way.

And the other man, bereft of this confidence. His supply compromised, a plugged well or a broken pipe, just a trickle flowing up, not enough to even out the rough edges of nervousness and insecurity, of herky-jerky body language with creaks and squeaks and uncomfortable angles. This was her man, the one who didn't just want her but needed her, and not just passingly but desperately. This was the legacy of her upbringing, the result of her own finite supply of self-confidence, her own valuation of herself in the world: Kate needed, badly, to be needed. She'd gravitated toward men who tended to need her more than want her. She'd married the one who'd needed her the most.

The new man was again staring at her, staring at him, challenging her, knowing that she was considering him, wanting her to know that he was considering her.

She couldn't help but wonder what it would be like to be with a man who absolutely didn't need her, but merely wanted her.

◆ ◆ ◆

KATE DIDN'T NOTICE anyone order or deliver or pick up the third bottle of Champagne, but there was no way this was still the second. She was hot, and thirsty, and she took a long sip, and then another, before Julia tugged her back into the throbbing crowd on the dance floor, everyone in the same motion and to the same beat, everyone sweaty, the strobe sweeping slowly across the room, the mirror-ball twinkling.

Dexter was engrossed in conversation with a staggeringly beautiful woman who read headlines for a news station. She wanted to move to Washington, this French newscaster, to cover politics; she was pumping Dexter for information he didn't really have. Kate didn't begrudge him his obvious thrill, basking in the glow of attention from an unattainably gorgeous woman.

They were all plastered.

Julia had undone yet another button on her blouse, crossing the neckline between sexy and exhibitionist. But half the women in the club were the same degree of naked.

Kate looked away from Julia, through the obstacles of lights and forms, her eye drawn toward the far wall, where Bill was slouched next to an attractive woman, who turned her head into the side of his, and may or may not have licked his ear.

Kate glanced at Julia, her eyelids resting heavy against her cheeks, oblivious.

Kate again scanned the roiling sea of flesh. Now it was Bill who was turning into the young woman's neck. She smiled, and nodded. Bill took her by the wrist and led her away.

Julia's eyes were now open, but she was looking nowhere near her husband.

Kate watched Bill recede with the girl down one of those halls in clubs and bars that lead to privacy, to restrooms and broom closets and storage rooms, to back doors that empty into alleyways. To places where people go, late at night, groping and squeezing, unzipping trousers and pushing aside panties, breathless and urgent.

Kate blinked, long and slow, letting her eyes stay closed for a few loud techno beats. Julia glided away, was dancing with a tall, dangerously thin young man, her lips moist and partway open, teeth glinting, tongue sliding slowly across her lip. One of Julia's hands was resting against the flat of her stomach, then this hand rose to her breast, cupping herself, then fell again, past stomach and down to hip, thigh. Her head was thrown back, extending her glistening neck; her eyes were hooded, open but barely, looking not at the man she was dancing with, but across the room, and not in the direction of her own disappeared husband, but in the direction, Kate knew without turning, of Dexter.

It was three thirty in the morning.

◆ ◆ ◆

THE BOULEVARD DESERTED of muscular bouncers and nubile girls, not a taxi nor a person in sight, but suddenly out of nowhere there were two of them, hoodies and baggy jeans and piercings and scraggly beards. One shoving Dexter hard against the wall. The other with the quick, unmistakable movement of a flustered young man raising a gun.

Kate could replay the next couple of seconds frame by frame, stop-motion, in her mind. There was Dexter's panicked face, and Julia's frozen horror, and Bill's impressive, impassive calm. *"Je vous en prie,"* he said. *"Un moment."*

Kate was off to the side of the main confrontation, ignored. It would be easy for her. The path she could take to end this scene was clear: the swift kick to the side of the head, the rabbit punch to the kidney, then wresting away the weapon. But if Kate did this, then everyone would wonder how the hell she had the nerve, and the technique, and she wouldn't be able to explain.

So Kate turned her thoughts to whether she'd miss anything she was about to hand over to these thugs. Muggers don't shoot tourists on central-Paris streets, do they? No.

But then the odd thing happened. Bill took hold of Julia's handbag, and extended it toward the gun-wielder. This was clearly not how these boys wanted the transaction to proceed, both shaking their heads.

"Tenez," Bill said. Kate could see that he knew what he was doing, and why, pushing the bag toward the weapon, getting too close, forcing the other man to step between Bill and the bullets to grasp the booty, which was when Bill lunged into the unarmed man, using him as a shield while he reached out and yanked the barrel of the gun, effortlessly, brazenly.

Everyone froze for a beat, cutting their eyes from the weapon to one another, heavy breathing, mouths agape, calculating their next possible actions . . .

The young men ran away, and Bill tossed the gun into the gutter.

8

Monday afternoon, and it was pouring.

Kate stood alone in front of the school, resting her umbrella so low that her head was touching the striped nylon, the aluminum ribs sitting on her shoulder, trying to safeguard the few undrenched portions of her body. Everything below the waist was soaked, squishing, unsalvageable.

Sheets of big, heavy drops were flooding from the dark, dense sky, pounding the concrete, thrumming the grass, loudly splattering in the deep puddles that had pooled in every dip or swale, crack or crevasse.

The mother groups were neatly divided by nationality. There were the self-sufficient groups of blue-eyed Danes and blond Dutch, of high-heel-wearing Italians and ultra-healthy Swedes. The intermingled English-language groups dominated by pale Brits, with chunky Americans and ever-smiling Australians and aggressively friendly Kiwis, the occasional Irish and Scot. There were the hyper-insular Indians, and the utterly unapproachable Japanese. Individual roving Russians and Czechs and Poles, hoping to attach themselves to Western Europe, ingratiating, firm-handshaking, trying to get invited to join the EU, ignorant—willfully?—of the universal futility of trying to get invited to anything, ever.

There were even a few men scattered around, not talking to one another, each in his own independent orbit of strangeness.

Technically, Kate was no longer hungover from Saturday night. But she was still physically tired from the lack of sleep—the children had awoken at seven A.M. on Sunday, oblivious to their parents' late night—and her body still felt nonspecifically wrong.

She also felt a psychic unease, partially attached to what she may have witnessed of Bill's infidelity, partially to Julia's inappropriate exhi-bitionism aimed at Dexter. Partially to Bill's heroic behavior—overly heroic?—in the face of muggers. And partially to her own desperation, back at the hotel, in the bathroom, the door locked against any sleepwalking children, descending famished on Dexter, begging him for more, harder, while uncontrollable images flitted through her imagination, of people who were not her husband, and sometimes not herself, their slickened bodies, their lips and tongues . . .

It was now raining even harder. She wouldn't have guessed that was possible.

Kate couldn't put her finger on exactly what had happened to the four of them, late on Saturday night in Paris, and whether it was good, or bad, or both.

✦ ✦ ✦

"LISTEN," DEXTER SAID, "I'm going to be late tonight." Again.

Kate and the boys had changed out of their wet things, into soft sweats and slippers, enfolded in fleece. But she was still having a hard time shaking the chill of the latest in a long series of drenchings. "Everything okay?"

"Yeah. I'm going to play tennis. With Bill."

They hadn't said a word about Julia and Bill since they got into separate taxis at four thirty in the morning on the avenue George V, four days ago.

"He has an *abonnement* for a court at a club, and his regular partner canceled."

An image ran across her brain, Bill shirtless in the locker room, unbuckling his belt, pushing down his . . .

Kate deposited the phone in its cradle, next to the laptop, facing onto the usually majestic view, which was now a vast expanse of cloud and fog and rain against the browns and grays of the leafless trees, the slates and blacks of the stone roofs, the beiges and tans of the stone fortifications and rock outcroppings and cobblestone streets.

It was dreary, and she was alone again, back from another Wednesday afternoon in the windowless basement of the sports center at Kockelscheuer, talking about bikini waxes. She used to be a person who did things. Not just run-of-the-mill normal-job things, but life-and-death things. Illegally crossing international borders. Eluding police. Hiring assassins, for God's sake. Now she was folding laundry. Could her life really have become this?

"When is Daddy coming home?" Jake asked, his teddy clutched to his chest, his brother silent at his side, both boys cold and tired and wanting their dad, again.

"I'm sorry, sweetie," Kate said. "He won't be home till after you're asleep."

Ben turned angrily, quickly, and walked away. But Jake stayed. "Why?" he asked. "Why can't he be home?"

"Oh, he wants to, sweetie. But he has other things he needs to do, sometimes."

The boy wiped a tear from his cheek. Kate gathered him in her arms. "I'm sorry, Jake. But I promise that Daddy will give you a kiss when he gets home. Okay?"

He nodded, fighting back more tears, then sulked off and joined his brother, who was already busying himself with Lego.

Kate sat down at the computer. She moved aside files—LUXEMBOURG RENTAL FURNITURE and LUXEMBOURG SCHOOLS and LUXEMBOURG UTILI- TIES. She waited for the machine to locate the wireless signal. She stared at the screen, second-guessing what she was about to do. What she was hoping to find, and whether or not she wanted to.

It didn't occur to her that she was doing exactly what she was expected to.

But before she could do anything, the phone rang again.

✦ ✦ ✦

"THANKS SO MUCH," Julia said. "I feel completely lost with the Inter- net down."

"No problem." Kate shut the door behind Julia. "I know exactly how you feel. Boys, say hello to Julia."

"Hi!"

"Hello!"

They ran back to the kitchen, the excitement of the doorbell finished, to their kitchen service: Ben was peeling carrots, Jake cutting them into chunks. Both were standing on stepstools at the counter, concentrating hard, being careful with their sharp tools.

"You've got sous-chefs," Julia said.

"Yes." The boys were prepping for a *poule au pot,* the cookbook open on the counter, under a shelf containing a half-dozen other cookbooks, all mail-ordered from Amazon's warehouses in England.

Julia wandered into the living room. "Wow!" She'd noticed the view. "This place is great."

"Thanks."

They were now in the living room, through two doors and around one corner from the children. Well out of earshot. If they were ever going to mention Saturday night, it was going to be now. But they weren't.

"So the computer is in there," Kate said, gesturing at the guest room.

"Thanks again. I really appreciate it. I'll probably be ten minutes?"

"Whatever you need." Kate left Julia alone.

✦ ✦ ✦

THE CHILDREN WERE asleep, and Dexter was at tennis with Bill, and Kate was alone, in the gray glow of the screen, her hands resting softly on the smooth keys, pointer fingers caressing the ridges on J and F. She felt a warmness, a tingling. She was looking for an activity, to relieve her boredom. And a picture, to enrich her fantasy.

She typed: B I L L Space M A C L E A N

The first page of the search revealed one cohesive personality with that name, but it wasn't the one she was looking for. She scrolled through page after page of results—seven, eight, nine pages, scores of links—but no one turned out to be a currency trader, recently moved from Chicago to Luxembourg, age around forty.

No Facebook. Nor LinkedIn. No university alumni updates, or high-school rosters, or society-page photos, or periodical references.

W I L L I A M Space M A C L E A N

A slightly different assortment of links, but mostly the same. On some second-tier professional-networking site, there was a page for a William Maclean of Chicago, profession listed as finance, nothing else. No picture, no links, no bio, nothing hard.

She tried other spellings—*Mclean, McLean, Maclane, Maclaine*—but the results were almost exactly the same. No one she found was him.

✦ ✦ ✦

"WHAT ABOUT SANTIBANEZ?" Evan had asked.

"I heard that was Leo," Kate had answered.

"Yeah, everybody heard that. You know anything more specific?"

Now that this conversation was finally taking place, Kate was relieved. It had been a long time coming. She was surprised it was so roundabout, so full of interrogations and executions and assassinations that obviously had nothing to do with her.

"Nope."

Evan glanced down at his pad. "He was killed in Veracruz. Two to the chest, one to the head. No abduction, no butchery, no spectacle." Just like she'd been trained.

This was the moment in the conversation—the debriefing, the interrogation—when she finally understood the point of this endless litany of violence: they were reminding Kate that even though she'd been out of the field for five years, she'd still not cleansed herself of the stench of dirty ops. She never would.

"So it didn't look like it was done by anyone in the narcotics business. What it looked like was something done by someone in our business."

And they would always know it.

"Santibanez, he once ran with Lorenzo Romero, didn't he?"

Romero had been a CIA informant who'd fed his handler misleading intelligence, in exchange for huge sums of cash from the *narcotraficantes*. Unfortunately, the misinformation got his handler shot in the head and dumped in Tampico harbor. The whole Mexico division agreed to dole out retribution, and Kate, the sole female in the group, would have the easiest time getting the notorious womanizer into an unguarded, private predicament.

"Like I said, I don't know anything specific about Santibanez."

"Okay." Evan nodded, eyes down on his pad. "How about Eduardo Torres?"

Kate took a breath, neither too deep nor too shallow. At last, here it was.

✦ ✦ ✦

DEXTER WAS IN London when the move-out-move-in happened: the rental company showed up at eight in the morning, with a little crane, and retrieved all their furnishings—the couches and beds, linens and dishware, toilet brushes and vacuum cleaner. Chairs, bureaus, a desk, a dining table. All out the window, by ten in the morning. Papers signed, truck closed and driven away, gone.

It was another dark and rainy autumn day. The window had been open all morning. The apartment was cold and empty. Kate was alone, again.

Alone and waiting for the shipping container to arrive after three weeks pending customs clearance. The same orange container that had departed her curbside in D.C. two months ago, where she'd stood alone in that other empty house, papers signed attesting that everything was packed and loaded and attached to a black cab gaudily decorated with neon outlines of impossibly busty women, bound for the port of Baltimore to be loaded onto the freighter *Osaka* to cross the Atlantic in eleven days to Antwerp, then to be attached to a cab owned by a Dutch freight company, an undecorated white cab that was pulling around the corner right now, here, in front of this empty apartment, and she was alone again while her husband was working at the same job on a different continent, and her children were in school learning the same things, and the stuff in the container was the same, and the big differences being where she was, and who she was. In the middle of Europe, the new Kate.

✦ ✦ ✦

"DEXTER SEEMS LIKE a great husband. Is he?"

Conversations with Julia often become much more personal than Kate wanted. Julia wore her need for intimacy on her sleeve, practically begging Kate to open up to her. Despite Julia's bluff of outgoing confidence, she was tremendously insecure. She'd been unlucky in love, unconfident in relationships, and uncomfortable in intimacy. She'd been lonely her whole life, much like Kate, until she'd chanced into Bill. But she was still operating on lonely-person principles, still worried that her happiness could be wrenched away at any moment, for reasons out of her control.

Kate didn't know how to answer Julia's question—even a private answer, to herself. Her relationship with Dexter had improved right after they'd moved—Dexter had been unusually attentive, and they'd been closer, cozier. The change had done them good; the move was good for their marriage. Though not yet good for Kate, as an individual.

But then Dexter had become increasingly absent, traveling who knows where. She barely had the energy to listen to his itineraries. Also more and more evasive, distant, and distracted when he was home.

Kate couldn't decide whether she needed to break the promise she'd made herself to not be suspicious of her husband. And if she gave in to the urge, and let herself be suspicious, of what? Cheating? Having some type of psychological crisis? Was his job falling apart, and he wasn't telling her? Was he angry at her about something?

She couldn't guess the realm where the problem dwelt. Or even if there was one. And although she felt the vague need to talk about it, she felt a stronger compulsion to keep her concerns secret. She'd always been comfortable with the unsaid; secrets are what she did.

Kate looked Julia in the eye, through this door to another level of their relationship, and decided not to walk through it. As she'd been doing her entire life.

"Yes," Kate said, "he's a great husband."

◆ ◆ ◆

KATE SETTLED INTO a routine.

On Tuesdays and Thursdays, after drop-off, she did her French home-work, then went to class. Kate's instructor, a disturbingly young and good-natured French-Somali woman, was impressed with Kate's rapid progress and natural-sounding accent. French wasn't difficult for Kate, after all those years speaking Spanish, mastering the nuances among dialects, Cuban and Nicaraguan, northern Mexican and eastern Mexican.

Two or three days a week, she went to the gym. She'd accepted the recommendation of Amber—always exercising, yet never fit—and joined a bizarre institution that offered ham sandwiches and cappuccinos but neither towels nor early-morning fitness classes; the doors didn't even open until nine.

Kate drove around, looking for things. She drove thirty minutes to a big toy store in a shopping plaza in Foetz, pronounced *futz*. She was searching for an item that was proving to be elusive, a Robin action figure. Not a big surprise, because who wants Robin instead of the readily available Batman? Ben, that's who.

She went to Metz, forty-five minutes away, looking for an immersion blender.

She drove the main byways of Luxembourg—route d'Arlon, route de Thionville, route de Longwy—poking in and out of shopping plazas and malls, eating steam-table buffet lunches at Indian restaurants, bland tikka masala, greasy naan.

She sat at the computer, researching weekend destinations, hotels and attractions, flights and highway routes, restaurants and zoos.

She got the car washed, at a variety of locations. In one, she got stuck for a half-hour. A solicitous jumpsuited employee kept checking on her every few minutes. At one point, he mentioned that she was welcome to call the police.

She had her hair cut. There was a lot of bad hair in Luxembourg, and she couldn't quite avoid becoming a victim, just on the cusp of being able to communicate that she did not want the features—mullets and bangs and spikes—that the hairdressers specialized in.

She bought window shades and area rugs, place mats and shower caddies.

She purchased and installed an extra towel bar in the master bathroom. Which entailed buying an electric drill. Then returning to the hardware superstore to buy the bits that had not been included with the drill. Then returning again for the diamond-tipped masonry bits that she'd need to push holes through whatever was behind the plaster coating of her walls. Each round-trip to the store took an hour.

She met other women for coffee, or lunch. Mostly it was Julia, but sometimes Amber, or Claire, or anyone; there was no one who she wasn't willing to give a try. Dutch and Swedes, Germans and Canadians. She was her own ambassador.

Also her own babysitter. She lay on the floor with the boys, building things out of Lego or wooden blocks, pushing around the cardboard cutouts of thirty-six-piece jigsaw puzzles. She read aloud book after book after book.

On occasion, she met her husband for a meal. But not often. Dexter worked a long day every day, and most evenings.

She looked forward to date night—ostensibly once a week but frequently canceled due to work, or travel. Date night in Washington hadn't been important; it was optional. But now it was something she felt herself needing, the opportunity to share the detritus of housewifedom, to elicit and receive sympathy, validation.

So much of it seemed devoid of value. She walked around the apartment, picking up toys and clothing, straightening piles, filing papers. She washed the boys' hair and soaped their armpits and supervised them on the fine arts of wiping their butts and brushing every tooth and peeing directly into the bowl, not just in its general direction.

She went grocery shopping and lugged bags. She prepared breakfast and packed lunches and cooked dinner and washed dishes. She vacuumed and mopped and dusted. She sorted laundry, dried it, folded it, put it into drawers and on hangers and hooks.

When she finished the chores, it was time to start each and every one of them again.

And her husband had no idea. None of the husbands knew what their wives did every day, during the six hours when their children were in school—not just the endless chores but the pastimes, the cooking classes and language lessons, the tennis instruction and, in special circumstances, affairs with tennis instructors. Meeting everyone for coffee, all the time. Going to the gym. The mall. Sitting around playgrounds, getting wet in the rain. One playground had a gazebo, where they could get less wet.

Dexter didn't know about any of this. Just as he hadn't known how Kate had truly spent her days back in Washington, when she'd been doing something completely different from what she'd claimed.

Just as Kate didn't know, now, exactly what he did all day.

"Bonjour," Dexter answers. *"Comment ça va?"*

Kate looks around the gallery, empty except for the Spanish couple, the man running a constant low-volume commentary. He fancies himself a connoisseur.

"Ça va bien," Kate answers.

They moved from Luxembourg to Paris a year ago, at the start of the new school year, in a new school in a new city in a new country. By New Year's, Kate had concluded that neither of them was making sufficient progress toward fluency. So she convinced Dexter that they should speak only French on Tuesdays and Thursdays. Today is a Thursday, nine months later. But for this conversation, they need to speak English; they need to communicate on a different level.

"I just ran into an old friend," she says. "Julia."

Dexter is silent for a second, and Kate doesn't push. She knows he's considering the meaning of this woman's arrival. *"Quelle surprise,"* he says flatly. "It's been so long."

Neither Kate nor Dexter had seen Julia since her hasty but not unexpected departure from Luxembourg, the winter before last.

"Can we make it for drinks tonight? Bill too is in Paris."

Dexter pauses another beat. "Okay. It'll be fun to catch up."

"Yes," Kate says. But she isn't thinking of the fun they'll have. "So how about seven o'clock, at the café in the Carrefour de l'Odéon?"

"Sure," Dexter says. "That's perfect."

The café is around the corner from their parking garage, and a half-block from a busy Métro station. It has tiny windowless bathrooms, no back rooms, no back entrance. There is nowhere for anyone to hide, no way for anyone to sneak up from behind. The tables on the *terrasse* offer unobstructed views of the entire intersection. It's the perfect place for a drink. And the perfect place from which to escape quickly.

"I'll call Louis and reserve a table," Dexter says. "I'll let you know if there's a problem."

Kate knows there won't be a problem, not with Louis and a table. But she can imagine many other problems, most of them ending with the pink fifty-euro note and the bill pinned under the heavy glass ashtray at the café, the hurried steps around the corner, the quick buckling into the soft seats of the station wagon with the kids already secured in the back, waving good-bye to Sylvie the nanny, the race to the Seine and across the Pont Neuf and onto the fast-moving roadway beneath the quais, streaming into l'autoroute de l'Est, light traffic and a wide high-way east on the A4 and then north on the A31 and into a different nation and on different roads, eventually narrow and curvy and hilly, until finally, four hours after pulling out from the parking garage beneath the Left Bank, coming to a stop at the stone gates of the white-painted farmhouse on a tree-dotted plateau deep in the sparsely populated Ardennes Forest.

And in the downstairs washroom of the little stone house, behind the panel of the nonfunctioning heating register, a small steel box is affixed with strong magnets.

"Okay. And oh, Dexter? Julia told me to pass along a message."

The hurried drive to the Ardennes is something they practiced. A test run.

"Yes?"

"The Colonel is dead."

Dexter doesn't respond.

"Dexter?"

"Yes," he says. "I got it."

"Okay then. *A bientôt.*"

And inside the box in the farmhouse's bathroom, neat stacks of crisp bank notes, a million euros, untraceable cash. New-life cash.

The Spanish couple has left the gallery. Kate is alone, looking at the photo-graphs, images of water and sand and sky, water and sand and sky, water and sand and sky. A relentless series of parallel lines in blues and tans, in shades of grays and whites. Hypnotizing lines, abstractions of place that are so abstract they're no longer place, just line and color.

Maybe the beach, Kate thinks. Maybe a faraway beach is where we'll live next. After we disappear from here.

9

It was tricky to call anyone in America, because of the time difference combined with the school schedule. All morning she was free, available; but everyone on the East Coast was asleep, at breakfast. By the time it was nine A.M. in Washington, she was picking up the children, she was with them, she was at the grocer's and butcher's and baker's, on play-dates and at the sports center, driving and cleaning and cooking. By the time she was no longer busy—children clean and abed, dishes washed, house tidied—she was exhausted, introverted, watching last season's HBO shows on iTunes, the laptop hooked up to the television via thick, multipronged cords, digital-media life support.

There was only one person in her time zone she could call. She dialed the long number, which was answered on the first ring. "Hello."

"Hi," she said. "I'm bored." She didn't say her own name, nor his. No names on the phone, ever. "In fact, more bored than I've ever been. In my life."

"I'm sorry," he said.

"I'm doing laundry."

"That's *good*," he said. "It's important to dress your family in clean clothing."

Kate realized that this conversation—lonely, laundry—sounded exactly like an asset reporting into a case officer, in code. "Tell me something interesting," she said.

"Interesting? Er . . . let's see. No American president has been an only child. They've *all* had siblings. If not biological, at least by marriage."

She'd known Hayden since the beginning of her career. After all this time, it was easy to forget how noticeable was his world-weary drawl, his Locust Valley lockjaw. Nobody sounded like him, in Luxembourg. Not even British men.

"That's a four."

"Oh, *not* fair. Statistically, twenty percent of American children are singletons. But not one American president grew up that way? Come *on*."

"Okay, I guess it's a five," she said, not fighting the impulse to smile, despite her awful mood. Hayden's fun facts always cheered her. "I'm lonely."

"I know it's hard," he said. "But it will get better."

Hayden had lived his entire adult life abroad. He knew what he was talking about. "I promise."

❖ ❖ ❖

"MAYBE DADDY WANTS to tell us what he did today."

Jake and Ben didn't look up from their brown slices of Böfflamott, *My Bavarian Cookbook,* page 115. Even if they'd known that an attack had just been struck by one of their parents, they'd also have known that it wasn't their battle.

Dexter didn't say anything.

"Or maybe Daddy thinks Mommy isn't intelligent enough to understand his job."

He stopped chewing.

"Or maybe Daddy just doesn't care that Mommy's curious."

Jake and Ben exchanged a quick look, then both turned their eyes to their father.

Kate knew she wasn't being fair. She shouldn't be doing this. But resentment was getting the best of her. She'd scrubbed three toilets that afternoon. Toilet scrubbing was at the very top of the list of chores she hated.

Dexter put down his fork and knife. "What exactly do you want to know, Kat?"

She winced at this purposeful use of her ex-name.

"I want to know what you *do*." Kate had never pried into Dexter's work life, at least not to his face. They'd always been a couple who'd given each other a lot of space. It was one of the things she most appreciated about her husband: his willingness to not know. Now it was Kate who wanted to know. "What did you do today? Is that too much to ask?"

He smiled, for the benefit of the kids. "Of course not. Let's see, today.

Today I plotted out one phase of a penetration test that I'm going to perform in a couple weeks."

That sounded like experimental sexual intercourse.

"A pen test is when a consultant like me tries to breach a system's security. There are three main approaches to intrusion. One is the purely technical method: finding some hole, some tear in the system that you can get into, rip open, and march around at will."

"Like what?"

"Like an unmonitored computer. One that's hooked up to the system and not password-protected. Or if it is password-protected, the user name is something easily cracked, or still on its default setting. Like a user name of *user* and a password of *password*. Some systems can be cracked in a few hours. Others might take months. And the longer it takes, the more likely it is that a hacker will give up, look for an easier target.

"The second approach is purely physical: breaking into a facility. Sneaking past the guards, coming in the window, up through the basement. Or pure force: arriving with manpower and gunpower. The physical approach is not my specialty."

"I shouldn't think so."

"What does that mean?"

"Nothing. What's the third approach?"

"The third is usually the most effective. Social engineering. This is when you manipulate a person to gain access."

"How do you do that?"

"All the methods revolve around basically the same principle: making people think you're on their team, when you're not."

Social engineering. That had been Kate's career.

"And the most effective are a combination of all three—social engineering to get physically on-site, where you utilize technical skills. This is how you shut down governments, steal major industrial secrets, cheat casinos. And, most relevant to me, this is how you rob banks. This is a bank's worst nightmare."

Dexter took a bite of beef. "That's why we're here." And a sip of wine. "This is what I do."

✦ ✦ ✦

KATE STARED OUT her window, over a cliff, down hundreds of feet into the Alzette gorge, across a quarter-mile of modern steel bridge, and old railroad aqueduct, and medieval fortifications and lush green lawns and dense forests and black-roofed houses and towering church spires and rushing river, across to the slope that fell from the Kirchberg Plateau's glass-and-steel office buildings and, on top of it all, an immense amount of bright blue sky. It was a spectacular view, a view of limitless possibility. A view that encapsulated Europe.

Then she turned her eyes back to her computer. The website for Julia Maclean Interior Design was nothing if not well-produced. Professionally produced. It was heavily reliant on mood music and slowly fading images, on varied typefaces and banal phrases. There were a few dozen images of pleasant but unremarkable residential rooms. According to one of the pages, the aesthetic intent was "Eclectic Traditional," which seemed to mean pairing expensive-looking American antiques with African tribal masks, Chinese stools, and Mexican ceramics.

There were no testimonials from clients. No celebrity endorsements. There was no page of local press mentions, no links to other features. The biography read:

> Julia Maclean, an Illinois native, studied architecture and textiles at college, and has a master's degree in fine arts with a specialty of interior design. She held a number of prestigious internships before launching her own firm, and in the past decade has earned a loyal following for her whimsical yet traditional approach to refined interiors. Equally at home amid the modernism of Lake Shore Drive or the traditionalism of the North Shore, Julia is one of the most sought-after decorators in the greater Chicago area.

On the contacts page, there was an e-mail address, but no brick-and-mortar location, no phone or fax numbers, no names of employees or colleagues, partners or references.

Across every attractive page of the entire website, there was not one piece of hard information traceable to any real person or place.

Kate had seen websites like this before. They were legends. Cover stories.

✦ ✦ ✦

"BOYS!" KATE YELLED, ignoring her husband momentarily. Not ignoring; just not responding. "Breakfast!"

She put the crepes on the dining table, one spread with Nutella, the other with Speculoos, both rolled tightly. There didn't seem to be any frozen waffles in this country; certainly no Blueberry Eggos. Luckily, the children were proving to be flexible when it came to eating different forms of sugar at breakfast.

What they weren't flexible about was not seeing their father on a daily basis. Kate was discovering that she was unable to bear their complaints about his absences, which felt a lot like accusations of her unsatisfactory parenting. If the boys needed him so much, it must be because they didn't love her enough. QED.

She knew rationally that this was not true. But she felt irrationally that it was.

"No." Kate turned to Dexter, angry and showing it, purposefully. "I don't remember you saying any damn thing about going to Sarajevo this week."

She tried to settle herself, to remind herself that business travel was rarely if ever optional; it was stressful, not relaxing; lonely, not fun. And Sarajevo was one of the last places on earth Dexter wanted to go. He bore a grudge against the whole ex-Yugoslavia region for the murder of his brother.

"Well," he said, "sorry. But I am."

Kate shouldn't resent him for leaving, for leaving her by herself with children in a strange land, alone and lonely. But she did.

"And when are you back?"

The children settled themselves into chairs, staring at the television. In Washington they'd never seen a single episode of *SpongeBob SquarePants;* they didn't know it existed in English. What they were watching was *Bob l'Eponge.* A French invention.

"Friday night."

"What are you doing exactly? In Sarajevo?" This would be Dexter's second trip to Sarajevo, along with one each to Liechtenstein, Geneva, London, and Andorra.

"Helping some of the bank's clients tighten their security."

"The bank doesn't have people for that?" she asked. "In Bosnia?"

"This is what they pay me for: to make customers comfortable. This is what I do, Kat."

"Kate."

He shrugged. She opened her mouth to scream at him, but couldn't, wouldn't, in front of the children.

Kate slammed the bathroom door. She leaned on the sink, scrubbed clean by none other than herself. She stared into the mirror, tears welling. She wiped one eye and then the other, but it was no use, she was crying now. Overwhelmed by the indelibility of her aloneness, her outsideness. Unable to imagine how she will ever feel like one of those other women, content in this life, sitting at a café table and laughing at the trials and tribulations of unwanted-hair removal. Having a great time. Or at least creating the compelling appearance to her, to one another, to themselves, of having an enjoyable life.

Kate and Dexter didn't have an enjoyable life, not yet. They'd procured notarized copies of their passports and birth certificates and marriage certificate, to apply for residency permits. They'd opened bank accounts and taken out insurance policies, bought mobile phones and small appliances and Ikea's bureaus and frozen meatballs. They'd driven to the second-largest city in the country, Esch-sur-Alzette, to buy a used Audi wagon with an automatic transmission and under fifty thousand kilometers. It had taken a couple weeks of online browsing to find such a car, a time frame that corresponded precisely to the length of time they didn't realize that the word *break* meant station wagon.

They were ticking off items on a to-do list that was magnet-attached to the fridge. There were nineteen items on the list. They'd crossed off fifteen.

The final item was underlined: *Make a life.*

Maybe this whole thing was a terrible mistake.

◆ ◆ ◆

"I DON'T KNOW anything specific about Torres," Kate had said.

"Anything nonspecific?"

Kate had struggled not to cut her eyes away from Evan. She'd been expecting this line of questioning since the very beginning of this process. She'd been expecting it for a half-decade.

"Torres had no shortage of enemies," she said.

"Yes. But at the time of his demise, he was at a low ebb. It was an odd time for him to be taken out."

Kate managed, barely, to maintain eye contact. "Grudges," she said, "are timeless."

Evan's pen was poised above his pad, but there had been nothing worth writing down. He tapped the ballpoint against the paper, four slow taps, keeping a beat.

"Yes," he agreed, "they certainly are."

✦ ✦ ✦

"WELL, WELL, WELL. Isn't this a pleasant surprise?"

Kate was walking in the Grand Rue, lined with bakeries and *chocolatiers* and butchers, lingerie shops and shoe stores, pharmacies and jewelers. The pedestrian route was semi-open to traffic in the mornings, for deliveries. Small trucks were inching down the street, or parked in front of stores, idling. Shopgirls were unlocking doors, carrying boxes, checking hair and makeup; deliverymen were operating hydraulic lifts, pushing dollies, carrying bulky boxes. And here was so-called Bill Maclean, nonexistent currency trader from Chicago.

"Yes," Kate said, "it certainly is. What gets you out of the office this morning?"

Kate had been wanting to tell Dexter about her research. She'd been partially amused by her discovery that the Macleans were on some level fictional. But she also imagined scenarios in which they were fugitives from bankruptcy, or in the witness-protection program, or mobsters in hiding. Bank robbers, murderers, dangerous criminals on the lam. Or maybe, even, they were CIA.

But there were a few impediments to telling Dexter about any of her suspicions. First was that Bill was rapidly becoming Dexter's friend. His only friend. The two men had played tennis again followed by dinner again, and Dexter had come home late, and happy.

As a couple, Kate and Dexter had been to a wine tasting organized by the American Women's Club; they'd been to a school mixer; they'd gone to the movies and the theater. They'd been invited to another family's house for a dinner, and they'd hosted a different family. They knew some people. But it was really Kate who knew a few women, and Dexter was merely along, as a husband, making small talk with British bankers and Dutch lawyers and Swedish salesmen. But Bill Maclean was Dexter's, and Kate didn't want to take that away. She didn't want to seem to be trying to take it away.

The second impediment was that she didn't want to acknowledge that part of her impetus to Internet stalking was a long habit of trusting no one. A habit whose genesis was the self-knowledge that she herself was untrustworthy.

"Uh-oh." Bill was smiling mischievously. "Looks like you've caught me."

"At what?"

Third was she absolutely couldn't admit that some of the motivation—a tiny part, but more than nonexistent—was sexual attraction.

"Well, my wife has left town. She went to Brussels this morning."

Kate had reconciled herself to saying nothing to Dexter about the Macleans's phantom nature. Not until—not unless—she discovered more. Or until she tried to discover more and failed to unearth anything, which would be its own discovery.

"So I'm walking around the *ville*"—Bill took a step closer, then another, then he whispered in her ear—"looking for a woman who I can spend the day in bed with."

Kate's mouth dropped open.

Bill's smile grew, then he laughed. "Just kidding," he said. He hefted a small shopping bag. "I needed something at the computer store."

She slapped him on the chest, not too hard. "Bastard." She stared at him, intrigued; he stared right back, playful. This could be a fun thing. Maybe it would benefit both Kate and Bill, perhaps in a way all four of them. A harmless little flirtation. Everyone has them.

"That was quite a maneuver you pulled in Paris," Kate said. "Very brave. Very manly."

"Oh pshaw." Facetiously. "It was nothing."

"Where'd you learn how to do that?"

"I didn't learn anything," he said. "That was just my lightning-fast reflexes."

This didn't seem true, but Kate knew better than to push. "Is Julia really in Brussels?"

"Yes. She went to see an old friend who's passing through, for whatever reason it is that people go to Belgium."

"An old friend from college?"

"No."

"Where'd Julia go to college, anyway?" Kate kept her eyes glued to Bill's, looking for a sign of evasion. There was none.

"University of Illinois."

"And you? What's your alma mater?"

"Wow."

"Wow what?"

Bill looked left, then right. "I didn't realize that I'd be on a *job* interview, here on the street. As you know, all's I was hoping for was a midday dalliance." He grinned. "But now that we're in it, I have to ask: how much does this particular position pay?"

"That depends," she said, "on a number of factors."

"Such as?"

"Well, where'd you receive your undergraduate degree?"

A quick look of confusion—maybe concern—flitted across his eyes, his forehead. But around the mouth, the smile remained frozen in place. "Chicago."

"University of?"

"That's right."

"Not bad. Your major?"

"I got around."

She arched an eyebrow.

"Let's call it *interdisciplinary*."

"Hmm. And graduate school?"

"None."

"I see. Most recent position?"

"Senior partner for a boutique currency trading firm."

"Why'd you leave?"

"Went out of business," he said, with something that sounded like finality; this part of the game was over. But Bill was still wearing a small smug smile, the supremely confident look of one of those guys who's competent at everything, at skiing and tennis and auto repairs and finish-carpentry, at communicating in languages he doesn't speak, at tipping porters and bribing cops, at foreplay and oral sex.

"Listen," he said, taking a step toward her, again, "to tell you the truth, my current gig is pretty good, and I just started it; I'm not really looking for a new one. So"—again, leaning in too far, his mouth right beside her head, his lips to her ear, making the hairs on her neck stand on end—"are we going to bed, or not?"

Bill was pretending it was a joke. But no one makes this joke unless it's not one. It's an excuse to open the door to a possibility; it's an announcement, loud and clear, that the door is open. "Your husband, I believe, is also out of town."

Although Kate had never been unfaithful, she'd been invited. More than a couple of times. It was this type of supposed joke that had been one of the more common forms of proposition.

Kate felt a chink in her armor, in her lifelong struggle against men like Bill: slick men, manipulative men, dangerous men. The opposite breed of beast from the man she'd married, the more civilized type that she'd willed herself, intellectually and pragmatically, to choose.

"No," Kate said, shaking her head, but smiling, "we're not going to bed," fully cognizant that her answer sounded equivocal. Although she would never end up going there, she felt compelled to let Bill lead her along.

"If you say so," he said.

✦ ✦ ✦

KATE HAD LET down her vigilance, and had allowed the boys' mess to migrate to the guest room, the office, the space where she now sat, waiting for the suddenly slow DSL connection to refresh a page, looking disgustedly around the room at the giant plastic vehicles—a human-limb-sized airplane, a helicopter, various police and fire vehicles—that were littering the floor. She felt compelled to clean up, but also repelled; she couldn't stand picking up toys.

The screen blinked back to life, the page finished loading. There were three campuses for the University of Illinois: Urbana-Champaign graduated seven thousand per class; six thousand at Chicago; five thousand at Springfield. Some quick calculations ended at a universe of fifty thousand female U of I grads in the possible time span. How many could be named Julia?

As for Bill: there were fewer than fifteen hundred graduates per class at the University of Chicago, and there was no maiden-name issue.

Kate stared at the phone number on the screen, the handset in her hand. Was she really going to do this? Why?

Yes. Because she was innately distrustful, and professionally suspicious. Because she was bored. Because she couldn't help herself.

"Yes," said the woman at the registrar's office, in the broad, flat Midwestern accent that neither Bill nor Julia seemed to have inherited from their homeland. "We had a William Maclean class of '92. Could that be who you're looking for?"

"I imagine so. Is there any way for you to e-mail me a photo?"

"No, I'm sorry. We don't keep photo records of our alumni."

"What about a yearbook?" Kate asked. "He must be in the yearbook."

"Not all students choose to include their photos in yearbooks, ma'am."

"Is there any way for you to check?" As sweetly as possible. "Please?"

No response. Kate thought the line had been disconnected. "Hello?"

"Yes, ma'am. I'll check. Please hold."

Kate used the ensuing silence to wonder whether Dexter would ever examine their phone bill. And if he did, whether he would ask Kate why she was placing calls to Chicago, of all places; he of course knew she had no friends in Chicago. And if he did look at the bill, and ask her about it, whether she would answer with the truth, or . . . maybe she would claim this was some type of customer-service issue, something involving . . . what? . . . what could be the fake reason—

"I'm sorry, ma'am. It looks like William Maclean was one of those students in the class of '92 who chose not to include his photo in the yearbook."

"That's too bad." Not to mention incongruous: the man Kate knew was not someone who would forgo a portrait. And he never would've been.

10

Alone again. Not really alone: with the children, but no husband.

Kate sat down at the computer, again.

What would be the most logical, obvious reason to create fake identities? She opened the browser, her mind meandering . . .

Her first thought, her strongest instinct, was that it would be to hide from something horrible. Something unforgivable and unforgettable that one of them had done. A crime. A murder, and he—she?—had been acquitted, but their lives ruined. So they left the country.

Or it could have been nonviolent, white-collar: he was an embezzler, a crooked accountant. A CFO cooking the books, and he'd sold out the CEO in return for immunity. His reputation was ruined, his social standing unrecoverable, so they were starting afresh.

Or it was her. She could've just served a ten-year sentence for—what? Corrupting a minor? DWI manslaughter? He'd waited for her, neither patiently nor faithfully, but waited nevertheless. She was released. They changed their names and left the country.

Kate opened a spreadsheet, ready to type in names and dates and criminal acts. She returned to the web, and found the Chicago news sites. She started browsing, one crime at a time, looking for photographs of the accused, the convicted, the acquitted, the released.

◆ ◆ ◆

"I'M SORRY TO tell you," Evan had said, "that we're not going to lift your cover."

This was as Kate had expected, after all she'd done, and seen. In a way, the permanent cover was a relief, removing her own decision making from the equation. If she was forbidden to tell anyone, she didn't have to decide not to.

"I see. Okay."

Evan considered her closely, probably trying to determine the extent to which she was disappointed, or frustrated, or angered by this decision. She wasn't any of those.

"And that, Kate, is it."

"Is what?"

"We're finished." ·

Kate glanced at her watch. It was eleven thirty in the morning. "For today?"

"Forever."

"Oh." She didn't push back her chair, or stand, or move in any way. She didn't want this part to be over. Because when this part was over, it was the end of the whole thing. Her whole career. "Really?"

Evan stood. "Really." His hand out. The bitter end.

◆ ◆ ◆

KATE'S STREET TURNED gently and then ended abruptly, like many European streets. In the States the streets were all long and straight, extending for miles, stretching as far as anyone could see, dozens or scores or hundreds of blocks. Europe vs. America, in a nutshell. The French don't even have a word for the idea of a city block.

A barrier stood at the entrance to the rue du Rost, red and white diagonal stripes on a strip of steel sitting atop sawhorses, RUE BARRÉE painted in neat stenciled block letters, black paint. A policeman stood at inattentive attention, chatting up a woman in a short apron. A waitress on a cigarette break.

Kate walked past the palace gates, watched the guards notice and dismiss her. She looked one in the eye, a fresh-faced man wearing rimless glasses, and attempted a smile, but he didn't react. The parking area back there was filled with cars, and people, and activity.

She crossed the street and entered a building and buzzed a bell.

"Come on up!" Julia exclaimed through the intercom.

The elevator was tiny, like her own. It must have been challenging for the architects and engineers, finding a way to carve elevator shafts into all these ancient buildings.

"Welcome." Julia was holding the door open with one hand, using the other to usher Kate inside. There seemed something antiquated in the gentility of this gesture; something mannered, but not ironic. Something odd. "So nice to have you over, finally."

Kate walked in tentatively, still not used to wandering around people's homes in the middle of the day. Back in Washington, the only places she'd wandered in daytime besides her own offices were field trips to the State Department or Capitol Hill. When she'd socialized at night, it had usually been in restaurants, at theaters. In public places. It felt intimate to be in Julia's apartment, alone with her, in the middle of the day. It felt illicit.

"Thanks for having me." Kate passed through the foyer into a long room that served as living and dining rooms, with a bank of windows in the western wall. Through every window was a view of the *palais,* richly swagged curtains and wrought-iron gates, balustraded balconies and sandstone turrets, an unfamiliar flag flying on top.

Julia noticed Kate staring at the palace. She followed Kate's gaze to the flagpole. "The flag is up," Julia said. "This means the grand duke is in residence."

"Really?" Kate asked. "That's true?"

"Yes. And it's lowered when he's not in the building."

"But that flag? That's not the Luxembourg flag."

"Oh?" Julia joined Kate at the window. "You're right. That's the Italian flag, I think. That means an important Italian is visiting. The prime minister, maybe? Or the president? What do they have in Italy?"

"Both." Kate reminded herself to not be too much of an expert. Added, "I think."

"Well"—Julia shrugged—"one of them's over there now."

"I bet you never lived across the street from a monarch before."

Julia laughed.

"Where *have* you lived?"

"Different parts of Chicago."

"Your whole life?"

"Nearly." Julia turned away. "I'll go make the coffee. A cappuccino for you?"

This was typical of Julia's discreet evasion. She never outright refused to answer a question, but rather responded without specifics, deflecting the question back at the asker, turning the conversation away from her history without drawing any attention to the redirection. But that's exactly what had captured Kate's attention, aroused her suspicion.

Sometimes, Julia simply found an excuse to leave the room.

"A cappuccino would be great."

Kate looked into the palace yard, a ground cover of tan gravel under a canopy of pines and chestnuts. A dozen cars, nearly all of them deep blue Audi sedans. For license plates, the cars had panels of two stripes, blue and orange, with no numbers or letters or any identification. The single non-Audi, the car parked nearest the porte cochere, was a vintage Rolls-Royce, grand and gleaming in a blue that matched all the other cars—or, probably, it was vice versa. The Rolls's license plate consisted solely of a crown.

Royalty. Very different from merely rich.

A handful of Luxembourgeois military were loitering in the backyard, near a cluster of men in different uniforms; these must've been Italians. A few security-looking guys wearing black suits stood off to the side, looking more alert than the uniformed personnel.

Kate could hear the crunch of gravel under the hard soles of the patent-leather shoes of the tall man who was striding across the yard, wearing a cutaway military jacket with epaulets. The Luxembourgeois military came to attention and saluted the man as he strode by, not pausing or slowing down or glancing at anyone.

The Italian military didn't salute, but they did bring their bearings erect, and they stopped talking and watched him until he'd entered the porte cochere, his heels clicking on the wood tiles, a much quieter driveway for horses' hooves than one paved in stone.

She began to turn from the window, but something caught her eye: on the second floor, up near her level, someone was opening a towering French door to a narrow balcony. An elegant man in a dark suit stepped outside, and surveyed the scene in the yard below. He reached into his jacket, pulled out a packet of cigarettes, and bumped one out. He lit the cigarette with a gold lighter, and leaned on the low stone wall.

Kate could see now that his necktie, which at first glance looked like solid navy, was a deep-hued paisley in blues and purples; it was a lovely tie.

As the crow flies, this man was not more than thirty yards away.

It would, Kate couldn't help thinking, be an incredibly easy shot.

✦ ✦ ✦

THE MAN ON the palace balcony took a deep drag of his cigarette, exhaled a big puff, then three perfect smoke rings. Kate could see his eyes scanning the pebbled lot below.

This was exactly the type of setup Kate had used at Payne's Bay. An innocuous seasonal rental with a perfect sight line. But in Barbados it had been a three-hundred-yard shot. Here, you'd barely even need a scope.

"It's sort of addicting, isn't it?" Julia asked. "Watching the goings-on over there."

"Mmm," Kate said, distractedly. Her original suspicion was that the Macleans had fled the States to escape something. But now she was becoming convinced of the opposite: they'd come to Luxembourg to accomplish something specific. Was it completely unreasonable to think it was an assassination?

◆ ◆ ◆

KATE TURNED OUT the light and turned to Dexter, the taste of red wine mingled with toothpaste, moving through the paces, grabbing this and licking that, paint-by-numbers sex, not particularly satisfying nor in any fashion problematic, just another unremarkable in a series of uncountables.

And after, a drink of water, pajamas pulled on, breath not all that difficult to catch.

"Listen, tomorrow night I'm playing tennis with Bill," Dexter said.

She didn't turn to Dexter, in the dark. "You have a good time with him, don't you?"

"Yeah. He's a good guy."

Kate stared at the ceiling. She wanted, needed, to talk about this with someone, with this exact someone. As much as Kate had been resenting Dexter, and this new life of hers, he was still her best friend. But she was worried—no, it was beyond the uncertainty of worry; it was awareness—that this would cross some line in their marriage, a line that no one acknowledged until you were on its precipice. You know the lines are there, you feel them: the things you don't discuss. The sexual fantasies. The flirtations with other people. The deep-seated distrusts, misgivings, resentments. You go about your business, as far away from these lines as possible, pretending they're not there. So when you eventually find yourself at one of these lines, your toe inching over, it's not only shocking and horrifying, it's banal. Because you've always been aware that the lines were there, where you were trying with all your might not to see them, knowing that sooner or later you would.

"Why?" Dexter asked. "You sound like you have something on your mind."

If Kate said, "Dexter, I'm afraid that Bill and Julia aren't who they claim," he would be angry. He'd be defensive. He'd have all sorts of possible, plausible explanations.

"You have something against Bill?"

Eventually Dexter would confront Bill, nonconfrontationally. And he'd be fed a line, which Dexter would swallow. They were in the witness-protection program, is what Kate suspected they'd claim. They couldn't discuss the details, the veracity of the story couldn't be confirmed, couldn't be proven or disproven. That's what *her* story would be, if she were in Bill's shoes.

Kate wasn't sure which she most wanted to avoid: fighting with Dexter about Bill's possible secrets, or revealing to Dexter—finally—her own.

So she lay there, feet splayed, looking up at the dark ceiling, trying to figure out a way to say something to her husband.

In hindsight, this was the moment—not a unique moment, but a specific one that she remembered, later—that could've changed so much. All the craziness hadn't started; she hadn't yet begun stockpiling new secrets, each addition compounding the ones that preceded, a vicious cycle, out of control.

Lying in bed, wanting to start a conversation but unable to bring herself to begin, and eventually saying nothing other than "No, of course not. Bill is great."

The most important non-action of her life.

At one end of the hall is the linen closet, neatly organized shelves and cubbies filled with floral-print bedclothes and plush white towels. At the other end is the closet where they keep the luggage. Kate turns the battered brass knob that's set into the ornately molded plate that's screwed to the gleaming creamy paint of the paneled closet door.

The large pieces are stacked one upon the other on the floor, a trunk and two full-sized suitcases. These big things are what they use to pack for the summer on the Côte d'Azur, or a few weeks in Umbria. But what she pulls down are two midsize wheelies and a tote.

Kate wheels one of the bags to the boys' room. She packs three days' pants and shirts, socks and underwear. In the adjoining bathroom, she pulls a toilet kit from the shelf above the mirror, into which she dumps their toothbrushes and toothpaste. She grabs the first-aid kit from the basket below the sink. Little boys do a lot of bleeding, wherever they go; European playgrounds are a lot less padded than American ones. Kate long ago tired of searching for plasters and antibiotic cream in Belgium and Germany, in Italy and Spain. So now they travel with their own supply.

She walks to her bedroom, through it, into the dressing room. She unfolds a luggage stand and lays the bag on it, adds her own things automatically, thinking about many subjects, none of them clothing. By her most recent reckoning, she has packed their bags forty-three separate times in the two years they've lived in Europe. Back in her old life, before the kids were born? Hundreds of times.

Kate finishes the autopilot packing. Before they depart, she will remember something: a phone charger, the boys' current books, passports. She always does, when she's packing while distracted. So she doesn't zip the bag closed, and leaves it on the stand, ready for whatever she will remember later.

She has no idea how long she's packing for. She could be packing pointlessly, for nothing. Or for one night or three, or for a few weeks or a month. Or forever.

But this is what they'd discussed, she and Dexter. If someone showed up, if they thought they were compromised, they'd pack for three days. Easily transportable luggage, not notable to anyone as being a lot of stuff, just a jaunt somewhere. If it turned out they were away much longer, they could always buy whatever they needed. They had plenty of money. And their money could be used to buy them flexibility somewhere else, later. Which is what they might not have here in Paris, now.

Kate retrieves the second wheelie bag, brings it to the other side of the dressing room, props it on the other luggage stand. Dexter's.

Matching luggage. She never would've guessed that one day she'd become a woman with a ten-piece set of matching luggage. This is yet another persona that she has fallen into, without quite intending to.

Kate is again standing in her long, elegant hallway, its wallpapered surfaces lined with photos of her children, skiing in the French Alps and frolicking in the Mediterranean surf, on canals in Amsterdam and Bruges, at the Vatican and the Eiffel Tower, the zoo in Barcelona and a theme park in Denmark and a playground in Kensington Gardens. The hallway doors are all flung open, to the public rooms and private rooms, light streaming from a variety of sources, at different angles.

Kate sighs. She doesn't want to leave Paris. She wants to stay here, to live here. She wants her children to answer "Paris" to the question "Where are you from?"

All she needs is a little something different, here, to round out her life. She needs to scratch an itch. Moving to Bali or Tasmania or Mykonos isn't going to do it. The problem is—the problem will always be—within herself, rooted in her distant past, back when she made the fateful decisions to become the person she became, back . . .

. . . back in college . . .

Something occurs to her, and she sets off down the hall, quickly.

11

Kate stared at her computer in front of the window, the view now dark and cloaked in fog punctuated by hazy points of light. Dark somber Impressionism, with electricity.

Jake and Ben were on the floor, playing diligently, sitting crisscross applesauce. Kate took her hands off the keyboard, and sighed.

"Mommy, what's wrong?"

She looked down at Jake, big concerned eyes under an innocent, unlined forehead. "I haven't found what I'm looking for."

"Oh," Ben said. "Do you want to play with us?"

Kate had spent the equivalent of a full workweek searching for criminals who could've been Bill or Julia. She'd found nothing.

"Yes." She folded the laptop. Gave up being a spy, and went back to being a mom. "Yes I do."

❖ ❖ ❖

THE DRYER'S BUZZER went off just as Kate cut a tomato in half. She distractedly set the tomato down on a piece of paper towel. After ten minutes of laundry folding, the tomato's juices had bled onto the towel, radiating along the fault lines of its fibers, dark red tendrils reaching out, grabbing Kate's consciousness and dragging her back to a hotel room in New York City, a man lying on the floor, blood oozing from a crater in the back of his head, seeping into the pale carpeting in the same pattern as this tomato's juices, on this paper towel.

And then the unexpected woman had been standing there, mouth open, frozen.

Years before that, it had been Hayden who'd explained about blood. "Shakespeare was no dope," he'd said to Kate, crossing the Ponte

Umberto I. The day's training was completed, and her trainer was taking her to dinner, at a trattoria behind the Castel Sant'Angelo. "The thing that *tor*tured Lady Macbeth was Duncan's blood. The same thing will torture you too, if you allow it. *Out, damn'd spot!*"

Kate looked at Hayden. Over his shoulder was the majestic dome of St. Peter's, bathed in the golden light of sunset. He too turned to admire the view.

"Once you see some things," Hayden said, "you can *nev*er forget them. If you don't want to have to see them for the rest of your life, it's better not to look in the first place."

They turned away from the Vatican, started walking again toward the old prison. *"Who would have thought the old man to have had so much blood in him?"* Hayden was CIA via Back Bay and then Groton and Harvard, just like his father and grandfather before him. Kate suspected they all quoted literature that was never less than a few hundred years old.

"Remember, Kate," he'd said. "They *all* have a surprising amount of blood in them."

Fifteen years later, staring at her soiled paper towel, Kate realized why she'd been planning a family trip to Germany.

✦ ✦ ✦

THE CHILDREN WERE upstairs, playing dress-up, loudly. Wearing gladiator helmets, which the boys called *gladier helmicks*. Kate didn't have the heart to correct them. If she allowed these childish mispronunciations, maybe they'd stay younger, longer. Then so would she.

Kate shut the guest-room door. Punched in the digits.

"What do you have for me today?" she asked.

"Hmm, let's see . . . Charlie Chaplin once entered a Charlie Chaplin look-alike contest, and *lost*. He didn't even make the *finals*."

"Nice. That's a seven. Maybe eight."

"Well thank you very much."

"Listen, I'm planning a family trip to Bavaria." Kate knew this conversation was being recorded. Maybe monitored in real-time, someone in headphones listening for a minute and then calling in his boss, and his boss calling a colleague, all of them sitting around with headphones plugged into a panel of jacks, wondering what this exchange was about. It was an unusual link again, from this open private line in Luxembourg to the office in Munich. "Any advice for me?"

"Ba*va*ria! Wonderful. I've a plethora of suggestions." Hayden rattled off the names of hotels and restaurants, directions, sights.

When he was finished, Kate said, "I also thought we might get together, you and I."

If Hayden was suspicious about this, he didn't let on. But of course he wouldn't.

✦ ✦ ✦

"BONJOUR?" THE UNCERTAIN voice crackled over the intercom.

"Hi!" Kate semi-screamed into the microphone. "It's Kate!"

Pause. "Kate?"

"Yes!"

"Oh . . . Hi. Come on up."

The doorbell buzzed, a weak little hum, like a malfunctioning toaster. Upstairs, in the dark stunted hallway, Julia was leaning on her door-jamb in a terry-cloth robe, trying to smile but not much succeeding. It was nine A.M.

"Sorry for not calling. I'm having a bit of a morning."

"No worries," Julia said, sounding odd. Julia didn't say things like "No worries."

"I rushed out this morning," Kate said, "and forgot not only my phone, but also my house keys. All I have is the car key. Could I use your phone? I need to call Dexter."

"Of course."

Julia walked into the guest bedroom, retrieved a landline from its dock on the desk, and thrust the phone at Kate.

"Thanks. Sorry again to bother you. And Bill. Is he here?"

"No. He left a few minutes ago."

Kate knew this. "Thanks again."

Kate dialed Dexter's office. When she'd hatched this plan, she'd considered making this call a fake one—dialing a nonexistent number, or her own mobile, then having a pretend conversation. But if she was right about Julia and Bill, they'd catch her; they'd find a way. Maybe Bill would quiz Dexter; maybe Julia would check the phone records.

So it had to be the real thing. And for extra verisimilitude—with Julia, with Dexter, with herself—Kate had also contrived to rush out of her apartment, and had purposefully left her keys and phone sitting impotently on the kitchen counter.

"Bonjour. Dexter Moore."

99

"Hi," Kate said. "It's me. I forgot my house keys. Could you meet me at home?"

"Jesus, Kat."

She knew he would be pissed; she was counting on it. He'd left for work at seven in the morning, a busy day, a Big Day. That's why she was doing this today: so he would be angry, and she could therefore say, "Don't give me grief, Dexter," and roll her eyes at Julia and hold up an indulgence-begging finger, and walk into the guest bedroom for privacy, to have a phone-fight with her husband, alone.

Kate looked around the room quickly but carefully, taking in everything. The bed was made neatly, but not perfectly; of the four pillows, one bore the unmistakable wrinkles and deep folds and misshapenness of something that had been slept on, then not fluffed out.

"I forgot my keys, by mistake," Kate said. "I didn't spit in your eye, on purpose."

A book sat on the bedside table near the used pillow, a paperback with a simple cover depicting farmland, a female author, the words A NOVEL under a long, vague title; chick lit. A water glass. A tissue box. Lip balm.

It was Julia who was sleeping here, in this bed that was not in the master bedroom.

"I'm about to walk out," Dexter said, "to a meeting."

The desk was small, tidy. The laptop was closed; there were no readable papers lying around, other than a couple envelopes, addressed to a street in Limpertsberg and to an entity called WJM, S.A. This was a *société anonyme,* similar to the *société à responsibilité limitée,* which was continental for *Ltd*. This, she assumed, was William J. Maclean, Inc.

There was a file drawer, but no way that Kate could chance opening it; that would be impossible to explain, if she got caught.

The peripheral device was a big affair, a scanner and photocopier and printer all-in-one. There was a small pile of business cards on the desk. Kate pulled a handkerchief out of her jeans and used it to shuffle through the cards, her fingers not touching the stack of paper. One of them was for a tennis club; Julia didn't play tennis. Kate plucked this one out with the hankie, slid the card into her pocket.

"I understand, Dex, and I'm sorry."

She walked to the bedside table, safely out of Julia's sight. She used the handkerchief to pick up the lip balm and drop it in with the pilfered business card.

Kate wondered if this was an unhappy marriage, or if Julia was a standard-issue insomniac, or if she had a cold and didn't want to disturb her husband last night.

Or if this was something far less ordinary.

✦ ✦ ✦

"AND DEXTER WILL be late," Kate said. "He's always late returning from meetings; somehow, everything takes longer than he expects it to. So we don't need to be back till one."

"Okay." Julia called out from the bathroom, where she was fixing her makeup. Kate knew Julia well enough to know that she never left the house without looking as perfect as she could.

Kate wandered over to the windows that faced the palace. The flagpole was flagless; no royalty in residence. The yard was empty of vehicles. A single guard stood at the back gate, weapon resting on his shoulder, bored. This window was certainly a great vantage.

But the crucial thing, Kate knew, was being able to get out. Just like a bank robbery, or an extramarital affair: getting in is the easy part.

"So shall we?" They were headed to a mall, to while away the morning.

"We shall." Kate pushed a small button on her watch, and walked away from the window on the rue de l'Eau, out the apartment door, into the tiny elevator, and six levels down, into the garage, where they climbed into Julia's Mercedes, and exited onto a different street, the rue du St-Esprit, a narrow cobblestone lane that was a few confusing turns away from the *palais,* and after fifty yards St-Esprit made a dramatic ninety-degree turn on a steep descent before dead-ending into the equally narrow cobblestoned lane called rue Large, which climbed steeply through a medieval arch before ending at rue Sigefroi, which a couple seconds later merged into the Montée du Clausen, aka local route 1, a road that would soon present the choice of speeding away at a hundred kilometers per hour along every point of the compass, to Germany or France, to the airport or the countryside, to anywhere.

Kate checked her watch: under two minutes from the window to unimpeded freedom.

They were foreign nationals, bearing false names, living across the street from a target-rich environment, with a vantage that couldn't be clearer, an escape that couldn't be quicker.

This was just circumstantial evidence, Kate knew. And maybe she wasn't even genuinely suspicious. Maybe she'd tricked herself into suspicion so she'd have an excuse to investigate them. To have something to do. Anything.

She was having a hard time distinguishing among the levels of implausibility of various scenarios that were floating around the murky swamp of her imagination. On the one hand, it seemed highly unlikely—it seemed nearly outrageous—that a hit-man team would come to Luxembourg to assassinate someone. She couldn't deny that. But she also couldn't dismiss this as a rational explanation for why a pair of people with secret identities would rent a flat that would allow such an ideal opportunity on assassinate-able characters.

Other scenarios revolved around flight. But could these people really be fugitives?

Or of course the worst-case scenario: could they be in Luxembourg for Kate?

Only a single thread of her past could extend to the present, reaching out across five years and the Atlantic to yank her back, to wrap itself around her neck and strangle her.

Kate had always known that she hadn't heard the last about Eduardo Torres. There were loose ends, unanswered questions; there was evidence. Plus no one had ever unearthed Torres's fortune, which was widely believed to be tens of millions of dollars. The money was assumed to be squirreled away in a European numbered account.

And here Kate was, newly retired before forty, living in the world headquarters of numbered accounts, with a husband who was an unparalleled expert in the security of numbered accounts.

Kate looked awfully suspicious.

But so did Bill and Julia. She needed to dig deeper.

12

It was lightly drizzling, or misting, or whatever it's called when minuscule bits of water, too fine to feel distinct drops, are drifting down out of the sky.

The wipers were on their slowest setting. Three seconds between swipes, during which the windshield clouded up, became almost too wet to see through, and then *swoosh,* clear again.

The ignition was ignited, the headlights lit, the tuner tuned to France Culture. Kate was having a tough time following the thread of the talk radio. The general subject seemed to be Baudelaire. Or at least *Baudelaire* was the word she recognized, repeated over and over. Or it could've been *beau de l'aire* they were talking about, perhaps some type of beautiful atmosphere. Which was sort of the opposite of Baudelaire.

A business card from a podiatrist was posed in the passenger seat. She could claim that she was early to her appointment. She'd say she had maybe a heel spur, wherein her heel hurt, but there was no exterior evidence that any non-physician could visually check. So she was sitting in her warm and dry car, trying to learn French by radio osmosis, listening to impassioned academics wage the obscure but apparently permanent Baudelaire war—what were the sides? what were the issues?—while she waited for whatever half-hour-on-the-dot was next. That's when her pretend appointment was.

No, she would answer, she had no idea that Bill's office was here. How could she? She'd memorized this address from the envelopes in his guest room.

Tall stone town houses were flush up against the sidewalk, with almost-gardens in front, tiny patches of grass, the stray denuded shrub. The buildings were gray or tan or putty; the sidewalk was paved in light gray concrete, the street in dark gray asphalt. The cars were shades of silver and gray and sometimes black; the sky a sodden slate. It was a colorless landscape, washed out by rain and the expectation of it, designed and constructed to match the dismal weather.

Kate had been sitting there for nearly an hour, and she still had more than three hours before she needed to be on her way to pick up the children. Three hours, and no one would know what she was doing, or where she was doing it, or for the love of God why.

Unless someone had tampered with her car, and for example installed a battery-operated GPS transmitter in the hollow under the supple gray leather of the passenger seat.

Bill emerged at 11:40. He looked both ways before descending the small staircase to the sidewalk. He had changed into tennis clothes, white shorts and a warm-up jacket with red and blue racing stripes down the sleeves. In this cold rain he looked comically incongruous, a Monty Python skit.

He hustled to his tidy little BMW, a plaything of a car. He gunned the engine, shifting gears aggressively, tearing through the quiet streets, on his way to a twelve o'clock court in Bel-Air. And then lunch. All with Dexter.

It had been Julia's suggestion, proffered to Kate—"Don't you think they should play during the day? So they could be with us at night?"—who in turn had passed it to Dexter. "It will do you good," Kate had said, "to get some exercise." In Washington, Dexter had exercised in the evenings. But now he was usually working after dark. And when he didn't need to be working, Kate wanted him home, with the children. With her.

That's how it came to pass that Kate had two luxurious hours when she knew Bill would not be in his office, at this building. So she waited another five minutes, to make sure he hadn't forgotten his water bottle or can of balls, his cell phone or knee brace, anything; then she waited an extra five, just to be extra-sure. And to procrastinate.

She glanced at herself in the sun-visor mirror.

This was a bizarre moment: this crossing-over from a hypothetical plan to a concrete caper, giving in to what may turn out to be an utterly outlandish idea, possibly letting go of some important tether to sanity. Deciding yes: I will do this. But not deciding it 100 percent, because that would be admitting too much to herself, about herself, that she didn't want to admit. But deciding it 95 percent, enough to take the possibly outlandish action, but not enough to believe beyond a reasonable doubt that this wasn't just a goof, a lark, but an actual non-insane plan.

Kate pulled the brim of her new rubberized yellow rain cap as low as it would go. Her normal cap, bought in Copenhagen a month ago, was a vivid multicolor. There was a lot of attractive foul-weather gear in Scandinavia; there was a lot of foul weather. But today's cap was a cheap something she bought yesterday, at a discount store in Gare. She would throw it away later today.

She picked up the envelope from the passenger seat, and wrote Bill's building address on it; inside was a special offer from a bicycle shop, a 20 percent discount on any bike. She'd picked up this flyer at the bike shop yesterday, when she was still debating this possibly insane plan.

She got out of the car, tugged on her leather gloves, and walked across the street.

Of the five buzzers, the fifth was unlabeled. The first had a Luxembourgeois or German name; the second an easily pronounced French name, Dupuis; the third was Underwood. The fourth read *WJM, S.A.*

She wrote *Underwood* on the envelope.

She rang Bill's bell. If someone unexpectedly answered, she'd claim she was looking for Underwood. But the only other activity she'd seen of this building was a dowager who'd left at eleven, carrying a folded-up shopping bag, and returned an hour later with the same bag, now looking far heavier than possible, the old woman listing to one side, tottering under the weight. Kate had watched her struggle up the slope of the street, an interminable climb, while the woman's mouth constantly moved, her lips pursing, her cheeks dimpling: the contortions of a native French speaker, keeping the facial muscles toned for all those nasal vowels that can be properly pronounced only with strong lips. This must have been Mme. Dupuis.

Kate rang again. There didn't seem to be any security cameras here at this door. But these days, cameras could be anywhere. She kept her eyes well below the brim of the cap.

She rang Dupuis.

"Booooooooon-jourrrrrrr!" Yes, that was the voice of the old lady.

"Bonjour, madame," Kate answered. *"J'ai une lettre pour Underwood, mais il ne repond pas. La lettre, elle est très importante."*

"Ouuuuiiiiii, mademoisselllllllllle."

The old woman buzzed. Kate pushed open the windowed door, then let it swing shut of its own accord; it closed with a noticeable rattling of the window.

Kate climbed the stairs, turned a corner, and saw Mme. Dupuis waiting at her door.

"*Merci, madame,*" Kate said.

"*De rien, mademoissellllllllllle. Au deuxième étagggggggge.*"

Kate climbed to the second floor, pushed the envelope under the Underwood door, then hustled down the stairs. She opened the front door, let it rattle closed. But she stayed inside. She stood still for a minute. Then she crept back up the stairs.

As she was rounding the corner toward the second flight, she heard voices, a man and a woman. *Damn.* Kate spun her head around: nowhere to hide. She could run to the basement, but what if they were going down to the garage? If there's one thing Kate didn't want, it was to be caught hiding.

She would bluff her way past them. She turned the corner, and started climbing the stairs. As the couple turned into the stairwell, Kate glanced up, feigning surprise, smiling. "*Bonjour,*" she said.

"*Bonjour,*" the man said. He was echoed quietly by the woman. The pair waited at the top of the narrow stairwell, allowing Kate to pass.

"*Est-ce que je peux vous aider?*" the man asked.

Kate returned a blank stare, even though she knew exactly what he was asking.

"Can I 'elp you?" he tried in English.

"Oh!" Kate smiled. "No, thank you. I'm visiting Bill Maclean?"

The man gave her a tight grin; the woman remained silent.

Kate brushed past them. "*Merci!*"

Her heart was racing. And this would be the easy part.

◆ ◆ ◆

BILL'S OFFICE WAS on the top floor, one of two doors in a short, well-lit hall; the first door was unlabeled. She tried his door, but of course it didn't open. She walked to the window at the end of the hall, and turned the handle to open it—all the windows in Luxembourg worked the same way, with side hinges and top hinges.

She swung open this window, leaned out, surveyed the windows and ledges, possible means of entry. Evergreens shielded the view from the neighboring building.

Kate retreated through the stone-tiled hall. There was a mat at Bill's door, the name of his company on a brass plaque, a buzzer. There were three locks, and one of them looked like a doozy. The lighting came from two upward-facing sconces, and the big uncurtained window. Nothing in this hall was immediately apparent to be a security camera.

She knelt at his door. She reached into her back pocket and took out a small leather pouch, well-worn covers bound by a no-nonsense rubber band, holding an assortment of miniature screwdrivers and rubber-handled pins and needle-nose pliers. She set to work intently with the tiny tools in her fingers, her face just inches away. She wouldn't bother with the two easy locks—low-grade pieces of security, more deterrents than preventatives—unless she could pick the high-end one.

While it was true that she had privacy up here on the top floor, and the luxury of uninterruptable time, she didn't have forever. And lock-picking had never been an area of particular expertise for her. Locks were not an important part of the Latin American experience—anything worth locking was worth guarding with a live armed body.

What had been important in her line of work were maps, which she was expert in reading. And guns, which she was expert in cleaning, repairing, and firing. She'd needed to master a variety of Spanish dialects, with special emphasis on slang, especially the many vulgar words for genitalia. She'd grown up in a declining city in coastal Connecticut that was undergoing a massive influx of Latin Americans. She'd had plenty of opportunity to learn gutter Spanish, on the streets, as well as proper Spanish, in her own home, from the low-paid babysitters whom Kate's parents had been able to afford for after-school care, back when she and her sister were still innocent little girls, released from first or third grades at three o'clock into the waiting arms of short, round women named Rosario and Guadalupe.

It had been sporadically necessary for Kate to pilot civilian helicopters and propeller planes. She'd learned how to do both, but not exhaustively, in addition to the standard-issue paramilitary training that she'd undergone during her months on the Farm.

She'd tasted, tested, and snorted small quantities of cocaine from different geographical areas, as well as smoked a sampling of the hemisphere's marijuana. She knew what it would feel like if someone slipped her a roofie or a dose of LSD.

She could memorize any number up to ten digits long, after hearing it once.

She could kill a person.

But what she couldn't do was pick this lock, and she didn't want to waste time on a lost cause.

She approached the second door, the unmarked one. The same brass handle as Bill's, the same buzzer. No plaque, no mat. She reached up to the molding that surrounded the door frame, and ran her finger slowly along the half-inch-wide horizontal surface up there, hoping to find a key to this uninhabited space. No such luck.

She stood stock-still, listening for noises.

Nothing.

Kate set to work quickly but calmly on this lock, an easy one. Within thirty seconds the off-the-shelf apparatus clicked quietly open.

She entered a large, dusty, empty room with one window. She opened the window, and leaned out. As expected, there they were: the windows to Bill's office. In between was a narrow ledge that ran across the bottom of all the windows. This could be done; she'd done something like this before. She took a deep breath and climbed out the window.

✦ ✦ ✦

KATE STOOD ON the nine-inch-wide ledge in the rain, clinging to the side of the building, three stories above the ground.

There was a lot that could go wrong here. One was that someone would see her through the thick stand of evergreens that separated this building from its neighbor, so she had to move quickly.

Another was that she could fall and die, so she had to move carefully.

She side-shuffled a few inches at a time, her face pressed up against the damp stucco.

She heard a sound behind her and below. She turned her head too fast and too carelessly, and scraped her cheek against the wall. The sound was a tree limb brushing against the roof of a car.

It now felt like her cheek was bleeding, but there was no way to check. She couldn't get either hand up to her face without losing balance.

She kept going, another few inches, and another, staying balanced, steady, slowly . . . and another few inches . . . and then she was there, at the sill to Bill's window.

Kate paused, allowed herself a few seconds of respite before moving on to the next task.

She was scared, but she felt comfortable with her fear, like the strange pleasure of rubbing a sore muscle, which doesn't accomplish anything except make you more aware of the pain.

This is where she belonged, up here on this ledge. This is what had been missing from her life.

She removed the tiny flat-head screwdriver from her tight back pocket. She ran it alongside the seam of the window, carefully, smoothly, until she found the catch.

She paused, then gently pulled the screwdriver up.

The lock didn't release.

She tried again, pulling even more gently.

Again, nothing.

Kate willed herself not to panic, in this panic-worthy predicament. Yet more slowly, she ran the thin, sharp head between the jamb and the frame.

She'd practiced this, on her own window. In the middle of the night, when no one could see. It had taken her twenty minutes, out on that sill, forty feet above the cobblestoned path, but she'd finally figured out how to move a screwdriver up against the catch, and rotate the head ever so slightly, to not only release the catch but also to unlock the window so it would swing open on the vertical hinge, not tilt open on the horizontal.

This window mechanism was the same as her own; they were all the same.

She'd practiced. This had to work.

This *had* to work.

She tried again, slowly, slowly, gently . . . *click*.

Kate applied pressure with her knee into the hinge side of the window, and the whole panel swung open slowly. She crouched on the sill, her hands flat against the exterior stucco for balance. She paused, then dove forward into the room, breaking her fall with her hands, rolling softly over yet another polished stone floor, large marble tiles, just like everywhere else in Luxembourg.

She lay still, catching her breath, trying to slow her racing heart. She'd expected that her pulse would accelerate, but this was too much; this was more than she could remember in a long, long time.

Kate shouldn't continue while in such a thorough state of panic; she didn't want to make any stupid mistakes. She closed her eyes and lay still, willing her body to calm itself.

Then she stood and looked around.

♦ ♦ ♦

ON THE FAR side of the room was an exercise bike, parked in front of a small television; also a weight bench and a collection of dumbbells, barbells, and plates, all on a rubberized mat.

There was a desk with a laptop computer, a printer-scanner, a telephone, a scratch pad, a few ballpoints. Some sheets had been torn off the pad. Kate removed the topmost remaining sheet, folded it, put it in her backpack; she'd examine the paper later.

The laptop was open but asleep. She pressed a key to wake it up.

This computer is locked. Please enter your user ID and password. No sense even trying.

Inside the desk, language dictionaries, more pads and pens. Files hung in a drawer made for hanging files: bank records. A few different accounts, with money flowing back and forth among them, a few hundred thousand total, the sums moving up and down, down and up, over and over, the cycle of investments and dividends, withdrawals and transfers.

The name was Bill's, the address this apartment's.

There were magazines, journals, newsletters. General-interest business, and specialized business, and technology, and news. Stacks of them. Kate reached into a pile and pulled out an issue of *The Economist*. All the paper smooth, unruffled, un-dripped-upon with coffee, un-ring-stained by a water glass. Unread, maybe. Or maybe read neatly, without sloppy spillage of beverages. Bill seemed like a neat guy.

Kate leaned back in the swivel chair, looking around without focus while her mind drifted, trying to stumble upon what she should be looking for.

There was a small bedroom. Queen-sized bed, made up sloppily. Soft sheets. Four standard pillows and a large sham. Another spare bed, rumpled. Who sleeps here?

In the drawer of a bedside table, a box of condoms. A depleted box that once held two dozen prophylactics, with only a handful remaining. Who screws here?

Kate lay down next to the condom drawer but kept her feet off to the side, not sullying the sheets. She pressed her face against the top pillow. It smelled like shaving cream, or aftershave or cologne. It smelled like Bill.

She reached her hand out to the bedside table, around back of it, feeling . . . feeling . . . nothing there. She slid her hand underneath the table, patting down the particleboard of another piece of Ikea furniture . . . nothing.

She bent her arm, reached her hand under the bed, under the wooden slats that supported the mattress . . . and there she felt something, leather . . . and she moved her hand a few inches . . .

Kate yanked, knowing exactly what she was pulling out to the side of the bed, then up in front of her. She could see through the bedroom door in a direct sight line to the front door, where, without even intending to, she was now instinctually aiming the Glock 22 that Bill kept in a holster taped to the underside of this bed.

PART II

Kate stands in the French doors of the sitting room, rugs piled upon rugs, high ceilings, wedding-cake moldings, shelves filled with books and bowls, vases with cut flowers, ornate frames for small oil paintings, distressed gilt-edged mirrors.

This thing has been bothering her, rooting around in her subconscious, bumping against the facts and suppositions down amid the foundations of her current beliefs about her life, her husband, how their history came to pass. This thing knocks against memories, forcing her to reexamine them, from the new vantage of another possible explanation to everything. Something about college . . .

Kate strides across her living room to the oversize books, bunched together on an extra-tall shelf. She pulls down Dexter's yearbook. She takes a seat on the settee, the book heavy in her lap.

She thumbs the corners, following alphabetical order, then opens the book prematurely, turning one page and another, until she finds a much younger version of Dexter Moore. The puffy haircut, skinny tie, unlined forehead.

She's now become convinced that she will indeed find what she's looking for.

That duplicitous bastard.

Kate heard the name only once, nearly two years ago, in Berlin. She's almost positive that it ends in *owski,* which will help her confirm, when she eventually finds the right face.

She turns to the beginning of the head shots, last names beginning with A. She closely examines each image, all these two-decade-old pictures, girls and boys who are now men and women, her age. Page after page, patiently. Suddenly this thing seems so obvious, so inevitable.

It doesn't take her long to find it. Not long at all. Except of course the two years that she didn't know she was looking for it.

Now, a total paradigm shift. All the pieces of the puzzle are moving, swirling, disorienting. Kate had been under the impression that she'd solved this puzzle long ago.

She gazes down at the familiar face staring back at her, the optimistic look of a college senior, posing for posterity.

The possible explanations are bombarding Kate, machine-gun fire, too heavy to evade, nothing to do but hide and wait till it subsides, and she can come up for air.

Kate catches sight of movement across the sitting room, quickly realizes that it's herself, a small tuft of her hair in the mirror on the far wall, a tiny corner of herself moving, detached from the whole invisible part. She stands, carries the heavy book back to its unremarkable space on a shelf in the middle of her family room, in the middle of her family's life. The best hiding spots are not the most hidden; they're merely the least searched.

Now that Kate possesses this new information, now that the yearbook has given up its secret, now that Kate recognizes this new reality, she feels unparalleled betrayal. But she also feels new options presenting themselves. New doors opening. She can't make out what's beyond these doors, but she can see the light streaming through.

This has changed everything.

13

Kate was annoyed with Dexter. It had taken him too long to increase the cruise-control setting to 160 kilometers per hour, up from the default 130 of the speedometer's red line. But still, at a hundred miles per hour on the A8, half the cars on the road were going faster.

She was annoyed with the children in the backseat, complaining about the mediocre movie on the portable DVD player that kept toppling over whenever Dexter took a turn too sharply, causing them to shriek.

But mostly Kate was annoyed with herself. She was obsessing about all the mistakes she'd made. Her shoe print in the mud; her muddy footprints in the dust of the vacant next-door suite; her moist footprints on the clean floors of Bill's. Her hair and skin fibers in his bed—maybe actual hairs *on his pillow,* just lying there in high relief, begging to be picked up, examined, DNA-mapped. What other moronic mistakes could she have made?

She'd even scraped her face, a splotchy raspberry on the cheekbone. The injury was easily explained to Dexter—a mishap in the garage, while unloading groceries—but nevertheless suspicious. Not to mention careless and stupid.

She'd behaved like a goddamned amateur.

Plus there'd been the two neighbors on the stairs, as well as old Mme. Dupuis. Witnesses, easily findable; practically inevitable.

Kate watched the unremarkable German countryside roll by. The Saar Valley, hulking industry and glass-and-steel office parks scattered among thick rolling forest, with big-box stores and auto dealerships snug against the *autobahn,* smokestacks and warehouses and access roads converging at traffic-choked intersections.

This had been the messiest mission of her career. But this wasn't her career anymore, was it? She'd resigned three months ago.

✦ ✦ ✦

ROTHENBURG OB DER TAUBER in the biting cold, half-timber everywhere, painted facades, lace curtains, beer halls, sausage shops, an immense Christmas market, medieval fortifications, stone walls with arches and turrets. Another version of a fairy tale, another postcard of a place. Another town-hall tower to climb, entertainment for little boys: going high or going fast. The stairs—how many? Two hundred? Three?—wound around the increasingly narrow walls of the tower, worn and uneven and rickety. At the top, they had to pay a guy, semi-official, with a missing eye. The children couldn't stop staring.

Then they were outside on a tight catwalk, in a gusting, biting wind, high above the town square and the streets that radiated out to the city walls and the countryside, the river, the hills and trees of Bavaria. Dexter pulled down the earflaps of his hat, a red plaid hunting cap lined with rabbit fur, something Kate had bought him for Christmas a half-decade ago.

Kate looked down at the market stalls, the tops of the tourists' heads, ski caps and green felt fedoras, laughably easy to kill.

So what if the Macleans were assassins? What was her responsibility? This was not her job, not her problem. They were not going to kill her, or Dexter. So what business was it of hers? None.

And if they'd come to Luxembourg to kill someone, who?

And who *were* they? They certainly weren't Mob; there was no way that Julia, at least, was in organized crime. They weren't Islamic militants. They had to be American operatives of some sort. Maybe they were Company, or Army Special Forces, or Marines black ops? Private contractors? Were they in Europe to do the dirty work of covert American foreign policy? To assassinate someone who came to Luxembourg to hide ill-begotten money—a Ukrainian oligarch, a Somali warlord, a Serbian smuggler?

And what did she care about the irrelevancies of dirty money?

Or was it someone whose death would be more immediately relevant to American interests? A North Korean diplomat? An Iranian envoy? A Latin president with a Marxist agenda?

Or were they merely hired guns on a civilian mission, a grudge, a corporate intrigue? A CEO? A bank president? A private banker who'd embezzled a fortune from a now very angry billionaire?

Maybe it was something utterly convoluted. Maybe they were going to assassinate an American—the secretary of the treasury? of state?—then frame it on a Cuban or Venezuelan or Palestinian, create the excuse to grandstand, to retaliate, to invade.

There were so many people to be assassinated for so many reasons.

Here a few hundred feet above Germany, she felt like Charles Whitman atop the observation deck in Austin, figuring out whom to pick off with a rifle.

Even though she'd made an unconscionable number of mistakes, it had still felt good out there at Bill's window; it felt like that's where she belonged. Not in a sports-center basement, talking about the loyalty programs of grocery stores. But out on a ledge, without a net.

Kate was increasingly convinced that she was never going to be a happy stay-at-home mom. If there was such a thing.

"Come on," she said to her family, eager to move on, to control what she could. Dexter was snapping pictures of the shivering children, bundled against the cold, red-faced and runny-nosed. "It's freezing up here."

✦ ✦ ✦

"I'LL SEE YOU back at the hotel at six."

"Okay," Dexter said, meeting Kate's kiss but barely glancing at her; it was just a pursing of the lips, not even a proper perfunctory peck. He was sitting on a window ledge, on the ground floor of the science museum.

Kate now had her four hours of liberty. Some of the mums in Luxembourg called this "being let out," like a high-strung terrier released through the kitchen door into the fenced-in yard. They went together, little groups of three or four women without husbands or kids, to London or Paris or Florence: forty-eight hours to shop and drink and eat, perhaps to meet a stranger in a bar and, under cover of a false name and inebriation, take him back to her hotel room for as much and as varied sex as possible before it was time to kick him out and order room-service breakfast. Suited and booted.

Kate made her way through the cold hurrying lunchtime crowds of downtown Munich, through the food vendors in the Viktualmarkt, the town-square Marienplatz and its Rathaus glockenspiel, the pedestrian-only high streets—was there a single city left on the continent without an H&M and a Zara?—and up to ritzy Maximillianstraße, leading away from the opera, as ritzy streets do, sprouting fur coats and fur hats, giant sedans idling at the curbs with liveried drivers behind the wheels, boutiques manned by multilingual salesgirls conversant in the vocabulary of silk and leather in English and French and Russian, neatly packing sturdy, recognizable little shopping bags.

Kate strolled into an opulent hotel lobby, and found a pay phone, and dropped in coins, and dialed the number that she'd lifted from Bill's office, 352 country code first; she imagined the number would be a local Luxembourg one. The piece of paper she'd stolen had been blank, but bore the imprint of what had been written on the prior sheet, easily retrieved with the side of a pencil tip, lightly brushed.

She was correct. "Hello," the woman answered, in American, "this is Jane." Upper Midwest accent, mildly familiar, though Kate couldn't picture the owner of it. "Hello?"

Kate didn't want to risk this woman recognizing her voice.

"Hello?"

Kate hung up. So: Bill was calling an American woman in Luxembourg named Jane. Kate had the definite sense that this was sexual. A sense heightened by being alone in this sexy, swanky hotel, the possibility of taking the elevator upstairs, opening a door to . . .

Of course it would be Bill. Now more than ever, now that she knew he was dangerous. He was a criminal, or a cop, or maybe, like many people she'd come across, he was both. He was handsome and sexy and charming, and brave, and he kept a gun under the bed where he had sex with women who weren't his wife. Women perhaps like Kate.

She left the hotel, trotted across the street to a taxi stand, climbed into one. "Alte Pinakothek, *danke,*" she said. She looked out every window, in all directions, satisfied that no one was following. Even so, she asked the driver to pull over on Ludwigstraße.

"Is half-kilometer to museum," he said.

"Is good," she said, handing over ten euros. "I want to walk."

Up ahead, the university Metro station beckoned with the lights and movement of the bars and shops and restaurants that cluster at subway stops everywhere. But the sidewalks near Kate were unpeopled. She walked past the thick, forbidding stone buildings, the wind whipping around corners, freeze-burning her ears and nose.

Kate was excited but in control. She felt good again, as she had out on that ledge, her pulse quickened, walking purposefully through unfamiliar foreign streets, all her senses attuned, her mind sharp. People had written her off when she'd left the Directorate of Operations to become an analyst in the Directorate of Intelligence. When she'd taken herself out of the field, out of the danger. When she'd written herself off, sitting in a comfortable chair behind a smooth desk.

Again she felt a tingle, her libido coming alive with the rest of her sensory input.

Suddenly, perversely, she blamed Dexter for her attraction to Bill. If Dexter were around more, if he were more attentive in every way—in *any* way: if he said thank you more, or called once in a while to do something other than say he wasn't coming home, or fucked her more frequently or more passionately or more creatively, or if he would just fold a single goddamned load of laundry—then maybe she wouldn't be walking down this street, fantasizing about getting into that bed with the gun strapped to the bottom.

This was all nonsense, she knew. Transference of her own guilt onto an innocent party, an excuse to be angry at someone who wasn't herself. She told herself to focus.

She traversed the windswept plaza in front of the Old Picture Gallery with not another person in sight. The crisscrossing paths created over-sized angled shapes of grass, giant geometry, punctuated by far-flung metal sculptures, bordered by leafless trees. It seemed to get colder as she approached the imposing building; its arched windows looked light-less within. She felt as if she were going to a mysterious court, presided by an omniscient judge.

Off to see the Wizard. She'd attempted to show the movie to the boys, giving into Jake's insistence. But both children fled the room within the first ten minutes, terrified.

Kate paid for her ticket and declined the audio tour; she held on to her handbag and coat. She climbed the stairs, wide and airy expanses of gleaming marble, step after step. She began at the beginning, with the Early Dutch and then Early German Painting, not particularly inter-ested. She moved into the big galleries filled with oversize works by blockbuster artists—Raphael, Botticelli, da Vinci. A pair of Japanese tourists were in here, as everywhere, engrossed in their headsets, cam-eras dangling.

A man alone, his wool overcoat draped over his arm, stood in front of a da Vinci *Virgin and Child*.

The sun was skimming the southern skyline of downtown Munich, casting distinct rays through the massive windows. She checked her watch: 3:58.

Kate moved into the gallery in the dead center of the building, packed with big Rubens canvases. *The Death of Seneca,* the philosopher surprisingly buff. *The Lion Hunt,* brutal, barbaric. And the biggest, *The Great Last Judgment,* a heaping pile of naked humanity, being judged from above by Christ, in turn judged from above by His Father.

"It's incredible, isn't it?"

She glanced at the man from the other room, overcoat over arm, wearing a sport jacket and necktie and pocket square, flannel trousers, and suede shoes. Horn-rimmed glasses, carefully groomed silver hair. He was tall and slender, looked like he could've been anywhere between forty-five and sixty years old.

"Yes." She turned her eyes back to the massive canvas.

"It was commissioned for an altar in Neuburg an der Donau—the Danube, to Yanks like us—Upper Bavaria. But the people—the priests, that is—weren't crazy about all this *nu*dity." A flick of the hand at the painted flesh. "So the painting hung in the church for only a few decades, often covered, hidden from view, before they got rid of it."

"Thanks," she said. "That's interesting."

She looked around the room. No one else here. She could see a security guard in one of the adjoining galleries, keeping a close eye on a family with a pair of young children, schoolboys, a whiff of wildness coming off them, menaces to museums, to the weltanschauung of a German museum guard.

"Actually, it's only semi-interesting. Not more than a four. A generous four."

The man laughed. "Good to see you, my dear."

"And you. It's been a long time."

14

"So are you still enjoying Munich?" Kate asked. "It's been forever, hasn't it?"

Hayden let out another burst of laughter. He had indeed been in Europe forever, his whole career. He'd been in Hungary and Poland for the thick meat of the late Cold War. Here in Germany—Bonn, Berlin, Hamburg—for the arms buildup under Reagan, the ascent of Gorbachev, the collapse of the USSR, the post-Soviet readjustments, German reunification. He was in Brussels for the birth of the EU, the dissolution of borders, the euro. Back to Germany when the whole continent started to respond to the influx of Muslims, the reassertion of reactionary forces, the reemergence of nationalism . . . Hayden had arrived in Europe at the Berlin Wall's midlife; it had now been gone for two decades.

Kate had arrived at the Company with the Wall already down. Latin America was the future—our hemisphere, our borders—even though the Sandinistas had been defeated and Clinton was making noise about normalizing with Castro. It didn't seem at the time that she was walking into that book in the middle of the final chapter. It just seemed like the middle, with the ugliness of the Iran-Contra debacle behind them, the abstractness of the Communist threat dissolved. The future would be concrete, action-oriented, home-turf-relevant results.

And it was. But little by little, year after year, Kate felt herself—her sphere within her directorate—becoming increasingly pointless, a sinking feeling of inefficacy that was hyper-accelerated on September 11, when it could not have mattered less who was in the ascendancy for mayor of Puebla. Although the CIA as an institution rededicated its mission on September 12, Kate as an operations officer never recovered her sense of relevancy. Or irrelevancy.

Throughout it all, Hayden had been right here.

"Love Munich," he said. "Here, let me show you some *smaller* pictures."

Kate followed him into a cozy room, one of the northern galleries that faced the entrance plaza, now in the full shadow of gloaming. He walked past the paintings, to the window. She followed his gaze to a man leaning against a lamppost in the foreground of the vast cold plaza, smoking a cigarette, looking up at the windows. Looking up at them.

"So how was the Romantische Straße? The children must've loved that silly castle Neuschwanstein. They're how old?"

"Five and four."

"Time flies." Although Hayden had no children of his own, he recognized that many people, at a certain point in their lives, begin to measure time not by their own forward progress but by the ages of their children.

Hayden was still looking out the window, watching the man in the plaza. A woman hurried down the steps. The man stopped leaning on the lamppost. As the woman neared, he tossed his cigarette, and locked arms with her, and they walked together, away. Kate wondered if she and Dexter would ever again walk arm in arm, as they had when they were first dating.

Hayden turned from the window, and approached a small, tidy, dark still-life. A little Flemish masterpiece of light and shadow. "The tallest people in the world," he said, "are the Dutch. Six-one, on average."

"For men?"

"For the whole lot of them. Men *and* women."

"Hmm. That's a five."

"Five? That's all? You're tough." He shrugged. "So, what can I do for you?"

Kate reached into the inside pocket of her tweed jacket, handed over the print, the candid photo taken in that Parisian nightclub, seemingly ages ago, but in reality only a month and a half in the past.

Hayden barely glanced at the print before putting it in his pocket. He didn't want to be seen standing in a museum, looking at a photo in his hand.

"There's a phone number on the back."

"A prepaid mobile?"

"That's right," she answered, blushing in anticipation of the criticism he was about to level at her. But Hayden could see in her blush that she was already punishing herself for using her home phone to set up this meeting; he didn't need to mention it.

"Do you know who they are?" Kate asked.

"Should I?"

"I thought maybe they're with us."

"They're not."

The family with the young children—French—was now in the adjoining gallery. In the gallery beyond the French, maybe sixty yards away, another lone man stood with his back to Kate, wearing his overcoat. He was even wearing a hat, a brown fedora. Indoors.

"Are you sure?" she asked.

"As sure as one can be."

Kate wasn't entirely convinced, but at the moment there was nothing further she could do about it. "The man on the right is my husband." She spoke quietly, nearly a whisper, but careful not to actually whisper. Whispers drew attention. "The man on the left calls himself Bill Maclean, a currency trader from Chicago, now living in Luxembourg."

They started walking again through another well-lit southern gallery, their footsteps echoing through the immense room, under the gaze of saints and martyrs and angels.

"He's not?"

"No."

Hayden walked by another Rubens, *The Fall of the Damned*.

Kate glanced up at the painting, horrors upon horrors. "The woman is supposedly his wife, Julia. A little younger than Bill. A Chicago-based decorator."

Hayden paused, gazing up at *The Sacrifice of Isaac*. Abraham was about to kill his only son, his hand covering the young man's eyes completely, shielding Isaac from his imminent fate. But an angel had arrived just in time, grabbing the old man's wrist. The blade falling away, airborne, still dangerous looking, this free-floating weapon. A rogue knife.

"Do you want to tell me what you're thinking?" Hayden asked.

Kate continued to look up at the immense Rembrandt, at the range of emotion on old Abraham's face, the horror and grief but also relief. "These people are not who they claim to be," she said. "Those are not their names. Not their careers."

She turned her eyes from the canvas to Hayden, and caught a glimpse of the other man, crossing a doorway, a hint of his profile, not enough . . .

"So?" Hayden asked. "Who are they? What's your theory? What are we looking for?"

"I think," she said, voice as low as possible, "they're going to assassinate someone."

Hayden raised his eyebrows.

"I know it sounds dubious."

"But?"

"But they live across the street from the monarch's palace, with a perfect vantage on multiple unprotected areas. And the security is pitiful. The palace has all the trappings of a secure environment, except for the actual security. If you were looking for one really great place to kill someone, this would be it. If you were looking for a venue to take out a very high-value target—a president, a prime minister—you couldn't ask for much better."

"Can't that just be coincidence?"

"Sure. Their apartment is a nice place to live. But they have weapons. At least one."

"How do you know?"

"I've seen the gun."

"I have a gun. You too, maybe. And we're not going to ass*a*ssinate anyone."

Kate gave him a what-are-you-kidding look.

"Are we?"

"Come on. You know what I'm saying."

"All right," he admitted. "I'll grant you that the weapon warrants some suspicion. But there are hundreds of reasons why someone would have a weapon—"

"An American? In Europe?"

"—and only one of them is assassination."

"Yes, but very few of those reasons are good."

Hayden shrugged, screwed up his face in a way that suggested he had an opinion he was reluctant to share.

"And what about the false names?" Kate asked.

"Please. Who *doesn't* have a false name?"

"Normal bankers moving to Luxembourg, that's who." Kate was losing patience; Hayden didn't seem willing to admit even a possibility that these people were killers. "I've known quite a few assassins in my time."

"So have I."

"And you know that this is how they operate; this is what they do."

In fact, this is exactly what they'd done when Kate hired a team to take out a Salvadoran general. They'd rented a house up the beach from where they knew the general would turn up, sooner or later: a Barbados vacation villa owned by the general's primary arms dealer. The team ended up needing to wait nearly two months, developing deep, rich suntans, and vastly improving their golf games. They even learned to surf.

Finally one evening, at cocktail hour, the woman pushed the nose of her rifle out the second-floor bathroom window, and took a fairly easy three-hundred-yard shot—she could've hit her mark at twice the distance, maybe thrice—across one rooftop into the pristinely manicured beachfront garden where the general was reclined on a chaise, a bottle of Banks beer in his hand, and suddenly a large hole in the middle of his head. The other half of the team had the engine running, bags in the trunk, private jet waiting on the tarmac on the east side of the island, thirty minutes away from the brand-new crime scene at Payne's Bay.

Kate caught another glimpse of the man in the other gallery. She kept the corner of her eye on him. "And something happened in Paris. We were attacked late at night, and he fought off the muggers . . . his behavior was too, I don't know, too . . ."

"Too professional?"

"Yes."

"Okay, I'll indulge you: if they *are* assassins, who's their target?"

"No idea. But there are important people traipsing through the palace all the time."

"That doesn't exactly narrow it down, does it?"

Kate shook her head.

"Listen, I don't . . . how can I put this? . . . I don't think it's credible that anyone would hire assassins in a man-and-wife team for—how long has this been going on?"

"About three months."

"For a quarter-year, on the chance that this arrangement will eventually afford a takeable shot on, frankly, anyone. No matter how insufficient you think the security is at this palace, an entire different level can be established any*where*, at any *time*, in forty-eight hours."

She saw the man in the other gallery move closer.

"I'm sorry," Hayden continued. "I agree that these characters sound suspicious. But I think you've misread the situation. They're not assassins."

Kate suddenly knew that of course he was right. She couldn't believe she'd invested so much in such a harebrained theory; that she'd so willfully constructed a scenario so obviously contrary to fact. She'd been an idiot.

So why were the Macleans in Luxembourg? Kate's consciousness chased something into a corner of her mind, a dark corner that she tried—but rarely succeeded—to forget.

"And if you don't mind me asking."

"Yes?"

"What's it to you?"

Kate couldn't think of an answer other than the truth, which was something she couldn't admit: that she was afraid they were pursuing her, because of the Torres debacle.

"You might want to just let this go," Hayden said.

She turned to him, saw the look of warning. "Why?"

"You might not like what you find."

Kate searched Hayden's face for more, but he wasn't giving it. And she couldn't ask for it without explaining why.

"I have to."

He stared at her, waiting for her to elaborate. But she waited him out.

"Okay." Hayden reached into his pocket, removed the photo, and handed it back to her. "I'm sorry. I can't help you. I'm sure you understand."

Kate was expecting this. Hayden had become an important person in Europe; he couldn't afford to walk down blind alleys.

The hat-wearing man was now in a different adjoining gallery, his back still to them. Kate took a couple steps around the perimeter of the room, trying to get a look at his face.

"How long are you in München?"

They walked into the next gallery, passing the young family and their security-guard escort. Hayden stopped in front of a Rembrandt. Kate looked around but didn't see the fedora'd stranger. And then she did, in the adjoining room.

"We're leaving the day after tomorrow," she said. "We're going to Bamberg for a day, then home. Back to Lux."

"*Beau*tiful little city. You'd love Bamberg. But."

She turned to him. "Yes?"

"Instead you could go to Berlin. To see a guy."

✦ ✦ ✦

THE MAN IN the next room was edging closer, now in a position that seemed an awful lot like he was trying to listen to their conversation.

Kate widened her eyes at Hayden, and inclined her head toward the adjoining gallery. Hayden understood, gave Kate a nod. He quickly glided to the wall, his soles falling silent on the floor, his body springing into tightly controlled, elegant action. Standing stock-still, in his foppish clothes and fussy hair, Hayden had looked like any other middle-aged man. But something else was visible in his gait, in the way he waved his arm to point at a painting. Like Travolta, near-dancing in *Pulp Fiction,* the coiled energy visible just below the surface. Now, sprung into action, Hayden was singularly spry. He slid into the next large gallery, while Kate hustled to the smaller one.

She saw nothing. Kate looked both ways down the long hall, windows on one side, unseen galleries on the other.

No one.

She started walking. In the next gallery she glimpsed Hayden in the adjoining large one, the two of them making parallel pushes, pursuing, flushing.

But still no one.

Kate sped up, now hearing the sound of the French schoolboys, and she caught a flash of an overcoat sweeping through a door, and the Japanese startled at Hayden rushing past, but no sign of the overcoat, and Kate moved faster now, the building coming to an end, the top of the stairs, she turned a corner and looked down—

There he was, taking the last few steps at the bottom of the sweeping staircase, turning the corner, his coat trailing after him.

Kate and Hayden ran down the stairs, a security guard yelling at them—*Halt!*—and turned the corner and descended more stairs and another corner and then the lobby was spread out below them, and they froze, breathing heavy.

They were looking at a huge room that they'd last seen empty. It was now packed, the population of multiple tour buses disgorged here, hundreds of people in coats and hats, buying tickets and queuing for the coat check, seated on benches and standing.

Kate scanned the crowd, walking slowly to change her vantage, Hayden strolling in the opposite direction. They descended the steps at opposite sides of the room and waded through the crowd, retired Germans from the provinces, checked wool coats and loden pants and sheepy-looking scarves, beer on breath, hearty laughing and red cheeks and thin flyaway hair.

Kate caught a glimpse of something on the far side of the crowd, and she anxiously pushed her way through the thick humanity—"Excuse me, *bitte,* excuse me"—until she was at the glass front doors, watching the man in the flowing overcoat and brown fedora near the end of the plaza as a car pulled to a stop in front of him. He climbed into the driver-side backseat, his face still turned away.

As the car pulled from the curb, the driver turned toward the museum for a split second before returning her eyes forward to her route in the Theresienstraße. It was a woman wearing big sunglasses.

The car was a hundred yards away, and the light was dim, but still Kate was pretty sure that the driver was Julia.

✦ ✦ ✦

"IT SEEMS LIKE we should go," Kate said. "When's the next time we're going to be this far east?" They were walking through the Englischer Garten in the failing light, a landscape of browns and grays, an infinitely intricate latticework of leafless branches silhouetted against the silvery sky. "Otherwise, we'll have to fly. And let's face it, we're not going to buy four plane tickets to Berlin."

"But then why wasn't Berlin a part of our original itinerary?" Dexter asked, fairly.

Frozen grass crunched underfoot. The boys were scouring the ground for acorns, which they were shoving into their pockets. It was some sort of competition. "I wasn't looking at the whole of Germany."

"I have to work on Monday."

"But you can do that from Berlin, right?"

Dexter ignored her rebuttal. "And this'll be another two days of missed school. You know I don't like that."

They walked down a swale and up again, Kate's feet slipping in the slick piles of leaves. "I do know that," she said. "And I agree. But this is *pre*school."

"For Ben. But it's kindergarten for Jake."

Kate glared at him. Did Dexter imagine she didn't actually know what grade Jake was in? She struggled to ignore the condescending remark; a fight would be counterproductive. She answered as levelly as she could, "I know." Her breath emerged in big white puffs in the cold dry air. "But this is why we wanted to live in Europe. For us and for the kids: to go everywhere, see everything. So let's see Berlin. Jake can get back to his ABCs on Wednesday."

Kate knew that she didn't have a moral leg to stand on. Her position was indefensible, and she hated defending it, pretending that something was for the children's good when it was really just something she needed. Or just wanted. This was the specific type of dreadful feeling that she'd hoped to avoid by quitting the Company. The exact type of lie for which she'd thrown over her career to not utter.

They paused at the edge of an iced-over pond, the shoreline buttressed by boulders, long low branches dipping down to rest on the glassy surface.

Dexter put his arm around Kate as they gazed at the serene, frigid tableau. They rubbed shoulders up and down for warmth. "Okay," he said. "Let's go to Berlin."

✦ ✦ ✦

KATE FORCED THE boys to pose at Checkpoint Charlie, in front of the YOU ARE NOW LEAVING THE AMERICAN SECTOR sign on Friedrichstraße. Kennedy was here in '63, on the same visit that included his *"Ich bin ein Berliner"* speech, delivered down in Schöneberg. Then in '87, up at the Brandenburg Gate, Reagan challenged Gorbachev to tear down this wall.

Americans liked to deliver bombastic speeches here in Berlin. Kate followed that tradition with an impassioned version of her stump, If You Don't Start Behaving Right This Instant. It was probably the chocolate that was the culprit, she announced. So a solution could be that they never eat chocolate, ever again, in their entire lives.

Their eyes were wide with terror; Ben started to cry. Kate relented, as usual, with a variation on "That's not what I *want*. So don't make me do it."

They quickly recovered, as they always did. She set them off into the undulating rows of monoliths of the Holocaust Memorial, thousands of concrete slabs, rising and falling. "If you come to a sidewalk," she called out, "stop!"

The boys had no idea what this place was; there was no way she'd explain it.

Dexter was back at the hotel, wi-fi'd and caffeinated. Another man was suddenly beside her. "You have something for me," he said in English. She was shocked to recognize him as the tweaked chauffeur who'd shuttled the family from the Frankfurt airport, their first day in Europe. Hayden had been keeping his eye on her, still. Maybe always. Upon reflection, this wasn't so shocking.

Kate nodded at the man in recognition, and he returned the nod. She reached into her pocket, handed over the ziplock bag that contained a tube of lip balm and a business card from a tennis club, pilfered from the Macleans' apartment.

"Same time tomorrow, north end of Kollwitzplatz, Prenzlauer Berg."

Fifty yards ahead, Ben yelled, "Hi Mommy!"

She looked down the long row of slate-gray slabs, her little son dwarfed by the immense stone next to him. She waved, hand high in the air. "Okay," she said, turning back to the man, who'd already vanished.

◆ ◆ ◆

IT CONTINUED TO feel good, to be on this mission in Berlin. Even if there was a chance that the mission was entirely in her imagination. Maybe this was what had been missing in her life, why she felt so bored, so worthless, so unhappy.

But what mission did she want? Maybe she didn't need the type with weapons and secret identities and coded calls and mortal peril. Maybe her family could be her mission. She could approach her children—their education, their diversions—as a job, as a problem to be solved. There was nothing standing in her way of making her life better, a nice normal life, helping with homework, turning her attention to *Mastering the Art of French Cooking,* and mastering the art of French cooking.

But first, she still needed to find out who Julia and Bill were.

Kate stopped walking at the entrance to the playground in Kollwitzplatz. "I'm going to get a coffee," she said to Dexter. "You want anything?"

"No thanks."

She crossed the street and entered a café and took a seat away from the window. A harried-looking waitress hurried from the kitchen, her tray laden with food for a large, boisterous crowd in the corner. The door opened again, and the man came in. He sat across from Kate.

She gave him a once-over: a thirty-something in a scruffy beard and cowboy shirt and jeans and sneakers under a peacoat. Indistinguishable from the hipsters who lived in Austin and Brooklyn and Portland, Oregon or Maine. This was globalization: everyone everywhere was interchangeable. You could be anyone anywhere to do anything. This New Wave–loving, pill-popping, Williamsburg-looking van driver was a spy.

"I don't have much time," she said.

"Yes. I see you brought an entourage."

The waitress rushed past without glancing at them.

"So?" Kate asked.

"Those people are Craig Malloy and Susan Pognowski."

"Pognowski?"

"Yes, it is a Polish name. She grew up in Buffalo, New York. And the Malloy man is from near Philadelphia, Pennsylvania."

The waitress stopped by, holding menus. Kate ordered a coffee to go. The man wanted nothing.

"They're married?" Kate asked.

"Hmm? No. They are not married."

"So who are they?"

"It is interesting," he said, leaning across the table, smirking.

At that moment someone delivered the punch line to a joke at the big table, and everyone roared with laughter. A stein was slammed onto the table. A small delivery truck that had been idling outside shifted into first gear and drove away, leaving in its wake an extra clarity to the sounds that remained. A sizzle from the kitchen when the waitress emerged carrying a large bowl of fries. A peal of laughter from the schoolyard around the corner. A shout from her own eldest son, across the street, on a climbing apparatus.

When the noises died down, the man said, "They are American FBI."

Kate was dumbstruck, eyes and mouth wide open, stock-still.

FBI? She tried to process this information, her mind swirling in different eddies, chasing different ideas. She stared out the window at her children playing, at Dexter seated on a bench, his back to Kate, facing the weak sun hanging in the southern sky.

"And also interesting?" the man continued. "They are on loan."

Kate turned her eyes to him, confused.

"To a special task force."

She raised her eyebrows.

"At Interpol."

15

Kate walked to the Wednesday market in the Place Guillaume, flowers and produce, butchers and bakers, fishmongers and a roast-chicken truck. There was a wiry little Frenchman who was a passionate advocate for his alpine cheeses. A Belgian who offered nothing but onions and garlic. There was a fresh-pasta stand, and one for wild mushrooms, and one for olives. There was a surreally talkative woman selling the specialties of Bretagne, and a roly-poly red-faced couple peddling the cured meats of the Tyrol who didn't speak a word of French, much less English.

She waited in a shivering queue for roast chickens, lost again in speculation. The good news—if she was inclined to label the silver lining here—was that she wasn't going crazy. The so-called Macleans really were aliases for feds. But what were they up to? Hayden's man in Berlin didn't have any further information, couldn't get it, not without arousing suspicion, which he point-blank admitted he wasn't willing to do. She couldn't argue with him. Well, she could, and she did, but hopelessly.

Kate shared with many of her CIA brethren a lifelong disdain for the feds who reported into the Hoover Building. The animosity between the spies and the cops was almost entirely irrational, born from the political considerations of the men who'd run both agencies, distrusting one another, playing poorly in the sandbox, vying for the attentions of the succession of dads who'd lived in the mansion on Pennsylvania Avenue.

But whether Kate respected the FBI or not, these agents were in Luxembourg. Why?

It could have nothing to do with her. They might be pursuing a fugitive: a murderer, a terrorist. This criminal possessed a numbered account in Luxembourg, millions of euros—billions?—that could be withdrawn by him only, in person. So sooner or later, he was going to show up. That's what Bill and Julia were doing in Europe: waiting to arrest a bad guy.

They might be investigating a money-laundering operation, drugs or arms, dirty cash being washed in the anonymous machines of Luxembourg's banks. They were monitoring the couriers who were coming and going past the lax customs station at Lux's tidy little airport, suitcases filled with dollars that had been carted away from American ghettos to the cartel's headquarters in South America and then packed into suitcases that were checked into Air France and Lufthansa flights from Rio or Buenos Aires bound for Paris or Frankfurt with connections to Luxembourg. The couriers would be leaving Europe with clean cashier's checks. So the FBI agents were keeping records; they were building a case.

Kate ordered her *poulet fermier* and a *petit pot* of the potatoes roasted in the fat that dripped off the roasting chickens.

So why be here in Luxembourg? Why would the FBI loan agents to Interpol and send them to the Grand Duchy?

There was of course Dexter to consider. What could he have done? Why was he in Luxembourg? He could have embezzled from one of his clients. He could be at this very moment hacking into a corporate database, buying stock on stolen inside information.

Or.

Kate tucked her thermal bag of chicken and potatoes into her canvas grocery tote. It had now been a long time since she'd used a plastic bag.

Or, obviously: Interpol might be after her, at long last. The minute she walked onto Torres's floor at the Waldorf—no, the minute she'd walked into Union Station in D.C. and paid cash for her Amtrak ticket to New York—she'd had a premonition that one day there would be consequences. And they'd present themselves when she least expected them.

Kate's bag was now overflowing with her attempt to purchase normalcy for herself—calla lilies, a baguette, vegetables and fruits and her chicken and potatoes. The load was heavy.

She would avoid Julia, give herself a cushion of privacy. This was not a long-term solution; in fact, it may turn out to be counterproductive. But it was what she needed now, along with flowers for the dining table, and a mind-clearing immersion in cooking.

Kate turned from the square into a vehicular street, and the sidewalk was suddenly crammed with nuns. There must've been two dozen of them, all old. Kate wondered where they grew the young ones, keeping them hidden from the world, like seedlings in a climate-controlled greenhouse.

Kate stepped off the curb, giving the sidewalk over to the aged sisters. She walked on the cobblestones, the deep fissures between them filled with minuscule rivulets, a Lilliputian canal system, miniature Holland.

The nun in the lead looked at Kate through small wire-rimmed glasses. *"Merci, madame,"* the nun said, softly.

As Kate walked by the others, each said the same thing, an endless chorus of gentle *Merci, madames,* all accompanied by quick glances to Kate's eyes.

Then they were gone, out of sight. Kate turned around, looked up the empty street, wondered fleetingly if the nuns had been there at all, or if she'd simply imagined them. The remnants of their piety hung in the air, smothering Kate in guilt.

✦ ✦ ✦

KATE WAS SITTING again in the sports-center basement, unable to pay attention to the chitter-chatter humming around her. A phone rang, somewhere down below, from the depths of someone's bag. No one made a move to answer. Halfway through the second ring, Kate realized that it must be her own disposable mobile. She'd never before heard it ring.

Kate yanked her bag into her lap. "Excuse me." Foraging around, standing up, walking out of the café, into the stairwell. "Hello?"

"Hello."

"Give me a minute . . . I just need to get . . ." She was at the top of the stairwell, passing the men's locker room. "Somewhere private." Into the cold and the wind and the dimness, the grimness of Northern Europe at four-fifteen P.M. in late autumn.

"So they're FBI," she said. To satisfy her curiosity, Kate had again called the Chicago alumni office, then the dean, who reluctantly revealed the old address of William Maclean's parents, who after another few phone calls Kate found in Vermont, eventually on the phone with Louisa Maclean, who said that twenty years ago—the summer after graduation—her son Bill, driving a rented Vespa on the treacherous coast road in the Cinque Terre, had lost control and crashed into a stone retaining wall. The wall stopped the moped's forward progress, a crushed heap on the side of the road. But Bill had been flung over the low wall, and plunged two hundred feet to the rocky beach.

Bill Maclean died in July 1991.

"Yes," Hayden answered, "I heard."

"I need to find out what they're doing."

"Why? Now that you know they're not *criminals*, you don't need to worry about your, like, *val*uables. And they're not going to assassinate anyone over at the *palais,* and create a huge *traf*fic jam. So what's it to you?"

This is when it occurred to her that she was investigating the Macleans in order to avoid investigating her husband. Manufacturing an exterior enemy to demonize, as every politician knows, is far more expedient than confronting the interior one.

"Because they're in my *life,*" she said.

There was a big ripe silence from the other end of the line, and Kate joined in it, both of them tacitly agreeing to skip over the conversation that neither wanted to have. One that began with Hayden asking, "Do you have something to hide from them?"

"Okay," he said. "There's someone you can talk to, in Geneva. Kyle."

Geneva. Hayden started to explain how to make contact, but Kate's mind was stuck at the previous stage, running through the scenarios that would allow her to hop a flight to Switzerland for a quick meeting.

This was the type of thing she used to do all the time: pop down to Mexico City or Santiago, claiming she'd gone to a conference in Atlanta. But that had been back when she'd had a grab bag full of excuses; back when it hadn't been Dexter's job that was unpredictable and demanding. Back when she'd had freedom to go wherever she needed to go, whenever she needed to go there.

"I . . ." She paused, unwilling to say aloud what she'd concluded: it would probably take her weeks to get to Geneva. She was suddenly wistful for the amount of flexibility she'd had in her old existence. It certainly hadn't seemed so at the time.

"Yes?" Hayden asked.

"What about Paris? Or Brussels? Or Bonn?" Places she could get to and back in one day, with the kids; she could tell Dexter it was a mental-health day.

"The guy for you is in Geneva."

"But," she said, "I can't get to Geneva." This was the same type of humiliation she'd felt as a teenager, reluctant to admit to her friends that she couldn't go out tonight, had to stay home and tend to her dad's colostomy bag, her mom's bedsores. The embarrassment that you weren't independent, your decisions not your own to make. "Not immediately."

"Your *sched*ule is your own business."

"Isn't there any way I can do this digitally?"

"Sure. If you *knew* the guy, and he *trust*ed you, and you could guar-an*tee* a secure connection. But you've got none of that. So no."

"Okay," she said. "I have a strange question: is it possible they're after me?"

"No."

Kate waited, but he didn't elaborate. "How do you know?"

"Because if anyone was after you, it'd be us," Hayden said. "It'd be me."

✦ ✦ ✦

IN THE MORNING she drove Dexter to the airport, where he rented a car for a day-trip drive to Brussels. He returned home just in time for dinner, edgy, distracted, more distant than ever. He could barely pay attention to dinner-table conversation; perhaps he'd gotten so unaccustomed to dining with his family that he'd forgotten how.

When for the fourth time one of the kids asked "Daddy?" and he didn't answer, Kate threw down her fork and left the table. She understood that he had to work, and he had to travel. But what he didn't have to do was be absent even when he was present.

She steadied herself in the kitchen, trying to calm down. She stared at the doormat, the console table that held the keys, the mail, the mobile phones and bowls filled with coins, the small rug where they all parked their shoes, the little ones and the big ones.

Dexter's shoes were muddy. Very muddy—caked on the bottom, spattered up top. It had been raining all day, steadily, but Kate didn't imagine that the landscape of downtown Brussels included expanses of wet soil through which Dexter would have to trudge on his way to the bank offices.

She stared at the muddy shoes, trying to avoid suspecting him. She'd promised herself that she would set aside suspicion after she married him.

But all people have secrets. Part of being human is having secrets, and being curious about other people's secrets. Dirty fetishes and debilitating fascinations and shameful defeats and ill-begotten triumphs, humiliating selfishness and repulsive inhumanity. The horrible things that people have thought and done, the lowest points in their lives.

Like marching into a New York hotel and committing cold-blooded murder.

Kate couldn't pull her eyes away from Dexter's shoes. Just because she'd found out the Macleans were dirty didn't mean her husband was clean.

Her mind flashed back to three years ago, midwinter, Washington, D.C., cold and blustery. She'd been rushing across I Street to a meeting at the IMF, huddled against the wind, kicking herself for not calling a car. A taxi was disgorging a passenger in the circular driveway of the Army and Navy Club Library, and Kate rushed to grab it, but someone descended from the club entrance and climbed in. Kate stopped in her tracks, swiveling her head around to look for another cab. This cold snap was unexpected.

Her eyes fell on a bench across the street, on an angled path in Farragut Square. Not the first bench next to the sidewalk, nor the second; this bench was fifty yards into the park. And sitting on it, wearing the unmistakable red plaid hunting cap that she'd mail-ordered from Arkansas, was Dexter. With an unfamiliar man.

❖ ❖ ❖

AFTER DEXTER FELL asleep, Kate sat in front of the fire and made a list. A list of the possible reasons for FBI agents on loan to Interpol to be here, in Luxembourg, entwined in the life of an ex-CIA. Kate assigned numerical values to the possibilities' strength. She couldn't help but assign the lowest values—ones through fives—to all the explanations that had absolutely nothing to do with herself or Dexter. Then there were some Dexter possibilities that received ones through sevens. Most of them on the harmless side.

But it was the scenarios that revolved around herself that scored the eights and nines, regardless of Hayden's assurance that these agents weren't after her. It was more than possible that this was a mix-up; there had always been dishonesty and cross-purposes between the Bureau and the Agency. Or it could be that they were protecting her, watching for someone else who'd be coming after her. Or admittedly her departure from the CIA was abrupt, and possibly suspicious, and maybe some other evidence existed to draw attention, and so she was a suspect in a crime of which she was not guilty.

She carefully placed her list into the glowing embers of the dying fire.

That cold, windy night back in Washington, the old six-over-six windows rattling in their decaying mullions, Kate had struggled with whether—how—to question Dexter about his visit to Farragut Square. In the end, all she could bring herself to ask was "Do anything special today?" And all she'd received in response was "Nope."

She'd put that aside, sealed in an envelope deep inside her, to be opened only if required. She didn't want to know, unless she absolutely had to, her husband's secrets.

16

"Hi," Dexter said. "How's everything?" There was static on the line, as there often was when he was calling from these tax shelters, these criminal havens, these places where he went, probably to help crooks hide their money, or whatever he was doing that required him to lie to his wife.

Kate sighed, exasperated with the children, angry at her husband. "Fine," she said, walking away from the kids. "It's all wonderful."

"Really? You sound . . ."

"What?"

"I don't know."

She looked out the window, at the eastern sky sliding from weak day-light to dreary night without any discernible sunset.

"Everything's okay?"

Everything was not okay, not at all. But what was she going to say, on this open line to Zurich? "Yes," she answered, staccato, the spit-out syllable signaling that this subject was now closed. "So when are you back?"

Pause. "Yeah. About that."

"Goddammit."

"I know, I know. I'm really sorry."

"Tomorrow is Thanksgiving, Dexter. Thanksgiving."

"Yeah. But the people I work for don't know from Thanksgiving. To them, tomorrow is Thursday."

"Whatever it is, can't it wait?" she asked. "Can't someone else do it?"

"Listen. I don't like this any more than you do."

"So you say."

"What does that mean?"

Why was she picking a fight? "Nothing."

Silence.

She knew why she was picking a fight: because she was furious, because the FBI and Interpol were for some reason in her business, because she'd once made a horrible decision that would haunt her forever, and because the one person in the world she'd trusted without reservation was lying to her.

Perhaps his lie was about something benign. And maybe his lying had nothing to do with her anger. After all, he didn't force her to have a morally wrenching career. He didn't force her to keep it a secret. He didn't force her to have children, to sacrifice her ambition, to quit her job entirely. He didn't force her to move abroad. He didn't force her to take care of the children, to do the cleaning and shopping and cooking and laundry, all by herself. He didn't force her to be alone.

"Can I talk to them?" he asked.

Different zingers kept popping into her brain. She uttered none of them. Because it wasn't Dexter whom she was furious at. It was herself. And perhaps Dexter wasn't lying to her at all, and never had.

She put the phone on the counter, walked away from it, as if from a moldy peach.

"Ben!" she cried. "Jake! Your father's on the phone."

Ben ran up to her. "But I need to poop!" He was panicked. "Can I poop?"

She was picking a fight because it was Thanksgiving, and she was not thankful.

✦ ✦ ✦

KATE SPRAWLED ON the sofa, flipping channels, Italian game shows and Spanish soccer matches and bleak BBC dramas and a limitless assortment of programming in French or German. The children were finally asleep, after a frustrating conversation about Dexter's absence: the boys lamenting it, Kate trying—heroically, in her estimation—to suppress her irrational desire to condemn him, and to instead explain it supportively. Trying to be supportive to her husband and her children; trying to remember that this was also supportive to herself.

She heard the laughter of teenagers spilling out of a bar a block away, the high-pitched squeals reverberating on the cobblestones. She caught strains of English. These were little expats, sixteen- and seventeen-year-olds, smoking Marlboro Lights and drinking Red Bull–vodka concoctions until they threw up in the foyers of the small apartment buildings that surrounded the pubs, whose Portuguese cleaning ladies arrived to work before sunrise, their first order of business to examine the nearby foyers, towing an industrial bucket on steel casters with a mop sitting upright in the wringer, cleaning up teenagers' vomit.

It wasn't Dexter's fault, her anger. It was her own. All the decisions that led to this point had been her own. Including the one not to suspect him of anything.

She stared at the flickering screen, a Dutch channel, an undubbed American made-for-television movie from the mid-eighties. The hairstyles and the clothes, the cars and the furniture, even the lighting, all of it looked like exactly what it was. Amazing how many clues there are in a single screen shot.

Kate could no longer ignore her suspicion of Dexter. She was now aware that ignoring it was exactly what she'd been doing.

She also didn't want to confront him, to demand an explanation. He wasn't stupid enough to construct an implausible, unpracticed lie. Quizzing him wasn't going to accomplish anything other than to alert him that she was suspicious. Asking him questions wasn't going to be how she found out what was going on. If he were willing to answer truthfully, he'd have told her the truth to begin with. He hadn't.

Kate knew what she had to do next. But first she needed Dexter to come home. Then she needed him to leave again.

◆ ◆ ◆

"HELLO FAMILY!" DEXTER yelled from the door. He was holding a bottle of Champagne.

"Daddy!" Both boys came running into the hall, limbs spinning, cartoonish, jumping into their father's arms, violent, acrobatic hugs. Kate had set them up at the dining table, lined with newsprint, two fresh sets of watercolors, brushes, a whole battery of water cups. The theme was Things I Want to Do on Our Next Holiday. Kate had led off by painting her own Alpine scene, beginning a PR campaign for a revised Christmas plan, while also engaging with the kids in an activity. Two birds. In turn, the boys had created their own snowy scenes, which Kate had affixed to the fridge door. "Manipulative bitch," she'd have to admit, would be an accurate description of herself.

"What's that for?" Kate pointed her chef's knife in the general direction of Dexter's wine bottle, crested and gold-foiled and beaded with condensation.

"Daddy, come look at what I painted!"

"One minute, Jakie," he said, then turned back to Kate. "We're celebrating. I made—*we* made—twenty thousand euros today."

"What?! How wonderful! How?" Kate had managed to convince herself that there was no upside to being snidely suspicious. What she had to be was upbeat suspicious.

"Remember those derivatives I mentioned?"

"No. What does that even mean?"

He opened his mouth, then shut it, then opened it again to say, "It doesn't matter. But anyway, I liquidated a bundle of financial instruments today, and twenty K was the profit." Dexter was still opening cabinets, looking around. He didn't know where they kept their wineglasses.

"In there." Again, Kate pointed with the blade. Now that he was so much closer, the knife seemed inappropriate. She put it down.

He popped the cork and poured, foam rushing to the top, settling slowly. "Cheers."

"Cheers," she answered. "Congratulations."

"Daddy! *Please!*"

She carried the bottle into the dining room. Dexter settled at the table, trying to figure out the subjects of the boys' drying watercolors. The artwork was rather abstract.

He looked happy. Now, she thought, was as good a time as any. "I've been thinking," she said, "that instead of the Midi, we should go skiing. For Christmas."

"Gee"—his standard prelude to facetiousness—"you don't want this money to have any time to cool off, do you?"

"No, that's not it. I was thinking this before . . . you know. All our hotel reservations are cancelable. And there are still open spots at some ski resorts."

"But the South of France," he said, "you know it's in the top five."

The top five. Right now this list was Paris, London, Tuscany, the Costa Brava, and the broad notion of southern France—the Riviera or Provence, maybe Monaco, which although technically not France, was probably the same thing, except for certain logistical details.

Dexter had told Kate about this list in London, a few weeks earlier. The British-run international school had been unaccountably closed for something British, so they'd hopped the early flight to City Airport, dropped their bags at the hotel by ten A.M., and were off in the dismal late-autumn weather, private squares and wrought-iron gates, austere facades and cozy-looking carriage houses in the cobblestoned mews. And the beautiful sounds of English, everywhere.

They paused at the majestic sweep of limestone mansions on Wilton Crescent, the curving cap to Belgrave Square, security cameras everywhere. Dexter had insisted they come to this neighborhood, this street. She didn't understand, at the time, why.

Kate watched the children running up the sidewalk, excited by the mere shape of an arced street. It didn't take much.

A vintage Rolls and a brand-new Bentley, both gleaming ebony and mirrored chrome, faced off at the curb. Dexter glanced at a house number, then took a few steps to stand in front of the next. They were exactly the same. "Maybe one day we'll live here."

She guffawed. "We're never going to have this much money."

"But if money were no object? Where would you live? Here?"

She answered with a dismissive shrug. Foolish daydreams.

He told her his top five, and she got into the spirit. Suggested swapping out Costa Brava for New York. "Maybe someday," he said. "But I don't want to fantasize about living in the States. Not now. Just where we'll live in Europe"—he smiled—"after I get rich."

"Really? When is it exactly that you'll be getting rich?"

"Oh, I don't know." Trying to be coy. "I've got a plan." He didn't elaborate, and it didn't occur to her that he really did have a plan to get rich. Could he?

"Skiing?" he now asked, surrounded by the children and the output of their imaginations. "How would we get there? We're not going to sit in the car for twelve hours."

"That's one option, yes."

Dexter looked up, as if peering over the top of reading glasses that he'd never worn, never owned. A gesture learned from film.

"I agree it's not the best option," Kate said. "We could fly."

"To where?"

"Geneva," she said offhandedly, as if this were not the sole reason for the ski trip.

✦ ✦ ✦

THE PRE-DINNER CHAMPAGNE was followed by a bottle of white Burgundy with the veal stew, then Kate took out the Armagnac for Dexter to sip—a glass, two—while she put the children to bed. Then they talked about skiing and vacations while drinking more brandy, music on, a fire burning, foreplay on the couch, energetic sex on the floor. They were up late, with a lot to drink.

So in the morning Dexter slept in, as he always did after Armagnac. When Kate returned from dropping the kids at school, he was still at home, a rarity. He was collecting his things, on his way out. They shared a tender kiss at the door, which she shut behind him, the large heavy slab clicking quietly into its lock.

Kate stood in the foyer, next to the console table, a few little flat slivers of dried mud sitting in the corner, pushed up against the molding, the physical remnants of wherever he'd gone last week, when he'd claimed to have gone to Brussels.

Her keys were still in her hand, her coat still on. Kate waited until she heard the elevator stop humming, then she followed.

✦ ✦ ✦

SHE FELT HUMILIATED—she felt depraved—that this was what she needed to do to find out where her husband's office was. She trailed him across town, not particularly carefully. Never once on his ten-minute walk to the boulevard Royale did Dexter turn around to see if anyone was following. He made no attempt to evade anyone, or catch anyone, or hide anything.

He walked through the public spaces on the ground floor of a nondescript building, eight stories tall, late-sixties concrete, outdated, ugly, functional. The semi-outdoor hallways were lined with workaday businesses, dry cleaner and sandwich shop, *tabac* and *presse,* pharmacy and Italian restaurant. Wood-burning pizza ovens were everywhere in Luxembourg, all over Europe; so was fresh mozzarella. The pizza was generally pretty good.

Dexter entered the glass-walled lobby and pressed the elevator-call button and waited, then stepped into the elevator with another man of the same vintage. He rode the elevator to either the third or fifth floor.

Kate walked around the perimeter of the bunker-like building, all entrances visible to the guard at the lobby desk. She examined the windows: ledgeless, all four facades facing different busy streets, crowded sidewalks filled with retail shops, a block away from the civic center and central bus depot, officials everywhere, uniforms and weapons and surveillance, the boulevard lined with international banks, the streets filled with cars of the bankers pulling into their private garages, the

subdued gray Audis and BMWs that the family men drove, the extrava-
gant yellow Lamborghinis and red Ferraris owned by the bachelors.

A busy hub of business and government. A secure environment.
Much more secure than Bill's. There was no way she'd be able to come
in through a window.

Here, she'd have to enter through the front door, in broad daylight.

17

"Mommy! Come quick!" Jake was suddenly standing in front of their table at the playground, panicked, panting.

Days had passed in a cold thick fog of kitchen mopping and grocery shopping and pot scrubbing. Of purchasing presents for the boys' teachers, and guiding the children while they drew holiday cards for their best friends, and attending Christmas concerts. Of end-of-year coffee mornings and moms' lunches. Of visits to Christmas markets.

Kate had plenty of excuses for Julia. Day by day, putting distance between them, a cushion, padding, protection for whatever explosion was on the horizon. Spending more time with British Claire, or Danish Cristina, or anyone.

"What's wrong, sweetie?" Kate asked Jake. "Is Ben okay?"

"Ben is fine."

Kate let out a sigh of relief.

"But Colin isn't."

Claire shot up. They all ran down the grassy slope to the pirate ship, where a cluster of small children were surrounding a boy who was lying on the pebble-covered ground, blood pouring out of a gash on the top of his head.

"Darling," Claire said, examining Colin's head. The boy was stunned. She turned to Kate. "I'd rather not take Jules to hospital with us. And I'm afraid that Sebastian is, of course, in Rome." She unwrapped her cashmere scarf, dabbed it on Colin's head a few times, then held it firm and still, trying to stop the bleeding. The boy's face was covered in blood. "Would you mind terribly," she continued, remarkably calm, "tending to Jules for a bit? I suspect we'll be a few hours at the *clinique pediatrique*."

"Of course."

Claire glanced at her watch. "It'll be supper time before long. But Jules'll eat anything, won't you, dear?"

"Yes Mum."

"That's a good girl."

Claire smiled at Kate weakly but genuinely. She gathered her younger child in her arms, and set off for her car, and the hospital, and the type of ordeal that Kate most dreaded: a child's health was at stake, urgently, here, in a foreign land and a foreign language, alone.

Kate had always known that she herself was a strong woman. But it had never occurred to her that there were strong women everywhere, living mundane lives that didn't involve carrying weapons amid desperate men on the fringes of third-world wars, but instead calmly taking injured children to hospitals, far from home. Far from their mothers and fathers and siblings, from school chums and old colleagues. In a place where they had no one to rely on except themselves, for everything.

✦ ✦ ✦

THE NEXT DAY Kate stepped into the narrow cobblestone street, another festive shopping bag adorned with another ribbon, for another birthday party, at a children's play space in a strip mall in suburban Belgium.

"Oh my God!" It was Julia, standing in front of her, with an older man. "How *are* you?" Julia leaned in to kiss Kate on both cheeks.

"Hi, Julia. Sorry I haven't returned your calls, I was just—"

Julia waved it off. "Listen, Kate, this is my father, Lester."

"Please call me Les."

"Dad, this is Kate. One of my closest friends."

"A pleasure," he said.

Kate examined this unlikely man, considered this unlikely encounter. "It's *so* nice to meet you."

This Les character was wearing the standard-issue uniform of the retired American, the khakis and golf shirt and walking shoes. The fleece pullover with THE HIGHLANDS emblazoned on the breast, an embroidered midswing golfer; a souvenir from a corporate retreat, circa late nineties. The type of thing that a law-enforcement manager would wear if he were trying to appear to be someone who's just a little bit not him.

"You're visiting?" Kate asked. "From?"

"From home! Yes, I decided it was finally time to come check out this little burg of Julia-kins'. It's a beautiful town, isn't it?!"

Kate reeled from the brazenness with which this man didn't answer her question. "The week *after* Thanksgiving," she said, "is not when people typically travel to see family."

Lester smiled. "What can I say? I'm unconventional."

"Listen, Kate." Julia laid her hand on Kate's arm. "What are you doing tonight? Do you think you and Dexter could join us for dinner?"

Kate's eyes widened, and her mind unwittingly raced for an excuse to beg off before she realized that would be supremely stupid. "Of course."

◆ ◆ ◆

"DADDY!"

"Hey Jake how are ya?"

"Daddy, look what I made!" Jake held up a few pieces of cardboard—deconstructed cereal boxes—that had been glued, taped, and stapled to halved water bottles. Kate had been saving recylcables for this. She'd also been collecting scraps of cloth—orphaned socks, old sweatpants—for a different project. She'd added recipes to the repertoire of children-friendly cooking—peeling and dicing apples for applesauce, pounding veal for schnitzel. She'd begun to treat the boys' activities as a proper activity of her own, instead of as an interruption to other things she should be doing.

"This is great," Dexter said unsurely, examining the oddly shaped structure. "What is it?"

"A robot!" As if it couldn't be more obvious.

"Of course. It's beautiful," Dexter said. "It's a wonderful robot." He turned to Kate. "So it's Julia's dad who's visiting? And you found someone to watch the kids?"

"The sitter should be here in a few minutes. We're meeting them at the restaurant at seven. But it's just Julia and her father. Bill can't make it. Or won't."

"Okay then." Dexter glanced at his watch, turning his wrist jerkily to see the face. "So what are you kids doing? What should we do? Daddy's home for a little while before dinner so we can do whatever you want so what do you want to do?"

"Lego!"

Dexter seemed nervous and edgy and filled with too much energy. Hopped up on something. Could he be doing drugs? That would certainly be an astonishing development.

"Okay, Lego it is! Let's go." He opened the closet door, grabbed the toolbox. "One of their bureau drawers is loose," he explained, without prompting. Kate hadn't noticed any loose drawer. And she was surprised at this uncharacteristic interest in domestic repairs. "You boys get started on the Lego while I do something about the drawer."

Dexter was not that type of guy.

♦ ♦ ♦

"SO WHY ARE you two here? In Luxembourg?"

They were in a corner booth at a brasserie on the Place d'Armes. The plaza was being filled with the wooden stalls of the Christmas market, strung with lights, festooned with wreaths. The clamor of hammering and the hum of portable electric generators wafted through the doors whenever they opened, accompanied by a chill. You never really needed to take off sweaters and jackets in wintertime Luxembourg. A chill was never far away.

"My job," Dexter said. "I work in banking."

"Banking? No! There can't be *bank*ing in Luxembourg!" Lester's red-faced joviality and harmless sarcasm were straight out of the father-of-a-friend textbook. He had changed out of his golfing gear into a navy blazer, pressed khakis, a button-down oxford. Directly from the office, leaving the tie in the Buick. A caricature of himself.

"Where are you from, Les?" Kate asked.

"Oh, we got around, didn't we, Julia-kins? But now I live near Santa Fe. You ever been down that way?"

"Can't say that I have."

"What about you, Dexter?"

He shook his head. Dexter's manic energy had been spent; now he was quiet, shy.

"Beautiful country," Les said. "Just beautiful."

"And you're from Chicago?" Kate asked.

"We lived there awhile, that's right."

"I've never been there, either."

"Huh. But I bet you all get around Europe? That's what Julia tells me everyone does, here. That right?"

"I guess."

"So I'm going to—where am I going? Let's see: Amsterdam, Copenhagen, Stockholm. You got any suggestions for me?" Les looked from Kate to Dexter to Kate again, acknowledging that right now, she was going to be the one speaking for her family.

"What are you looking for?" she asked.

"Hotels. Restaurants. Sights. What have you. I've never been up this way before, probably never will again. Figured I'd see this part of the world before I die."

Kate smiled. "Of those three, we've been only to Copenhagen."

The food arrived, large plates filled with brown and beige—pork shoulders, lamb shanks. Kate's came with buttered spaetzle *and* buttered potatoes. The minced-parsley garnish was the only green thing on the table.

"Where'd you stay?" Les asked. "Nice hotel?"

"Not bad."

"How many stars?"

"Four, probably. Maybe three."

"No, I'm 'fraid not. In my dotage, I've become strictly a five-star guy."

"Can't help you then, Les." Kate glanced at Julia, who was also quiet, sheepish-looking.

"What about restaurants?" Lester asked. "That's a good-eating town, isn't it?"

She smiled. "Again, Les, we're going to have to disappoint you. What with the kids, and a budget, we don't really seek out the finest dining."

"A budget? I thought all you Luxembourg bankers were richer than Croesus." Looking at Dexter now.

"That may be," Dexter said. "But I'm not a banker. I work *in* banking, but my job is really more like I.T."

"I.T.?" Les looked shocked. "Well, I'll be."

"Is that so unusual?"

"No, no, not at all. It's just I wouldn't've expected that a Luxembourg bank would hire an American for any type of I.T."

"Why's that?" Dexter asked.

"It's sort of become the specialty of the rest of the world, hasn't it?"

Dexter cut his eyes down to his food. "Well, it's more about security, what I do. I'm a security consultant. I help banks ensure that their systems are secure."

"And how do you do that?"

"The main thing is I try to put myself into the mind of an attacker. What would he do? How would he do it? I try to orchestrate the attack myself, and find the points of weakness that a hacker would exploit. I ask myself, What is he looking for? How is he going to try to find it?"

"You talking about computer weaknesses?"

"Yes. But also human weaknesses."

"Meaning what?"

"Meaning the types of weaknesses that make humans let down their guard. Trust people they shouldn't trust."

"You're talking about manipulating people."

"Yes." Dexter and Lester were staring at each other. "I guess I am."

◆ ◆ ◆

IT WAS AFTER sex when Kate most wanted to talk to Dexter. To tell him that Bill and Julia were FBI agents. To tell Dexter that she knew he was lying to her about something, and demand he explain.

During her entire career at the CIA, pillow talk had never played a role. But now she understood what an asset it could have been, having sex with people to get information. She wondered whether this insight would've changed her past behavior.

She stared at the bedroom ceiling, again, failing to start the conversation. Even with the new possible opening of "Lester is not Julia's father," she couldn't bring herself to do it.

Dexter would be going to London in two days. She could wait.

18

"You don't have to do this," Dexter said, gathering his things. "I can take a taxi." He closed his carry-on bag, a quick aggressive zip. "Is it that you enjoy visiting our tidy little airport? Or are you really that desperate to get rid of me?"

"Counting the seconds," she said, purposefully not looking at him.

He picked up his key ring from the hall table, slipped it into his computer case. It was the same sterling ring that the real-estate agent had presented to Dexter when they'd closed on the D.C. house, his initials engraved on an oval fob. Kate had received her own, but she'd long ago relegated it to her jewelry box. Matching key rings were an invitation to disaster.

Now Dexter's ring held the Luxembourg apartment's keys, and two unfamiliar keys that she assumed were for his office, and one small key that she knew was a bicycle lock, rarely if ever used. Plus a memory stick with a hardened case, tamper-resistant and tamper-evident, with secure encryption keys and even self-destruction circuitry. This device had not been casually purchased from Eurobureau; this was a serious little gadget.

"This trip is to London?" she asked, pulling the door shut behind her.

"Indeed."

Down in the parking, Dexter deposited his computer bag and sturdy plastic Samsonite into the way-back, on the newly washed black carpet, professionally cleaned a few weeks ago in the parking of the *centre commercial* in Kirchberg, by appointment, while Kate shopped above—groceries and DVDs and Christmas toys, a twelve-pack of new underwear for the boys, growing too quickly to fit into anything for more than a few months at a time, their old briefs obscenely small and tight, somehow embarrassing.

Kate opened the driver's door but then paused, pretending to make the decision to remove her coat. She walked to the rear. She glanced at her husband, nervous, worried about the mirrors, despite her certainty that they were not angled for this, not the side-views and not the rearview; she knew positively that Dexter simply could not see her in the mirrors.

The garage's overhead light extinguished itself, its automatic timer expired. Now the only illumination was from the tiny bulbs in the car, single-digit watts scattered at places where you might otherwise bump your head, or trip.

Kate reached across Dexter's bags, and carefully put down her coat, the heavy pile of navy wool and silk lining and brass buttons. She coughed to cover the sound of opening the zipper of his nylon bag. She grabbed his keys tightly to avoid jangling. Coughed again to close the zipper, then slid his keys into her pocket in concert with slamming the door. She began to—

Dexter was beside her. Kate held her breath, frozen. Caught.

He stared at her, and she at him, for seconds. A dim forever. "What are you doing?"

She didn't answer; couldn't.

"Kate?"

In the dark, she couldn't see the expression on his face.

"Kat?"

"What?"

"Can you move out of the way, please?"

She took a step back, and Dexter popped the hatchback. Grabbed his computer bag. He threw Kate a glance. The trunk light had gone on, and she could read his face: confusion, worry. She was paralyzed. What was about to happen here? To her whole life?

Dexter unzipped the bag. He reached his hand in, feeling around. Glanced again at her, quizzical, then continued to rummage around, his brow furrowed.

Kate couldn't move a muscle.

Finally Dexter pulled his hand out of his bag, looking at it, at the thing he was holding: a piece of plastic wrapped with wire.

She still didn't move. She still couldn't.

"I thought I'd forgotten my charger." He held the thing up for her to see: proof that he hadn't forgotten it, for both of them, much to their vastly different types of relief.

✦ ✦ ✦

KATE STAGGERED TO the front of the car, collapsed into the driver's seat. She turned the ignition, shaky, and switched on the headlights, and hit the remote to open the garage door. She shifted into drive while Dexter was buckling his seat belt.

Kate had lied to many people in her life, profusely; she'd regularly been a breath away from getting caught. But it was very different when it was your husband, and the thing you're lying about is no longer yourself, but him. It was inconceivable to treat it as a game; it was impossible to pretend that it wasn't real life.

"You okay?" Dexter asked.

She knew that her voice still wouldn't work. She nodded.

The drive to the airport took ten minutes. Dexter made a meager attempt at small talk, but Kate responded with grunts. So he gave up, granting her the space of her silence.

She spun the car around a short arc of a roundabout and cruised into the efficient little airport. It was a one-minute trip from the kiss-and-fly parking to the check-in counter. Almost never any queue—none—to check in, and rarely a soul waiting at security. Distances here measured in steps, instead of the kilometers marched in Dulles or Frankfurt. From the door of their apartment to any gate, the journey was twenty minutes.

"Thanks," Dexter said, a peck and a smile, climbing out the door. Elsewhere in the kiss-and-fly other men were climbing out of the passenger seats of other German cars, gathering bags and feeling around pockets for passports, uttering variations of what Dexter said now, to his wife, "See you in a few days," all with something else on their minds.

✦ ✦ ✦

KATE EXITED HER building just as her phone began to ring, another incoming call from Julia Maclean. Kate hit the Ignore button, again.

She set off in the light drizzle of a cold December rain, a degree too warm for snow. Retracing the footsteps of the previous time she'd followed her husband across town. This was the same route as her walk to French class, or the good butcher, the post office. The same walk that launched her daily peregrinations, the myriad missions of the housewife. But today Kate was something else.

She marched through the lobby without a glance at the guard, punched the elevator button, rode to the third floor with a pair of

Italian bankers on their way to five. She didn't know where Dexter's door would be—she hadn't followed him into the elevator, back when she'd followed him—but she suspected it would have no label, no plaque, no name on the door. She quickly found such a door, near the end of the fluorescent-lit corridor. The first key she tried opened the lock—easy!—and she pulled the door.

Kate stepped into a tiny vestibule, dimly lit, another door a few feet in front of her, room enough for two people in here, tops. Designed for one.

A keypad, numbers glowing red, confronted her on the opposite wall.

How many combinations would she be allowed to try? The system would shut down after what? Three false tries? Two? Would she get the chance to be wrong even once, before the system turned off, or sent an SMS to his phone, or an e-mail to some account?

Numbers were streaming through her head, or ideas of numbers: their anniversary, their children's birthdays, his own birthday, hers, or possibly his mother's or father's, his childhood phone number, an inversion of any of these, a replacement code . . . ?

The only way it would be possible to guess his code? If he were a moron.

♦ ♦ ♦

SHE WAS HOME again when her mobile rang, an unfamiliar number, a long string of digits, must be from a different country.

"Bonjour." She didn't know why she answered in French.

"It's me."

"Oh, hi."

"I forgot my key ring," Dexter said. "Or, worse, I lost it."

"Oh?"

"I need it. I need something from the flash drive on it."

She glanced at his keys, sitting in the ceramic bowl on the hall table, exactly where he would have left them, if he had left them, on purpose or by accident.

"What do you propose?" she asked, trying to keep her voice flat, unemotional, uninvolved in what he should imagine was his own private drama.

"Are you home?" he asked.

"Yes."

"Can you look for them?"

"Where?"

"Where I keep them."

"Okay." She walked through the hall, stood at the table, staring at the keys in the bowl. "No, they're not in the bowl."

"Can you check the car? Maybe they fell out when I was looking for my charger."

"Sure." She went to the basement, looked in the empty trunk. "They're here."

"Thank God." His voice was crackly; phone reception was poor, down in the garage.

She didn't respond. Walked back to the elevator.

"Listen," he began, but didn't continue.

"Yes?"

He was thinking, she guessed. She let him do it. "Do me a favor."

"Of course."

"Take the key ring to the computer."

"One minute." Kate walked into the guest room. Sat at the laptop. "Okay."

"The computer on? Pop in the memory stick."

She slipped the device into its slot. "Done."

"Okay. Double-click it."

A dialog box popped open.

"The user name," he said, "is AEMSPM217. Password is MEM-CWP718."

What the . . . ? She jotted down these sequences before typing them, keeping a record for herself; these were too complex to memorize on the spot. Her mind was racing, trying to figure out what these numbers could mean, but nothing was occurring to her. Nothing familiar in any of that. "What *are* those numbers?"

"They were created by a random-number generator. I memorized them."

"Why?"

"Because that's the only way to get a totally unbreakable code. Now, please, double-click the top icon. The blue I."

This launched an application, the screen blinking on an unfamiliar logo, then a small window, another series of letters and numbers, gibberish.

"Read it to me."

"Is this randomly generated?"

He didn't answer.

"Why do you need it?"

"Kat. Come on."

"Goddammit Dexter. You tell me *nothing.*"

He sighed. "This is a program that creates dynamic passwords. It's how I unlock my computer. A new code every day."

"Isn't this a little ridiculous?"

"It's what I *do,* Kat. It's ridiculous?"

"No, not—I didn't mean . . . I'm sorry."

"Okay. Can you read me the code, please?"

"CMB011999." She jotted it down as she read it, and he repeated it.

"Why don't you keep this program on your computer?"

He sighed again before answering. "It's crucial to silo the components of a multi-stage security apparatus. No matter how good the security, any computer—mine included—is hack-able. Any computer can be stolen. Seized by law enforcement. A computer can be exploded, or imploded. Set on fire with a liter of kerosene, bludgeoned with a nine-iron, erased with a portable low-voltage electromagnetic pulse."

"Huh."

"So that's why I memorized the randomly generated codes, and that's why I use dynamic passwords created by an external device. Does that satisfy your curiosity?"

"Yes."

"Wonderful. Then can I get back to work now?"

They hung up. Kate stared at the dialog boxes, then sprang out of her chair.

◆ ◆ ◆

OUTSIDE AGAIN, SLICKENED cobblestones and dense cold fog, through the quiet blocks near home and across the somber Place du Théâtre, a concrete cap to the public parking beside the small theater, into the narrow tree-lined sidewalks of the rue Beaumont, expensive children's clothing, expensive chocolate, expensive antiques, expensive women walking in and out of the expensive restaurant doors at lunchtime, Japanese and Italian, then the busy intersection with the avenue de la Porte Neuve, then back on the charmless boulevard Royale, nervous.

Kate pulled on her gloves.

Back in the concrete bunker of an office building. Back in the empty elevator, the long gray hall; back in the small dark vestibule. The fingers of her right hand hovering next to the glowing keypad. She could feel the electricity from the keys, jumping the centimeter to her fingertips, coursing through her. The tingle of anticipation.

The code couldn't be today's daily code; it wouldn't make sense that Dexter would need to rely on the flash drive to get into his office. It would be—it should be—something he'd memorized; it would be the same every day. It would be the password he'd revealed to her, reluctantly. She'd told this to herself ten times, twenty, on the short walk over here: it would be the same password. It had to be.

Was it impossible that entering a wrong code would lock her into this tiny room until the police arrived? Or *electrocute* her?

She didn't need to look at the slip of paper in her left hand. She typed the M, then the E, and then in a rush the MCWP, the 718.

She hit the button with the green arrow, and waited . . .

"Code bon."

The lock clicked. She exhaled, and pushed open the door.

Another man's private office, private room, secret from real wives, pretend ones. Papers in here. Framed pictures, Kate and the boys, singularly and in groups. Even a wedding picture, a black-and-white, an unfamiliar print, something she didn't even know he possessed, much less had framed and shipped across an ocean and hung on his secret wall. It relieved her, this picture, this proof of something good.

A desk, a desktop computer, a phone, a complicated-looking calculator, a printer. All the normal stuff, pens and a stapler, file folders and Post-its, paper clips and binder clips.

Bookshelves filled with file boxes, big handwritten labels on their fronts, TECH and BIOMED and MFTG and REAL EST DERIV. Piles of newspapers, *The Financial Times* and *Institutional Investor*.

She didn't understand what this stuff was. No—she understood what it was, but didn't understand why it was here.

Kate sat in the swivel chair, tall and ergonomic, breathable mesh and adjustable height. She looked at the display screen and keyboard and mouse and speakers and headphones and external drive and an odd track pad.

She pressed the power button, and listened to the hum, and watched the screen flash. At the prompt, she entered the user name and password, holding her breath, again worrying that the laptop and the desktop wouldn't share the same security, but then again insisting to herself that they should.

They did.

The screen blinked from black to white, the hard drive hummed, and a dialog box opened, a red exclamation point, an instruction: AWAITING THUMBPRINT.

Kate looked at the odd pad on the desk, and understood it, defeated again.

She powered down the computer.

Kate stood at the bookshelf, pulling out the contents of file boxes, paging through the thick sheaves of professionally printed earnings reports, prospectuses, investor-relation brochures, shareholder-meetings minutes, glossy paper and multicolored pie charts and stock histories, x and y axes, big boastful numbers in bottom right-hand corners, measured in hundreds of millions, thousands of millions.

There were letter-size spreadsheets and graphs, annotated and folded, dog-eared and corrected. Numbers circled, arrows drawn. Margin notations scrawled.

This office? This was not the office of a security specialist. This was the workplace of an investment banker. Or a fund manager, or a financial adviser. This stuff belonged to someone who did something other than what her husband did; this room was inhabited by someone who was not her husband.

Kate looked again around the room, her eye running across the well-aligned tops of framed photos, to the windows facing out onto the slow-moving traffic, the office building across the street, similarly ugly but from a different architectural fad. Then she caught sight of her reflection, and the reflection distracted her from the real view, and she let her eye wander around the reflected room, the backward office, inverse-world, the corners at their opposites, and in one of them, in one of the corners was a thing, up there where two walls met a ceiling, and she spun around, panicked, *panicked,* at first turning to the wrong corner, then finding the correct corner, the thing, she took a single step to it, then another, and she realized—she confirmed—that the thing she was looking at, up there in the corner, that thing, a device, it was also looking down at her, a coin-sized piece of glass, encased in plastic.

A video camera.

✦ ✦ ✦

FORTY MINUTES LATER and she was sitting in her car, waiting for three o'clock, again. The trifling rain had become a steady downpour, unignorable, frigid.

She watched the other mothers scurrying onto campus, gripping umbrellas, clutching raincoats closed against their bodies, water flowing off nylon and leather and rubberized canvas. Some of them were pushing infants and babies, in car seats and strollers, through the freezing deluge. How awful.

Because of the rain, the swarm was more concentrated around the precise turn of the hour. On nicer days, the women arrived on a staggered schedule, beginning as early as two thirty. On nicer days, it was less noticeable that they were a herd.

That video camera.

Kate couldn't last a full minute without her mind returning to that camera. When would Dexter check the footage? Was the video streaming to a server, monitored by someone—who?—regularly? Or was the surveillance being recorded? Could Dexter check remotely, from London? Or would he have to wait until he returned to Luxembourg, to the physical office, which wouldn't be for another two weeks, after New Year's?

Were all those paper files even his property? Or were they owned by his client, whoever that was? Perhaps the security camera was the client's as well? Perhaps the whole nonsensical contents of that office weren't really Dexter's?

Kate climbed out of her car full of unanswerable questions, into the rain, falling into step, joining the herd, turning onto campus just as the first children were being released through the garage-like glass-and-steel doors, stomping in the puddles, free, oblivious to the awfulness of the weather. Oblivious in general.

When exactly would she get caught? And by whom?

✦ ✦ ✦

KATE KEPT RETURNING to the phrase *benefit of the doubt*. She should give it to Dexter; he should give it to her. This should be in wedding vows. More important than richer or poorer, sickness and health, have and hold, parting at death. Benefit of the doubt.

How could she explain? What rationale could she give him for why she stalked him to his office, stole his keys, broke in, snooped around?

Maybe she could maintain the farce that his keys had fallen in the trunk. Maybe she could claim that when he'd given her the codes over the phone, she couldn't resist.

Or maybe she could go on the aggressive: she could blame her invasive curiosity on his excessive secrecy. *If you had told me anything,* she could say, *anything whatsoever, then maybe I wouldn't have felt the need. Your fault,* she could accuse. *You made me do it.*

But how—*how?*—could she explain why she knew where his office was?

And, flipping the whole damned thing around, what could *his* explanation be?

He could be doing exactly what he claimed: he was a security consultant for a bank, and he worked exclusively electronically. All his work, all his information, was on the computer that she couldn't access. Nothing professional was on paper. All that paper in his office? That was spare-time paper, amateur-hobby paper.

Or? Or what?

Dexter was definitely adding a consistent amount of money to their checking account every month, and not withdrawing anything abnormal. Someone was paying him to do something. Who?

And then of course there was the non-coincidence that Julia and Bill were FBI tasked to Interpol, in all likelihood investigating either herself or Dexter. Why?

Kate felt like she'd lived for so long when no one knew the truth about her, about who she was. Now the tables were turned, and all these people were arrayed on the other side, unknown, unknowable. What she did know, unfortunately, was that she had to reconsider everything she'd ever willed herself to believe about her husband.

She leaned over the boys, reaching across their laps to secure their seat belts, the hard cold metal of the buckles chilling her skin, the sharp edges digging into her flesh.

Of course, Dexter could be completely innocent. There could be the explanations she'd already thought of, or ones she couldn't imagine, for his office. And the guilty one would be herself. She was Interpol's target. The crime was Torres.

She climbed into the driver's seat.

What she couldn't figure out was how that old event would tie into any current investigation. There was either five-year-old evidence against her, or there wasn't. But nothing about her life in Luxembourg was even tangentially relevant to what had happened in New York, the thing she'd tried hardest to bury. The thing that made her understand that she could no longer be an operations officer. Made her realize that she was no longer strong enough and rational enough to maintain objectivity. To separate her parental panics from her professional responsibilities. She could no longer trust herself to behave correctly; she could no longer be trusted. She had to resign. So she'd resigned.

But quitting didn't change what she'd already done. The piece of her past that she'd never be able to outrun.

19

The ambassador stood at the rear of the entry hall, beside a round table with an oversize vase packed with a towering assortment of flowers, branches and limbs and fronds and blooms sprouting willy-nilly in all colors, shapes, and sizes. It was an utterly anarchical arrangement. A non-arrangement.

"Welcome," he said, "I'm Joseph Williams," extending his hand to Dexter. "And this is my wife, Lorraine. So pleased you could join us for our annual Christmas party."

They all shook hands, two sets of two, crossing in an awkward X, awkward chuckles.

"Of course," said the wife to Kate, "we've met." She winked, as if they shared a secret, a history. But there was nothing to it; this woman was just one of those winkers.

"Of course," Kate said, vaguely remembering a coffee morning, maybe at school. There had been so many. Coffee everywhere, all the time.

"So, Dexter?" the ambassador asked. "You new here?"

"Nearly four months."

"Why, that's an eternity in Luxembourg, isn't it?" The ambassador shook with laughter at his own joke, which wasn't really a joke, and wasn't funny. "We've been here two years, feels like twenty. Isn't that right, dear?" The ambassador didn't wait for an answer, didn't expect one. He put his hand solicitously on Dexter's shoulder. "You settling in okay?"

Dexter nodded, visibly tired. He'd just arrived from London an hour earlier. He still hadn't returned to his office since Kate had let herself in, looked around, been caught on candid camera. And he wouldn't have that opportunity for another week and a half. They were leaving for Geneva in the morning.

"Good, good," the ambassador said. "Well, we're so glad you could come tonight. We have so few chances to gather the whole American community. Please, get yourself something to drink. The *crémant* is flowing freely." He laughed again, red-faced and moist-looking, at another unfunny comment. He was either drunk or an idiot. Possibly both.

Kate and Dexter took their polite leave as another couple arrived, the blast of cold from the door, the booming voice of the ambassador's forced jocularity following them into a sitting room, fussy furniture and precious bric-a-brac, little brass statues and plaques, etched glass and inlaid mahogany, a surfeit of throw pillows on striped-silk upholstery.

"Well, hello there." Amber walked up with another woman, who Kate remembered was from somewhere in the U.S. totally unexpected. Oklahoma? She talked about church a lot. And described everything as super-something. She was super-psyched to have bought this super-cute blouse at this super-trendy store.

"Hi," the woman said, too loudly. She stumbled, sloshing wine. "Oops!"

"Jesus," Dexter whispered in Kate's ear. "When did this party start? Yesterday?"

"I'm Mrrnda," the woman said to Dexter. "Please-a-meecha."

"Miranda?" Dexter asked.

"'S'right."

"Nice to meet you. How's the *crémant*?"

"Super-tasty."

Kate looked around the room at this sea of mostly unfamiliar faces. This party was dominated by the sizable contingent who'd circled around themselves as Americans, exclusionary, flag-pin-wearing. Behaving as if they hadn't chosen to live in Europe, but had been moved against their wills, and were putting up a brave resistance. Freedom fighters.

Kate, on the other hand, had made the decision to try to be friends with the non-Americans, with all the other people of the world she could meet in Europe. Somehow, though, Julia had happened. Had snuck in, around the perimeter. As if on a mission.

A waiter appeared with a silver platter of rolled-up ham. Everyone shook their heads, rejecting him and his cured meat.

Kate saw Julia in the next room, examining the commemorative photos that lined the wall. Kate scanned for Bill, her eyes skimming the peaks and valleys of the few dozen heads surrounding a buffet table and a bar. He was off in the far corner, next to a pretty woman who appeared to be seething at him, giving him the business at low volume. Bill looked marginally contrite; he looked like he was pretending to be contrite.

Jane, that was the pretty woman's name. Plain Jane, who wasn't so plain, wearing a beautiful green dress, slinky and low cut, shoulders bare. She was some type of officer in the American Women's Club, her husband second-in-command—or something like it—here at the embassy. An alpha American couple.

Now Kate understood: Jane was the woman whom Kate had called from Munich, testing the phone number that she'd pilfered from Bill's office. Kate had been to Jane's house, for a coffee morning. That was where she'd met the ambassador's wife.

Kate set off for the living room, and Julia. Their exchange would be impossible to avoid, so Kate wanted to get out in front of it, control it.

Julia felt her coming, or noticed through a reflection in a picture's glass. She turned slowly when Kate was a few feet away. They cheek-kissed, left and right. Kate smelled gin. It would've been impossible to miss it. "Merry Christmas," Julia said.

"You too."

"So where have you been? I haven't seen much of you." Julia had left a few messages that Kate hadn't returned; Kate hadn't been able to figure out a way to interact with Julia, knowing what she knew.

"Oh, you know, the holidays." Kate didn't elaborate, and Julia didn't ask for an explanation. Although they were operating at different levels of awareness, they both knew their relationship fell somewhere short of a truthful answer here. Somewhere that included the possibility that one woman would avoid the other, and not explain why. Somewhere that could just as easily be defined by dishonesty as by the opposite.

"It was nice meeting your father."

Julia smiled. "Thanks. He sort of surprised me."

"Ah."

"So are you excited for the South of France?" Julia asked. "That'll be a great trip."

"Oh," Kate said, "actually, we changed our minds."

"Really?" There was something in Julia's tone, in the forced curiosity on her forehead, that made Kate think this was not news.

"We're going skiing instead."

"Skiing? You're kidding. So are we!"

The last Kate knew was that Julia and Bill were going home for the holidays. Back to Chicago. "Where are you going?" Kate asked, suddenly sure what the answer would be.

"French Alps. The Haute-Savoie."

Sure enough. "You too?" Kate tried to muster an enthusiastic response. But she couldn't get out from under a smothering blanket of paranoia.

"Incredible! We'll have to get together. We'll *ski* together. Bill will be so happy."

Kate forced a smile. "Dexter too."

"Dexter too what?" Dexter asked, ambling over. "Dexter is too handsome?" Leaning in to kiss Julia's cheeks. "Dexter is too sexy?"

Julia slapped his chest. "Dexter too will be excited that we're all going to be in the Alps together."

His head swiveled to his wife, an accusation in his eyes.

"I know what you're thinking," Kate protested, "but this is *not* a conspiracy. I didn't know a thing about this. Julia? Tell him."

"She didn't know a thing about this," Julia agreed. "I promise. Bill and I just decided last-minute. A couple days ago."

"You're lying," Dexter said, half playfully, half not. "I'm surrounded by women, lying to me."

❖ ❖ ❖

NO ONE REALLY ate. People picked and nibbled, but there was never a sit-down, never a required-dining moment, so for the most part the forks went untouched. All solid sustenance was delivered with the fingers. But mostly what the partygoers consumed was liquid.

Kate wasn't sure whether she'd had five glasses of wine, or six. The easy-jazz piano had been replaced by a light-FM assortment of classic rock, low volume. Then someone raised the volume on the easy-listening. Hotel California; you can never leave.

She stood in the center of the small sitting room, swaying slightly. A certain measure of clarity was cutting through the alcoholic fog, bringing into focus what might very well be an alternate reality, in which none of these people were who they claimed to be. Just as Kate knew that she herself had not been, for a very long time, who she claimed to be.

It was looking increasingly likely that Dexter was not who he claimed to be. What the hell was all that material in his office? What was he up to?

Kate looked around, and found Julia cornered by one of the fathers from school who everyone agreed was closeted-gay. She couldn't see Bill anywhere. Nor Plain Jane, for that matter.

Kate grabbed a fresh superfluous flute from a tight grouping on the bar, inverted bowling pins. She wandered with purposeful aimlessness back through the small sitting room, letting her forefinger play against the tops of the tactile knickknacks, various varieties of cold and smooth, glass and brass and sterling silver. As she came around the corner to the hall, she pulled her phone out of her purse and pressed a button to ignite the screen. "Yes," she said to a private Snuffleupagus, "is everything okay?" The dark-suited functionary guarding the door glanced at her, and she threw him an apologetic smile. "No, darling," she fake-protested into the phone. "It's not a bother, tell me what the problem is." She wanted the guard to feel he was intruding, standing there where he was supposed to, listening to her listen to a problem, an intimate problem being explained by Darling. The guard pursed his lips, turned, and took a few steps out of the center hall, toward the kitchen, or office, or some type of service room, giving a woman some privacy. Social engineering indeed.

"Of course," Kate said, her voice dripping with concern and sympathy; Darling was ill. She started walking up the stairs, out of sight and soundless on the plush red carpet. The upstairs hall extended in both directions, dim in one, dark in the other. She took the dark path. The doors were all open, but no lights were on, no slivers of illumination angling into the hall. Kate walked slowly, cautiously, into the first room. A small, nearly empty bedroom. The curtains were closed, the darkness nearly total. She left.

A door at the far end of the dim hall swung open, bright light spilling out. She saw a leg emerging, stockings and heels; Kate jumped backward into the bedroom.

"Oh don't give me that crap," the woman hissed. "It's the goddamned Christmas party, Lou. You should be here." The phone conversation receded down the stairs.

Back into the hall, to the next room, bigger, an office with a desk and couch and coffee table. A study. Open curtains, light filtering in from the street, through the bare branches of trees, illuminating one wall, the light chopped by a tree, a wood-cut pattern. There was a door against this semi-lit wall, open partway.

Kate heard breathing.

She peered through the slightly open closet door, to the floor, where the light fell brightest, and saw pants crumpled at the top of shoes, and above that a stockinged calf held in the air, and above that a quick glimpse of the thick dark between open legs being split, curved and veined and glistening, sliding slowly all the way out before slipping back in, and above that the pushed-up skirt, and above that the blouse yanked askew and a nipple and the arched neck and open mouth and flaring nostrils and tightly clamped eyes, lids jammed together.

"Ungh," the woman grunted. The man quickly raised his hand to her mouth and covered it. He let his thumb slide between her lips, and the woman took it between her teeth, enamel glinting.

Kate was frozen. She couldn't stop watching, listening. She could even smell it.

The woman moaned.

The woman's eyes were clamped even more tightly shut, head further back. Kate couldn't pull herself away.

"Oh. God." The woman was convulsing, her head lolling in and out of the weak light. Barely enough light to confirm that it was Plain Jane. And the man, of course, was Bill.

Kate crept away, back toward the door, ever so slowly, quietly, carefully . . . almost there . . . one more step—

"Shit!" Bill spat out.

Kate turned the door's corner, into the hall, just in time to hear Plain Jane ask "What?" in a hoarse whisper. And then again, *"What?"*

Kate scampered down the dark hall. Down the well-lit stairs, feet sliding on the plush rug, gliding. The guard looked up at her, his mouth open in protest, but he never managed to decide what to say. She breezed past him, into a hall. She would hide in the restroom for a minute. She pushed down on the door's lever, but it didn't budge. Locked.

At the end of the hall, a brass panel was inset into what must be a swinging door. The kitchen. Kate took a step forward, but then the door began to open, and she froze.

It opened wider, and she heard laughing from a man, giggling from a woman, both sounds—both voices—familiar, very familiar, and then the door was wide open, the man coming out first, followed by the woman.

Dexter. With Julia.

✦ ✦ ✦

"KATE," JULIA EXCLAIMED, all cheer. It seemed false, like the cover that a woman would lay when pretending that she wasn't doing something wrong.

Dexter was flushed.

Kate felt the need to explain her presence, but it was these two who needed to explain themselves. She stifled herself.

"Hi," Dexter said, short and unconvincing, non-incriminating.

Kate looked from one to the other, her husband to her fictional friend, back again. This wasn't coming out of nowhere, but it was also not expected. At least, not what she expected out of Dexter.

They all stood there in the hall, these three, each second an eternity. Julia said nothing more, neither did Dexter. Every millisecond of silence made them seem more and more guilty.

"What're you two up to?" Kate finally asked.

They glanced at each other, Julia and Dexter. Julia giggled again. These two suddenly seemed like brother and sister, or two old friends, not a pair of adulterers.

"Come," Dexter said, taking Kate's hand.

The kitchen was large and professional, a big work island, multiple ranges, hoods, open cabinets and hanging pots, speed bars, bottles with pour tops, big battered pots.

Julia headed to a drawer, pulled it open, and removed something. "Here," she said.

Kate was confused. She looked down at the offering, then back up at Julia.

Dexter made his way to the far end of the room, a big steel-doored appliance, refrigerator or freezer. He too was removing something, shutting the door, turning to Kate.

She looked at her husband's offering, and her friend's. Ice cream, and a spoon.

Kate couldn't shake the feeling that she'd caught them at something illicit, something hidden. Not the ice cream, nor the obvious thing. Something else.

Kate wanders the streets of St-Germain-des-Prés, lost in thought, trying to unravel the meaning of her discovery, an explanation for the incontrovertible evidence in the yearbook. The evidence that Dexter and the woman who now called herself Julia did not meet two years ago, in Luxembourg. They met two decades ago, in college.

The morning rain has given way to high patchy clouds that rush across the sky, leaving in their wake bursts of harshly bright sunshine, a blustery wind roiling the clumps of fallen leaves.

She walks through the *terrasse* of the Flore, where the whole family took a break after the boys' school interview, and before they rashly chose their apartment, last year. A famous café, its white-and-green china easily recognizable. This is guide-book Paris, Picasso's Paris. Kate's home.

This is not a life she ever expected.

The past year in Paris was a vast improvement on the prior year in Luxembourg. And this coming year, she knows, will be even better, by degrees. She likes the new friends she and Dexter made last year; she expects she'll like them even more this year. Plus there will be new people. She has realized that she likes new people.

She turns into the rue Apollinaire in front of the jaunty stripes of Le Bonaparte.

Kate likes tennis too. She took up the game a year ago, first in an exhausting flurry of thrice-weekly lessons, to make rapid progress so she could join the round robin of moms from school who play in the Jardins du Luxembourg. By the end of the year, she'd become one of the best players in the group. But she's neither young nor tall nor fast, and she's never going to be any of those things, so she's also never going to be a great player. Just good enough. And she can play with Dexter.

Now that he doesn't work so much, and doesn't need to travel at all, they have ample time—and plenty of money—to do enjoyable things together, constantly. They are permanent tourists, in Paris. Their life is a certain type of dream come true.

But Kate can't deny that she still wants something more. Or something else. She's never going to be one of those women who opens a children's shoe store or a home-decor boutique, importing stylish plastic from Stockholm and Copen-hagen. She isn't going to immerse herself in studies of the Old Masters or the

Existentialists. She's not going to wander around with a Bristol pad and a box of pastels; nor with a laptop, pecking away at a pointless novel. She can't imagine leading walking tours for small groups of retirees, progressing from the best bakeries to the best cheese shops, uncovering the covered markets, shaking hands with the falsely friendly proprietors.

There are a lot of things Kate knows she does *not* want to do.

Although hers is by any standard a good life, Kate can't deny that she's bored, again. She's been through this before; she has more self-awareness this time. Which is leading to her conviction that there's only one solution to that problem. And this afternoon she's conscious that the solution might now be within her grasp, courtesy of the revelation in the yearbook, and how she'll be able to use this new information.

It isn't surprising to Kate that she was lied to by the undercover agent. She was never much aggrieved by that tautology. But her husband's betrayal is another matter. There has never been any doubt in Kate's mind that Dexter loves her, and their children. She isn't concerned about his fundamental nature: he is a good man. Her good man. Whatever the explanation of the enormity of Dexter's and Julia's duplicity, it must accommodate the undebatable reality that he's good, not bad.

Kate has already thought through a half-dozen scenarios, and dismissed them all. She picks up afresh with Julia's message, a few hours ago: the Colonel is dead.

She turns at the chamfered corner of Le Petit Zinc's elegant door, oozing Art Nouveau out onto the sidewalk, the warm afternoon light setting aglow the sand-colored stones of the buildings in the rue St-Benoit.

This is an elegant spot, an elegant corner. An elegant turn . . .

Kate stops stock-still in the street, eyes frozen in front, mind racing in a circle to come all the way around to the beginning, to the certainty, to confirmation, to the brilliance of it.

She knows what happened.

20

Kate pulled her hat low, shelter against a gust of wind blowing cold down from Mont Blanc looming in the distance, the white-peaked Alps folding over themselves, Alp over Alp, all the way down to Geneva skirting the shores of Lac Léman.

The ice cream was a plausible explanation. They'd had too much to drink, most of the food in the dining room was gone, they didn't want any more ham. No one wanted any more ham. Everywhere everyone went, there were ham sandwiches. In bakeries and butchers, supermarkets and cafés. At the kiosks in malls, in the vending machines in offices, under glass domes on the counters at gyms, on airplanes. Goddamned ham sandwiches, everywhere.

So they'd gone to the kitchen, looking for something nonham to eat. Questionable judgment, wandering through the private spaces of the embassy. A drunken semi-caper. Completely believable.

Kate walked through Paquis, near the train station, North Africans and Arabs, couscous restaurants and souvenir shops, chunky Turkish prostitutes smoking cigarettes in the doorways of cinder-block buildings, skinny men in baggy jeans lurking in shadows. This would be a good place to buy a gun; this was the type of neighborhood where she'd done that before. Kate was halfway thinking she should have a weapon.

She crossed the Rhône at the Pont du Mont Blanc, ducked into the Jardin Anglais, wintered over, unpeopled, the wind here frigid and biting, tears springing from her eyes.

Kate had to keep reminding herself that she hadn't discovered anything definitively *wrong* in Dexter's office. All the material there could be a legitimate part of his job. She didn't understand his job, and never had. She had no idea what it entailed.

But Jesus, that video camera. How was she going to explain to him why she'd broken into his office? And how?

Luckily—or not; who knew?—it didn't appear that Dexter had been alerted yet to her break-in. Or if he had, then he was certainly not the man she thought she'd married.

Kate passed a familiar-looking woman on the sidewalk, tall and dark-haired and heavy-eyelashed. Kate couldn't place her, then she did: a flight attendant on this morning's hop. The LuxAir stewardesses in their sprightly blue scarves practically threw the ham sandwiches at passengers as soon as the plane was airborne, eager to get the snack under way on the short flight. They were all short flights, on LuxAir.

Kate headed up the hill on the rue Verdaine, the architecture now looming chunks of medieval stone, tight cobblestoned streets, a promenade along a park, fortifications, arches, terraced sidewalks. This part of Geneva reminded her of Luxembourg, of Arlon, of everywhere.

Snowflakes began to flutter, drifting softly to the street lined with eighteenth-century *hôtels particuliers,* massive arched doors leading to courtyards, a matching suite of three imposing buildings leaning against one another, like fashion models posing for a homoerotic shot, skin-on-skin-on-skin.

It was certainly possible that Dexter and Julia were having an affair. They could be meeting at Julia's apartment, weekday mornings, while Bill was in his strange office lifting weights or masterfully fucking Jane—possibly both, at the same time—and Kate was at some coffee morning, sitting around with a bunch of women bitching about the absence of their husbands, while her own was around the corner, in bed with her best friend.

Or had they simply dipped into the kitchen, buzzed, and kissed for five minutes?

Or was it a harmless flirtation, a diversion, staying alive, un-old, un-dead?

On the rue de l'Hôtel de Ville, nearly all the antiques shops were closed, neatly handwritten signs announcing the vacation, *fermé* until early January. No presents to be purchased. Unimaginable, in the States, that any store would be closed two days before Christmas.

If it were really an affair? What would Kate do? Could she understand this, ignore this, forgive this? Did Dexter still love her? Was he bored, or curious, or horny, or selfish, or terrified of mortality? Was he having a midlife crisis? Had he done this before? Was he an inveterate philanderer? Had he been cheating all these years? Was it turning out that he was an utter bastard, and she hadn't been aware of it? For nearly a decade?

Or was his infidelity a crime of opportunity? Had he been seduced, unfairly? Plied with liquor and teased and eventually propositioned, an offer he couldn't refuse?

At the apex of the hill, the street opened out onto the Place du Bourg-de-Four, cafés and a fountain in the middle of a wide, irregularly shaped expanse of cobblestones. Kate checked her watch—2:58—and took a seat on a caned chair, next to a propane-powered heater throwing warmth into the air, spitting into the ocean. She ordered a café au lait from a handsome, self-satisfied waiter.

Or was it something more sinister than sex?

Across the *terrasse* a mother and daughter in matching fur hats smoked matching cigarettes, long skinny tobacco toothpicks. The mother caressed a miniature dog in her lap, some type of white fluffiness. The daughter said something, but Kate couldn't hear; they were too far away. Good.

Her coffee arrived with a foil-wrapped cookie in the saucer, as always, everywhere.

The waiter continued on to the mother and daughter. They laughed at something he said as he leaned on the back of a chair, flexing, flirting. Kate heard footsteps behind her, a man's hard soles falling on stones. She didn't turn. The man took a seat at the next table, separated from Kate by the heater and its glowing cap, a flying saucer.

The waiter returned. The man ordered hot chocolate. He opened his newspaper, carefully folding *Le Monde* into a prim packet. He wore a gray overcoat, red scarf, skinny jeans, pointy black shoes with green laces. His skin scrubbed and shiny, face shaved extremely closely, more hairless than Dexter was ever able to shave. The same look as the boys in Dupont Circle, something about their entire faces that broadcast their orientation.

Kate put her tote on the table. She removed a guidebook to Switzerland, and a messily folded map of Geneva, and a pen and small notepad.

The waiter delivered the man's hot chocolate.

She took the camera out of her pocket, held it aloft, and leaned toward this man. *"Excusez-moi,"* she said. *"Parlez-vous anglais?"*

"Yes, I speak English."

"Would you mind taking a picture of me?"

"Not at all." He scooted his chair over, and took her camera.

Kate looked around for the right backdrop—a fountain, attractive buildings, snow in the grass. She moved her chair a few degrees. She pushed aside the guidebook, out of the frame of the upcoming picture. There was a photo shoved between the pages of her guidebook.

"Are you visiting Geneva on your way to a ski trip?"

"Yes. We leave tomorrow. To Avoriaz, for a week."

The man directed her to move to the right, and snapped again. The waiter reemerged, asked Kate and the man if everything was okay, then returned to the mother and daughter. He was probably the reason the women were here.

The man rose into a crouch. He leaned forward, extending the camera, and put it on Kate's guidebook. As his hand retreated, he pulled the photo out of the pages, slipped it into his coat pocket. Then he picked up his cup, and took a long drink of chocolate.

"Three days," he said. "Maybe four." He placed a giant coin onto the table; some of these Swiss franc pieces were practically sporting goods. Why did they need a different currency? Goddamned Swiss.

"Then I will find you."

✦ ✦ ✦

IT STARTED SNOWING when they were halfway up the mountain, the snow noticeably heavier as the car climbed, traffic slowing, the shoulder littered with pulled-over station wagons whose drivers were kneeling in the gravelly slush, installing chains. Switchbacks one after another, straightaways of barely a few hundred yards, the downhill side of the road falling away steeply past jagged outcroppings and tenacious pines and precariously perched timber-framed chalets.

By Monday morning three fresh feet had fallen and the clouds had fled in the night, dawn breaking pink-gray out the bedroom window that faced the center of the resort, the Village des Enfants and the cafés and shops. When Kate padded into the living room, she gasped at the view, which had remained completely cloaked in cloud and mist and swirling snow for their first thirty-six hours on this mountain, but now was crystal clear, picture-perfect Alps, Alp after Alp after Alp, all cloaked in white, spray-painted snow.

✦ ✦ ✦

JULIA SKIED OVER from the edge of the trail, gliding effortlessly. "My God," she said. "How great is this?" She kissed Kate on the cheek. Bill also skated over, shook hands with Dexter, slapped him on the upper arm.

The snow was blindingly white, the visibility seemingly infinite in every direction, as if the entire world had been placed under a microscope, the lens freshly wiped. The view to the north encompassed four folds of mountain range, then a sliver of the lake, then the mountains on the far side, tiny notches under an immensity of clear sky.

"Shall we?" Bill asked, pushing off with his poles.

"Let's roll!" said Dexter, more enthusiastic than before. Gung-ho, now. He'd been unconfident, terrified, in the difficult skiing of the heavy storm, the summit lift depositing skiers into a total whiteout nine thousand feet up, above the tree line, no forests to mitigate the elements, nowhere to hide, no way to see the boundaries of the pistes, visibility at thirty yards, one second away from the farthest you could see. After a single trip to the top, Dexter had refused to ski the summits, and instead retreated down the mountain, to the quiet trails that snaked among the trees.

"I want to see where the hell I'm going," he'd said. Cruising down that easy trail, Kate had lost herself in his unintentional bit of philosophy. She too wanted to see where the hell she was going. Wondered whether that was ever again going to be possible.

Now they were back at the summit, a completely different experience in this blazing sunshine. Kate pulled her goggles off the top of her helmet, fitted them around her eyes, the soft foam pressing gently into her cheekbones, her forehead, sealing her eyes inside this pink-tinged cocoon. *La vie en rose*. A flash in her mind of the blood in the carpet radiating from Torres's head, his lifeless unstaring eyes, the sound of the baby crying.

Kate shuddered the thought away. She skied to the lip of the piste, a quick drop-off onto a wind-whipped face, swirls of snow slithering across the surface.

"I'll go first," Bill said, and launched himself over the ledge. Dexter looked none too sanguine about this trail, but he dutifully followed. Then Julia.

Kate remained at the top, looking down on these three people, all waiting for her to throw herself off a cliff.

✦ ✦ ✦

KATE PAUSED AT a wide turn on a broad trail. It had been three days since her meeting with Kyle in Geneva, and it was time for him to come skiing out of nowhere, pull to a stop, and tell her . . . tell her what?

Tell her that these FBI agents were investigating something that had nothing to do with Kate or Dexter. This was what Kate wanted most in the world, now: that improbable news.

Kate waited a few more seconds, a half-minute, staring at the fluffy white landscape, the marshmallow fields. No one arrived.

She gave up, set off down the hill, her turns silent in the soft powder, the poles at the sides of the trail counting down to the bottom, where a half-dozen trails converged at three lifts and a handful of cafés, hundreds of canvas chairs arrayed in the sunshine, people lying around with jackets off, smoking cigarettes and drinking beer, eleven in the morning. Dexter and Julia were at one of these cafés, boots unbuckled, resting.

Kate joined Bill. They skated through the milling crowd, pushed through the gates, planted their poles. They turned to face the oncoming chair clanging around the bend, the steel bar at the front of the seat attacking the crooks of their knees, slamming into them, forcing them to sit quicker and harder than expected, butts stinging.

No one else joined them on the lift. It sped away, at first along a level area, then up a steep angle to cross an exposed rock face lined with a spiderweb of dark mineral veins. A varicose rock.

"It's exhilarating, isn't it?" Bill asked.

The lift leveled out to cross a shallow valley, a dale cut into the side of the mountain, a rushing brook surrounded by pines half-buried in snow, high steep banks and frigid-looking water, stones in the bed, thousands upon thousands of stones, pink and gray, white and black, brown and tan, large and small and medium.

"When you're speeding down, not sure what you're going to encounter next."

The chair passed the dale and climbed another rocky face, then a long rough slope, icicles and snowdrifts, immense boulders strewn, balls tossed around by giants. They were now very high from the ground, one of those spots in a two-thousand-foot ascent when the lift is more than the normal twenty feet up, but rather fifty, sixty feet.

The chair slowed. Then stopped.

Exposed to the wind, the cold. Swinging back, an equal and opposite reaction to what had been their forward momentum. Newton's Third Law, here above the mountain. Swinging forward, then back. Forward, back.

Creaking.

A shudder ran down Kate's spine. This was a mistake. She shouldn't be here, alone with Bill.

The wind picked up, howling, pushing the swing of the chair into a bigger arc, the hinge's creak louder. The extra-harsh coldness of a stalled lift on a windy day; raw exposure.

Kate looked up, to where the chair was connected to the cable by a clasp that looked like the end of a shoelace.

"Sorta scary, isn't it?"

It was called an aglet, the shoelace tip.

Bill leaned forward, looked down. "If you fell from here, do you think you'd die?"

The aglet-like fixture was clamped to the cable as if with giant pliers. Kate could see the seam where it could be opened.

"What do you think?"

Kate looked at him. She could see through her rose lenses something new in his face, an expression she hadn't seen before. Something hard.

"You ever been afraid for your life, Kate?"

✦ ✦ ✦

EDUARDO TORRES HAD been living in a suite at the Waldorf, the hotel where presidents stay when they stop in New York for photo ops at the United Nations and a Broadway theater, a game at Yankee Stadium. Torres, however, wasn't staying in the presidential suite. He wasn't a president, never had been. But he thought he should be. And not just president of Mexico. Torres had a grandiose vision for a pan–Latin American supra-state—el Consejo de las Naciones, the Council of Nations—of which he would be leader, in effect the head of the western hemisphere and the half-billion people who lived south of the U.S. border.

But first he had to mount a triumphant return from unofficial exile. When he'd lost the election, he'd not conceded graciously; instead he'd objected vociferously. He'd incited violence, which in turn instigated revenge violence, and led to a generally unsafe environment for the ex-general. So he'd fled his Polanco compound to Manhattan, where he didn't need to employ an entire regiment merely to make a restaurant secure for dinner. In America he could feel safe with a handful of body-guards.

Torres had spent the previous year trying to build alliances and raise money for the next election, or a coup, or who knew what path he imagined for his ascendancy; he was delusional. No rational players were willing to offer him any support of any sort.

He was getting desperate. His desperation was making him

increasingly unviable, which in turn was making him increasingly desperate. A vicious cycle.

Kate, meanwhile, had just taken a trip to southern Mexico, which would turn out to have been her final overseas mission. She'd held a series of not particularly clandestine meetings with local politicians, trying to befriend—or at least un-alienate—whoever would be next, the generals and entrepreneurs and mayors who would mount their own presidential campaigns, sooner or later. Kate sat in courtyard gardens, purple bougainvillea climbing whitewashed walls, sipping cups of strong coffee in colorful ceramics delivered on hand-forged silver trays, absorbing their bombast.

Then she returned to Washington, to her husband and six-month-old firstborn. She was walking on G Street, returning to the office from lunch, when a town car pulled to the curb. The driver lowered his window.

"Señor Torres would appreciate a few minutes of your time."

Kate quickly weighed her options, her responses. No matter how irrational Torres was becoming, there was no way he would do harm to a CIA officer in Washington.

"He is at the Ritz. He is available now."

Kate climbed into the backseat, and five minutes later walked into the hotel lobby, where a bodyguard met her and directed her to Torres's suite.

"Absolutely not," she said. "He can meet me in the bar."

Señor joined her in the lounge and ordered a bottle of water and asked about her well-being, a grace period that lasted thirty seconds before he began to pontificate. She listened for a half-hour to his tale of woe, to his vision for Mexico, and Latin America. He made an impassioned yet wholly ludicrous case for why the CIA should support him.

As an audience, Kate strove to seem dubious and pessimistic but fundamentally noncommittal and decidedly nonconfrontational. She'd known Torres for a decade. She didn't want to piss him off unless she had to.

Torres asked the waiter for the bill. He told Kate he'd be returning to New York in the morning, and looked forward to their next conversation at her earliest convenience. She said she'd discuss it with her superiors.

He nodded slowly, closing his eyes, as if expressing deep gratitude. But he didn't say thank you.

Kate rose.

That's when Torres reached into his jacket and removed something from his breast pocket. He laid it on the gleaming cherry table, but said nothing.

She glanced down. It was a three-by-five print, glossy paper. She leaned over to get a closer look at the sharp, clear image, obviously taken with a powerful telephoto lens.

Kate straightened her back, deliberately slowly, trying to stay calm. Her eyes flickered up from the photo to the man across the table.

Torres was staring into the distance, as if this implicit threat had nothing to do with him. As if he were merely a messenger, and this were an ugly business between Kate and someone else.

21

Bill slid in front of Kate, down a steep, ungroomed trail, thick woods on one side, the other a rocky cliff lined with trail-limit poles—black-tipped poles, expert-slope poles, well beyond Kate's abilities. He seemed determined to take her to the next level, or she was going to refuse to be taken there, or she was going to try and fail. But in any case, it would be different.

Kate struggled down the mogul-infested slope. A pair of fearless teenagers zoomed past and were gone within seconds. Kate and Bill were alone again in the deep silence of a tall snowbound mountain on the French-Swiss border.

She traversed the bumpy field to where the mountain came to an abrupt end at the intersection with the sky. As she neared the cliff's edge, she could see more of the view out beyond the mountain, but she couldn't see any of the side itself; the drop-off was too steep. A fantastically terrifying sign was planted here, a pictogram of a skier falling, windmilling, one ski off, a pole in the air. Certain death, is what this sign promised.

Bill was tight behind her. "You're doing great," he said.

Kate wasn't reassured. She decided to stop but then didn't, kept going, and decided to stop again but again didn't, went faster, and faster, getting more nervous, and she could hear Bill's turns behind her, and she could see the fall-away off to her left, thirty feet down to an outcrop of boulders, another twenty to the bottom of the ravine, and her left ski slipped out, toward the edge, nearing air . . .

She turned sharply toward safety, digging into the snow with her edges, pushing hard with her downhill ski, quickly coming to a snow-throwing stop—

Realizing, too late, that she was stopping with too little warning. She was still in the microsecond process of this realization when she heard yelling—

Felt his pole trying to knock her out of the way—

His ski tip rushing across hers—

The full collision, the impact on her hip and torso and shoulder and arm, then she was airborne, being propelled toward the edge of the trail, the ledge of the slope, falling down the piste and sideways, in the direction of a long, fatal drop, the poles no longer in her palms but still attached by nylon straps to her wrists, spinning batons, only one ski still secured to her boot, and she tried to remember if she'd ever heard any advice—anywhere: in Girl Scouts, or at training on the Farm, or even on ESPN or who knows maybe PBS—about what is the best position to be in when you fall fifty feet off a cliff onto a rock?

◆ ◆ ◆

KATE TRIED TO lift her head, but couldn't. She couldn't move her neck, her shoulders, her arms. She couldn't see anything except a faint tinge of rose to the near-total blackness. Her face was pressed into the dense granular snow. The cold had suffused her skin, and she imagined her face muscles chilling, being flash-frozen, like sockeye salmon on a North Pacific trawler, their eyes permanently immobilized while looking off to the side.

It felt like a tremendous weight had pinned her at the spine, paralyzing her.

She tried to wiggle her toes, but couldn't tell if she succeeded; goddamn ski boots.

She began to hyperventilate.

And then the weight on her spine might have shifted. And then it definitely did shift, at first increasing in pressure, then decreasing, then disappearing completely.

Kate heard something.

She thought she could move now. She did, turning, rolling her torso and shoulder and neck, turning her face from the snow, her goggles still mostly covered but not completely, so she could make out the world again with her eyes, and that thing she'd heard before, she heard it again, and it was a voice, and she could see through the patches of snow that it was Bill, and he was standing above her, asking if she was okay.

And she was.

◆ ◆ ◆

DARKNESS ADVANCED QUICKLY in the mountains. By three, the sun's angle had become oblique, the blue-tinged light flat, shadowless.

Kate arrived by herself to the bottom of an easy cruiser trail, a respite from Bill's aggression. She hustled to the gates of the high-speed quad while there was no one waiting, intending to get on alone. But another skier pulled up to her side.

It was a man; it was Kyle. Finally.

The gates opened, and the two of them pushed up to the red line painted on the rubber matting, turned to face the oncoming chair. Then another skier arrived to Kate's other side, invading their privacy. Damn.

The three sat down with a group thud. Kyle closed the safety bar. *"Bonjour,"* he said, barely audible through the grating of the chair pulling out.

Kate lifted her goggles off her face. She looked over at this Kyle character from Geneva, then stole a glance to her other side, at the third skier. She did a double take as she realized it was Dexter, grinning at her.

"Sweetheart," she said. "You snuck up on me." Loud enough to ensure that Kyle heard, unmistakably.

"Yes I did," Dexter said, exultant in his sportiness. "How's it going?"

"It's beautiful," she said. Wondering if Dexter had heard Kyle's hello.

Dexter was leaning forward, looking over Kate, at Kyle. Double-damn. "You two know each other?"

Please, Kate thought—prayed—let Kyle not be an idiot.

"No," Kyle answered.

"You said hello."

"Just being friendly."

Kate stared ahead while these two men talked across her, zipping through the sky.

"I'm Dexter Moore. My wife, Kate."

"I'm Kyle. Pleased to meet you."

"You staying here?" Dexter asked. "Or visiting from another resort?"

"Day-tripping, actually. Up from Geneva. I live there."

The chair rumbled through a support tower.

"We're skiing with some other Americans today," Dexter said. "Friends from Luxembourg. That's where we live."

Kyle couldn't figure out how to continue this conversation; nor how to stop it. Kate didn't know what the hell to do about this. So she just sat silently, while the men made small talk.

✦ ✦ ✦

185

BILL TOOK OFF his Muppet mitten, and Kyle did the same, and the two shook hands, introductions all around.

"We found this lonely American on the mountain," Dexter explained. They were standing on a wind-blown ridge, with a sharp drop-off onto a steep mogul field to one side, an unskiable cliff to the other, cordoned off with a slack yellow rope that would do nothing to slow people down, much less stop them, on their way off the edge.

Bill gave Kyle a once-over. "You don't say."

Kyle smiled, big white teeth gleaming out of winter ruddiness.

Dexter checked his watch. "We have to go. Ski-school pickup is in a few minutes." He turned to Kyle. "Want to join us for après-ski?"

Kyle hesitated, but not too long. Not long enough for anyone to think it was anything other than a man considering an unexpected social invitation. "Sure," he said. "Love to."

The light was failing, the sun out of view, over a jagged summit to the southwest. The five Americans traversed the ridge in a snaking line, their ski edges scraping loudly against hard-packed crud, interspersed with soft whooshes through the softer snow, the rustle of nylon rubbing nylon, a clank as a pole hit a boot. Kate heard Bill close behind, and couldn't stop the shiver running down her spine.

No one said anything.

Around a bend and the *centre de la station* came into view, the cluster of tall buildings surrounding the Village des Enfants, the horse-drawn carriages moving with surprising speed, all of it cloaked in fresh snow, dotted with sharp pinpoints of electric lights, a complicated foreground against a simple backdrop of canyon and valley and more mountains and the immense broadness of the cerulean sky.

"Who's Kyle?" Bill asked.

Kate shrugged dismissively. "Guy from a chairlift."

"Yeah," Bill snorted. "Like I'm a guy from a tennis club."

Kate's brain went haywire. She didn't understand what Bill was saying. Her mouth was open, then she closed it, then opened it again, but she couldn't think of anything to say without giving something away. But saying nothing would also be giving something away. "I don't know what you mean by that."

A gust of wind blew the loose snow into the air. The sky seemed to be dimming by the second.

"Are you going to tell me?"

Bill stared at her for a second, two, but then skied away without saying anything.

There was only one explanation: he knew. He knew that she knew.

Kate pushed off, following Bill down the hill and around a bend and across a plateau and into the thick humanity swarming around the center of the resort, parents pouring into the children's area, big hugs and high fives and toddlers crying from the relief of finally seeing Mommy after a seemingly interminable and possibly terrifying day.

Dexter skied through the gates of the ski school, while Julia and Bill volunteered to go to the nearest café and claim a big table. Kyle and Kate were left alone, standing side by side in the middle of the main path, surrounded by thousands of people.

"You're not going to like this," he said.

Kate watched Dexter lean over to gather the children in big hugs, one in each arm. Even through the crowd and the gear, under the helmets and the goggles, Kate could see the giant smiles of unmitigated joy on the boys' faces. Reunion.

"What they're investigating," Kyle said.

Kate turned to him. "Yes?"

"It's your husband."

❖ ❖ ❖

KATE WISHED SHE was surprised; but she wasn't. She also wished she wasn't relieved; but she was. At least a little. Whatever her husband had done, it couldn't be as bad as what she herself had done.

"What do they think he did?"

Dexter was removing the boys' bright-yellow identifying vests—PREMIER SKI—that made them look like miniature contestants in a grand slalom.

"Cyber theft."

"Of what?"

Julia had suddenly returned. "We're over there," she said.

Kate's heart skipped a beat—a few beats.

"That bistro with the green awning," Julia continued. Kate could barely hear her through the din; there's no way Julia could've heard their conversation. Could she?

The children were approaching, carrying their skis across their chests, followed by a grinning Dexter. Kate gave the boys hugs, trying but failing to distract herself, even minutely, from the dreadfulness that was assailing her.

Everyone trudged through the snow and crowds toward Bill, seated alone in the middle of a huge picnic table, like a disgraced executive at the end of a board meeting.

Kate needed less than a minute more, maybe just a few seconds, alone with Kyle.

They all settled at the rough-hewn table, accepted delivery of hot chocolates topped with whipped cream, and giant mugs of frothy beer, and plates of apple galette.

"So," Bill said, "Kyle, is it?"

"That's right, Bill."

"You live in Geneva?"

"I do."

"Interesting town?"

"Not terribly."

"You look familiar. Do we know each other?"

Kate was going to explode.

"I don't think so."

Bill nodded, but it wasn't a gesture of agreement. "What do you do, Kyle?"

"I'm a lawyer. But you'll have to excuse me," he said, rising, "because I'm a lawyer who needs the men's room."

Kate felt Bill's eyes on her, felt his suspicion of Kyle oozing across the table, the slime of it covering herself. She pretended to people-watch, skiers in snowsuits and bright jackets and helmets, children in snowball fights, dogs barking, waitresses carrying trays filled with steins, grand-mothers in furs, teenagers smoking cigarettes.

Kate pushed herself across the bench. "Excuse me," she said, not meeting any eye.

She could feel Bill and Julia staring at each other, knew they were sending signals, having a whole conversation about whether to follow Kate to the restroom, and which one should do it, and whether it should be overt or surreptitious.

"I'll join you," Julia said. Of course.

Kate walked among tables, and waited for a horse-drawn carriage to pass, and a pair of squealing girls to run by, and one spun just in time to get hit in the face by a snowball, triggering an instant nosebleed and high-pitched crying. A big thick drop of blood hit the icy snow, and another drop, then a flurry of a few, a small splattering there at the girl's feet. Her mother arrived, scolding what was obviously a pleased little brother, pressing a napkin to the girl's injured nose, the blood spreading through the snow. That same pattern again, writ small. Spreading blood.

✦ ✦ ✦

KATE HAD PASSED a difficult night after the unpleasant conclusion to the unscheduled meeting with Torres at the hotel; she was without question afraid of him. It was a long painful night of hand-wringing and plotting and counterplotting.

Kate hadn't been able to fall asleep until she'd made up her mind, with a heart-stopping finality, at three in the morning. She was awakened two hours later, when Jake cried to start his day. She fed him, and sat with him, and cooed at him, staring off into the lightening sky over the stockade fence that separated her barely tended garden from the scrubby, weedy yard of the multi-unit rental to the east.

Kate didn't know it yet, but she was pregnant again. Not intentionally. But also not disappointingly.

Twenty-four hours later she was on the Amtrak to New York, an unreserved seat purchased with cash at a ticket counter in Union Station, wearing oversize eyeglasses with clear lenses—her vision didn't need correcting—and a blond wig. She then walked from Penn Station up- and across town, thirty minutes through the crowded meat of Manhattan, with a quick stop to buy a Yankees cap from a sidewalk shop exploding with China-produced merchandise. She wore the cap low, blond bangs brushing her eyelids.

Kate entered the Waldorf-Astoria not on Park Avenue but through the quieter Forty-ninth Street entrance. She got off the elevator at a few minutes after nine. It was too early for there to be a large housekeeping presence on the floor—too many guests would still be asleep. But it was late enough that the businesspeople would be gone. It was a quiet time of day on a hotel guest floor.

Kate knew that Torres was not an exception to the Mexican-time rule. He was often late for meetings, sometimes by as much as an hour. And he neither saw anyone nor did anything before ten in the morning. Kate had honestly never understood how they accomplished anything in that country.

Kate knew he'd be alone in his room at a time like 9:08 A.M.

She didn't encounter anyone in the plushly carpeted hall until she came to the bodyguard who stood at Torres's door. He was a squat, angry-looking man in a cheap black suit that was way too tight. The early-morning shift wasn't the A-team, not the big imposing guys who would sit at restaurant bars at night. This morning guy was B-team. At best.

When Kate was just a few feet away, she smiled demurely at the

189

bodyguard without slowing down or breaking stride, to all appearances continuing on to some other room down the hall, drawing her hand out of her coat pocket, the switchblade already open, her arm shooting across her body, the knife sinking smoothly and quietly into the man's trachea, his eyes wide, registering his dire situation, his arms attempting to rise but too late, his body slumping, sliding down the wall while she supported his weight under the armpits, to avoid the alarm-inducing thud of a heavy body hitting a hard floor.

✦ ✦ ✦

KATE NEEDED TO get Julia in front of her, and she was running out of space, out of time. Kate limped for a few steps. "Excuse me," she said. "My sock has bunched up. You go ahead."

Kate leaned over, avoiding Julia's gaze, which Kate knew would have been calling bullshit. But if Bill knew about Kate, then Julia knew about Kate. And Bill and Julia probably both knew who Kyle was, or some approximation of it. And they were either going to confront Kate now, or they weren't.

She was calling their bluff, in this transparent bit of playacting, leaning on a chair in an empty dining room. Kate dallied, unsnapping her boot slowly, waiting for Julia to move on, worried that she wouldn't. Then she did.

✦ ✦ ✦

"SHHHH," KATE HISSED, inclining her head toward the ladies' room. "She's in there." Kate tugged Kyle down the hall, away from the doors. "Quick."

"They think he stole money."

Kate's eyes were drawn to the goggles around Kyle's neck, which made her wonder about hidden microphones, though she couldn't imagine how anyone could gain anything from eavesdropping on her now.

"How much?"

"Fifty million."

"*What?*" Kate could barely prevent herself from staggering. "How much?"

"Fifty million euros."

✦ ✦ ✦

SHE SPLASHED HER face, stared at herself in the mirror, dripping wet. The things unsaid between Kate and Dexter were large beyond comprehension. They'd been growing every day for months, for *years,* for their entire relationship. But now the lies and secrets were accelerating. The growth was exponential.

How could she not tell this to her husband?

On the other hand, how could she tell him? How could she explain her suspicions, her actions, her contacts? Would she tell him about breaking into Bill's apartment? Would she tell him about Hayden in Munich and the agent-chauffeur in Berlin and Kyle right out there, sitting at the table? With the children? How would she explain any of this without admitting that she was CIA? Without opening that bottomless can of worms?

She was trapped—she had trapped herself—under an oppressive veil of silence.

◆ ◆ ◆

"WHAT YOU HAVE to do—what I have to do—is try to put myself in the mind of the attacker, the hacker. What would I do if I were trying to break into a system?"

Dexter was leaning back in the banquette, unshaven and snow-burned and wild of coif and not exactly steady of eye, explaining his job to Kyle, of all people.

"So I have to poke around, to find the weaknesses. Is it the system architecture? The firewall? The software-update protocols? Or is it the physical plant—the office layout, the mainframe access, the confusion of a lunchtime rush? Or is it social engineering that's going to be too easy? Are the employees trained, at all, to be aware of security issues? Are there sufficient procedures for choosing and changing and protecting their passwords?"

Kate glanced at the kids, obliviously eating, ravenous, digging into their thick soups like escaped prisoners, devouring fries and baguette between hearty slurps. Jake paused for water, came up gasping, and set upon his soup again.

The children were red-faced and chapped-lipped, and the buxom waitress wore a low-cut gingham blouse, and the maître d' was a picture of jolly rotundity. The people all looked like they'd been painted into the scene, itself set-designed with vintage sleds and wooden ski poles hanging on the walls, a person-high stack of wine bottles, a towering fire in the stone fireplace. Thick planks for tabletops, pots of fondues and bowls of potatoes.

Dexter pushed aside the remainder of his *tartiflette,* another meal in shades of white, and took a long pull of beer from a huge mug, then continued pontificating. "The best hacker isn't merely expert at the technical aspects of systems design and engineering, of ports and code and software vulnerabilities. No. That's what makes a good programmer. What makes a good hacker is the devious social engineer who can identify and exploit the greatest weakness in every system, every organization: human frailties."

Kyle was rapt.

"And once I've figured out a way for a hacker to get in, I have to think about how he plans to get out without being detected."

Julia and Bill exchanged a quick look that Kate barely noticed.

"There are a lot of ways to get caught extracting anything from anywhere. Just ask the bank robber doing thirty years in a federal pen. Getting in and getting the money are the easy parts. The hard part, always, is getting out. Especially undetected."

◆ ◆ ◆

KATE HAD TAKEN a deep breath and rapped—carefully—on the door, a soft polite *knock-knock*, like a room-service waiter, or a considerate spouse.

This was the type of operation that needed to take less than a half-minute, quickly in and immediately out, completely reliant on the element of surprise. A hard knock on the door would've ruined the surprise.

She counted the seconds—six, seven—while fighting the urge to knock again, another way to cede the surprise—eight, nine—until the handle turned, and the door opened a mere crack, and Kate threw all her weight into it, shoulder first, knocking Torres away.

He stumbled backward into the suite's sitting room, trying to avoid completely losing his balance and falling on his ass, while also coming to the horrifying realization that he had erred gravely. That somehow, of all the mistakes he'd made in his adventurous, eventful, and satisfying fifty-seven years, of all the many people—hundreds of them, thousands—he'd pissed off, it was astoundingly this *chica* who was finally going to kill him, right now. He should have never hired that photographer to take those pictures through her living-room window in Washington. Should never have printed up those glossies of the mother and her little boy, reading a book on the sofa. Should never have laid that picture on the table in the hotel lounge. Should never have made that implicit threat on her life, on the safety of her family.

He opened his mouth to plead for his life, but didn't get the chance.

It was when Torres was still falling to the floor—two sound-suppressed bullets in the chest, one in the head, no way to not be dead—that Kate heard the baby cry, and looked up to see the young woman walking through the door from the bedroom.

PART III

"Kate! Hello!"

Carolina is waving as she approaches. Another expat woman on another narrow Parisian sidewalk, smiling, this one a Dutch mom from school. Another woman who owns a large set of matching luggage, purchased somewhere within a mile of where they stand in the rue de Verneuil, a hundred yards from the somber Pont Royal that crosses the Seine to the Louvre and the Tuileries.

Carolina starts talking, a gushing stream of enthusiasms and exclamations. She's an excitable woman, socially ambitious and hyper-friendly, nearly pathologically outgoing, producing a constant stream of invitations across a broad swath of the Left Bank expat community. The Dutch, Kate has found, are very outgoing.

Kate can't quite pay attention to the chitchat, watching Carolina's mouth but barely understanding the monologue, something about the refurbished café around the corner in the rue du Bac, and when they'd have their first moms'-night-out of the school year, and there was a new American from New York—had Kate met her?

Kate stands there grinning and nodding at her friend, at this woman she has known for a year, this woman she sees nearly every day, sometimes two or three times per day, at the school's giant green door in the cobblestoned street, and at the café next door and the restaurant up the block, at the *tabac* and the *presse*, in the playgrounds and parks, in the Musée d'Orsay and playing tennis and drinking coffee, shopping for children's clothes and red wine, for shoes and handbags, curtains and candlesticks, talking about babysitters and housekeepers and the legroom on transatlantic flights, and ten-piece sets of matching luggage.

This woman whom Kate may never see again, this conversation their last. This is the expat life: you never know when someone you see every day is going to disappear forever, instantly transmogrifying into a phantom. Before long you won't be able to remember her last name, the color of her eyes, the grades that her children were in. You can't imagine not seeing her tomorrow. You can't imagine you yourself being one of those people, someone who one day just vanishes. But you are.

"I'll see you tomorrow?" Carolina asks. She thinks this is a rhetorical question.

"Yes," Kate answers, a thoughtless assent, but she realizes that in actuality she's deeply agreeing with something else entirely, committing herself to a plan that has been batting around her brain for the past hour.

Kate knows now she will not be needing the weekend bags packed for the forty-fourth time, nor the gassed-up Audi. Her family will not be going anywhere. Not tonight, nor tomorrow.

There's another life that Kate can live, here. And she now knows how to make it happen.

22

Pop!

Kate spun, startled by the sound of another cork yanked out by Cristina, who was too rushed and maybe too drunk to twist it out slowly, instead just yanked the thing, letting the liquid effervesce into a towel, wiping down the bottle, pouring the wine quickly, sloppily, spilling. There must have been a lot of empty bottles lying around the kitchen.

Tonight was their first social occasion since skiing and dinner with the so-called Macleans, a week ago. They'd returned to Luxembourg yesterday.

Cristina refilled Kate's glass, a heavy crystal. Did these people really own dozens of crystal flutes? A thousand dollars'—more?—worth of glassware? For New Year's Eve?

Kate noticed Julia in the next room. The last they'd spoken had been standing in the flurries outside the restaurant at the resort, cold fake cheek kisses, distracted by the tired children and the surprisingly agreeable company of Kyle and the new knowledge that these FBI agents suspected her husband of stealing approximately seventy-five million dollars.

Kate still hadn't said anything about it to Dexter.

The most common language at this party was English; everyone here spoke it. But since the hosts were Danish, there was a lot of that buzzing around too, indistinguishable to Kate from Swedish and Norwegian, barely separable from Dutch and German. Kate could deal with Romance languages; she could communicate in all of them, even in a pinch Portuguese, which had some wigged-out sounds. But these northern tongues? Gibberish.

Julia made eye contact. Kate took a deep, calming breath.

Dexter was wearing jeans and a black shirt, the same as a few other men here. But Dexter's was the only black shirt that was untucked, while the others all wore thick belts with status-symbol buckles, silver or gold logos, a big serifed *H,* a boxed-in *G;* these buckles were the point. It would not have occurred to Dexter to buy a belt with such a buckle, to tuck in a shirt to display such a symbol. That was not her husband; she knew him, and that was not him. But of course she didn't really know him.

Kate looked around at the men. These bankers with their platinum watches and alligator wingtips, their stretch denim and silk-cotton blends with iridescent mother-of-pearl buttons and hand-stitched buttonholes, talking about their carving skis and fully catered Swiss chalets, their villas in Spain and first-class flights to Singapore, next year's Audis and last generation's Jaguars, the dollar versus the euro, earnings reports, short positions. Money: earning it, spending it. Eating it, drinking it, wearing it.

Dexter had given Kate a watch for Christmas, gold, leather band, simple and elegant. The price was right there in the *vitrine* on the rue de la Boucherie, everyone in town could see it: 2,100 euros. All the husbands came shopping to the center streets twice a year, for Christmas and for their wives' birthdays. They gazed in the windows of the same retailers on the same streets, considering the same prices that all the women considered, so everyone who cared knew exactly how much every bag cost—that midsized one was 990 euros, that one with the bigger pockets, 1,390.

And these women, all these mothers, all these ex-lawyers and ex-teachers, ex-psychiatrists and ex-publicists. Expat exes. Now they were cooks and cleaners; they went shopping and lunching. They carried price tags on their arms, projections of their husband's income and willingness to spend it on nothing. On matrimonial goodwill.

Had Dexter become one of those men, behind her back? If so, he was still hiding it. And Kate was still letting him. Because she didn't think that confronting him, when all she knew for certain was that the FBI suspected him, would do any good. She was going to need to be the one to discover the truth. And she had as good a shot as anyone. Better: she had access to his computer, his possessions, his daily schedule. His history. His mind.

"Hello, Kate," Julia said.

Kate couldn't read the look on Julia's face. Couldn't determine what level of truth, or what depth of continued deception, they were agreeing to stand on, here in the middle of this crowded party. Honesty is a consensual continuum.

Did Julia know that Kate knew she was an agent? And also knew what her mission was?

Kate swallowed her pride, or disgust. Her protectiveness and hostility. "Hi Julia."

✦ ✦ ✦

WHAT COMPLETE LONELINESS is this? Surrounded by people, suffused with untruth, unable to tell anyone anything real. Vague acquaintances, casual friends, intimates, even her single soul-mate, the one person in the world, her partner, her ally, her everything. His head was thrown back in carefree laughter, his eyeglasses askew, hair mussed, crooked smile. She loved him so much. Even when she hated him.

Kate considered her husband, the secrets between them, the distance those secrets created. Her secrets: her secret life. The spying on him she'd already done and planned on doing, the massive wall of untruths that was growing taller every day, with every conversation they didn't have, every admission she didn't make.

Kate climbed the stairs. Quietly, alone, past the parents' floor to the kids', an out-of-the-way bathroom. Primary-colored plastic crap on the bathtub ledges, shampoo bottles decorated with unfamiliar cartoon images—TV shows produced in France, Germany, maybe Denmark. A few tubes of toothpaste in various stages of crusted-over sticky disgustingness, the universal uncontrollable in kids' bathrooms.

Kate sat down. Across the tiled room, a full-length mirror, an invitation—a challenge—to observe your own nakedness. Kate stared at herself, fully clothed in black skirt and nylons, black sweater, ebullient necklace, excessive earrings, this brand-new expensive watch. Stupid jewelry.

It seemed so obvious now: of course she would be drawn to a man with a secret life. Of course she would be attracted to someone who had something slithering under the surface, something unseemly, somewhere secret.

She had forcibly willed herself to believe that she'd left this behind when she chose Dexter: a world where people were defined by their duplicities. And in her life, filled with deceptions, this had been her largest: self-deception.

Dexter had said that the best hacking is done by exploiting human frailties. Kate had always known, of course, that she had her own frailties. Everyone does. But she'd never before been aware of exactly what hers were. Now she was.

Did she know her husband, at all?

Kate began, once again, to cry.

✦ ✦ ✦

THE CLICK OF the door, and Dexter was gone, back to the office for the first time since before Christmas. Back to that room that Kate had broken into. Back to the computer she'd failed to access, the files she'd riffled. Back to the video camera suspended in the corner.

It was the day after New Year's. The first day back in the home routine since Kate had learned that her husband was probably some type of criminal. Back to grocery shopping, lugging, unpacking, stowing. Loading and unloading the dishwasher. Sorting and folding the laundry, tiny load after tiny load. Whites and lights, darks and brights.

There was black ice early in the morning, a thin sheet of invisible danger lining every paved surface, cars sliding and crashing everywhere, on small streets and highways, the steep ramps of driveways. Kate was thankful they lived in the center, where the early-to-work bankers' traffic melted the downtown ice before she sank into the heated seats of her car at eight sharp, weaving in and out of the casualties. The Porsche that slid into a stone wall, the Ferrari towed from a tree trunk. Emergency lights glowing in the dark gray fog.

Dexter was at the office now. If the video was the first thing he checked, then he already knew.

Kate must've glanced at her mobile phone a hundred times, assuming that she'd missed Dexter's call, with every glance expecting to see the new voice mail alert, listening to the message, *"What the* fuck *were you doing in my office?"* But the message never appeared. The only person who called was Julia. Kate didn't answer, and Julia didn't leave a message.

Dexter had gone to work later than normal, and now he was home earlier than expected. "I'm going to London in the morning," he said. "This is my last trip for a while. My last business trip. But you remember we're going to Amsterdam for the weekend, right?"

"Of course," Kate said.

Dexter had made all the Amsterdam arrangements, because it was one of his old friends who was passing through on business, an early-career buddy from their shared days low in the ranks at an ISP.

They'd reconnected through social media. Thought it would be fun to see each other, after all these years, in Europe.

So it was the first of their family trips that Kate hadn't booked from home. From the laptop computer that Julia had once used for ten minutes, to check her e-mail, when her Internet service had been down.

✦ ✦ ✦

DEXTER AROSE WELL before daylight. Kate stayed in bed, unmoving, staring at the dark wall as he hurried through his shower, dressing. When she heard the door close, she got up.

Kate started her investigation in the predawn darkness with the computer. She accessed their aboveboard bank accounts, the one in Luxembourg and the one in Washington. The American checking account had minimal online security—nothing more complicated than a user name and a password. But the Luxembourg account required a long, abstract user name, a string of meaningless numbers and letters. Then a similar password. Then a complex access-code grid, to which Kate needed to insert the correct numbers and letters from a jigsaw-puzzle-like key.

If that was the security rigmarole for 11,819 euros, she could only imagine the complexity for a 50,000,000-euro account; 50,000,000 stolen euros. These types of codes were too complex for Dexter—for anyone—to memorize. There would have to be a record of the account numbers and security protocol somewhere. It wouldn't be at his office, in an institutional building in the civic center surrounded by a variety of law enforcement. A place that could be raided, a building that could be shut down, a property that could be seized.

He must be keeping the information in the apartment.

Kate began to open and quickly close every file on the hard drive or the shared drives or the clouds, files that were not her own, looking for similar information for a different account.

When the boys woke up hungry, an hour later, Kate had still found nothing on the computer. This was what she expected. As Dexter had mentioned, any computer could be compromised. But Kate had to be thorough and patient.

It had to be here, somewhere.

✦ ✦ ✦

IT TOOK TWO hours to make her way through the file drawer of the home-office desk, through every single piece of paper, every envelope and folder, looking for handwritten notes, A1-sized sheets that had been output from their printer, scrawls on phone bills, anything on which Dexter could have recorded a code.

Nothing.

Kate turned her attention to the books he'd chosen to bring to Europe, a handful of novels, foreign-language dictionaries, travel guidebooks, technical manuals. All she discovered was that he particularly admired a few lines in *A Confederacy of Dunces*.

She examined every notebook scattered around the house—the boys' tiny pads and midsized ones, big composition books and giant drawing pads, trying not to get distracted by their artwork. Ben in particular had gone through a phase of portraiture that was comically focused on socks.

American-bank checkbooks, deposit slips, check registers. Photo albums. The children's passports. Bedside drawer. Medicine cabinet. Coat pockets. Kitchen drawers.

Nothing.

✦ ✦ ✦

AT TEN THIRTY Dexter returned from London, exhausted. It seemed like he'd left years ago, instead of this morning. They barely spoke— not a bad flight, meeting was all right—before he collapsed into bed, a hardback on his chest, a dense volume about financial markets.

He still hadn't mentioned anything about the video camera in his office. He hadn't said a word about anything that mattered.

She lay down beside him, picked up her magazine, opened to the table of contents, turned pages, trying to read but merely skimming, eyes wandering over words and images.

Soon Dexter fell asleep. Kate kept her eyes on the magazine, killing more time, turning pages quietly, staring at photographs, deconstructing them into their constituent pixels, abstractions of forms and color. It was a two-month-old glossy from the United States, outdated celebrity gossip and irrelevant cultural commentary and a long piece of political journalism that seemed like it was from not only a different country and continent, but from a whole different world. A planet where she used to live but now could barely recognize.

Kate waited five minutes after Dexter's snoring commenced. Then crept out of bed.

She tiptoed downstairs, in the dark. She took his wallet to the bath-room, and shut the door. She locked the door. She removed every single item from his wallet, one by one: credit cards and IDs, receipts, various denominations of different currencies.

Kate examined everything, and found nothing.

She plucked a tea towel off its kitchen hook, carried it to the desk where Dexter's mobile phone sat, plugged in to its charger, red light glowing. She wrapped the phone in this towel, to mute the beep when she unplugged it. She returned to the bathroom and sat on the toilet, scrolling through contacts and memos and recent calls, any application that provided an opportunity to type and save a string of digits or letters.

She discovered that he hadn't made any calls during his day in London. As she scrolled through his list of calls made or received during the past sixty days, she discovered that Dexter had never made any international calls whatsoever during any of his business trips, except those home to her.

She closed the phone, considering the oddness of a series of business trips that required not a single phone call. No secretaries to confirm meetings, no logistics to be arranged—no cars to beckon, no tables to reserve. No meeting follow-ups or previews. No details to discuss, ever, with anyone?

This didn't seem terribly likely.

This was impossible.

Either he hadn't gone on these trips, or he had another phone.

✦ ✦ ✦

WHEN KATE USED to imagine what she didn't want to do—how she didn't want to investigate Dexter—this was the exact image in her brain: creeping through her own home in the dark of the middle of the night, picking through her husband's private things while he slept.

This was why she'd promised herself that after they were married, she'd never investigate him again. She didn't want to do this, didn't want to feel this way.

But here she was, carrying his nylon briefcase into the bathroom, locking the door. She felt around the interior pockets, unzipping, unsnapping, ripping Velcro, not expecting to find anything, but then something . . . what? . . . a silk tab at the bottom of his case—

Her pulse raced. She pulled this square black centimeter, suddenly hopeful. She lifted a sturdy nylon panel, and there it was: a hidden compartment. And inside, a phone. An unfamiliar little piece of plastic and metal.

She stared at this first bit of positive proof, the entrance to the rabbit hole from which she might never reemerge. She considered putting the thing back into its little pocket, the briefcase back into the hallway. Instead she could go upstairs, shake her husband awake. *What the fuck is going on, Dexter?*

But she didn't.

She powered on the phone. The screen blinked to life. She stared at the cool blue glow, the app icons, the reception bars. She hit the phone icon and the recent-calls button and stared at the list, the walls of the rabbit hole closing in, deepening, while she scrolled:

Marlena, yesterday at 9:18 A.M.

Marlena, the day before at 7:04 P.M.

A London number, country-city code 44-20, unsaved to contacts, at 4:32 P.M.

Marlena the day before that, and again, last Monday night.

Kate opened the contacts list: just two. Marlena, with a London number. And Niko, with a prefix she didn't recognize. Kate memorized both.

Marlena and Niko: who the hell were they?

◆ ◆ ◆

DEXTER WOKE LATE. He ate breakfast with Jake and Ben, and didn't return upstairs to shower and shave until they all left for school. Lazy deadbeat, all of a sudden, after four months as an unrepentant workaholic.

But when Kate returned home he was gone. Back to the video camera that had recorded her. Back to his unexplainable office. Back to his secret phone, his unfamiliar contacts, his fifty million stolen euros. Back to his other life.

Kate could barely breathe.

She set to work again. She dug through their basement storage, sifting through the American electronics that wouldn't work here. She examined the back of the old television, the insides of lamp shades, the slots in the toaster, the filter of the coffeemaker. The box of old Tupperware, mismatched glassware, impulsively and wastefully purchased Chinese bowls. The summer tires for the car. The bicycle pump. The luggage. The luggage tags.

Among all this unused, unusable detritus was a wardrobe box, KATE'S WORK CLOTHES, dark wool suits and starched white blouses, collars just shy of frayed. Her old life, crated up and forgotten in a basement.

She went to the bakery, ordered a ham sandwich. Waiting, trying to figure out how she could begin investigating Marlena and Niko, other than calling their numbers. That would be traceable; she would be noticed.

If Dexter didn't check the video footage, who did? What was the camera there for?

She looked in his sock drawer, underwear drawer, T-shirt drawer; the pockets of jeans and suit jackets and overcoats; the inside stitching of his belts. The linings of his neckties. The bottoms of his shoes, heels of shoes, insoles of shoes.

She collected the children from school, bought pastries, then parked them in front of the television, cartoons in French. *Bob l'Eponge* was, it seemed, always on.

She examined the liner notes to CDs, the big pockets in photo albums, the backs of photos, sitting there on the couch, with the children.

"Mommy?" Jake asked. "I'm hungry."

She'd forgotten to feed her children.

◆ ◆ ◆

KATE DIDN'T HEAR Dexter come in. The range's exhaust fan was on; she was sautéing.

"Hi."

She jumped, her right hand attached to the sauté pan, lifting it, chicken flying, the edge of the pan hitting her left forearm, quickly searing a line into her flesh, dropping the pan onto the vitro-ceramic cooktop, clattering. She yelped, short and loud.

"Oh!" Dexter said, rushing into the kitchen, but then helpless, no idea how to help.

Kate ran to the sink, turned on the water, put her arm under it.

"I'm sorry," he said. "I'm so sorry."

For the past few seconds, she'd forgotten about the video camera and the money and Marlena and Niko. But now she remembered.

He put his hand on her shoulder. "Sorry," he said again, kneeling, picking chicken off the floor, throwing it away. Then he gathered the pieces off the cooktop, put them back in the pan. "We can still eat this, right?"

She nodded.

"Should I go get the first-aid kit?"

The faint red line was two inches across the pale flesh of the inside of her forearm. She held it under the stream of cool running water. "Yes. Thanks."

She looked at her husband. At his eyes, locked with hers, worry across his forehead. He'd never burned himself cooking. He didn't cook enough to make kitchen mistakes. He'd never peeled his thumb with a peeler, nicked his fingertip with a paring knife, scalded his arms in boiling water, burned bubbles on the back of his hand with splattering fat.

What he'd done was steal fifty million euros.

Dinner came and went. The adults read some books to the children, then read books to themselves, then Dexter fell asleep, without having mentioned anything about any video.

She lay awake next to him, sleepless.

Marlena and Niko.

✦ ✦ ✦

"WHAT ABOUT DEXTER?" Claire was asking. They were waiting for three o'clock at school.

"Excuse me?" Kate was completely absorbed in her own obsessions. She still hadn't discovered anything more of any value: no account records, no leads on Marlena and Niko, no information about anyone stealing fifty million euros from anyone, anywhere in the world. Plus the family was driving to Amsterdam that night, and Kate hadn't yet packed. Dexter would be home at four thirty, itching to hit the road. She was running out of time.

"I was saying that Sebastian is *worth*less around the house. Is Dexter handy?"

"No," Kate had to admit. "He's not particularly useful. I do the household stuff."

"You build the Ikea rubbish?" Claire asked. Kate had once built a chest of drawers composed of 388 individual pieces. "Yes," she admitted. That chest had taken four hours.

"Sebastian will try," Claire said. "But only if I beg him."

"Is same with Paolo," Sophia agreed.

"With Henrik," Cristina said, leaning in, lowering her voice, "I have to blow him to get him to change a lightbulb."

Kate knew Cristina was kidding about the fellatio. But maybe it wasn't a bad idea, because Dexter didn't ever—

He did, Kate realized, attend to a mundane household repair, unbidden. Just once.

✦ ✦ ✦

SHE DUMPED THE socks and underwear on the bed, stacked the shirts and pants, dropped the sweatshirts and sweaters, impossible to keep folded.

She attacked with the cordless screwdriver, *bzzz-bzzz,* opening this screw and that, removing this panel, turning over this strip of particle-board, that length of fiberboard, that piece of ABS plastic. Deconstruct-ing the bureau in the boys' room, the one piece of Ikea furniture that Dexter had tended to, well after the fact of assembling it, the so-called repair that he'd made—when? One month ago? Two?—that she hadn't noticed was necessary.

She flipped over the bureau's frame, upside down, and she leaned over the upended bottom, the rectangle of one-by-fours that gave the thing its shape, and she unscrewed them, detached them from one another, pulling them apart.

Nothing. She couldn't believe it. She was sure—she was positive—that this was it.

She examined the cut ends of the one-by-fours, looked in the holes vacated by the bolts that held them together, the first one, and the sec-ond.

She sighed.

At the bottom of the leg, there was . . . was there? . . . a slit in the wood that she hadn't noticed when the bureau was upright, and she tried to slip her forefinger inside, but it didn't fit, neither did her pinky, and she grabbed the screwdriver, and shoved it in there . . . angling it . . . pressing down and pulling out at the same time . . . sliding . . .

It fell to the rug. A slip of paper, folded over into a tight little rectan-gular packet.

Lying there.

She picked it up, this small piece of paper, and unfolded it to the size of a chewing-gum wrapper, and stared at the meaningless-looking handwritten numbers and letters.

23

Her watch, the expensive Christmas present, read 3:51. Kate looked around at the wreckage of the boys' room, the clothes everywhere, the bureau disassembled, parts strewn, tools scattered on the floor.

Dexter would be home in forty minutes—thirty-nine—ready to start on the long drive to Holland.

Kate picked up the small slip of paper. Laid it flat on the floor. Removed her phone from her pocket, snapped a photo, checked to ensure everything was legible in the image. Then she reinserted the slip of paper neatly into its slit of a hiding spot. ·

She retrieved the screwdriver, working from the memory of other Ikea assemblies, joining pieces, banging dowels, twisting bolts, turning screws.

At 4:02, Jake appeared in the doorway.

"Mommy? What are you doing?"

"Nothing, sweetie."

"Mommy? *Bob l'Eponge* is finished."

Bzzz-bzzz. "Is there something new on now?"

"Yes, but I don't like it."

Bzzz-bzzz. "There's nothing I can do about that, sweetie."

"You can change the channel."

"Goddammit, Jake!" she yelled, no warning. The kid stumbled on his terror. "I have to do this! Let me do what I need to do!"

He started to cry, and skulked away. She felt awful, but also panicked.

At 4:13, the frame was completely reconstructed.

Kate sighed, halfway relieved. How long could the drawers take? She set to work on the first, timing herself. It turned out to be more confusing than she'd expected, and took her four minutes. There were six drawers.

She rushed. The second was easier—no more confusion—but there were still a lot of screws to turn. It took under three minutes. But she wasn't going to make it.

"Mommy?" It was Ben now.

"Yes?" Without turning around to look at him.

"That's Daddy's furniture."

"Yes," she said, "it's true, he fixed it the last time."

"But he did a bad job? So you need to do it again?"

Oh. How can she explain this? "No," she said. "It just broke again."

This was a problem; this was a totally unexpected problem. She stood up, and walked over to the kid. "But don't tell Daddy about this, okay?"

"Why?"

"Because he'd be sad."

"Because he did a bad job?"

Yes, she thought to herself. He did do a bad job. "That's right."

"Oh."

"So let's keep it a secret. Okay?" Asking her child to lie, to his father. This was fucking dreadful.

"Okay." Ben smiled; he liked secrets. He left.

The third drawer took two minutes, but so had the discussion with Ben. It was 4:27.

Kate looked around desperately. Dexter would be late, of course; he was always late. Never home when he said he'd be.

Except when they were leaving town.

There was no way she could finish. She picked up a drawer front and jammed it onto a bottom and sides, no screws, no back, no glides. It held together. She picked it up gently and slid it into the frame, slowly, slowly . . . the front fell off, clattering to the floor.

"Daddy!" downstairs.

She picked up the front piece. She jammed it again, banged with the heel of her hand, and it stayed in place.

"Hi!" he yelled up to her in the stairwell, still downstairs.

"Hi!" she yelled back. Kate repeated the jam-bang with another drawer. She heard them talking downstairs, husband and sons, but couldn't hear what they were saying. Sort of like the grown-ups in *Peanuts*.

Jam-banged another drawer.

She heard his leather soles clicking on the stone stairs.

There was still one more drawer. She wouldn't make it, she didn't even have time to gather the pieces together. She picked up the final drawer front, the bottom one, with her right hand. With the left hand she dragged a large plastic bin filled with Lego. She placed the drawer front where it should be, and shoved the bin against it, pinning it in place.

"We all set?" Dexter asked from the top of the stairs, rounding the corner.

She surveyed the extant mess, the clothes, the—*shit!*—toolbox. She grabbed the orange blanket from Jake's bed and tossed it over the tool-box just as Dexter arrived in the doorway.

"Are we ready?" He glanced around. "What's going on here?"

Kate brushed hair from her forehead, pinned it behind her ear. "I was sorting through their clothes. They have a lot that's too small. Gotta get rid of it."

His eyes settled on the bureau, not quite flush against the wall. "Huh."

"Sorry, I got derailed."

She walked across the room, away from the bureau, away from her attempted concealment of the thing. She picked up the overnight bag she'd brought into their room this morning—why hadn't she packed this morning?—and carried it to the bed.

"This'll just take a minute," she said. "Are you packed for yourself?"

"Yes," he said. "I did it this morning. You?"

She shook her head.

"Here," he said, picking up the bag. "I'll pack for the boys."

She was speechless.

"Which are the piles of too-small stuff?" he asked.

"I, um . . . I got rid of them already."

"Oh?" Eyebrows raised. "What did you do with them?" Suspicious. Or just curious?

"I put them in the, um . . . the . . . in the textile recycling bin. In the basement."

"Is that for clothing? I thought that was for old towels. Sheets. Things like that."

"Clothing too," she said. "They sort it at the center." No idea if this was true.

"Huh. Okay, then." His hand was on her shoulder. "Go pack."

Could she deflect this? Could she send him down to keep his children company? Could she tell him any lie that would prevent him from being alone in this room? No.

Did he *want* to be alone in this room? Did he realize exactly what was going on?

"Thanks," she said. "Sorry I didn't pack earlier." She left, turned into the hall, and stood there, ears straining to hear what he was doing. The sounds were too faint, a rustle, breathing. Nothing like a plastic bin moving; no dresser parts clattering to the floor.

She chose her things as quickly as possible. This would be one of those forty-eight-hour trips. Like Strasbourg, Bruges, Cologne. They'd done it enough that she knew not to overthink or overpack. This trip didn't need to be very different from leaving the house for the day, twice.

She carried her pile back to the boys' room, rushing down the hall, anxious—

Dexter was standing in the middle of the room. Folding Jake's orange blanket.

The toolbox, uncovered, open. Cordless screwdriver lying on the rug, next to the orange-and-black heavy-duty plastic box.

Dexter was staring at her as he folded. He didn't say anything.

She walked across the room, to Ben's bed, where the weekend bag sat, open, half-filled with the boys' clothes. She placed her things inside, zipped it shut.

Kate watched Dexter lay the folded blanket on the bed, then walk out, still silent. She threw a glance at the bureau. The bottom drawer panel, completely unattached to the frame, had slipped open a few degrees. It was still leaning against the plastic bin, not lying on the floor. But it was obvious, to anyone who looked, that it was not attached. That it had fallen off or been removed. That something was wrong.

Had Dexter looked?

❖ ❖ ❖

THE CANALS OF Amsterdam shimmered in the cold night, the water forming a rippling blanket of pinpoints of light, reflections from the streetlamps, restaurants, bars, houses. All the houses' blinds were undrawn, curtains open, people sitting in their living and dining rooms, reading the newspaper or drinking a glass of wine, family gathered around the dinner table, children watching television, all of it on display to neighbors, to strangers, to the world.

Dexter found a parking spot near the hotel, on the canal, inching the car forward, slowly, carefully, no barrier between the cobblestoned street and the ten-foot drop to the water. He bought a parking permit from a vending machine for forty-five euros, stuck the ticket in the window, good for twenty-four hours. A few months ago, Dexter wouldn't have known how to do this. But now it was second nature, muddling through instructions in languages he didn't speak, pressing buttons and swiping credit cards, sturdy tickets stowed in wallets to be validated and reinserted in machines upon exit, or flimsy slips displayed on dashboards, fluttering to the floor when the door opened on a windy day.

Dexter was a lot more competent than he used to be. He knew how to park.

They crossed a bridge, the canal lined with grand brick houses, tremendous expanses of lit-up glass, glossy doors all painted in the same shade of dark green, almost black. She ran through her imaginary conversation, again. *Dexter,* she'd say, *Julia and Bill are FBI working for Interpol. They think you stole fifty million euros. I know you have a secret bank account, and I'm inclined to think you did it. But the important thing, now, is to figure out how you don't get caught.*

Dexter would ask, *How do you know about the account?*

Kate would tell him about dismantling the dresser, discovering the slip of paper.

So this snooping came out of nowhere?

It's at this point in the conversation when her imagination fails. It's this question she can't imagine answering; it's this subject she can't fathom explaining. *Not exactly,* she'd say. Then what would the next words be? How would she start telling the story that leads inexorably to *I was in the CIA for fifteen years*?

She pushed away that subject again—the hundredth time, the thousandth, who could count?—on this Amsterdam street, cold and tired and hungry.

"How about here?" Dexter was standing at the door to a brown café, wood-paneled walls, un-tableclothed tables, big smoky mirrors, rows of bottles on thick shelves, all the wood unadorned and brown, hence the name.

They were shown a table in the main room, the last available, the others occupied by cheerful couples and crowds, Friday night. Everything on the menu looked good; all the specials described by the waitress sounded delicious. They were starving. They should have eaten on the road, but didn't make that decision until it was too late, and the rest areas had fallen away on the outskirts of the city.

They'd given the kids snack bars. The glove box was filled with snack bars.

The waitress brought beers and sodas, brown and orange in heavy glasses, satisfying clunks on dark tabletops. The boys were coloring in activity books, as usual. The adults knew how to park in foreign cities; the children knew how to amuse themselves in restaurants, away from home. Home itself far away from home.

"What were you doing with the toolbox?"

Out of nowhere. A sneak attack, five hours after the fact.

Kate didn't answer, mind racing.

Dexter didn't expand or clarify or repeat himself, giving no excuse for extra delay.

She couldn't remember the lie that she'd prepared, earlier, for an earlier conversation. "I, um . . . the window . . ."

She saw that Ben was paying close attention. It wasn't clear if he thought this was funny, or serious; if he was going to rat her out, or not. A smile crept up his lips.

"I had to fix the window shade." Quickly deciding: "Boys? Let's go wash up."

"I'll take them," Dexter said. "C'mon, Ben. Jake."

Dexter stood, taking the boys by their little hands, leading them away. Halfway across the room, Ben turned back, and smiled at his mother, mischievously.

◆ ◆ ◆

BECAUSE AMSTERDAM WAS his trip to meet his friend—his idea, all the way—it was Dexter who'd chosen the hotel, made the reservation. This hotel seemed more expensive than their normal. Four stars, but definitely edging up toward five, not down toward three.

While Dexter checked in, Kate and the boys waited in the hall, on a velvet-tufted love seat with a carved wood frame, surrounded by ornate flocked wallpaper, thick plaster moldings intersecting with the fifteen-foot ceilings.

"Ben," she whispered, "did you tell Daddy what I was doing?"

"When?"

"Upstairs? In your room?"

"I mean, when did I tell him?"

"In the bathroom, at the restaurant? Or, I don't know, *ever*? Did you *ever* tell him?"

Ben glanced at his older brother, as if for explanation, or support. But Jake was cuddled against his teddy bear, sucking his thumb, nearly asleep. No help.

"About the bad work that he did?" Ben asked.

"That's right," Kate said. "Did you tell him?"

Dexter glanced around, smiled at Ben, turned back to the clerk.

"No," Ben said. He too was smiling.

"Ben? Are you telling me the truth?"

"Yes, Mommy." Still smiling.

"Then why the big smile, sweetie?"

"I dunno."

✦ ✦ ✦

THE CHILDREN FELL asleep immediately in the fold-out sofa, leaning toward each other, separated by the cheerful-looking teddy bear, ragged and thin, losing weight and dingy.

Kate understood that it had been absurd of her to refuse to be suspicious of Dexter. But at least she was aware of why she'd been absurd: a liar doesn't want to think that other people are liars, because then the other people should suspect her of lying too, because she is, and she'll get caught.

Dexter emerged from the bathroom, white boxers and a white tee, springy tufts of hair curling out of the pale skin along his legs and arms, extra-pasty. A pale man in the depths of a sunless winter.

He lay down in bed, hands folded in lap. He didn't pick up anything to read, didn't say anything.

Jake snorted, a rutting animal, then began to snore. Dexter lay unmoving, inactive. Kate didn't want to glance over, didn't want to see what expression he was wearing, what he was thinking. She didn't want to start any discussion, didn't want to get into it.

But she also did. Desperately. She needed this—needed something—to come out in the open. She needed to stop adding secrets, needed to stop generating questions.

She closed the guidebook in her lap, a flurry of resolve, the sound of her thoughts deafening, turning to him, opening her mouth, her pulse pounding in her brain, starting to speak, ready to get it all off her chest, or get some of it into the open, or something, she wasn't sure, but she spoke. "Dexter," she began, turning to him, "I—"

She froze, midsentence, midthought, mideverything. He was sound asleep.

✦ ✦ ✦

THEY WENT TO the Van Gogh Museum and the flower market, not much to see in the dead of winter. Bulbs for sale, trowels, seed packets.

217

They agreed that the Anne Frank Museum would raise too many unpleasant topics and unanswerable questions, so they skipped it.

When it was time for a bribe for the children, they entered a toy store. Gave the boys carte blanche for any box of Lego. Any small box. "I'll take care of this," Dexter said, only vaguely aware of the discussions, considerations, and negotiations that were about to ensue.

So Kate stepped back out into Hartenstraat, Saturday-afternoon crowded, everyone bundled and behatted, smoking and laughing, on bicycles and foot. She saw a familiar figure, out of the corner of her eye, at the end of the intimate block. It was a posture and a bearing Kate recognized, a height and weight, under a big dark hat, a wool cloak. This woman was facing a shop window, a large reflective expanse of immaculate glass.

This woman didn't expect Kate to emerge from the store so quickly, after just ten seconds. The woman hadn't counted on that. So she'd let herself relax, marginally unhidden, relatively unguarded. And she'd been caught.

Kate unlocks the desk drawer, and the lockbox. She hefts the Beretta, much lighter without its magazine. The smooth black metal is cold in her hand.

She glances at a photo on the desk, a little snapshot in an antique leather frame, the boys laughing in the surf in St-Tropez. More than a year ago now, bronzed and blonded by a summer of sun, teeth glinting white, golden light shimmering off the Mediterranean, late afternoon in late July.

In the end, Dexter left the where-to-live decision up to Kate. He claimed that he preferred the countryside or small-town options, Tuscany or Umbria, Provence or the Côte d'Azur, even the Costa Brava. But Kate suspected that Dexter never really wanted to live in any countryside. Instead, what he wanted was to lose an argument. He wanted to make her feel like she'd won something, like this decision had been hers, despite him.

Kate couldn't help suspecting that he'd been manipulating her about every-thing, all the time. A huge reversal, after so many years of believing that he was the least manipulative person she knew.

Her probably superfluous argument for Paris was on behalf of the children. So they would grow up educated and cosmopolitan, not sheltered and spoiled; she didn't want their sole areas of competence to be tennis and sailing. The grown-ups could always move to Provence when the children had gone to university.

Kate leans back in the chair, the pistol in her palm, thinking about these people: this other couple, strangers who she thought were friends who were pretending to be enemies. And her surprisingly diabolical husband. And her own behavior, both questionable and justified. And what she's about to do.

She snaps the Beretta's clip into position. She lifts a hardened panel in the bot-tom of her handbag—very similar to the compartment in Dexter's old briefcase, where he kept his secret phone. She drops the handgun into the bottom, then replaces the panel.

Kate reaches across to a cluttered bookshelf, unplugs a mobile from its charger. She hasn't powered up this phone for more than a year and a half, but she keeps it charged. She turns it on, punches in the long number. She doesn't store numbers like this one in address books of any sort.

She doesn't recognize the voice on the other end of the line—a woman saying, *"Bonjour"*—but she didn't expect she would.

"*Je suis* 602553," Kate says.

"One moment, madame."

Kate looks out the window, over the gabled rooftops of St-Germain, the Seine and the Louvre to the right, the glass domes of the Grand Palais straight ahead, the Eiffel Tower to the left. The sun is peeking through clouds behind her, unseen, painting a golden wash over the city, gilding her lily of a view, almost too perfect.

"Yes, madame. The ladies' lounge in the Bon Marché. Fifteen minutes."

Kate glances at her watch. "*Merci.*" She hurries out the door once again, down the elevator and through the lobby and breezeway to the street, the rue du Bac merging onto the boulevard Raspail, weaving south through the dense lunchtime crowds, pushing her way into the department store, onto an escalator, brushing past slowly ambling women to the anteroom outside the restroom, where a pay phone is ringing.

"Hello," she answers, closing the door behind her.

"*Lovely* to hear your voice," Hayden says. "It's been so long."

"Likewise," Kate says. "We need to talk, in person."

"Is there a problem?"

"Not really, no. It's a solution."

He doesn't reply.

"Can we meet at four?" she asks.

"In *Paris*? I'm afraid not. I'm, well, not *near.*"

"But you're not far. And if I'm not mistaken, you have access to a plane." Hayden was promoted last year, despite a lifelong career track in the field, not administration. He is now, surprisingly, deputy baron of Europe. A job that comes with use of a jet. As well as discretion on personnel, from the junior officers in Lisbon and Catania to the field chiefs in London and Madrid. Paris too.

He doesn't respond.

"Do you remember the fifty million euros stolen from a Serbian?" Kate asks.

Pause. "I see."

"Four o'clock?"

"Let's make it five."

24

Kate marveled at how deeply she'd buried her head in the sand. How she'd ignored what she should have seen, long ago: that the Macleans had been monitoring the Moores' every move, for months.

Jake waved at her from the other side of the store window. Kate waved back. Dexter and the boys were in another shop, a chocolate store, while she stood outside. She could see their eyes wide, their fingers pointing, their whole bodies begging. Kids in a candy shop.

Kate had chosen to pretend she hadn't seen Julia. She'd turned the other way up Hartenstraat, let her gaze linger in the opposite direction, giving the FBI agent an opportunity to scamper away, unsure whether or not she'd been made.

Now Kate stood in some other *straat,* her mind racing back to what she realized was the beginning of the surveillance: that rainy day—extra-rainy, pouring thick sheets—in late September—more than three months ago—in the parking lot of the Belle Etoile mall in Strassen. Julia claiming that she'd forgotten her phone in Kate's car. Insisting that Kate stay away, stay dry. Returning to the car alone, installing something subtle and unfindable, then returning to Kate with the slim smile of secret victory. Mona Lisa.

From that moment, Bill and Julia had always known where Kate was.

So the Macleans had known it the following Friday afternoon, when Kate and Dexter set south on the A3, crossing the border into France, cruising by the nuclear reactors at Thionville, veering off at Metz onto the A4 toward Reims. That turn was probably when Julia and Bill decided to give chase, to hop into his little BMW, racing to catch up, closing the gap during their remaining three-hour drive to Paris, slowing down to 140 kph only when their GPS alerted them to speed cameras. Or maybe not slowing down at all. What did the FBI care about European Union speeding tickets?

And while the Moores were finding a place to park in Paris, the Macleans were still on the highway, hurtling through Champagne, the vineyards littered with trucks parked for the night in the fields, harvest time. They located Kate's stationary station wagon in a grimy garage. They called around to the nearest hotels, one after the other, until they found the one where there was a junior suite registered to Monsieur et Madame Moore. The Macleans booked their own room nearby, set up surveillance.

The Moores were easy to follow. They moved in a large, slow group, took the Metro and never taxis, walked around crowded streets. They were out in public spaces, all the time.

The Macleans probably took turns—ten minutes on, ten off, trailing each other while they trailed the family—following, waiting for a good opportunity, a natural circumstance, a touristy spot late in the day, an easy chance meeting, an effortless insertion. They'd already called the Moores' hotel, verified that babysitting was available, knowing they could pull this off, knowing that Dexter and Kate would accept an invitation to a night out, to too much wine, to a fashionable club, to accelerated friendship, to instant intimacy.

That whole spontaneous Saturday night had been carefully orchestrated. That attempted mugging was play-acted, a sham.

This had all started a quarter-year ago.

Dexter was hiding something—was it really fifty million stolen euros?—and these FBI agents were tight on his tail. They were following his every move, through Luxembourg and Belgium and into Holland, now tracking him around Amsterdam. They were closing in on something, unwilling to allow Dexter out of sight for a weekend. Why?

The boys spilled out of the chocolate shop, victorious, their booty held aloft—"Mommy! Look!"—eager to show their mother what their father had allowed them to choose, innocent and naive.

Kate smiled down at her children, but she was shivering with cold and terror. "That's great, sweetie."

Whatever was going on, it felt like it was drawing to an end. Kate certainly hoped it wouldn't be a violent end. But she had to be prepared.

✦ ✦ ✦

KATE WAS ALONE, stopped in the middle of a bridge, looking up at the spectacular sky: the deep rich blue damask of dusk, the fast-moving puffy clouds, layers of whites and silvers and grays piled atop one another. The lights were on in the windows, on the fronts of bicycles, reflecting in the water.

Dexter had taken the boys back to the hotel for a predinner pay-per-view; they weren't meeting his tiresome friend Brad until eight.

On the far side of the bridge, the last of the boutiques fell away, like the end of a commercial stretch on a suburban road, the final Sizzler and Meineke under streetlights before the dark countryside. The funk of marijuana drifted from a pair of dreadlocked teens.

Kate found a bank, entered the small vestibule with the ATMs. She ignored the cards in their slits in her wallet, the everyday cards. Instead she reached her thumb into an interior pocket, a half-dozen pieces of plastic there, things she didn't need to carry in Europe, but did: laminated American Social Security card, old office ID, gym membership. And the bank card, the checking account in her old name. The account Dexter didn't know about.

She withdrew the limit: one thousand euros.

She also withdrew the maximum from their joint Luxembourg account, another thousand. She took cash advances from two credit cards, a thousand apiece.

Back in the street, the red lights began to appear, the women large and unattractive, southeast Asians, garters and high heels and sagging breasts spilling out of ornate lace.

Kate found a convenience store. She bought a packet of plastic bags, a roll of tape, a bottle of water. She was thirsty, nervous.

The streets grew narrower and the storefront windows denser, six girls in quick succession, good-looking dark-haired Europeans; then around the corner a few Africans, full-lipped and big-bottomed. There appeared to be departments. Like a department store.

She entered a well-lit café, clean and safe-looking from the outside, but rougher within. She ordered a Coke, left her coins on the bar, drank it quickly. She walked to the rear, found the sign for the toilet, pointing down a creepy-looking winding staircase. There were a couple men down there, a shady transaction, the stench of secrecy.

"Excuse me," she said, sidling past, locking the door. She took the baggies out of her coat pocket, tore one off along the perforation, tossed the remainder in the bin. She removed her wad of large-denomination bills. Peeled off a few hundreds, shoved those in her right pocket; some twenties were in her left. She put the balance of the four thousand euros into the bag. She pressed the air out, folded the packet tightly, wound it up in tape.

She sat down on the toilet. Pulled off her left boot. When she crossed her legs, she always did it right over left. She didn't know if she'd be crossing her legs—she didn't know how the hell this was going to go down, if at all. But better safe than sorry.

The boot had a low heel, but it would do. At the rear of the sole, back behind the arch, where the leather sole rose to meet the rubber-bottomed heel, there was ample space. In this space, she taped her compressed bagful of cash.

Outside again, men were shuffling their feet, making fleeting eye contact through the red miasma and the glinting expanses of velvet-framed glass. There were boisterous teenagers, groups of three or four, outdoing one another in bravado to compensate for inexperience. Besuited middle-aged men, some furtive, others brazen—regulars, or simply beyond caring what strangers thought, secure in the knowledge that here, everyone was pursuing their own agenda. Not unlike everywhere.

The coffee shops were full and loud and rank smelling, the pungent pot wafting through doorways and lingering on sidewalks.

A young man met her eye, a come-on to something. She considered and dismissed him, kept walking.

Along another canal, this one very different from what she'd seen of upscale Amsterdam, lined with sex shops and nightclubs and red-lit windows. The sound of drunken laughter spilling out of a bar, Australian-accented English, the titter of embarrassed women.

Another man made eye contact, this one older, harder. He nodded at her, and she nodded back. He said something in Dutch, and she slowed down, but didn't respond.

"You lookin' for sometin'?" West Indian accent, far from home. So was she.

"Yeah."

Gold tooth glinting. "What dat?"

"Something special," she said. "Something steel. With lead."

His smile disappeared. "Can't 'elp you wit' dat."

She reached into her pocket, removed a twenty. "Who can?"

"Go see Dieter. Up dere." Inclining his head, dreadlocks tumbling.

She continued up the sidewalk beside the narrow canal, the sounds and smells close beside her. In front of a live-sex club, promotional posters leaving no doubt about the show, a man in a shiny black suit, pointy-toed shoes, narrow leather tie, carefully watching everyone come and go. He met Kate's eye. *Guten tag.*

"Hi. You Dieter?"

He nodded.

"I'm looking for something. A friend told me you could help. It's steel."

Dieter looked confused. "Is a stolen thing?"

"No," she said. "Steel. Metal." She raised her hand, pointed at him with her forefinger, thumb straight up in air. Winked the thumb. Bang.

Dieter understood, shook his head. "Not possible."

She took two blue twenties out of her pocket, offered them. He grimaced, didn't accept the money, shaking his head again.

Kate retrieved another bill, this one a hundred.

Dieter glanced at the green piece of paper, easy to instantaneously assess the denomination. "Follow me," he said, folding his hand around the bill. He walked quickly, looking both ways again and again, ill at ease on a non-sex-trade mission. Across a bridge, down a narrow crowded street, attractive whores in every window, a popular stretch, the *Billboard* Top 40 section of the district, no specialty tastes here. A turn into a darker and smaller street, an alley really, just a couple red lights here, long stretches of brick wall.

Dieter stopped at a red window, and Kate stopped alongside him. The pretty blonde inside looked at him, and at Kate, then opened her door wordlessly. Smells of incense and cigarette smoke and ammoniac disinfectant. Dieter walked past the girl and her sordid little room, her neatly made bed framed in mirrors. The girl didn't meet Kate's eye.

They walked down a narrow hall, cheap wallboard, unadorned. At the end of the hall, a rickety staircase, low-ceilinged, badly lit.

Kate was getting nervous. She stopped walking.

"Come." A quick wave, not particularly reassuring. "Come."

They climbed the stairs, turned on a treacherous landing, climbed again to another recently constructed hall. The cheap flooring was vibrating, and Kate could make out a thumping hip-hop bass, and now vocals, a growling basso, and now synthesizers, the music growing louder, its English lyrics distinct, vulgar and brutal.

Kate stepped down off the carpeting and onto a tile floor, a wider hall, taller ceilings, moving from a slum to a mansion, somehow tucked away in here, a pair of large doors, paneled and painted, Dieter glancing back at her, then pushing the doors open—

Kate took in the anarchy of the tremendous room at a glance. Couches and settees and chaises, coffee tables and Persian rugs, tasseled lamp shades on alabaster bases, marble fireplaces and massive windows fronting onto the canal, a half-dozen girls in various states of undress, one of them with her head in the lap of a tattooed and pierced and furious-looking man, her head being thrust down and yanked up by the ears, and, in the middle of it all, a bright orange head, bent over a mirror-topped coffee table, then rising, throwing itself back, sucking the white powder in and shaking his head, long stringy hair slapping his face.

"Ahhhhhh!" he yelled. "It's fookin' bootiful." He wiped his nose, looked at Kate, then at Dieter. " 'Oo's this coont, then?"

Dieter shrugged. "She looks for something."

"You know 'er, then?"

"Not at all."

"Ookay, then."

Dieter shrugged, turned, and left, closing the doors behind him, glad to be rid of Kate and her disquieting inquiry.

"Angelique? Check 'er."

The girl rose languidly, six feet tall, topless, wearing nothing but panties and stilettos. The redheaded man watched her, his eyes filled with lust. Angelique was a fantastic specimen, not more than seventeen years old. She frisked Kate, then sauntered away, back to her chaise and her magazine. *Vogue*. A naked girl reading a fashion magazine.

"What you woont, then?"

"I want a piece."

The tattooed man seemed to be finishing up, pumping the girl's head up and down furiously, while she gagged and gulped and tried not to whimper.

"Ah woont a piece, too." He grinned. "You 'ere to gi' me a piece o' yoour poosy? Tha's nice ah-you."

Kate smiled broadly. "I want a fucking gun, you stupid Scottish prick."

"Ahhhh," moaned the other man.

"Whot? You listen ta this, Colin?"

"Ahhhhhhhhh." Colin bunched the girl's hair in fistfuls. "Doon't intrup me, Red."

"A fookin gun, you say?"

Kate didn't respond.

"Whot are you, soom kinda fookin bobby? Where's your wire?"

"No wire."

"Show me, then."

Kate looked him in the eye; he didn't blink.

"Or git the foock oout."

She waited another beat, another two, eyes glued, before she slowly took off her jacket, and dropped it to the floor, still staring straight at him.

She pulled her sweater over her head in one swift motion, her hair staticky. Reached behind her, unzipped her skirt, let it fall to the floor. She stepped out of it, hands on hips.

"You American?" he asked.

Kate was now wearing nothing except boots and underwear. She didn't answer.

"The rest." He flicked his fingers at her. "Take off the rest."

"Fuck you."

"Whot you need a gun foor?"

She wanted desperately to put her clothes back on, but she also felt a small victory with every passing second that she kept them off, gathering strength from her humiliation.

"Colin? Whot we got fer 'er?"

Colin was zipping up his black jeans, walking over, shirtless, his whole torso covered in an indecipherable jumble of faded ink. He leaned over the mirror-topped table and took a bump. Then he rose, walked across the room. Opened a desk drawer, looked inside.

"Beretta," Colin said.

"Oooh." Red smiled. "That's a nice goon. Just foound that on the street last week."

Kate didn't want to hear what bullshit story he was peddling to disavow this weapon.

"Let me see it."

In one fluid motion Colin popped the clip out of the Beretta and tossed the gleaming steel fifteen feet across the room, a perfect throw to Kate, who caught the thing easily. She took a moment to examine the weapon, partly to examine it, partly to convince Red that she was not to be fucked with. The 92FS was the Toyota Corolla of handguns. This one seemed to be in fine condition.

"Two thousand," she said. She didn't want to ask his price, didn't want to give Red the opportunity to frame the negotiation. The eventual price was pure negotiation, not tethered to any objective value. It could be worth fifty euros or twenty thousand; it was worth the intersection of whatever he could get her to pay with whatever she could get him to accept.

"Git the foock ootta 'ere. The price is ten."

She bent forward, picked up her skirt. Zipped it.

"Eight," he said, and she knew she would win. She put back on her sweater.

"Twenty-five hundred." She pulled her hair out of the collar.

"Git the fuck oout, you foockin coont."

She picked up her jacket, pulled it on.

"I woont take a penny less than five."

"I'll give you three."

"Foock you."

She shrugged, turned away.

"Four," he said.

"Thirty-five hundred. Take it." She smiled. "Or leave it."

He tried to stare her down, but then realized it was futile.

"Thirty-five hundred," he said. "*Ploos* a bloo job."

She couldn't help but laugh. "Fuck you," she said.

He broke into a broad smile. "That," he said, "woould alsoo be fine and fayer compensation."

❖ ❖ ❖

KATE INSISTED THEY go to the science museum on a pier in the harbor. Then after lunch a flea market in a church, where she lingered and haggled and bought this and that, a porcelain platter and sterling serving utensils. Then she wanted to sit somewhere and have a coffee, with some pastries for the kids.

Under the table, the new Beretta sat heavy in the bottom of her handbag, even heavier in the top of her consciousness.

Dexter admitted that Brad had indeed become an insufferable bastard in the decade since they'd worked together. He had moved to New York to do something extra-bullshit-sounding for tech start-ups. Throwing around the title CMO, talking about loft-buying and Hamptons-summering and blah-blah-blahing. Kate had always thought of Brad as unbearable, and was gratified that Dexter could finally see it, now that Brad had fully bloomed into the exceptional prick that had always been growing within. New York had nurtured his prickishness.

If Dexter really had fifty million euros sacked away somewhere, he was doing an awfully good job of not becoming a self-satisfied prick.

Kate ordered another coffee. She was pushing back the day, one o'clock to two, two to three, until she was assured that by the time the family returned to Luxembourg, it would be late, and the kids would have to go straight to bed, the lights in their room never even turned on. Dexter wouldn't have a chance to be alone in the boys' room, to examine the disassembled bureau, evidence of her suspicion, proof of her discovery.

They sped down the motorway in the flat Netherlands, an exit every couple of miles, a city at every exit. At sunset they were stop-and-go around the Brussels ring, then speeding south again through Walloon Belgium, sparse and dark and hilly, ravines and forests and nothing, nothing, more nothing.

Kate looked out the window into the darkness of the Ardennes, where the World Wars had been fought, hand-to-hand bloody. The Battle of the Bulge, the biggest and deadliest of World War II. That was sixty-something years ago. And now? Now there wasn't even a border between Germany and France and Belgium and Luxembourg. All that carnage over sovereignty and the integrity of borders, and now you didn't even need to show a passport to travel from Allied to Axis.

George Patton was buried in Luxembourg, walking distance to the kids' school, along with five thousand other American soldiers.

The German car was humming at 150 kilometers per hour, cutting through the fast-moving fog slithering across the blacktop. Up and down the dark quiet hills, rarely coming across other cars or trucks, the middle of nowhere in the dark of night.

The perfect place to disappear.

25

Eight o'clock in the morning. Five after eight. Seven after. Time—
now—to leave for school, already late, but Dexter still not out of the
apartment, barely awake, in the shower.

If Kate left, then Dexter would have the run of the apartment. He
could go anywhere, do anything. He could check the bureau and find
that she'd disassembled it. He could check the bin in the back of the
pantry and find the Beretta.

"Okay, boys," she said from the kitchen. She pulled the gun out of the
bin, dropped it into her bag. "Mommy's ready."

She couldn't live like this.

✦ ✦ ✦

"HELLO?"

She closed the front door slowly, quietly. *Click.* "Hello?"

She glanced at the ceramic bowl on the hall table, where he kept his
keys. Empty. "Dexter?"

She walked upstairs, double-confirming, through the hall to the master bedroom, their bathroom. As she passed the boys' room, she looked
at the bureau, unchanged, unfixed. She'd get to that soon enough.

Down the stairs and the hall and through the living room. She poked
her head into the kitchen, triple-checking. More nervous by the second,
practically trembling.

She sat at the desk. She opened the laptop. She checked her e-mail,
procrastinating. Responded to something trivial, read something irrelevant. Even emptied the spam folder.

Then there was nothing else to do, except what she'd sat down to do.

She opened the photo library of her telephone. She chose the image of

Dexter's slip of paper, the account numbers and passwords. There were no bank names. But how many banks could there be? How long could this take? A half-hour? An hour?

She rose. She walked to the kitchen, poured herself a cup of coffee. As if caffeine could possibly help.

She sat down again, hands poised above the keyboard, thinking. Start with the easiest: the bank where they kept their joint account.

She clicked the bookmark at the top of the web browser. The page jumped to the bank's welcome page, asking for account number and password.

She glanced at her phone again, the image, the numbers . . .

She hit the computer key for the first number, an eight, her middle finger resting there under the asterisk atop the numeral . . . thinking of something . . . this computer . . .

Julia popped into her brain. The day when Julia visited this apartment, her Internet connection supposedly down, to check e-mail. When Julia sat in this chair, at this computer, hands on this keyboard.

Now Kate realized: Julia hadn't been checking e-mail. She'd been inserting spyware, capturing Kate's screens and logging her keystrokes, surreptitiously e-mailing whatever she typed to Julia and Bill, showing them whatever she saw, so they could steal the Moores' account numbers and passwords, to monitor their bank balances and investment portfolios, to track their air-travel purchases and hotel reservations.

The Macleans had been tracking this computer's activity. But it hadn't been this computer that had booked the Amsterdam trip.

Of course! The Macleans didn't know where the Moores were going, or for how long, or why. Because Dexter had made the hotel reservations from his office. From his ultra-secure office, and his impossible-to-access computer. So the FBI didn't know if maybe Kate and Dexter were fleeing. On their way to the Isle of Man, or Hamburg, or Stockholm. Permanently moving, going into hiding, carrying false passports and duffels filled with cash.

So the FBI had pursued, nervous, making sure their suspect wasn't disappearing.

Kate removed her hands from this tainted keyboard, this compromised position.

❖ ❖ ❖

"HELLO, CLAIRE? IT'S Kate. Kate Moore."

"Kate! How are you?"

"Well, thank you." Kate watched a familiar face walk past her phone booth in the P&T. "Claire, I've an odd favor to ask."

"Anything, dear. Anything."

"Could I stop by and use your computer for a bit?"

✦ ✦ ✦

CLAIRE'S HOME OFFICE was tucked into a corner behind the staircase, facing out onto the driveway, the least appealing room in the big suburban-esque house. Kate watched a car drive past, and wondered if Julia or Bill would end up coming by, crawling along the street, keeping tabs on her.

She launched the web browser. Began with the biggest banks, their names plastered everywhere around town, on the tops of buildings, on sponsor banners at festivals, on the jerseys of cycling teams.

There had been two account numbers on Dexter's little slip of paper. The first number was paired with a user name and password and other information; the second had no accompanying information. Kate wouldn't even try the second number; it made no sense.

But the first one did. It was almost too easy, too quick: ten minutes after she'd begun, the fifth bank she'd tried, the first account number was valid.

She sucked in her breath, held it as she entered the password . . . also valid.

Then she had to choose the correct image from a choice of maybe thirty, which explained the note "dog" on the slip of paper. And then she had to match a puzzle against a string of letters on Dexter's slip of paper. Then a dialog box opened:

Accessing your account records.
One moment, please.

Accessing your account records.
One moment —

The screen went dark.

Kate froze, panicked, looking around quickly, wondering what this could possibly—

The screen lit up again, the summary page of the account, scant information, bare bones only, her eyes flitting around the screen, taking in all there was to take in.

Account holder: LuxTrade S.A.
Account address: rue des Pins 141, Bigonville, Luxembourg

There were no currency figures on the page, no amounts, just this inconclusive information, indicating nothing, proving nothing. Her spirits plunged.

Then she noticed the tab for ASSETS, and she grabbed the mouse, and moved the cursor, and clicked, and waited the frustrating millisecond while absolutely nothing happened, then the terrifying microsecond when the screen went blank, then the new screen flashed, white and blue, two lines in the middle of the page:

Savings account balance
409.018,00 EUR

That was a lot of unexpected money. But it was a far cry from fifty million euros. Kate let out a deep sigh of relief, leaned back in the chair, away from the computer. Whatever Dexter was doing, it wasn't stealing fifty million euros.

She stared at the screen, lost in speculation, her mind whirling . . . wondering what this could mean, the vast discrepancy between four hundred thousand and fifty million . . .

That's when she noticed the tab for the other account.

✦ ✦ ✦

SPEEDING ACROSS LUXEMBOURG in Claire's husband's sports car, west-northwest, two-lane roads and a short spell on a proper motorway, through roundabouts, merging, accelerating and braking, passing. Nothing on the radio, no music and no French culture, lost in her own labyrinth of explanations, pursuing one dead end after another.

She'd stared at the computer screen, mouth hanging open, for a full minute.

Current account balance
25.000.000,00 EUR

Then she'd logged off the bank interface and cleared the web browser's history and emptied the cookies and exited the program and restarted the hard drive, formulating her next steps.

She'd walked into the kitchen with a forced smile. Claire had been a bit nonplussed when Kate asked if she could borrow Sebastian's BMW. "My car has been making an odd noise," Kate claimed, "and the conditions are dreadful out there. I'd hate to break down on a day like this. I'll take my car to the garage tomorrow."

The land fell as she headed west into the valley of the Petrusse that ran down the center of the country. On the other side of the river the soft hills began to rise again, long low-grade ascents, plateaus, dips down to cross creeks and streams before continuing up.

There was a big difference between the fifty million euros that the FBI thought Dexter had stolen and the twenty-five-plus million in his accounts. Half. But this difference was in degree, not order of magnitude. The general idea was the same: a huge amount of money. An unearnable amount.

Kate sped through the forest, the trees close against the road, slender white-barked trunks straining skyward, lightward. The trees suddenly became whiter, and brighter, one of those full-frost zones that cropped up regularly in the countryside on days like this, the temperature just below 0 Centigrade, predawn fog clinging to every plane of every surface, under and over and sides, then freezing, encasing everything—trees and shrubs, twigs and evergreen needles, street signs and lampposts—in cloudy white ice, brilliant and blinding. Otherworldly.

There had to be a justifiable reason. Dexter was a good man. If he'd done a bad thing, there had to be a legitimate reason for it.

After all, she herself had done the very worst thing imaginable. And she was a good person. Wasn't she?

❖ ❖ ❖

HALF OF FIFTY million . . .

The car hurtled through the distinctive desolation of farmland in winter, cut back and barren and low, even the shortest structures seemingly towering, barns and granaries and single-story stone houses built right against the road, which had been a medieval footpath, later widened to a Renaissance horse path, then widened again and ultimately paved in the twentieth century for cars, the current form its briefest incarnation, at most 5 percent of this byway's lifetime, another sliver of Europe's history, tucked away on—as—a narrow road.

Where was the other half . . . ? It must be in that other account, the one whose number Dexter had written down without any other info, no user name or password. Why would he keep a written record of only one account? Of only half the money?

The car hummed on the weathered asphalt, in and out of forests, a preponderance of evergreens up in these highlands.

Because he had a partner. Marlena? Niko? Both?

Kate wasn't using Sebastian's GPS device. The whole point of driving his car was to avoid having her steps retraced. So she was using a map, which she now needed to consult regularly through the twisting unnumbered roads whose names changed every few kilometers, merging and dead-ending and doubling back.

Finally she was in Bigonville, on the rue des Pins, a supremely missable road, with no painted lines, thickly lined with evergreens. Street of pines, indeed.

Kate was now certain—99 percent, if not the full 100—that Dexter had illegally appropriated some large multiple of millions of euros. And this money was what was paying for her home and groceries and toys, for the diesel she'd put in the car yesterday morning, a sixty-three-euro fill-up, nearly a hundred dollars' worth of gas for the secondhand Audi.

The used car. That was where two irreconcilable realities bumped up against each other: what man bought a used car when he had twenty-five million euros in the bank?

Kate had suffered through dinner with that prick Brad in Amsterdam. There was a guy with extra millions in the bank. And he spent all his free time, all his energy, spending his money. His cars, his houses, his vacations. Just like the rich bankers here in Luxembourg, whose business was making money and whose passion was spending it.

Her husband was not one of them.

This small narrow road twisted and turned, dipped and rose, patches of snow and ice, dense forests and a winding creek that the road shadowed, never had been any budget to build a bridge, never would be.

The whole thing just didn't make sense.

The road abandoned the creek and began a steep climb, leveling at the top of another ridge, where the forest fell away, opening the landscape to a wide vista of repeating ridges, folds in the land covered in grayish white, the skin of an old sharpei. A rustic stone wall ran alongside the road, the big rocks cleared to make the field on the other side arable, the wall merely a byproduct, a place to put the rocks. It was an immense field, covered in low grass, brownish-green and fallow.

Kate saw the white-painted farmhouse with a black slate roof, just like every other roof in the entirety of the landlocked little nation, the house bookended by coppices of leafless oaks, a shady spot in the summertime. The grounds surrounding the house were crisscrossed by a series of low, semi-crumbling stone walls, looking like the base of a Roman ruin, delimiting giant rooms—dining halls and vomitoria and grand foyers.

She slowed to a crawl, a glance in the rearview, confirming again that she hadn't been followed. In every direction, there was no car or truck or tractor to be seen; the wooden shutters were closed. No sign of life or habitants, here at this protected house, secluded in the wide open by its coterie of deciduous bodyguards.

There was no space to pull to the side of the road, which fell precipitously into deep drainage ditches. The house's driveway passed through a narrow opening in the stone wall, and was barred by a chain, which Kate could see was secured by a padlock. On one of the stone pillars, a small white-enameled plaque, the number 141 in black. This was definitely rue des Pins 141, Bigonville, Luxembourg. The headquarters of LuxTrade S.A.

Kate had come to a complete stop in the middle of the road. There was no way to loiter here; no way to lay in wait for this house or its inhabitants or visitors. She looked around, left and right, front and back; there was no cover within a half-mile in any direction. There was no way to sneak up on this house.

This was an odd headquarters for a company worth twenty-five million euros. What this looked like was a safe house.

✦ ✦ ✦

THERE WERE A dozen moms for moms'-night-out, seated on bar stools circling a high table. Before a half-hour was out, most of them were plastered.

This excursion was supposed to get Kate's mind off her impossible situation. Plus she had to maintain a facade of a normal life. This had been part of her training, part of her career, part of herself: whatever was going on, live like a normal person. Do normal things, see normal people. Don't give anyone a reason to question you, investigate you. Don't give them any meaningful answers to prying questions that might be asked after you've disappeared. Don't create any suspicion that you were not who you claimed to be.

The gossip was flying rampant around the table, unfounded, malicious. This one's husband was diddling his secretary. That one's babysitter was the school slut. The Czech family that seemed so rich? Destitute. That loud vulgar Texan with the three kids? Undergoing fertility treatments to have a fourth.

That so-and-so was a such-and-such.

Kate couldn't stop trying to piece together what her husband was up to, and where he could possibly have gotten millions of euros in any way other than exactly what the FBI suspected: stealing it.

She discreetly slipped ten euros on the table when no one was paying attention, and she walked away, as if to the restroom. But she went to the door and grabbed her umbrella from the stand and exited to the street and the mist, the vaporous streetlights, the static-like rattle of the river rushing by, fecund with melted snow.

There were a handful of pubs clustered around the bridge in Grund, each with its own discrete micro-atmosphere of smoke and noise, the sound of TV rugby in one, a Euro-pop jukebox in another, sloppily drunk teenagers in a third, where a sign clearly prohibited entry by anyone under sixteen years old, thus attracting every sixteen-year-old in the city.

Kate walked across the bridge, entered the long well-lit tunnel cut deep into the rock upon which the *haute ville* was built, the rough-hewn walls hung with derivative art, the faint stench of urine, as in every urban tunnel, even in the most well-kempt cities. It was a hundred feet worth of ascent to her neighborhood atop this rock formation, good exercise if she tramped up the hill of the rue Large, but tonight she didn't want any. She wanted answers, not cardio; she wanted to be home, alone with her thoughts. There was a babysitter to pay and dismiss, a husband playing tennis with the FBI agent who was investigating him. What a goddamn mess.

A small crowd spilled out of the arriving lift, a pair of teenagers, a pair of banker types, a lone woman, meeting Kate's eye in some type of solidarity.

Kate was alone in the elevator, waiting for it to depart. She heard footsteps in the tunnel, someone rushing. It sounded like a man—heavy footfalls, long strides. She pressed the button, again and again, an irrational and futile but still takeable action.

The doors closed just as the man arrived, trying to insert his arm into the closing gap between the dimpled-steel panels, a split second too late.

The elevator was slow, rumbling, groaning on its cables. Kate stepped out onto the St-Esprit plateau, the administrative complex, the courts and national agencies, the plaza in the middle of all the hyper-clean buildings, the whole area well-lit but empty, silent.

Kate hustled across the cobblestones. She passed a nightclub, thumping music within but no one without. She turned a corner, ascending now, into another plaza. A bar here, a fountain, a fancy restaurant, an idling taxi. A middle-aged couple walking out of the restaurant, into the taxi.

She glanced over her shoulder; no one there. She hustled through the *place* and into a street, the pavement torn up, construction equipment idle in deep dirty ditches. She heard footsteps behind her.

Kate hurried, walking as fast as she could. She broke into a jog for a step or two, then speed-walked, alternating modes of rushing. She passed an intersection, a busy Italian restaurant down to the right, the grand duke's palace to the left, and she realized she was about to walk under the Macleans' windows.

The person behind her was definitely a man, shoes clopping quickly on the stones, keeping pace with her. She glanced back. A long dark coat, a brimmed hat. Was he the same man from the tunnel? Indeterminate age and size, hidden in the night. Indeterminate everything.

Kate looked at the Italian restaurant, considered dashing in for asylum. But she kept walking, quicker, passing a Chinese restaurant, a bar, then cutting down a steep alley, the shortest path to her home, unfortunately the creepiest, and she broke into a proper run, uncomfortable and unsteady in heels on steep wet cobblestones, reaching out to a stucco wall to avoid falling, scraping her fingers on the rough surface, turning a corner at full speed, planting her full-size umbrella to help her pivot, all concentration forward, homeward, nearly sprinting now, glancing into a dark passage, and changing her mind.

She ducked into the passage, which led to the front door of a building similar to her own, another medieval structure that had been renovated beyond recognition, stone walls covered in stucco, timber replaced, new double-pane windows hung, modern flashing installed around the chimneys.

She pressed herself flush against the wall, waiting, hidden, silent.

The footsteps grew louder, clip-clopping on the stones, the sound of a slip on the steep slope, and then nearly upon her, three seconds away, now two, now—

Kate spun off the wall and into the narrow street, her right arm raised, the momentum of her spin helping her fling her arm around at maximal speed, her right hand lying flat on the horizontal, a firm swing, and when the hand made contact with the man's neck she maintained the follow-through, chopping through the resistance of the flesh and bone.

The man dropped to his knees, hands grasping at his neck, struggling to breathe. She held her umbrella with both hands, and rotated it so the curve of the wooden handle faced the outside of the swing that she used to thwack him in the middle of the back of the skull, and he pitched forward, face-planting into the cobblestones, probably breaking his nose.

Kate knelt over him, confirmed he was unconscious, alive. She noticed he wasn't wearing a hat. This wasn't the man who'd been behind her thirty seconds ago.

She reached into his coat and pocket and removed his wallet, and quickly determined that she'd just beaten up a Swiss lawyer who lived on her block.

It's been a long time since Kate carried a gun, passing police and security cameras, trying not to be nervous. It's a familiar sensation, like the aggravation of an old injury.

She glances at the screen hanging above the Métro platform. The next 12-train bound for La Chapelle is due to arrive in one minute, the following in four minutes. She will wait for the second. She's supposed to be on the first of the 12s to arrive at five o'clock or later.

Kate looks around the platform. She toys with the idea of trying to figure out which is the person who's following her, but it's pointless. She understands the rationale behind the precautions. They need to make sure that she herself is not being followed, is not paired up with anyone unsavory, or indeed anyone at all. And she's not trying to evade anyone or anything. So it doesn't matter who's following her.

She flips through the pages of *Match,* photographs of all the people she expects to find in the pages of *Match.* She used to suspect that French celebrity gossip was different from the American version, superior. After a year of living in France, she now knows that it's not.

The second train is more crowded than the first was, the commuting crowd thicker with the turn of the hour. There is no seat for Kate. She leans against a wall near a door, shifting her weight, growing fidgety.

She can't help herself now: she wants to know who it is who's following her. She considers the normal assortment of characters who can be found on a five o'clock Métro. No one meets her eye for very long, and no one pointedly avoids it. It could be any of these people. It could be none of them.

The train stops at Solférino, and nothing much changes. Then Assemblée Nationale; still nothing. Then Concorde, the Métro slowing into this large, busy station, the crowded platform, waiting passengers walking toward the train as it's still moving. She hears a man's voice, low and gravelly, just as the doors open. "Transfer here. Go to Beaubourg, top café."

The door is open, and she is stepping out.

She never got a look at the man who gave her the instructions; she didn't even try. He was turning away even as his last sound was still hanging in the air, determined to be a wisp of a whisper in the loud din of the crowd.

Kate wends her way through the *correspondance,* up and down steps, around corners, long tunnels merging into longer ones, until finally she's on the platform as the number 1 is pulling into the station, jam-packed on this most central line, post-work crowds streaming into the car at each station, people pushing and rushing, five uncomfortable stops until she allows herself to be ejected with a thick mass, human effluvium, at Hôtel de Ville.

She is out on the street, walking away from the river, then without warning the hulking Tinkertoy behemoth of the Pompidou Centre is looming in front of her, primary colors and glinting steel against the bright blue late-afternoon sky.

Kate pays for her ticket, enters an elevator, its only passenger.

She knows her way around this museum. It's one of the places she comes with Dexter, to look at a new exhibition for an hour before lunching on the rooftop with the best view on all the Right Bank.

She enters the restaurant, nods at a waitress, heads to the corner table on the far side. A bottle of mineral water sits on the table, two glasses, one patron.

A woman at another table glances at Kate, flickering eyes back down to her coffee cup, the man with her studying his fingernails. The backup.

Kate's pulse is quickening. She's fleetingly aware of the loaded weapon in the hidden compartment at the bottom of her bag, of the other concealed weapons scattered around the handbags and shoulder holsters up here on this refined rooftop, sport jackets tailored loosely to hide ever-present hardware.

Hayden rises to kiss her, cheeks brushing cheeks, his late-afternoon stubble scraping her skin, dried out from the long outdoor summer and her general disdain of sunscreen. His breath smells of coffee and the aftereffects of a mint.

"Another museum," Kate says, taking her seat. "You're a big art fan, aren't you?"

"It's one of the main reasons I live in Europe."

"Yes."

"What's yours?"

"The adventure."

"Ah. Of course. We all *love* adventure, don't we?" Hayden pours her a glass of water, the bubbles hissing softly. He produces the tiniest of wry smiles, of which he seems to possess an infinite variety.

"So. You mentioned something about a bit of stolen money."

Kate takes a sip of water, steadying herself, preparing to be firm, unwavering. To not allow herself to be manipulated or short-changed.

"Yes," she says. She puts her glass down, turns her eyes to Hayden. "But I want something in return."

He nods.

"A couple of things, actually."

26

The door was labeled REGISTRE DE COMMERCE ET DES SOCIÉTÉS, in a small new low-rise office building, on a street that Kate had never before entered or considered. A woman sat behind a desk and a computer and an angular pair of magenta-framed eyeglasses.

Kate had memorized new vocabulary words, checked verb conjugations. She even had a pocket dictionary in, of course, her pocket. She was expecting a lot of unfamiliar language in the national registry of businesses. But after Kate's first sentence in French, the woman responded in English. "Of course. Please, what is the name of the company?"

"LuxTrade."

The woman typed, hit the Enter key with authority. "The président-directeur general," she said, "is Monsieur Dexter Moore."

"Is there anything you can tell me about the company?"

"It is described as an investor in the financial markets."

"When was it founded?"

"I do not know."

"I'm sorry, I meant when was it registered here in Luxembourg?"

The woman glanced at the screen. "Previous October."

"Thank you. Is there anything else you can tell me?"

"There is nothing else at all."

Kate turned to walk away, then stopped, turned back. "By 'previous October,' you mean three months ago, right?"

"No, madame. LuxTrade was registered in Luxembourg fifteen months ago."

Fifteen months ago? That was a year before they moved to Luxembourg. That was when Dexter had left the bank job to go freelance.

That was apparently when he'd launched the plan to steal an immense amount of money and hide it in Luxembourg. Fifteen months.

✦ ✦ ✦

IN A DAZE, walking back to the mall's garage along the broad, fast-moving avenue JFK, surrounded by the glass-and-steel office buildings, the glass-and-steel cars, these different shapes and sizes of containers of human life, a pedestrian on an un-pedestrian street. Heading into the wind, stiff and cold, painful when it gusted.

The boulevard was lined with bank offices, the S.A.s and the Sàrls, the different configurations available for protecting profits from taxes and lawsuits. There were cranes and earthmovers everywhere, new construction on office towers surrounding the new art museum, the new opera house, the new sports center, all the new public spaces financed by the skimpy taxes levied on the new money that found its way here, every day, hiding. Like LuxTrade's twenty-five million euros.

Kate climbed the steps and entered the glass-and-steel mall, among the living, breathing people for a few seconds, before descending in the big glass-and-steel elevator alone, not another person in sight.

Dexter registered LuxTrade, an investing company—or was it?— here in Luxembourg fifteen months ago. How could this be?

Kate heard the squeak of tires, the hum of an engine, the slam of a door.

She walked within the painted lines that demarcated the footpath, following the rules, looking around, listening.

The harsh clang, somewhere far away, of one shopping cart being slammed into a long row of others.

Kate walked toward where she thought her car was. She heard footsteps, not far away, but saw no one. She dismissed the fear that scampered across her brain, but then reconsidered, accepted fearfulness. She looked around again, more carefully, her ears alert for other sounds, preferably normal comforting sounds, but also abnormal terrifying ones.

It was a parking lot at midday in Luxembourg. This was safer than nearly anyplace in Washington, D.C., any time of any day. Not to mention all the other dangerous places she'd spent the better part of her career.

Kate's key was in her hand, her eyes darting. She heard footsteps and a trunk slamming, a car accelerating up a ramp, the clanking of a cart with a wobbly wheel, and then she saw—thank God—her car, the *thrump-thrump* of the doors unlocking, her heart racing, sliding behind the wheel, turning the ignition, shifting into gear, releasing the brake and accelerating, getting the hell out of here, her fear getting subsumed by embarrassment—how could she be so scared of the Auchan parking lot?—lowering the window to insert the parking ticket, the barrier raising, the ramp ascending toward daylight, exiting to the—

A rustle and a movement and a voice from the backseat, a low growl.

✦ ✦ ✦

"TAKE THE NEXT right," he said.

Kate considered her options. She could slam on the brakes and open the door and jump out of the car, run down the middle of the street, flag down the police.

Or she could refuse to go anywhere until he explained.

Or she could reach into her handbag on the passenger seat, pull out the Beretta, spin around, and put a few bullets in this FBI agent.

Or she could hear him out.

"Where are we going?"

Bill didn't answer, sitting in the middle of the backseat, eyes locked with hers in the rearview.

Kate turned the car as instructed, then again, around the monstrous roundabout with the steel sculpture in the middle. Someone claimed it was by Richard Serra, but that didn't make much sense to her. She stopped the car where she was told, a few hundred yards past the traffic circle, beside a narrow stretch of open parkland, a long sloping hill, benches and lampposts, an old man walking a small dog.

"Let's get out." Bill led her to a nearby bench. This was in the wide-open, very public; it would be tough to imagine this wasn't safe. That was, Kate was sure, the point.

Bill sat. Kate thought about heading to a different bench, randomly instead of purposefully chosen. But this *was* randomly chosen, wasn't it? It was becoming difficult to separate her own decisions from those made by others, for her, on behalf of themselves.

A car drove past, close behind another. One of them looked like Amber's. Kate had been on this street before, passed this park. Everybody drove this street.

"People will think we're having an affair," Kate said. She took a seat next to Bill on the cold slats of treated wood.

"That would be better than the truth."

A familiar car approached. Kate tensed, her mind drawn back to the gun in her bag. Julia climbed out, walked to the bench, sat on the far side of Bill. "Hi, Kate." The tight little half-smile of people greeting each other at a funeral.

Kate didn't say anything.

"Do you think a little fairy like Kyle Finley can access joint FBI-Interpol files and no one will know it?" Bill asked. "That no one will alert the field agents?"

Kate stared at Bill, then at Julia, then back at Bill. Now she understood that they were confronting her, and she could get information from them. What she had to do was not give any. "What's your point?"

"Listen," Bill said, "there's no easy way to prepare you for this."

Kate actually laughed.

"I guess you're already prepared. So here it is: Kate, your husband is a thief."

Kate was surprised at how surprised she was to hear the allegation out in the open, from the investigators themselves. It was a rare moment of clarity, of certainty. If nothing else, at least Kate was sure that this man believed what he'd just said.

"Tell me what you think you know."

"As far as we can tell, he committed his first crime last summer, when you were living in Washington. He stole a million dollars, hijacking an electronic transaction."

Kate didn't respond.

"There were certain markers," Bill continued, "in the electronic trail, clues that the stolen money had made its way to Andorra. But that the theft had been initiated from a computer in the States. So we started reviewing the profiles of Americans who were arriving to the Barcelona airport, the nearest airport to Andorra, which doesn't have one."

"One what?" Kate asked, buying herself a pause in this story so she could recall last summer, Dexter's short-notice trip to Barcelona . . .

"An airport," Bill said. "Andorra doesn't have its own airport. So, four days after the hijacking, one of the American arrivals to Barcelona was a man who happened to be one of the leading specialists, in the entire *world*, in the field of electronic-transaction security."

Kate crossed her arms across her chest.

"This man hired a car to continue his journey from Barcelona, a three-hour drive, returning the next day. Expensive car. Do you know where he went?"

She glanced at Julia, who was watching Kate intently.

"This man took his hired car to Andorra for a day, then back to the airport and home to the States. Then this man bought plane tickets to Frankfurt. Four plane tickets: two adults, two children. He put his house on the rental market. He put his car up for sale; he recorded a title transfer with the DMV. And his wife? She quit her job."

Kate looked Bill in the eye, and saw that he knew who she was, what she did. What she used to do. Kate glanced at Julia. They both knew.

"What does this sound like to you?" Bill asked.

Kate looked away, watched a trio of cars heading down the hill. Traffic had picked up on this already busy road.

"This looks like a criminal, fleeing," he answered his own question. "We already had a team investigating the million-dollar hijacking, but we got in touch with Interpol, to make it a joint op, so we could follow the suspect to Europe, with full authority and access. We—"

"Why?"

"Why what?"

"Why did you follow him? He stole—what are you claiming?—a million dollars? People steal a million dollars all the time. Why is this worth following someone abroad?"

"Because we couldn't figure out how he did it."

Kate didn't understand; she knew she was missing something. She shook her head.

Julia jumped in: "Since we couldn't figure out *how* he'd done it, we also couldn't figure out what would stop him from doing it again. From stealing *any* amount of money, anytime anyone was making a transfer, anywhere in the world."

Ah. That certainly was worth putting together a modest little covert op.

"Which is exactly what happened." Julia leaned forward. "In November—on Thanksgiving, in fact. Do you remember your Thanksgiving, Kate?"

Kate glared at this woman. This home-wrecker.

"I bet you were pretty angry. Your husband was off on a *business*"—air quotes—"trip. Did he claim to be alone?"

Kate wasn't going to give anything. She rubbed her hands together, for warmth. It seemed to be getting colder by the second.

"Well . . ." Julia shrugged. She reached into her bag, pulled out a large manila envelope. She removed something, papers maybe, from the envelope.

"He was in Zurich," Julia said, thrusting the pile at Kate. "With another woman."

Kate took the stack, snapshot-size photos, annotated with a pen, scrawls of dates and locations and names. Dexter with shady-looking men in a café in Sarajevo, Dexter in banks in Andorra, in Zurich. Dexter in a nightclub in London with a stunning woman. Kate turned over this photo, saw the date and name: Marlena.

"What is this?" she asked, struggling to maintain composure, to not fall apart completely and maybe permanently, right now. She hadn't been expecting this Marlena character to be supermodel-caliber. "What does this prove?"

"Each of those photos proves a different thing. All those things add up to the truth."

Kate couldn't tear her eyes from a Zurich photo, from last June, Dexter at a jewelry counter, leaning on the glass, standing next to this beautiful creature, smiling at her. Marlena. And behind this photo were more Zurich scenes with Marlena, with Dexter, coming and going from a hotel lobby, the hotel elevator. Having a meal in the dining room. Having *breakfast*. And then London, in a restaurant, on the steps of a white-brick mews house.

Kate shook her head. "Photoshop can create anything." She wasn't expecting to be this jealous, nor this worried. "With a decent printer, anyone can manufacture any history."

Kate's phone was ringing: Claire. Kate hit Ignore.

"You can keep those prints," Julia said, ignoring Kate's eminently ignorable objection. "Check them against your calendar. Your e-mails, phone records, whatever. You'll find that Dexter has *always* been where we're saying he's been. Opening up bank accounts, one after the other, numbered accounts across Europe. And consorting with this woman."

"You could have set up all this, after the fact," Kate said. But she was struggling to avoid believing that Dexter was living a double life as a criminal, with another woman who lived in Zurich or London. It wasn't a totally inescapable conclusion, but it was damn close.

"And while he was in Zurich," Julia continued, "he did it again. But this time he stole twenty-five million euros."

Bill's face flinched, a quick furrow of the brow, narrowing of the eyes.

"How much?" Kate asked. She remembered to act surprised; she tried to paint surprise across her face.

"Twenty-five million," Julia repeated.

Bill's mouth opened slightly, his eyes darted to the side. But then he closed his mouth and turned his eyes back to Kate.

"That's a lot of money," Kate said. Though not as much as Kyle had said was stolen. "Who'd he steal it from?"

"A Serbian arms dealer."

Kate glanced down at the photo that she was still clutching. Spectacular Marlena. Plus twenty-five million euros. Tough to compete with.

Kate pushed that thought aside. "Who *are* you?" she asked.

"You know who we are."

"You're FBI via Interpol?"

Julia nodded.

"You're senior-level cyber-crime task force. You've followed my husband to Luxembourg, on suspicion of stealing twenty-five million euros last November, plus a million dollars last summer."

"That's correct."

"And it's crucial to catch him because you have no idea how to stop him."

"Yes."

"Why are you telling me all this?"

Neither answered, waiting for Kate to draw the conclusion. Kate looked from one to the other, and she knew that she'd been correct. Knew what they were trying to do.

Kate's phone was ringing again, Claire again. Could be something important. What *isn't* important? She flipped it open. "Hi."

"Kate? Is everything okay?"

"Uh . . ." What a question. "Um . . ."

"Your boys are the last ones. Everyone else has left."

Shit! Kate glanced at her watch: it was fifteen minutes past pickup. "I'm so sorry," she said, apologizing to the wrong person, rising. Now she understood all the recent traffic on this street: moms driving from the mall to school pickup. "Thanks for calling, Claire. I'll be there in five minutes."

Kate pocketed her phone. "I have to go pick up my children."

Julia nodded, which looked like giving permission, which pissed Kate off. She turned and walked away, toward her car and the retrieval of her children, with her mind swirling, an eddy being spun around a new premise. A new plan.

27

Kate woke at two A.M. For a few minutes she tried to go back to sleep, but then admitted that she'd never succeed, and that she didn't want to. She padded downstairs in robe and slippers, the apartment chilly and quiet and echoing with secrets, un-home-like. She stared out the window, the dark chasm of the deep gorge, the streetlights, the occasional car driving too fast on the winding hilly icy streets.

She turned on the computer, and started opening files, again. All the same files she'd opened before, just last week. And rooting around the web pages of their bank accounts, again. She had found nothing last week. She would find nothing tonight. But this was what a suspicious wife would do, when her untrustworthy husband was asleep. This was what she had to do. Had to be seen doing.

At four A.M. she closed the computer. She used a thick marker and large, easily readable letters to write a short note, which she carried upstairs. She looked in on the boys, as she always did when she passed their room in the night. She watched them sleep for a minute, soaking in their innocence.

Kate returned to her bedroom, turned on a low-voltage reading light. She stood over the bed, staring at her husband, breathing deeply, mouth ajar, sound asleep.

She nudged him.

Dexter blinked awake, confused, staring at the piece of paper his wife was holding in front of his face.

Silence. Follow me downstairs, put on coat, out to balcony.

❖ ❖ ❖

TEN HOURS LATER Kate climbed the steps into the tiled entryway, held up three fingers to the maître d'. *"Trois, s'il vous plaît."*

"Je vous en prie," he said, arm extended, leading her through the dimly lit bar area, into the brighter back room.

This was where Kate and Dexter had eaten the night they'd signed the apartment lease. A celebration, with the children asleep, under the care of hotel babysitting.

Could that really have been less than a half-year ago? It had been warm. Outdoor seating straddled two sides of the cobblestoned street, a small plaza under a shade tree, perched at the edge of a cliff, a majestic view. Kate and Dexter ate at a white-clothed table under the gloaming, the street strewn with clusters of business-dressed young people, holding glasses, smoking cigarettes.

After dinner Dexter had taken her hand, tickled her palm. She'd leaned against him, feeling the warmth of her marriage, the promise of sex, soon.

That had been summer in Northern Europe. Neither of them had speculated what this place would be like in the dead of winter.

Kate now slid into the window seat, sitting sideways, half-facing the window—snow beginning to fall—and half-facing the clubby room, somber wallpaper and shaded sconces and dark, heavy furniture, obliquely lit by the silvery sunless daylight. She put her bag on the bench beside her, heavy with the weight of the Beretta.

The waitress deposited the menus on the table with the customary Luxembourgeois *"Wann ech gelift."*

Nearly all the tables were occupied by men, in pairs and quartets, neckties and jackets. Across the room, one woman sat by herself. She flipped her hair and glanced around, trying not only to attract attention but also to monitor whatever attention she could muster. A maneuver that would be attempted only by an unattractive single girl.

Everyone played to type.

Julia and Bill were standing in the doorway, grim-faced.

Kate herself had to maintain her type, to stay in her character.

"Hello," said Julia, draping her coat on an empty chair. "So. You wanted to see us?" Behaving as if this were a confrontational business meeting, the airing-out of a long-standing grudge.

The waitress was hovering. They ordered drinks. When the waitress was out of earshot, Kate said flatly, "You're wrong."

Julia nodded, as if agreeing with a fine idea, a proposal for a lakeside picnic on a clear spring day. "The problem is, Kate"—condescending smile—"that we can't locate any record of Dexter's employment contract with any bank."

Kate was surprised by the irrelevancy of this administrative detail. She could still picture the employment contract in question, tucked away in that innocuous-looking file about refinancing their mortgage. But then her mind flashed back to the embassy functionary who claimed that the American authorities should have received a copy of Dexter's work permit, from his employer. This was no minor administrative detail; this was part of their proof.

"Dexter's employment is confidential," Kate added, her own irrelevancy.

"Nor a record," Julia continued, a freight train beginning to roll, "of how his income is being generated. We've checked your bank account, of course. That is, your *normal* bank account, the one you opened in both your names, with credit cards and cash cards and statements mailed to your apartment. So we can see the regular income coming in, and the regular expenses going out. But what we can't see is *where* the income is coming from."

Julia paused, staring at Kate, letting this sink in before clarifying, "The transfers are being made from a numbered account," Julia said. "Nameless, anonymous."

"That's kind of the point of Luxembourg, isn't it? Banking secrecy."

"Have you met any of his colleagues?" Julia asked, continuing to ignore Kate's half of the conversation. "Have you ever seen Dexter's employment contract?"

This was the first allegation Kate could refute. Because she had in fact seen his contract, a brief, unremarkable document that he'd squirreled away inside a misleadingly labeled folder. But she stayed silent.

"Have you seen a pay stub? Has he received anything in the mail from his employer? Has he filled out any paperwork? Life-insurance forms?"

Kate stared at the battered old table. Of course the contract could be fake. *Was* fake.

"A business card? A corporate credit card? A key-card to access the offices?"

Their waitress delivered the drinks, loud thumps on the table, two Coke lights and a beer on the bare wood.

"Have you ever seen anything whatsoever—*any*thing—that would prove—not even prove, that's too strong a burden; that would *in*dicate—that your husband works for any company at all?"

Julia picked up her soda, took a sip. Didn't continue her attack.

"That's quite a collection of circumstantial evidence," Kate said.

"Circumstantial evidence may not be enough to convict. But it's almost always enough to reveal the truth. Isn't it?"

"Circumstantial evidence to bolster wild conjecture."

"Inescapable conclusions, actually." Julia was staring at Kate firmly with complete conviction, trying to convey her certainty across the table.

Kate looked away, out the window at the swirling snow. "What do you *want*?" she asked. "From me?"

After a long silence, Julia answered, saying exactly what Kate expected: "We want you to help us."

◆ ◆ ◆

"DEXTER."

He looked up from spearing a forkful of amuse-bouche, a something-something with something sauce. This was supposedly the finest restaurant in the country. The chef had won the most prestigious award in the world. That bestowment had been long ago, but still.

"I know," Kate said. Her entire body was tingling, bristling with anxiety. This was going to be a difficult conversation, with a lot on the line.

"You know what?" Dexter popped the unidentified food object into his mouth.

"I know you're not a security consultant."

Dexter stared at her, chewing his UFO slowly. "I'm not sure what you mean."

"I know about the secret bank account."

He stopped chewing momentarily, then started again, contemplatively.

Kate held her tongue. It was now his move, and she was going to wait him out. He swallowed. He picked the napkin out of his lap, dabbed the corners of his mouth.

"What," he said, "do you think you know?"

"Don't try to deny this." It sounded a bit more hostile than she intended.

"Who has been telling you what, exactly?"

There was ample space between tables. They had plenty of privacy, here in the middle of a formally dressed crowd, neckties and dark suits, pearls and quilted handbags.

"Nobody needed to tell me," she said. "I found the account with the twenty-five million euros, Dexter."

"No you didn't," he said, slowly and calmly, steeling himself. "Because it doesn't exist. I don't have an account with twenty-five million euros."

Kate stared at Dexter and his lie, and he stared right back. "Who spoke to you, Kat?"

She mumbled.

"Who?"

"Bill and Julia, that's who. They're FBI, on loan to Interpol."

Dexter seemed to consider this.

"They came here—to Luxembourg—chasing you, Dexter. This is a big operation, for a big crime, and you're the suspect."

A pair of waiters arrived, bearing white plates under silver domes, sliding the plates onto the table, lifting the domes in tandem. One of the waiters explained the dish, in what may have been English, or possibly Swahili, for all Kate knew; she didn't pay any attention.

"Did you steal the money, Dexter?"

He stared at her.

"Dex?"

He glanced down at his plate, picked up his fork. "After we eat this," he said, "we're going to the restroom for a minute."

✦ ✦ ✦

DEXTER LOCKED THE door. "Show me you're not wired."

She stared at him but didn't say anything or do anything.

"Show me."

"You're not doing this."

"I have to."

She was surprised at how invasive this felt. But of course this is what someone like him would do. So this is what he had to do.

Kate removed her blouse. She'd gone a long time without being strip-searched. And here it was, twice within one week. She unzipped her skirt, stepped out of it. Dexter pawed around the lining, the zipper. He wouldn't know a bug if it was stinging him on the nose.

Dexter handed her clothes back.

These days, transmitters could be anything, anywhere, any size. The one she was wearing now, for example: a small disk affixed to the underside of her wristwatch. The present Dexter had given her just a couple weeks ago, on Christmas morning in the Alps, primly wrapped in earth-tone plaid with a staid silk ribbon by the jeweler on the rue de la Boucherie. The Swiss-made watch that had been trucked to a distributor in the Netherlands and then collected in a van by the boutique in Luxembourg, then flown by Dexter back to Switzerland to be unwrapped by Kate in France, thirty miles from where it had been manufactured, then flown back to Luxembourg, where in the men's room of a downtown brasserie it had been upgraded by an undercover FBI agent, and eventually overlooked by an American semi-criminal here in this silver-wallpapered restroom, now.

Kate started buttoning up, zipping up.

Dexter opened her handbag, rummaged around: lipstick and compact and phone, pens and keys and packet of gum, who the hell knows what, all of it possibly recording or transmitting. Impossible for this bag to get a clean bill of health in such a cursory checkup.

She'd left the Beretta in the apartment.

"I'm going to put your bag in the car," Dexter said. "Meet me back at the table."

◆ ◆ ◆

SHE STUMBLED OUT of the restroom, into the hall. Steadied herself against the wall before taking another step on the plush carpet.

This was much harder than she'd expected. She'd been in similar situations before. But never with her husband. For many reasons, she thought it would be easier this time.

Kate tried to stay composed. She took a sip of wine, then a sip of water. She wiped her mouth with her napkin, and fiddled with her fork, and massaged the bridge of her nose.

Dexter returned to the dining room. "I'm sorry," he said. "I didn't want to do that."

The waiters slid immense white bowls onto the white tablecloth. The soup course. A few tablespoons of liquid, topped with what looked like lobster meat.

"Do you understand? That I had to?"

Kate stared into her soup.

"First of all," Dexter said, "I don't know anything about twenty-five million euros." As they'd agreed the night before on their cold balcony, scripting out this dialog, there would be three large lies in this conversation. This was the first. "And I haven't actually stolen any money from anyone." And this was the second.

"But the way I've been making my living, I admit that not all of it is entirely legal."

"So you're not a security consultant?"

"No, not anymore. I'm a day trader, in securities. I'd been dabbling for a few years, a hobby. Then a year and a half ago, I had a string of successes, and I was fed up with my work, so I . . . Kate, I'm sorry . . . I quit."

A busboy cleared their plates, smoothed the linen, retreated.

"So what do you do that's illegal?"

"I hack into corporate computers, to access inside information. Which I use to ensure that my trades are profitable." This was the third lie, delivered steady and calm. Well-performed.

A waiter visited to find out if everything was okay. A preposterous question.

"How much money have you made?"

"I've made about six hundred thousand euros from this, um, activity."

Kate gave Dexter a small smile, an encouraging nod. The past two minutes had been the hardest part of the conversation, the biggest challenge to the performance. Dexter had handled it well. The rest would be much easier. Much closer to the truth.

◆ ◆ ◆

THE WAITERS CEREMONIOUSLY lifted more domes, little breasts of some bird underneath, lacquered skin, viscous brown sauce in a glistening slick, little baby vegetables, a whole nursery school's worth.

"Who is this Marlena woman? They showed me pictures of you with a terrifyingly beautiful woman."

"She's a prostitute. She helps me by seducing men, and accessing their computers, which is how I hack into their systems."

"That's horrible."

He didn't defend himself.

"So you have no actual job. But I found an employment contract hidden away in a file. That's a fake?"

He nodded.

"But you have a work permit? We're here legally?"

"Yes. I own a business here."

"There was some problem, though? Back when we first arrived, at the U.S. embassy?"

"The problem was that I'd applied for the work permit much earlier than when we arrived here. And in the meantime——"

"The meantime being about a year?"

"Correct. In that year, the Luxembourg government started automatically sending copies of new work permits to the foreign embassies. I didn't know about this change in protocol. So in the normal course of affairs, in September, the embassy should've received a copy of my work permit, if I'd've received it when they—when you—thought I had; when I was claiming I had. But that's not when I received it."

✦✦✦

"WHAT DO WE do about them?" Kate asked.

"Who, the Macleans?"

"Yes."

"There's no evidence for them to find twenty-five million stolen euros, because I didn't steal twenty-five million euros. So there's nothing to worry about."

"How do we make them leave us alone?" Kate asked. "Make them go away?" She contemplated the second meat course, two tiny little lamb chops, perfectly pink, the Frenched bones arranged like crossed swords. New wine, glasses the size of a child's head, with a dark depth of red liquid, a horror film's bloody swimhole in an abandoned quarry.

"I think they're about to," Dexter picked up. "That's why they confronted you, after—how long have they been here? Four months?"

"What do you think they were waiting for?"

"To unearth evidence. For us to spend huge sums of money. To buy cars, boats, big houses on the Riviera. Luxury hotels, first-class plane tickets, helicopter tours of Mont Blanc. To do any of the things that we would do, if we had twenty-five million euros."

"So tell me how you think this ends."

"I don't think we need to do anything special," Dexter said. "Except I imagine we should stop having any relationship with Bill and Julia."

"What are the reasons?"

"We don't need to give them any reasons. They know exactly why."

"No, not for them: reasons for our other friends."

Dexter shrugged. He didn't care; he didn't really have any friends. "Bill made a pass at you?" he suggested. "Or Julia at me? Which do you prefer?"

Kate's mind flashed back to the embassy Christmas party, Dexter and Julia coming out of the kitchen. "Julia hit on you," Kate said. "It's more important for there to be a rift between her and me than between you and him."

"Makes sense."

Kate stared at the multi-component chocolate extravaganza that had appeared in front of her. "Okay. So we don't talk to them anymore. What else?"

"Sooner or later—probably sooner—they'll give up. They have no evidence. They're not going to find anything, because there's nothing to find."

Kate drove her fork down into the chocolate-encrusted torte, revealing layers upon layers of textures and colors, all hidden within the hard dark shell, looking for all the world like the simplest of concoctions.

"So they'll go away," Dexter said, himself breaking the smooth brown shell, sweetness spilling across his plate. "And we'll never see them again."

The man is the first one Kate notices, crossing from the other side of the intersection, from a bigger and busier and less exclusive café, a tourist place. Sunglasses are propped on his head, and he's wearing a bushy beard, in the current style of men in New York and Los Angeles; Kate has seen pictures in magazines. An actor in a candid photograph, Sunday morning on Beverly Drive, clutching a macchiato in a to-go cup with a sip-top.

Kate realizes that these two were sitting there in that other café, hiding behind sunglasses, watching her and Dexter arrive and wait. Kate is impressed, and marginally intimidated, by the thoroughness. After all this time, and they still have the energy.

It's a good thing Kate was careful with the sugar container when she sat down. It always pays to be prudent.

"*Bonsoir*," the man says. The woman initiates phony kisses all around.

The waiter arrives instantly, attentive to Monsieur Moore and his guests, as ever. M. Moore always leaves very large tips here. Everywhere, in fact.

"So how have you been?" Dexter asks.

"Not bad," Bill says. "Not bad at all."

The waiter arrives, presents the bottle to Dexter for inspection. Dexter nods. The waiter pulls out his corkscrew, and begins to peel away the foil around the bottle's neck.

"You live here now?" Bill asks.

Dexter nods.

The cork comes out—*ploop*—and the waiter pours a taste for Dexter, who obliges, nods. The waiter pours the wine, four glasses half-full, at the silent table.

The four Americans glance at one another, each in turn, unable to start a conversation. Kate is still wondering what this meeting could be for, and how she might make it fit her particular needs. She has her own agenda. She knows that Julia and Dexter probably have a different agenda, shared between the two of them and possibly Bill. Or maybe Bill has a completely separate agenda. Or maybe none.

"So," Dexter says, looking at Julia, then Bill. "I received a message. About the Colonel."

Julia rests her hands on the table, fingers crossed. The diamond of her engagement ring catches the light, twinkles. Who will Julia be marrying? Or is this ring just another prop, for a new cover?

"Yes," Bill says. He crosses his legs, getting comfortable to tell a story. "You know of course how someone stole a fortune from him during a transaction."

Kate notices that Bill doesn't mention the specific amount of money.

"I heard about that," Dexter says.

The two men maintain firm eye contact. A poker game, both of them bluffing. Or pretending to.

"Well, the Colonel's supplier in that transaction, a Russian ex-general named Velten, was livid about the failure of an immense amount of money to arrive in his Swiss bank account by the end of business."

"I can imagine."

"So the Colonel passed an unpleasant night in West London. Or rather it looked to the naked eye pretty damn pleasant, at a three-star restaurant with a spectacular Russian hooker named Marlena. But I'm sure it was angst-ridden, his night."

Bill swirls the wine around in his glass, takes a sip, letting the liquid sit in his mouth before swallowing.

"So," puckering his lips, "the Colonel woke in the morning, and started transferring his wealth — cars, jewels, yacht; chattel — to the General. Within weeks he'd sold his London flat, passed that money along to the General. Then he — "

"Where was it?"

Both men look at Kate, surprised at the interruption.

"Where was what?"

"The London apartment."

"Belgravia," Bill answers, turning back to Dexter.

"Where exactly?"

"Wilton Crescent."

Kate shoots a look at her husband, and he responds with a tiny shrug, guilty as charged, perfectly willing to accept the penalty of having a lot of money. Kate now understands why they stood on that curved street off Belgrave Square, in front of all those white mansions, fantasizing about where they'd live one day, when they were rich. At the time, it hadn't occurred to Kate that there could've been any meaning in the street address. Another of her husband's silent lies.

"The Colonel also sold a New York apartment. But the market was bad, especially in this rich-person pied-à-terre bracket. And he was short on time. So he had to accept a lowball." Bill turns to Kate. "I believe this was on East Sixty-eighth Street. Off Fifth."

"Thanks for that detail."

"You're quite welcome."

"So now he was out of assets," Dexter says, trying to get the story back to the story. "But he still owed a lot of money."

"Yes. The Colonel had been scrambling to put together another deal—a cache of surface-to-air missiles—but word had gotten out about his debacle in the Congo. So he was having difficulties. The General, meanwhile, had been a lot more patient than anyone could've expected him to be. This was a year after the debt was incurred."

"Why so patient?" Dexter asks.

"Because Velten wasn't out any actual money. It wasn't like he had to pay any type of retail for the MiGs; he stole them. So he was up quite a bit on this deal. Even so, he wanted the balance paid. He had a reputation to maintain, after all. Finally the Colonel did put together another deal. Which fell apart at the last minute."

"How?"

"I believe someone in U.S. law enforcement leaked word to the supplier that the Colonel was being closely monitored."

"Interesting," Dexter said. "What a bad piece of luck."

"Awful."

"Now the Colonel was out of assets," Dexter says, "and out of options."

"That's right," Bill agrees. "So what do you think he did?"

"I think he disappeared."

"*Absolument*. He hid out in Bali, or Buenos Aires, or wherever. Who knows where an illegal arms dealer ducks his angry, murderous supplier? But then after a few months he rather stupidly showed up in Brighton Beach. You know where this is?"

"New York City. The Russian neighborhood."

"*Exactement*. So he was visiting Brighton Beach, or staying there, or living there, whatever. I don't know all the details of his housing situation. But what I do know is that last Friday night, about eleven o'clock, he walked out of a restaurant with two companions, both middle-aged men like himself. A cheap joint, locals only."

Bill takes another sip of wine. Kate notices that Julia hasn't touched hers.

"The Colonel, he was never a particularly handsome man. But for a lot of his life, he had money and power, and with these assets he was able to attract some women. Or at least afford them. Now, though, nothing doing. So he and his similarly unappealing comrades were out on Brighton Beach Ave., in front of the restaurant, trying to pick up a couple young girls who were waiting for a taxi to take them into Manhattan, to go to a club, where they were planning to drink Cristal from some hedge-fund manager's bottle service before going home to screw professional basketball players. These were *hot* girls, claiming to be twenty-one years old. Which made them seventeen, eighteen."

"The Colonel and his friends were out of their league."

"Totally different sport. But they were persistent fuckers. The hostess was watching this harassment go down from inside, wondering if she was going to have to round up some waiters and busboys to intervene, or even call the cops. Then a plain white van pulled up. The side door slid open while the vehicle was still moving. Two masked men jumped out, and pop-pop, a bullet each for the Colonel's friends, both in the middle of their foreheads, blood splattering all over the girls. They were screaming their skinny little asses off. The hostess started screaming too. It was mayhem."

"And the Colonel?"

"Punched in the face, picked up off the sidewalk, dragged into the van, door slammed, tires screeching as the van tears away."

"I'm guessing there were no license plates on this van."

"*Rien.*"

"Then?"

"Then nothing, all weekend."

"It was a long weekend for the Colonel," Dexter offers.

"*Vraiment.*"

"What's with all the French, Bill?" Kate interrupts.

"It's a nice language."

"And?" Dexter is impatient.

"And so I'm practicing."

"No, not and-what-more-can-you-tell-me-about-French, you idiot. And what-happened-next-to-the-Colonel?"

"Gotcha. So Monday morning, a big Labrador retriever, off leash on the beach part of Brighton Beach, refused to come out from under the boardwalk."

"The Colonel."

Bill nods. "His arms?" he asks, rhetorically. "Cut off."

Kate gasps, taken by surprise.

"Legs are gone too."

"My God."

"The Colonel is now just a torso, attached to a head. And his eyes?"

"Yes?"

"They're open." Bill takes a sip of expensive red wine. "You know what this means?"

Everyone does, but nobody answers.

"He had to watch," Bill says. "The Colonel was forced to watch his own arms and legs, while they got cut off."

28

Dexter looked at Kate's note, then her face, then the clock. It was 4:06 A.M., the night before they would go to the restaurant.

Kate had been avoiding this, or looking forward to this, anticipating this, dreading this, ignoring this for what seemed like forever. Now that it was finally here, she wasn't surprised to find herself still reluctant to start it. Reluctant to end the part of her life when this conversation hadn't happened yet. Reluctant to find out what her life would look like after it.

She walked down the stairs slowly. She bit into her lip, suddenly on the verge of tears. In all her interior deliberations about this conversation, her main emotions had been anger and fear. Not sadness. But that was what was overcoming her, now that the moment was here.

Would they have a life together anymore, after tonight? Or was this it? The end? Was she going to pack a bag, wake the boys, take them to the airport, get on an early-morning plane, and fly to . . . where? To Washington? Who would rescue her in D.C.? Who could she go cry to?

Dexter was all she had. He'd been all she had for the entirety of her adult life. She remembered flying back from a mission in Guatemala, sitting on the cold military transport, staring at the riveted gunmetal wall, recognizing that there was only one thing, one person, she was looking forward to seeing in Washington.

With her back to Dexter, she wiped her eyes, pushing back the tears. They put on coats and boots and stepped out onto the cold, windblown balcony that hung over the deep dark gorge. The light from inside was dim, but sufficient for Kate to read Dexter's face. She saw that he knew exactly what was going on.

"Dexter," she said. She took a deep breath, trying to steady herself, but not much succeeding. "I know about the twenty-five million—or maybe it's fifty million—stolen euros. I know about the numbered accounts, and LuxTrade, and the farmhouse. I know . . . Dexter, I know you're not a security consultant for any bank here. I know that whatever you've been up to, you've been up to it for a long time."

The wind gusted into Dexter's face, and he winced. "I can explain."

"I don't want you to explain. I want you to convince me I'm wrong. Or admit I'm right."

Kate already knew the truth; that wasn't what she was hoping to hear now. The first thing she wanted to learn was whether Dexter would deny it. Whether he would make the choice to add more lies. Whether all hope was lost.

And for a split second, standing there fifty feet above the stone-paved path, Kate also wondered, however irrationally, whether Dexter would try to kill her, right now.

✦ ✦ ✦

KATE HAD IMAGINED the different possible paths of this conversation many times. If Dexter said A, then she would say B, and he would respond C, and on and on. She'd tried to imagine the best-case scenario, and the worst. She'd ranked their likelihoods. She'd considered a few exchanges that ended with her walking out the door with the children, never to see Dexter again; she'd even considered the possibility that her gun would be involved. The Beretta sat just inside the door, atop the radiator, hidden by a curtain that she'd bought at the Belle Etoile mall, hung from a rod she'd installed using the diamond-tip drill bits bought on her third visit to the big-box home-improvement store, not that long ago, but long enough that it was back when she was just another normal expat housewife. Back before her life had begun to unravel. Or before she knew it was unraveling.

When Dexter opened his mouth, all the possible scenarios seemed to rush at Kate at once, making it hard for her to hear him say, "You're right."

She didn't respond, and he didn't elaborate. They stood in the silent cold, not looking at each other.

"Why are we out here?" Dexter asked, eyes still off somewhere else.

"Because Bill and Julia are FBI agents, working for Interpol, investigating you. Our computer is, I'm positive, being monitored. Our car is bugged with a tracking device. Our phones are tapped. I'm pretty sure the apartment is wired."

He took a moment to digest this. "But it's safe out here?"

Kate shrugged. Then, finally, she turned to face her husband. His face was a worried wreck. This was good, she thought. If he was calm, if he didn't care, that would be much worse.

"Can I explain now?" he asked. "Please?"

She nodded.

"It's not a short story." Dexter gestured at the chairs and table, and waited for her to sit before he did.

"You remember that my brother was in the Marines?"

Where in hell was this coming from? "Of course," she spat out, more angry than she intended. "Yes," she added, trying to soften it.

"You know he was killed during the Bosnian war. But I never told you *how* he died."

"You told me he wasn't in the Marines anymore. He was one of those military advisers." Kate knew all sorts of things about these guys. "He was captured, and killed."

"That's right. Captured by a Serbian colonel named Petrovic. Ever heard of him?"

Kate shook her head.

"Petrovic wasn't well-known outside Europe. But in the Balkans, he was famous. For being sadistic. He was a recreational torturer. Do you know what I mean by this?"

"I can guess."

"He tortured solely for the fun of it. He got his kicks pulling out fingernails with pliers. Cutting off ears with butcher's knives. He removed arms with machetes, Kate. He mutilated people, killing slowly and painfully with a maximum of blood. Not trying to collect intelligence, but just because he liked to. Because it built his reputation as a barbarian.

"When they found my brother, Kate, he was missing all his fingers. And his toes. His genitals too. And his lips. His *lips,* Kat. Petrovic cut off Daniel's *lips.*"

A shudder ran down her spine.

"Petrovic tortured my brother to death, just for the hell of it, then left his mutilated body to rot in a back alley, picked over by stray cats and rats and packs of wild dogs."

This was much more awful than Kate could have imagined. Nevertheless, she couldn't connect this story and the millions of stolen euros. And she couldn't imagine how she hadn't learned this story before, back when she'd investigated Dexter's background.

"That's horrible. And I don't mean to be a totally impatient and unreasonable bitch about this, Dexter, but what the hell does that have to do with you stealing fifty million euros?"

"It's twenty-five."

"However-the-fuck-million euros! Goddammit, Dexter!"

"Because"—he took a deep, quavering breath—"because Petrovic is the person I stole it from."

✦ ✦ ✦

"OKAY," SHE SAID, gripping the sides of her chair, willing herself to calm down. "Explain this to me. How did you know?"

"How did I know what?" Dexter's voice was trembling, and Kate could see he was on the verge of tears.

"All of this? About your brother? About Petrovic?"

Dexter took another deep breath. "To begin with, there were photos of Daniel's body. In the original State Department report on his death."

"When did you see this report?"

"Late-nineties. Someone from State got in touch with my parents. Said that documents from the war had been declassified, including the report on Daniel's death."

"You saw this report?"

He nodded aggressively, head bobbing up and down. "A photocopy. The report ended with the information that Petrovic was alive and well, and making an exorbitant living as an arms dealer, selling weapons to the worst people on earth: Mexican drug lords, genocidal Sudanese, the Taliban."

"This was in the report on Daniel's death?"

"No. Separate info, from the same guy who'd gotten in touch. I met him a few years later. This guy didn't know much beyond what was in the report. But he did put me in contact with a Croatian émigré, a guy named Smolec, who knew a lot of military. And Smolec had the goods on the Colonel. They'd come up together in the Army, and Smolec knew everything the Colonel was up to."

This was the most cockamamie story Kate had ever heard.

"So I sort of put Smolec on retainer," Dexter continued. "To help me keep tabs on the Colonel. His comings and goings, his real-estate acquisitions, his weapons deals."

"Whose idea was that? For Smolec to monitor the Colonel? His? Or yours?"

Kate could see the hint of a smile on Dexter's face, a glimmer of relief.

She knew what he was thinking: if she was asking questions like these, she was trying to understand. Trying to forgive him. He was right.

"I don't remember," he said. "Maybe he alluded to how easy it would be, and I asked him to give it a try? It was a long time ago."

"Where did you meet with this Smolec?"

"In a park. Farragut Square."

Of course: this is what Dexter was doing that cold day when Kate had noticed his red cap from across I Street, the previous winter.

"Why were you doing this?"

"Good question. The truth is I don't really know. I had no plan, if that's what you're wondering. But the information was there, and it seemed like I should take it."

"Okay," Kate said, momentarily putting aside the implausibility of this entire scenario. "Smolec was monitoring the Colonel for you, I vaguely understand that. But here's what I don't understand, Dexter: you never mentioned this to me? Even though I worked at State?"

It occurred to Kate, despite the situation, that this was yet another chance for her to come clean. Just making a truthful clarification to this one sentence could be the pebble kicked off the mountain that started the landslide. But at this moment, the dirty one—the dirtier one—was still Dexter.

"It all started before I knew you," he said. "And what I was doing didn't make an excessive amount of sense. So I was ashamed. I didn't want you to know."

This struck Kate as stupid, but honest. "Okay. Then what?"

"A few years ago, a totally unrelated development, in my professional world. In the course of testing a security protocol, I discovered a back door of how someone might steal money electronically, during transfers."

"You just happened to discover this?"

"No. It wasn't a coincidence that occurred while I was browsing eBay. This was my *job*. This is what I did. I looked for possible security breaches, and closed them."

"Right."

"So also, I knew that electronic transfer was how the Colonel conducted his business. Regularly transferring millions, sometimes tens of millions, into and out of numbered accounts, on a regular basis. Executing arms deals, from his home computer."

"And you decided to rob him blind?"

"Yes. But I didn't want merely to empty his bank account; that's just thievery." The tremble was gone from Dexter's voice, and he was talking louder, quicker. Relieved to be able to explain this, to his wife. To his best friend. "What I wanted was to find a point when he was vulnerable, when he had a lot of money that wasn't his, in the middle of a deal. When he possessed a huge sum that he owed someone else."

"Someone who'd be unhappy to not get paid."

"Exactly."

"So this wasn't just a financial revenge you wanted to extract?"

"No." Dexter shook his head. "I wanted to get the Colonel killed."

Kate was surprised at Dexter's forthright vindictiveness.

"That's the whole point of this, Kate: justice." He forced a smile now, reinforcing the heart of his rationale. "I didn't steal the money because I'm greedy. I did it to punish one of the worst people in the world."

Kate considered this semi-justifiable explanation. "That's one way of looking at it."

"What's another way?"

"That you're a thief."

"I'm meting out well-deserved punishment."

"You're a thief and a vigilante."

"I'm making the world a better place."

"Possibly. But not in the way that we do things."

"Who's *we*?"

"Americans. That's not the American way of justice."

"The American way? You mean arrest, indictment, trial, sentencing, appeals, incarceration?"

Kate nodded.

"How do you pursue that for a Serbian citizen living in London?" Dexter asked.

"Treat him as an international war criminal."

"So try him in the Hague. That's not terribly American either, is it?"

"It's American to respect international law, yes."

He snorted.

"Of course," she said, "that wouldn't get you twenty-five million euros."

✦ ✦ ✦

A FREIGHT TRAIN rumbled over the rail bridge that spanned a spur of the gorge, cargo heading north, the train long and low and slow.

"So what was your first step? When?" Kate was beginning to put distance between her sense of betrayal, her anger, and Dexter's behavior.

She was beginning to take his side. Or at least beginning to be able to see things from it.

"About a year and a half ago, I registered a business here, an investment firm, a *société anonyme*. And I opened a numbered account for the S.A. I also began to closely monitor all the Colonel's activities, his accounts, his various transfers, looking for the types of opportunities I'd have, trying to figure out how to exploit them."

"How'd you do this?"

"On one of his business trips, to Milan, he used a hotel's open-access point to execute a web transaction, and this connection allowed me to install and hide a program to his hard drive, one that created a record of his screens. Every night at four A.M. Greenwich Mean Time, if his computer was on, it e-mailed me a record of his screen activity for the previous twenty-four hours. This didn't get me his passwords or anything like that; it just enabled me to see what he was doing. It enabled me to get my ducks in a row.

"Then in early August—a half-year ago—I was ready. Everything was in place. Nearly everything. But first I needed to confirm that I really could do this."

"How?"

"With a test. I was habitually hacking the firewalls of banks. One of them, in Andorra, was where a law firm parked funds before forwarding disbursements to its clients. The primary business of this firm was representing a single insurance company—a health-insurance company. A few years ago, in an egregious miscarriage of justice, this firm not only defended the insurer against a suit, but also held the plaintiff responsible for legal fees: a million and a half dollars. The firm kept their fee, a third of the total, in Andorra. Then they transferred the remaining two-thirds to the client. Or rather they attempted this transfer."

"A million dollars. You stole this?"

"That's right. Do you have any idea which insurance company this was?"

Kate's mind raced through the irrelevant possibilities, then realized it wasn't irrelevant. She hadn't given much thought to this company in a long time. Two decades.

"American Health," she muttered. One of Kate's primary occupations had once been corresponding with AmHealth. Debating them, filling out their forms, asking for meetings, begging and pleading that it was their obligation to approve her father's treatment, despite their fine print to the contrary. "You hijacked a million dollars from AmHealth."

"A million *dirty* dollars. That rightfully belonged to someone just like your father. Or rather just like you. The suit was brought by a daughter, on behalf of her dead father."

"This was your test?"

"I figured I might as well use an evil guinea pig. And it worked. I was ready to take down the Colonel."

"That's when we moved here?"

"Yes."

"Okay," she said, leaning forward. This whole thing was beginning to make sense. "Explain to me how it worked."

29

Dexter wasn't exactly the man Kate had thought he was. But it was becoming evident that he wasn't as different as she'd feared.

"First," he said, "I needed better access to the Colonel's computer. So I hired someone to help me, a young woman in London."

A wave of relief washed over her. "What's her name?"

"Marlena."

This was one of the two people Dexter called from his secret mobile phone. Kate imagined that Niko was the other one. "And what's Smolec's given name?"

Dexter looked confused, but answered anyway. "Niko."

This was the other contact. Two for two. That explains that.

"And this Marlena," Kate said, "what did she do?"

"She helped me access the computer."

"How?"

"She had sex with him," Dexter said.

"So she's a prostitute?"

"Yes."

"And have you been fucking her?"

He actually laughed.

"No, you do *not* have the right to laugh at any questions of mine whatsoever. You're going to need to earn that back."

"Sorry."

"So? Have you?"

He swallowed his smile. "You know what Marlena looks like?"

"I've seen pictures, yes."

"I realize that I'm an incredibly good-looking man, Kate. You and I both agree about that. But do you honestly think a woman like Marlena would sleep with me?"

"You're *paying* her. To have *sex*."

Dexter gave her a gimme-a-break look.

"Okay," Kate relented. "Go on."

"Marlena is a twenty-two-year-old Russian. This is the Colonel's, um, specialty. I put her in a situation—a hotel bar that was known as a place to find girls like her."

"So he knew she was a prostitute."

"Yes."

"And she just went to his apartment and hacked into his computer?"

"No, this had to be more of a long-term thing. So when they met, she gave him her service's number. He called—she's a call girl—and she went over. That first night, she put on an extra-special performance."

"Meaning?"

"The usual overacting. Plus a tender moment of pillow talk wherein she confided that even though she had sex with men almost every night, she'd never before in her life achieved such, um, satisfaction with a customer. She made it clear that she'd had a unique time, physically. And she'd love it if the Colonel could become a regular customer."

"He fell for this?"

"Who wouldn't?"

Kate was never going to understand the extent to which men were stupid.

"It wasn't until their fifth date when the Colonel left her alone long enough to ensure privacy, with the computer accessible. She installed something called a sniffer, which can find user names and passwords. By Marlena's next visit—their relationship had become weekly—I'd created a software package that she installed, which included a keystroke logger, which recorded every keystroke, and e-mailed me the records every minute.

"Then I had to spend a hundred hours cracking the algorithm of his dynamic-password system so I could log into his bank account without his knowledge. Pure drudgery. Another few weeks to build a fake web site for his bank."

"Why?"

"Because when people are transferring millions of dollars, they don't simply hit the Send button on their computer. They're also on the phone with a bank officer, confirming the transaction. The customer creates the transaction detail, then the bank officer executes the transfer. This is how banks prevent fraud."

"So how did a fake web site get around this security?"

"Because when the Colonel thought he was logging onto the bank web site, he was actually accessing a piece of software on his hard drive, not on the web. The strokes that he typed on his keyboard, the images he saw on his screen, had only a fictional relationship to the live activity of his account. The actual activity was being directed by me, remotely."

"So you're saying he thought he was online, transferring money. And he was on the phone, confirming a transfer. But you yourself were executing a different transfer."

"Correct."

"That's brilliant."

✦ ✦ ✦

DEXTER RETURNED TO the balcony, wearing his ski cap. He handed Kate hers, and she pulled it low over her ears, burning and tender from the cold. They resettled under wool throws.

"The Colonel was *always* putting together a big arms deal of some sort," Dexter said. "But the one I was tracking was extra-large, with comically bad Africans as the buyers. This would be my ideal opportunity, exactly the type of complicated transaction I'd hoped for. The Colonel was buying a fleet of MiGs from an ex–Soviet general, then selling the planes to a Congolese revolutionary faction. You know about the war in the Congo?"

Third-world carnage had once been Kate's métier; she was glad to be rid of it. But that didn't mean she'd gone clean. She would always be a political junkie. "Deadliest conflict since World War II," she said. "More than five million dead."

"That's right. So this deal of the Colonel's required trust from the general, Ivan Velten, which the Colonel had earned over a couple decades of partnerships. And it required that a few transfers happen nearly simultaneously, on the same day that the MiGs were delivered. Which happened to be Thanksgiving Day."

Kate nodded, acknowledging this explanation of Dexter's failure to be home.

"The morning of the transaction, the Congolese delivered their down payment to the Colonel, who transferred half of it to Velten. So half the jets were delivered to an airfield near the Angola border, flown at night from Zambia, where the General had been stashing the planes since he pilfered them from an airbase in Kazakhstan. At that point the Colonel was obligated to pay the General the next installment. He initiated the transfer, and the funds left his account. But the money never arrived to the General's account."

"Because you'd transferred it to yours."

"Yes. The Colonel now owed the General twenty-five million he didn't have, and he tried to figure out what had gone on. He called his banker, but she had records of their conversation, which included his approvals and confirmations for the same-bank transfer. Both the Colonel and Velten had their accounts at SwissGeneral. Transfers within the same bank are effective immediately, because the bank can verify the funds. I too had an account at SwissGeneral."

"So couldn't the bank trace the record of your transaction? Couldn't they find the account, in their own system?"

"Yes, they could've. I'm sure they did. What they found was an empty account opened by some guy I'd paid to open one a year ago, who never knew my name or saw my face. I'd immediately emptied this SwissGeneral account to an outside account."

"But couldn't they trace that transaction, too?"

"Yes, in the normal course of affairs, they could've. But they had a security breach that day, at their headquarters in Zurich. Much earlier—months earlier—I'd opened a safe-deposit box at this branch. The morning of the Colonel's transaction, I went to visit my box. I was taken to a conference room for viewing. From my box I removed a small wireless-access-point device—it looked like a computer's power cord— that I plugged into the router under the conference table, and left. The router accessed the bank's mainframe, and the device boosted a wireless signal, so I could access it from outside the building."

"Why didn't you access the system from within the conference room?"

"Because if I used the hard connection, the administrator could've run a trap-and-trace, and found out exactly where I was. Plus I didn't want to connect inside because I assumed their security would lock down the building when they discovered the breach."

"Did they?"

"Yes. But I had already returned to my hotel next door. My room faced the street. I positioned a directional antenna to capture the WAP signal."

"How did you know this would work, technologically?"

"I'd tried it before, on a previous trip. I'd tested the tech aspects, and also captured the passwords to the bank's firewall. I'd been able to analyze the architecture and logic to the system, the protocols and safe-guards used by their administrators. I wasn't able to do anything yet, but I knew what I would be able to do, when the time came."

"Which was what?"

"After I'd redirected the Colonel's transaction, then transferred the funds out of SwissGeneral to an account in Andorra, it took me a couple minutes to get into the part of the bank's system that recorded the routing and account numbers of the day's transactions."

"You wiped out those records?"

"That's right. And it was at that point when the system administrator noticed my intrusion, and shut down the system, locked down the building. By that point, I'd transferred the money to dozens of accounts all over the planet, every transaction a different sum. Then from all those accounts, back to one account. In Luxembourg."

✦ ✦ ✦

"WHAT DID YOU do at the office? Working all those late nights, week-ends . . . what was keeping you so busy?"

"There was a lot of systems analysis, of the Colonel's computer, and of course of SwissGeneral. Intrusion is time-consuming. It's a soul-crushing amount of legwork behind a tremendous amount of theory."

"But why did you have to do this late at night?"

"Most of the nights was something else: I was monitoring the Col-onel's communications—e-mails and phone calls—to stay on top of his deals. Often, I had to stick around to learn the outcome of an I'll-call-you-back-in-a-few-hours conversation. Waiting."

"Just waiting?"

"Yes. But I used this downtime to accomplish other things. A hobby, sort of: researching a very confusing category of securities."

"Why?"

"I figured that if the securities were created in such a complex fash-ion as to make it impossible for the layperson to understand, then the bankers must've been hiding something incredibly lucrative. And the circular logic of these arrangements—which I'm pretty sure were con-structed purposefully to obfuscate—appealed to the engineer in me. In any case, it's another form of stock-market gambling. In the past couple months we've earned a quarter-million euros from these investments. It's how I make my living now."

"I thought you make your living as a thief."

"No," he said. "That's what I do for fun."

✦ ✦ ✦

KATE SET DOWN the two mugs, the coffee's steam streaming in thick white clots into the frigid predawn air. She took her seat, re-bundled herself under the gray cabled blanket.

"How do you get caught?"

Kate was still wrapping her mind around the logistics of Dexter's scheme. Pushing away the more abstruse subjects—morality, honesty, matrimony, criminality—to focus on practicality, for tonight. For now.

"I can't."

"No? It's not possible?"

"No."

Kate was surprised—she was impressed—with her husband's outrageous confidence. Where did that come from? "What if the FBI finds the money?"

"It doesn't matter. There's no way they can trace every transaction, through every account. Through commercial banks and private banks, in open banking countries and tax havens, through the secrecy of Andorra and Switzerland and the Isle of Man and the Cayman Islands and of course Luxembourg. Also, Kate, these accounts no longer exist; the trails of their transactions have been erased. There's no way this can be traced to me."

"None?"

"Absolutely none."

"But what if they simply find the money? Like I did? How do you explain possessing all that money?"

"I don't have to. That's why the money is here, in Luxembourg. In banking secrecy."

"That's why we're here?"

"Basically."

"Speaking of which: can we go home? To America?"

"Sure."

"But . . . ?"

"But we shouldn't keep any substantial amount of money in any American bank, and we shouldn't transfer more than ten grand from any account to any other. We shouldn't buy any property in the U.S. We shouldn't spend any appreciable amount of money there. We also shouldn't earn any income there, so we shouldn't sell our house in

D.C.—we should just keep renting it. We shouldn't do anything to open ourselves up to the IRS."

Kate understood. They needed to hide from the IRS so they could hide from the feds. "The man you stole it from, the Colonel," she said. "Can he find you?"

"He's not looking for me. I framed someone. I set up a guy to look like he stole it from the Colonel. Another Serbian ex-Army thug."

"What happened to him? This other man?"

"Another lowlife got what he deserved."

What else did she need to know? "That account, the twenty-five million? It's such an even number. Not earning any interest."

"No."

"You don't want to have to report any income on it. Even here."

"Correct. Because we have to report our income here, there."

"Forever?"

"Forever. As long as we're American citizens, we need to file American taxes."

"What do we do about that?"

"We limit our income to what I earn through legitimate investments. But that doesn't mean we have to limit what we spend."

"Does your plan include spending that stolen money? Or did you steal it solely to take something from someone you hate?"

"My plan is we'll spend it."

Kate let that settle in her mouth. She rolled it around, like red wine. "When?"

"When it's safe. I guess when the FBI leaves us alone."

This comment made sense at the time, in the overload of information from Dexter's surprising narrative. It would be a long time before Kate noticed the flaw in the logic at the heart of this rationale: that if Dexter had been waiting for the FBI to leave them alone, he'd already known they were watching him. Before she'd told him.

✦ ✦ ✦

"TELL ME ABOUT the farmhouse."

"It's a mailing address; a banking address. It's out of the way. It's unmonitorable."

It would serve nicely as a safe house, if the need ever arose. But Dexter thought in terms of tax addresses, not safe houses. Safe houses were Kate's department.

"You rented a car to go there. When you claimed you went to Brussels. Why?"

"The deal was imminent. So I opened up a slew of new accounts, for a week, for the purpose of moving the money. The accounts' paperwork was mailed to the farmhouse. I needed to collect it. To shred it."

"I see. That was about when you hid the account records in the kids' bureau. Right?"

He looked ashamed at this revelation. "That was after the, um, transaction. When the secrecy of the account became much more crucial."

Kate recalled that night clearly. "And that was when Julia's supposed father showed up, wasn't it? When we had dinner with him?"

"Was it? I don't remember that bit."

This seemed implausible. Impossible. Kate was thrust back into doubt, suspicion, distrust. "Really?"

He shrugged.

"So who do you think he was?" she asked. "Lester was his name, right?"

"Probably their boss. Or a colleague."

They sat in silence, each pursuing a separate but parallel path of conjecture.

"Why don't you keep the account info at your office? Or at the farmhouse?"

"I don't want to have to go someplace," he said. "If we ever need to flee quickly."

"Why would we need to flee quickly?"

"If I'm about to get caught."

"But you said it's not possible."

"Still. I should take precautions."

Kate couldn't help thinking that the main precaution he'd been taking had been against her. And that brought her back to the security camera. She couldn't decide how much to push. Couldn't decide how desperately she wanted to know whether Dexter had seen the footage from his office. And hence whether he could backtrack through the myriad levels of her deceptions. She was still grasping her own secrets, tight to her chest.

"Isn't your office safe?" she asked, pushing a bit.

"Very."

"Do you have surveillance there?" Unable to stop pushing, now that she'd started.

His face still didn't reveal anything. "I bought a video camera."

Her heart stopped.

"But I never got around to networking it to my computer."

✦ ✦ ✦

DEXTER DIDN'T KNOW.

How much didn't Dexter know?

Dexter didn't know that Kate had stolen his key ring. He didn't know that Kate had broken into his office, riffled through his things. He didn't know that Kate had been suspicious of him long before Bill and Julia had told her to be. He didn't know that Kate had suspected Bill and Julia too. He didn't know that Kate had broken into Bill's fake office, that she'd made contact with an old Company acquaintance in Munich and new ones in Berlin and Geneva. He didn't know that barely weeks earlier Kate had thought maybe the investigators were assassins.

Dexter didn't know that he had been—his whole family had been—traipsing across Europe, chasing his own tail.

And he didn't know that his wife was CIA.

✦ ✦ ✦

THERE WAS STILL no hint of dawn in the sky, but cars and trucks and buses had become more frequent. It didn't need to be light to be day.

"Your last trip to London, right before Christmas? Was it to pay off Marlena?"

"Yes."

"How much?"

"Twenty thousand pounds."

"That doesn't seem like so much."

"It's not, purposefully. I paid her enough to get her to do the job, but not so much that she'd imagine she was involved in anything huge. I didn't think more money would buy more security; I thought it'd guarantee less."

Kate was surprised at Dexter's insight. "And what happened to Marlena, after your, um . . . what should we call it?"

"Transaction?"

"Okay, transaction. What happened to her?"

"She saw the Colonel night of, but canceled the next week's appointment. She hid, but stayed in London. In case something went wrong, and she needed to rekindle with him. She had a story ready about being attacked by a client, and being scared. I found a guy we could accuse."

"You thought of everything, didn't you?"

"Yes."

"So you're finished with her?"

"Yes."

"But she's alive."

"I know what you're thinking."

"And?"

"First of all, she doesn't know the full extent of what happened; she's aware of only her part of the puzzle."

"But still."

"I have a stockpile of evidence against her. That she committed multiple crimes."

"She could trade testimony against you for immunity, couldn't she?"

"It's a pretty long list. Some of her crimes are serious."

"Nevertheless."

"Yes," Dexter said, exasperation in his voice. "You're right. There's a minuscule possibility that someday she might be turned against me." He looked his wife in the eye, held her gaze. "But what am I supposed to do?"

Kate stared back. There was something in his look that seemed to be a challenge, a dare, for her to say aloud what she would say, if she were the person she used to be.

That person would say, *Kill her*. But this person wouldn't.

The unspoken subject hung in the air, nudging Kate with another chance, another possible segue to her own dishonest past. But this one, like all the others, turned into just another opportunity that she allowed to pass by. Instead her mind pursued a fresh offensive, turning the tables, as she always did when she should've been defending herself: why did Dexter keep this whole thing a secret from her?

Then again, who was Kate, of all people, to question anyone's motives for secrecy? She could think of good reasons—great reasons—why Dexter had kept this secret from her. She had no right to ask.

But isn't that what marriage is? Asking for things for which you have no right? "Why didn't you tell me, Dexter?"

"When?" he asked. "When would I have told you?"

Kate had rehearsed this very same argument herself, time and again.

"When I first thought of this ridiculous plan?" he asked. "When I hired a London hooker to seduce an old criminal so she'd be able to compromise his laptop? When we moved to Luxembourg so I could hijack an African arms deal? You'd've left me."

She shook her head: no, this wasn't true. Or was it? Kate had never imagined that Dexter might know everything about her. But tonight, for the first time, she had doubts. Because Dexter was much more clever, much more deceptive, and much more devious that she'd thought possible. She'd been wrong about him, all these years. How wrong?

✦ ✦ ✦

"SO HOW DO you think we handle the FBI?" he asked. Kate didn't realize at the time what a thoroughly disingenuous question this was.

She stared into space, puzzling out this challenge. "In the morning, I'll call Julia," she said, glancing at her watch. The children would be waking up any minute. "I'll arrange a meeting."

"Why?"

"Because I'm pretty sure they'll ask me to help them. Probably by wearing a wire. I'll feign outrage, but they'll press their case, promise how miserable they'll make our lives if I don't cooperate." Now that Kate was saying it aloud, this plan was beginning to sound like the exact right course of action. "So I'll agree to do it."

Dexter raised his eyebrows, leaned forward. "Then?"

"Then you and I will go someplace semi-public, as if we're trying to ensure that there's no surveillance. A neutral, unanticipated locale. A restaurant, I think . . ." Kate trailed off, trying to picture the right place. Trying to solve every last problem, all at once.

"Yes? Then?"

"Then we'll put on a show. For their benefit."

30

Their show was, finally, over. The car hurtled through the night, the straight two-lane road unlit and lonely, the wheels thrumming on the pavement, humming along through the countryside toward the glow in the distant sky above the city, above their home and their children, the resumption of a normal life, or the creation of a new one.

Dexter was driving faster than usual. Maybe he'd drunk too much at the restaurant, succumbing to the pressure of the performance for the benefit of the microphone and the FBI agents on the other end of the transmission. The device was still transmitting.

They allowed the silence in the car to wash over them, a warm bath of nontalking, nonperforming. For the first time in memory, the silence between them wasn't filled with layers upon layers of lies. But Kate was hyper-aware of the one big untruth that still hung between them.

She watched the road, the hypnotizing yellow line in the middle of the band of black. She was wavering, yet again. Then she suddenly grew more frustrated with herself than she could bear.

Enough.

"Dexter," she said, forcing herself into it before she had time to reconsider, "could you pull into the rest area up ahead?"

He took his foot off the gas pedal, shot a glance at his wife.

"There's something I need to tell you."

❖ ❖ ❖

THE REST AREA was a few miles south of the city, a massive complex crowded with parked eighteen-wheelers, with drunk teenagers spilling out of beat-up Skodas to buy beer and cigarettes and big bags of chips, with pierced young Dutch on long-haul road trips back from the Alps, with silent exhausted Portuguese laborers eating shrink-wrapped sand-wiches on their way home from mopping the ketchup-sticky floors of fast-food restaurants.

Dexter kept the car idling, the heated seats on, headlights off. He turned to Kate.

She considered the transmitter. She thought about asking Dexter to step out, into the grim seclusion of the parking lot. But of course the FBI and Interpol already knew everything she was about to tell him, so why bother?

"Dexter," she said, "I never wrote position papers."

It was hard to read his face in the dim blue glow from the dashboard lights. She fought the urge to look away, to hide her own eyes. Struggled against the long-ingrained habit of disguising her own lies, now that she was finally telling the truth.

"And I never worked for the State Department."

A tractor-trailer drove by in low gear, the rumble and grumble of the big engine, the rattling and clanging of the hardware. Kate waited for the noise to pass.

"What I did for a living . . ."

Then she changed her mind. Although Kate knew what she was plan-ning to say, she didn't know how Dexter would respond.

Kate glanced at the brightly lit building at the center of the rest area, the convenience store and the café area, the gleaming floors and neatly organized tables.

She unclasped the watch from her wrist, slipped it into the pleated leather seat pocket. "Let's go get a coffee."

◆ ◆ ◆

DEXTER DROPPED THE coin into the machine and pressed the button and waited for the sputter and hiss and burble of the espresso, spitting and spurting out of the discolored plastic nozzle into the flimsy dispos-able cup.

Kate took a sip of her cappuccino. It wasn't bad, this rest-area-machine coffee; it was hot and strong and decent. There was a lot of good coffee, everywhere in Europe.

They took seats at a pebbled-glass-topped table, lightweight steel chairs, a giant window facing the highway. Another couple was sitting on the other side of the room, the woman teary-eyed, in their own mode of crisis: a breakup, an unwanted pregnancy, an affair. Those people had their own troubles, wouldn't attempt to eavesdrop on anyone else's.

There was no point in preamble. Kate reached across the table, took Dexter's hands in hers. "I worked for the CIA," she said. "I was what you'd call a spy."

Dexter's eyes widened.

"My job was to run assets in Latin America. I worked a little bit in El Salvador, Venezuela, Nicaragua, Panama, and Guatemala. But mostly it was Mexico."

He looked as if he was about to say something, but he didn't.

"I started with the Agency straight out of college. It's all I ever did. It was a career I chose, in large part, because I thought I was incapable of loving anyone. My experiences with my parents, my sister . . . I was a numb person. I discounted myself from the possibility of genuine intimacy. I believed I'd never have my own family."

Kate squeezed Dexter's hands, emphasizing this, the most operative component of the multilayered apology.

"I thought I'd always be alone, Dexter. I thought I'd never need to lie to anyone I loved, because there'd never be anyone I loved. I was young, and I was damaged, and I couldn't imagine being not young, and not damaged. You remember how it was to be young?"

He nodded, still mute.

"It was impossible to understand how brief it is. It seemed like youth would last so long; it would last forever. But it's just a blink."

At the table on the other side of the cafeteria, the woman let out a short loud sob.

"So when you and I met, I of course didn't tell you the truth about what I did. I expected I'd dump you in six months. Or you'd get frustrated with how closed I was, and you'd get rid of me. I thought we'd never connect, just as I'd never connected with anyone."

Dexter was watching her intently.

"But I was wrong. It turned out I fell in love with you."

Kate's attention was caught by a man entering the store, glancing her way. She hoped that a day would come when she wouldn't be suspicious of everyone who walked by.

"I wanted to tell you, Dexter. Please believe that. I considered it thousands of times. Almost every day, for the entire time we've known each other. But when could I have told you? When should I have passed that point?"

This had been exactly the same rationale he'd used last night, out on their balcony, the legitimate coming-clean, after which they'd planned the fake coming-clean, performed tonight for the benefit of the feds.

Now, here in this rest area, they'd returned to the privacy of their marriage.

"Then we got married, and I still hadn't told you. How awful. Really, I completely admit it: this was awful of me."

Dexter gave her a tiny smile, a small concession.

"Then after Jake . . ." Kate paused, wondering how many of the details to tell him, how full her disclosure needed to be to count, to satisfy herself. "I transferred out of operations, became an analyst, at a desk in Washington. You don't know what this means. But it's . . . it's like quitting being the starting shortstop to become the first-base coach."

Dexter had once been an avid baseball fan. He gave Kate another pained-looking smile, but seemed incapable of speaking.

"I essentially threw away my career. But I stayed with the CIA. We needed the paycheck, and the health insurance, which soon you weren't providing for us."

Dexter let a grimace escape; she shouldn't have gone there. Health care in Luxembourg was, thankfully, universal and free.

"Anyway," she said, "the point is, I never did get around to telling you." Kate couldn't tell if he was angry, or sad, or outraged, or shell-shocked. Much later, she would realize that stoicism was all he could muster. He had never been trained for this type of confrontation. He was not naturally or professionally devious. Just by happenstance.

"And when we moved here, of course, I did quit. But at that point, why should I tell you the truth? How could I? I'd been lying to you for a decade. And now the lie was finally over. I had every reason to think it was becoming irrelevant, more every day. So why should I admit it? What good would that do? As I remember you once said, about the secrecy of your supposed—nonexistent—client, it would've been a big downside with no upside."

Dexter stared across the room, at nothing.

"Except I was wrong, Dexter, I know. I should've found a way, at some point, to tell you. But I didn't." She tried to make her eyes beg for forgiveness. "And I'm so, so sorry."

Dexter now gave Kate a cheeky smile, a smile that looked full of indulgence and superciliousness and condescension. A smile that someone uses when receiving an important and heartfelt apology. A smile of leniency paired with superiority. A smile that says, *I am willing to accept your apology, but now you owe me.*

Or at least that's what it looked like to Kate, at the time.

She wouldn't figure this out for another year and a half, but Dexter's was a smile of deep relief. A smile of someone who could finally stop pretending he didn't know something that he'd known for a long time.

✦ ✦ ✦

IT STARTED TO rain, as usual. Slowly at first, misting over the picture window that faced the highway. Then the loud patter of heavy drops on the glass atrium overhead.

A car made a turn that threw headlights in Dexter's eyes. "What did you do?"

"Mostly I met with people," Kate said. "I encouraged them to do things that we—the United States, or at least the CIA—wanted them to do. I persuaded them."

"How?"

"I gave them money, and information. I helped them organize. Sometimes I threatened them with bad outcomes if they were uncooperative."

"Such as?"

"Mostly the absence of things they wanted. Money, or weapons, or the support of the U.S. government. Instead their rivals would get that support. Or money, or weapons."

"But sometimes it was something else?"

"Sometimes I told people that they'd be killed."

"By you?"

"I usually left that part vague."

"And were they? Killed?"

"Sometimes."

"By you?"

"Not really."

"What does that mean, *not really*?"

Kate wanted to not answer this question. So she didn't.

Dexter looked away, about to ask a question he didn't want to. "Was it part of your job to have sex with people?"

"No."

"But did you?"

"Did I what?"

"Sleep with other people?"

"No," she said. "Did you?"

"No."

Kate took a final sip of her cappuccino, now room temperature, stasis with the ambient atmosphere. This was an unexpected turn into the irrelevant realm of sexual fidelity, the one deception in which neither had engaged.

"Did you ever kill anyone?" he asked point-blank.

She knew this was coming—she'd dreaded this—but still she hadn't settled on her answer. On how complete her answer would be. "Yes."

"How many?"

She didn't want to give a number. This was one of the main reasons she'd never told Dexter the truth. It wasn't merely the Agency's code of secrecy that she didn't want to break, and it wasn't her reluctance to admit that she'd been lying all those years. The primary reason she never wanted to have this conversation was she didn't want to answer this question, asked by this man, who would never again look at her the same way.

"A few."

His face asked for a greater degree of specificity, or honesty. But Kate shook her head. She would not give him the number.

"Recently?" he asked.

"Not really."

"Meaning?" There was impatience in his voice, exhaustion with her evasions.

"The last time was a few months after Jake was born. It was someone I'd known in Mexico." If she was going to have to tell him this, she was going to tell him the whole story. Nearly.

"He was a politician who'd lost a presidential election. He was planning another try, and wanted our support. My support. I'd written him off, and in fact that final trip I took to Mexico was to meet with other politicians, other guys who were considering a run. He found out about that. And when I came home, he kind of forced me to take a meeting with him."

"Forced you? How?"

"He sort of abducted me. Off the street. It wasn't violent, but there was definitely a threat to the situation. The meeting turned into a long harangue about why we—why *I*—should support him. Then he showed me a photo, taken through our window, of me with Jake in our living room."

Dexter cocked his head, asking to confirm if he understood.

"He was threatening me. If I didn't support him, harm would come to my family. I couldn't decide how credible this threat was. I wouldn't have taken it seriously at all, except for the fact that this man was a deeply irrational player. A delusional guy. And I had a baby. My first. Our first."

"So."

"So I couldn't see clearly any way to ensure that he left us alone. A guy like that, his reach is far longer than deportation, or imprisonment, or . . . or anything. If he wanted harm to come to us, harm would come to us."

"Unless you killed him."

"Yes."

"How? Where?"

She didn't want to give the murder-pornography frame by frame. Didn't want to recite her route across Manhattan, the length of the knife blade and the number of times she pulled the trigger, the color of the blood-splattered wallpaper in the hotel room, the man falling to the floor, the baby crying in the next room, the woman emerging and dropping the bottle, its nipple popping off and the milk spilling onto the carpet, the woman pleading *"Por favor,"* her hands up, shaking her head, asking—begging—for her life to be spared, her big black eyes wide, deep sinkholes of dark terror, while Kate trained the Glock on her, a seemingly eternal internal debate, while the baby sounded like he was the same age as Jake, late infancy, and this poor woman the same age as Kate, a different version of herself, an unlucky woman who didn't deserve to die.

"Dexter, I don't want to get into all the details."

She didn't want to tell him about the blood that was spreading through the carpet fibers from the tremendous hole in the back of Torres's head. Damn'd spot.

"Maybe someday," Kate said. "But not now. Okay?"

Dexter nodded.

"And what I realized," Kate continued, "was that it had become too easy to get to me, to rattle me. To make me behave in ways I shouldn't. I knew I had to leave the field; I had to stop interacting with assets."

That young woman had seen Kate's face. She'd seen that Kate had killed Torres and the bodyguard. That woman, that witness to cold-blooded murder, could send Kate to jail. Could wrest Kate from her baby, her husband. From her life.

"So after I killed this man, I went back to my office, and I asked for a reassignment."

Kate was aiming the gun at the woman's chest, holding her right wrist steady in her left palm, beginning to panic, wondering if she had the strength to do this. Wondering if she had the strength to not do this.

And in the next room, the baby cried out again, louder.

✦ ✦ ✦

IT HADN'T TAKEN very long to come clean, after so many years of so many lies. It was surprising how undifferent she felt, now that every-thing—nearly everything—was out in the open.

They both had a legitimate right to be furious with the other. But their separate self-righteous indignations seemed to be canceling each other out, and neither was angry. Worry was etched in Dexter's face. Kate thought this worry was for their future. Maybe he was wondering if they could make it, such liars, together. A marriage based on so many things that were not true. A life lived so falsely, for so long.

Kate didn't know that Dexter hadn't admitted all his lies. Just as she hadn't revealed every one of her secrets.

He opened his mouth, let it hang silently, struggling with something, then gave up. "I'm sorry too, Kat. I'm so sorry."

Sitting there in that rest area, she later realized, Dexter had been struggling with whether to admit the deepest layer of his deception. But he had decided against it.

And so had she.

31

Kate felt her way through the hall, fingertips trailing the pebbled wall-paper, to the glowing door of the boys' room. When she'd left before dinner, distracted, she'd failed to close their blinds. The streetlight streamed into their bedroom, bathing everything in a silver tint, a powder-coated world of little clothes and little toys and innocent little boys, with unlined foreheads and impossibly slender shoulders.

She walked to their beds, junior-size mattresses barely bigger than crib mattresses, but nevertheless referred to as big-boy beds. She kissed each head, fresh-smelling silky hair. Both children were sprawled in different ludicrous positions, limbs akimbo, as if they'd been dropped onto these small beds from a great height. *Plop.*

Kate looked out the window before closing the blinds. The babysitter was climbing into the passenger seat, Dexter behind the wheel, about to drive her across the bridge to the Gare, to her tight little street crammed with mediocre Asian restaurants. Luxembourg is a place where a great steak au poivre is half the price of awful Chinese food.

A taxi was parked at one end of the block, the driver blowing ciga-rette smoke out the half-open window, billowing up in violent-looking bursts, the dense warm smoke cohering in the cold night air.

In the other direction, Kate could barely see the outline of a figure under an oak planted in a clearing, the soil covered with a black iron grate. He'd probably be there till dawn—or maybe they'd take turns on this overnight sentry duty—making sure the Moores didn't flee. Stand-ing uncomfortably on the cobblestones, leaning against a sharp-edged iron rail, bundled and shivering, feet aching, tired and hungry and cold and bored.

But this was his job. And although Kate didn't know it at the time, he'd recently made a discovery that had amplified his motivation, which was now at a level that could be fairly characterized as obsession. So he had passion, to help him through the long dark night.

✦ ✦ ✦

KATE WAS AGAIN sitting on the balcony when Dexter returned. He dropped his keys in the bowl on the hall table, where he always dropped his keys. He walked across the polished stone tiles, the same tiles as on every other floor in Luxembourg, through the half-light. He stepped out onto the balcony, and shut the door behind him.

The rain and clouds had blown by. The night was now clear, stars twinkling.

"You can have me," Kate said, "or you can have the money." She'd made her decision, and it was nonnegotiable. She was convinced that she knew Dexter's essential character. Which was not a man who wanted to buy yachts and sports cars with a fortune's worth of stolen blood money. He'd wanted, simply, to steal it. "But you can't have both."

They faced each other across the cold darkness, for the second night in a row, a tremendous distance traveled in the intervening hours.

Dexter let his head fall back, stared at the sky. "Do you really need to ask?"

"I wish not. But I do."

He understood: the ground had shifted beneath their feet. It was now impossible to know exactly where she stood.

"You," he said, looking at her. "Obviously, I choose you."

She returned his gaze. Something passed between them that she couldn't put a name to, an acknowledgment, a resignation, a gratefulness, a hodgepodge of emotion between two people who've been married a long time. He reached his hand out, took hers.

"We leave that twenty-five million in that account," she said, "and never touch it."

"Then why keep it? Why not give it away? Build a school in Vietnam. An AIDS clinic in Africa. Whatever."

It had never occurred to Kate that she'd be able to dispose of a huge sum of money. That she'd be able to donate anything to anyone. She reconsidered her plan, her options, in this odd new light. They were silent for a few moments, lost in thought.

"I don't think so," she said. "We'll need to keep a cushion. A large stash of getaway cash. Enough to build a whole new life, from scratch, instantaneously."

"Why?"

"I'm not convinced there's no way for you to get caught. There's always a way to get caught. There might be evidence you don't know about. There's the girl in London; there's your Croatian source, wher-ever—whoever—he is. There's whoever those people spoke to, who-ever they slept with. There are those FBI agents and their records. There's Interpol."

Dexter slumped low in the chair. It was one o'clock in the morning.

"We'll need to be on the alert, for years," Kate continued. "Maybe forever. We'll need to be ready to disappear with a suitcase full of cash."

"Okay. But that's, what? A million? What about the rest of it?"

"We need to leave it alone. Sort of like escrow."

"Why?"

"Because someday, we might need to give it back."

❖ ❖ ❖

KATE WOKE WITH a start, in a sweat.

She padded down the dark hall, kissed the boys on the tops of their perfect heads, listened to them breathing, safe and sound.

She looked out the window. Bill was still out there, making sure she wasn't fleeing.

Dexter was fast asleep, the weight of the world lifted from his shoulders.

But Kate was wide awake, chased by the same demon that haunted her regularly, especially when she was trying to forget it.

❖ ❖ ❖

THE DESCENT WAS steep and narrow, a sharp ninety-degree turn in the middle of it, another difficult turn on the other side of the garage door onto the narrow stone-walled street, also steeply descending, more sharp turns. Kate guided the car carefully through the narrow streets, up and down the rain-slicked cobblestones, around tight corners. The radio was tuned to France Culture, the morning news, political scan-dal. She still didn't understand a quarter of the words, but she was semi-satisfied that she was getting the story. In the backseat the boys were discussing what types of things they most enjoyed cutting or chopping. Jake liked apples; Ben claimed, surprisingly, kiwi.

Kate had achieved that special level of fatigue that was almost hallu-cinatory. A feeling she remembered from her children's infancy, awake for the four A.M. feeding. And from the missions she'd run, awake for

the three A.M. break-ins, the five A.M. unscheduled flights from impro-
vised airstrips in jungle clearings.

She led the children through the morning mist across the campus, exchanging hellos and smiles and nods with a dozen friends and
acquaintances. She had a quick chat with Claire. She was introduced by
Amber to a newly arrived American, a freckle-faced young woman from
Seattle with a husband at Amazon, in the converted old brewery down
in Grund. Kate agreed to join them for coffee before pickup, six and
a half hours from now, the daily window of opportunity to shop and
clean and see movies and have affairs with tennis coaches. To live whatever type of secret life you could conjure. Or merely to have unsecret
coffee with other expat housewives.

Down the hill, extra-carefully through a dangerous construction
zone, across the railroad's grade crossing, up again, then down to cross
the river Alzette in Clausen, then ascending to the Haute Ville, past the
turnoff to the grand duke's *palais,* past the fat arrogant guard with the
tinted glasses, back to her spot in the parking garage. *Chirp-chirp.*

It had started to rain again. Kate set off on foot through Centre,
streets she knew by heart, every dip and turn, every storefront and
shopkeeper.

An old nun stood in front of St-Michel. *"Bonjour,"* she said to Kate.

"Bonjour." Kate looked at the nun closely, rimless glasses and close
habit under a dark felt coat. Kate now saw that she wasn't old, this nun;
she just looked it from afar. She probably wasn't any older than Kate.

Onto the montée du Clausen, dramatic vistas on either side of the narrow sloping plateau, wide-open views of browns and grays, wet dun.
The rain picked up, a cold steady downpour now. Kate pulled her coat
tightly around herself.

A train traversed the gorge on the high aqueduct-style bridge. On
the semi-frozen river below, a duck quacked insistently, sounding like
a grumpy old man arguing with a cashier. A trio of Japanese tourists
wearing plastic ponchos scurried across the street.

Kate climbed to the observation deck atop the fortifications, which
were cut through with a maze of tunnels. Hundreds of miles of tunnels
ran beneath the city, some of them large enough for horses, furniture,
suited-up regiments. During wars the town's populace would hide—
would *live*—in these tunnels, shielding themselves from the carnage
above.

Kate took the final step onto the platform. There was another woman up here, facing away, northeast toward the gleaming EU towers in Kirchberg. Standing atop old Europe, gazing at new.

"You're wrong," Kate said.

The woman—Julia—turned to face her.

"And you need to leave us alone."

Julia shook her head. "You found the money, didn't you?"

"Goddammit, Julia." Kate was struggling to keep herself composed. She wasn't terribly confident she was going to succeed. "It's simply not true."

Julia squinted into a burst of sideways-blowing rain. "You're lying."

In her entire career, Kate had never lost her temper during a mission, during a confrontation. But when the children were babies they'd sapped her spirit, defeated her patience, and she'd lost her temper regularly. It had become a familiar sensation, the tightness in her chest that preceded a loss of control.

"And I'm going to prove it," Julia said, taking another step toward Kate, wearing an insufferably smug smile on her preposterously painted lips.

Kate shot her arm up and hand out and slapped Julia across the face, snapping her wrist as she made contact with the wet skin, a hard stinging open-hand slap that left a big red mark.

Julia pressed her hand to her injured face, looked Kate in the eye, a look that seemed like satisfaction. She smiled.

Then she lunged, reaching for Kate's shoulders, her throat, pushing into her, driving with her legs. Kate staggered back, toward the stairs; she was going to fall down the stairs if she didn't regain her balance. Kate spun away, coming to a stop against the low stone wall that separated her from a seventy-foot drop.

Kate glanced around, looking at the dangerous cliff that surrounded her on three sides; Julia was standing at the top of the stairs on the fourth side, cutting off the escape route. The Japanese witnesses had disappeared. There were no other tourists, no other sightseers, midweek in a small northern European city in the middle of the winter, in the frigid pouring rain.

They were all alone.

Julia took a step toward Kate, face lowered, jaw tensed, glowering. Another step. Kate was pinned against the wall.

Julia was now just a few feet away. Kate suddenly cocked her arm and threw a quick punch. Julia ducked and spun and brought her hand out of her pocket, a shiny silver something rising.

Kate lashed out with a kick, her right foot knocking into Julia's hand and the weapon, but the two things didn't separate, while Kate lost her balance on the slick wet stones. She fell, first her ass and then the back of her head making painful jarring contact with the hard, dense, uneven sandstone.

Everything went black.

But for only a split second. Then Kate's vision returned in dots and stars and swirls of multicolored light, and she felt herself reaching into her pocket, and then her eyes could make out Julia regaining her balance, spinning back toward Kate, whose own arm was rushing up, a blur and the swish of fabric against fabric.

Julia was standing over Kate, aiming her gun at Kate's head. And Kate's matte black Beretta was aimed directly at Julia's chest.

✦ ✦ ✦

A BUS RUMBLED by on the street below, hidden from view, shifting gears to make the final push to the top of the steep Clausen hill.

The women stared at each other across the sights of their handguns. They were both soaking wet, water streaming through their hair, across their faces, in their eyes. Kate blinked the water away. Julia wiped her brow with her free left hand.

They continued to stare.

Then without warning Julia lowered her gun. She stared at Kate for a second, then nodded. It was the tiniest of nods, her neck slightly inclining, the angle of her face barely changing. Or maybe her neck and head didn't move at all; maybe the nod was just in the eyes, a blink. Her cheeks tightened, in what may have been a smile, or a grimace.

Kate would revisit this enigmatic look many times over the next year and a half. Julia was trying to communicate something to her, there in the pouring rain on the observation deck. But Kate couldn't figure out what it was.

Then Julia turned, and walked across the platform, down the stairs, and out of sight. Gone. For, Kate believed, ever.

✦ ✦ ✦

"DID YOU HEAR about the Macleans?"

Kate was standing at school, waiting for three o'clock. It was cold but cloudless and bright, the type of day that seemed commonplace back in the American Northeast, high-winter, but that seemed a rare pleasure here, a break from the everyday grayness, *la grisaille*.

The question came from ten feet away, off behind Kate. She didn't want to turn to face this conversation, but she did want to eavesdrop.

"What about them?"

"They're leaving. May have already left."

"Back to America?" This woman's voice sounded familiar. "Why?"

The giant door opened, and children began to emerge from the building, dazed by the glaring sunshine.

"I don't know. All I heard was that they're leaving. From Samantha. You know she works at Luxembourg Relocation Experts? She just received a listing for the Macleans' apartment. Checked with the broker, and found out that they're being released from their lease because they're returning to America, for work. Immediately."

Jake walked into the sunshine, looking around for his mother, finding her, his face lighting up, as it always did, every day. "Hi Mommy."

Kate turned and glanced at the gossiping women. One was a vaguely familiar face with vague bits of information. Kate felt this woman's eyes upon her, a known confederate of Julia Maclean, possibly tainted by whatever had forced the departed into their flight.

The other woman, the one with the familiar voice, was Plain Jane. She met Kate's eye, then looked down, in unmistakable shame. She probably thought this was about herself; her affair with Bill had ruined his marriage. We all see ourselves as the center of everything.

◆ ◆ ◆

THE WINTER EBBED away. They spent a week in Barcelona, warmer than the north of the continent, jacket weather instead of coats. A weekend drive to Hamburg. A weekend flight to Vienna. Foreign places, in foreign tongues.

Kate spent a solo weekend in wintry Paris, down on the Friday-morning TGV, a comfortable two-hour ride, then an invigorating walk from Gare de l'Est to lunch in a covered market, oilskin-covered tables and steam billowing from the Vietnamese stall, batter sizzling on the wide crepe pans, plates of architectural pigs' feet. Popped in and out of the grand department stores on the Grands Boulevards. Visited the Louvre.

On Saturday, late afternoon, she stood on the Pont Neuf, the river glinting smooth and silvery in the winter light. She retied her new scarf around her neck, tighter, warmer. She crossed back to the busy buzzing of the Left Bank, the cafés and brasseries packed for early-evening drinks and cigarettes, sunlight slipping away and replaced with electric. Waiting for a traffic light to change on a corner of the Place St-Michel, packed with hundreds of people, Kate noticed that the tree branch hanging over the intersection was beginning to bud.

✦ ✦ ✦

WHEN THEY LEFT Luxembourg for the summer holiday in the South of France, they thought they'd be returning in five weeks. Assumed they'd be sending the kids back to the same school, in new grades. But in that month on the Mediterranean they reexamined their plan. Did they really want to live in Luxembourg? Did they need to?

What they needed—what they *had* needed—was for Dexter to be able to open the ultra-protected numbered accounts that his scheme required. He'd needed to incorporate a *société anonyme* that would operate in a business to which no authority would give a second thought: financial-markets investing, in Luxembourg. They needed to pay income taxes somewhere that wasn't under the jurisdiction of the FBI.

Did it need to be Luxembourg? No. It could've been Switzerland, or the Cayman Islands, or Gibraltar, or any number of tidy little privacy-friendly nation-states. Dexter had visited them all, back in the year before they'd moved. He'd chosen Lux because it seemed like the nicest tax haven in which to live. It was a real place, not a remote island in the Irish Sea nor a country club in the Caribbean nor a rocky outcrop of the Pyrenees. It had a thriving expat community, good schools, easy access to the cultural riches of Western Europe.

And no one in America knew what Luxembourg was. When Americans heard you were moving to Zurich or Grand Cayman, they assumed you were hiding money, or on the run, or both. No one knew what you were doing in Luxembourg.

All in all, Kate had to admit that Luxembourg had been a good choice, for the whole family. But it ended up compromised by the way it started. And by the Macleans.

Now that the Luxembourg S.A. was established, now that Dexter was making a legitimate—and surprisingly lucrative—living through his investment enterprise, now that they had residency visas and E.U. driver's licenses, now that they'd filed income taxes in Luxembourg . . . now that all that was done, did they need to remain in Luxembourg?

No.

✦ ✦ ✦

IT WAS THE children who made friends on the beach at St. Tropez. And then the next day the grown-ups introduced themselves. And then the following day they were all together on the same beach again, and later in the week over lunch, chilled rosé and the cheerful babble of expat Americans on vacation. Kate listened to anecdotes of life in Paris, and the international school in St-Germain, and the newly soft real-estate market . . .

Then they were on the early flight from Marseille, the boys' hair washed and combed, shirts tucked, the taxi from the airport to the school, the quick interviews with the children and the longer ones with the adults. And then shaking hands with the admissions officer, smiling, listening to assurances that there were spots for the boys.

They had snacks and drinks at the Flore. Then they set off again, a sultry summer weekday. They came across the *agence immobiliere,* its windows festooned with glossy photographs of apartments. They introduced themselves, and went on a quick house tour.

In the morning, they signed the school's contract, and the apartment's lease.

◆ ◆ ◆

LUXEMBOURG SEEMED EMPTY in mid-August. Or empty of expats. Kate's friends were all on family holidays—the Americans in America, the Europeans in rented seaside cottages in Sweden, or whitewashed villas in the mountains of Spain, or pastels with pools in Umbria.

Kate walked around the old town, the familiar faces of the shopkeepers, the vendors in the Place Guillaume market, the waitresses on their cigarette breaks, the palace guards. All these people whose names she didn't know, who were part of the texture of her life. She felt like she should say farewell to each and every one of them.

She wished her friends were here, now. She felt the urge to sit in a café with Claire and Cristina and Sophia, have a final round of coffee, a final round of hugs. But it was probably better this way. She hated good-byes.

Kate returned to the apartment, a ham sandwich in a wax-paper bag, and resumed the task of sorting through the boys' toys, picking out the discards, the donations, the keepers. They were with Dexter at the pirate-ship playground, for the last time.

It would be easier, Kate knew, the second time around. The hard parts would be less hard, the fun parts more fun. Like with the second kid, Ben: it would be less intimidating, less difficult, less bewildering, with the benefit of the prior experience.

They still needed to maintain some type of Luxembourg residency, a place from which to file taxes, where they could pretend to live. The little rented farmhouse in the Ardennes, for a thousand a month, would serve perfectly. There was a pile of farmhouse-bound boxes shoved into the corner of the living room, packed with inexpensive lamps and cast-off dishes and mismatched flatware. With a lock-box where they would stash a million in cash.

The Colonel's money was otherwise untouched, sitting in the same numbered account, possibly forever. It was now twenty-four million.

Kate looked out the window at the expansive view, the broad swath of Europe in her sight line, this brief home of hers. Tears welled in her eyes. She felt a heavy weight of despair at the end of this. At the inexorable march of her life forward, toward its inevitable end.

32

The memories are beginning to fade, to take on an undefined tinge at the edges, a vagueness that creeps toward the center, eroding Kate's confidence that the events actually occurred. It would make a lot more sense if she had imagined this whole thing, her whole life. Now would just be now, attached to some other, more straightforward past.

It's been a year and a half since Kate and Julia were standing in the freezing rain on the exposed platform hanging over the monteé du Clausen, both armed and angry and unsure if one of them was going to have to kill the other.

Now in this Parisian café they meet each other's eyes sheepishly, like new lovers after their first fight.

Julia's body is leaning toward Bill's, pulled magnetically. There's something different in the way this woman and that man are together now. Perhaps more natural than they'd been before, back in Luxembourg. More something. Or maybe less.

"So," Julia says, "what have you been up to?" She directs this to Kate. Now that the men have finished the men's business of arms deals and dismemberments.

Kate glances at Dexter. He doesn't meet her eye, won't offer any guidance. He seems completely comfortable, as if there's no possible downside to this interaction, nothing that can go wrong, no bad turn it can take. Which makes Kate doubly sure that she's right about what really happened among them. Triply. Kate is immeasurably sure.

What she doesn't understand is how she's supposed to converse with these people, as if they're all normal, and this is a real meeting among genuine friends, or even a tense confrontation between foes. What degree of honesty could Julia be expecting? What type of conversation does this woman think they're going to have?

"Why Paris?" Julia asks. She hopes maybe a more specific question will generate an answer.

"Why not?" is Kate's terse response.

Bill holds up his hands, gesturing at their surroundings. "Because this?" he asks. "This is fucking awful."

There's a pleading in Julia's eyes. "Come on, Kate. I'm not asking for much, here. We don't need to be . . . friends . . ."

Kate turns her eyes down.

"But we don't have to be enemies, Kate. We're not enemies. We're not here . . . this isn't . . ." She trails off, stares off.

Kate takes a long look at Julia, hands folded, elbows on the table, leaning forward, eyebrows raised, head cocked at an angle, eager to hear any tiny irrelevant detail of any beside-the-point story. Anything. In this pose of avidness, Kate thinks she recognizes something odd: friendship.

"I . . ." Kate suddenly feels terribly sad. "What do you want me to tell you, Julia?"

"I don't know, Kate. Anything. Do you miss Luxembourg?"

Kate shrugs.

"I do," Julia admits. "I miss my friends. I miss you, Kate."

Kate has to look away, fighting the urge to cry.

"Ladies," Bill says, raising his glass. "Let's not be maudlin. To Luxembourg!"

Kate watches Julia raise her glass, slosh some wine on her lips, then replace the glass on the tabletop. "To Luxembourg."

✦ ✦ ✦

"So forgive my bluntness," Kate says, taking the step that no one else seems willing to take, "but why are you here?"

Julia and Bill exchange a quick glance. "We came," Julia says, "to tell you — to tell Dexter — about the Colonel."

"Ah." Kate nods. "I see."

Silence again.

"I don't understand," Kate picks up, "why that needs to be in person. In fact, I don't understand why you would want to do that at all. Dexter is, after all, someone you investigated — accused — of a major crime, of which you obviously still think he's guilty."

"We were also friends," Julia says.

Kate leans forward. "Were we?"

They stare at each other, the two women. "I thought so. I still do."

"But . . ." Kate tries to paint her bewilderment — her betrayal — all over her face.

"I was doing — we were doing — what we needed to do."

Kate is relieved that Julia isn't claiming she was just doing her job. At least she's being honest about that. Because her job was the last thing she was doing.

304

"There's something else," Bill says, rejoining the fray. "We wanted to tell you that now that the Colonel is dead, the investigation is closed."

"Completely?" Dexter asks.

For a moment everyone sits quietly in the loud Parisian twilight. Bill empties his glass, refills it. "Completely. And permanently."

◆ ◆ ◆

A blue-suited policeman is leaning on a car, flirting with a young woman who's straddling a moped, smoking a cigarette. Kate's eyes are drawn to the cop's carelessly dangling gun. It would be easy to overcome him, to seize his weapon while he's distracted with other, more French, priorities.

Kate turns back to her companions. Are any of these people ever going to come clean with her? Will she herself come completely clean with any of them?

For the past year, Kate had been thoroughly honest with Dexter. Or nearly. And she'd thought he'd been thoroughly honest with her. But she was disabused of that illusion this afternoon. Now she can't believe it had taken her all this time to check his yearbook; now she sees there was a tremendous degree of denial in that oversight.

It was just a small photo she found, poorly reproduced in washed-out color. Third row from the top of the page, second from the right: an unremarkably pretty woman with a big smile and pale pink lip gloss and feathered blond hair.

"So," Kate says, "what are you going to do with your half?"

The same unremarkably pretty woman now sitting across the table, eyebrows raised, smile wiped away, pretending to be surprised. "Our half of what?"

"Your half of the money."

◆ ◆ ◆

Neither Julia nor Bill responds in any way—no facial expression, no body movement, no sound, no nothing: the practiced non-response of the professional liar. But these two are too obvious about it. They're not as good actors as Kate would've thought; not nearly as good as she herself is. Maybe it's true what everyone in the CIA has been asserting for the half-century grudge match between the institutions: FBI agents are just not as good as CIA ones. Or maybe they, like Kate herself, are simply out of practice.

"What money?" Julia asks.

Kate smiles patronizingly. "Haven't decided yet?" She glances at each of her three companions, at the protective veneers they're all wearing, trying to mask the different lies they've told one another. The lies they're all continuing to try to maintain. Hoping these lies will carry them through the rest of their full and satisfying lives, despite the truths they've chosen not to tell the most important people in their worlds.

Kate keeps her eyes on the primary culprit, Julia. When Kate realized this afternoon that Dexter and Julia—real name of Susan Pognowski—had known each other in college, her first thought was that this was a plan they'd hatched together, way back then, or soon after. But she couldn't reconcile this scenario with the reality of her Dexter. He was not that type of person. He was not a manipulator. He was the type of person who got manipulated.

Kate realized that this was it—Julia had masterminded the whole thing, tricked everyone. There had never been anything sexual between her and Dexter, nothing romantic. Just an extraordinary degree of deviousness and a mind-boggling capacity for planning and foresight.

Staring at that yearbook photo for the first time, Kate was hurt, and angry, and betrayed, and confused. But walking the noisy crowded streets of Paris, she'd figured out the whole thing, piece by piece. And as the puzzle unfolded, Kate became less and less angry at Dexter, more and more astounded by Julia. Standing in the rue St-Benoit, at the elegant turn formed by the corner of Le Petit Zinc, Kate forgave Dexter. After she'd walked another block, she'd revised her entire life's plan. And by the time she entered her apartment a few minutes later, she was ready to take the necessary action.

Kate understands why Dexter had to keep this particular secret from her. Because admitting it would entail admitting something else—that he knew Kate was CIA but never acknowledged it—that he couldn't abide. He couldn't stomach the thought of admitting to his wife the full extent to which he'd lied to her.

Dexter doesn't know that he's been forgiven. All he knows is that his ultimate deception has just been unearthed. He's now bristling with anxiety, barely able to stay seated. Kate is reminded of how she used to buckle the children into their high chairs so they wouldn't escape during meals. She imagines herself reaching over and snapping Dexter into his caned café chair, buckling him in. This surreal image makes her smile.

Kate's smile gives Julia the courage to break the silence. "What the hell are you talking about?"

Which prompts Kate to say, "I'm talking about your half of the fifty million euros." And then for good measure she adds, "Susan."

✦ ✦ ✦

Bill nearly chokes on his wine.

"Please," Kate says, "interrupt me when I get something wrong. Okay?"

Bill and Julia and Dexter all glance at one another in turn, the Three Stooges. They nod in unison.

"No one here grew up in Illinois," Kate says. "Bill, you didn't attend Chicago. Julia, you didn't go to any branch of the University of Illinois. You created this Chicago background because you knew I'd never been there, had no friends there. We'd never get a six-degrees-of-separation game off the ground. Bill, you're sort of irrelevant. You two"—she points to Dexter, Julia—"you met in one of two places: you were in the same dorm, or some type of small class. I'm guessing first semester freshman year."

For a moment neither Dexter nor Julia answers, both in knee-jerk denial that their jig is finally up. "Dorm," Julia admits, the first of the two to arrive at the conclusion that the truth—or at least this truth—is no longer avoidable. "Freshman year."

"And something pushed your relationship beyond dorm-mates. What?"

"We had a class together, second semester," Julia says. "French."

"So you were fast friends as freshmen, when it was easy to become friends with anyone. Just like being an expat."

Kate has a flashback to the day she met Julia. That night, standing with Dexter in their bathroom, brushing teeth side by side, telling him that their new life felt like freshman year. And she'd met a woman from Chicago. Dexter had kidded that Kate couldn't be friends with this new woman, what with her pretend antipathy toward Chicago. He'd been so cool. Kate had never imagined her husband capable of such deception. She's impressed with Dexter, despite it all.

"But you gravitated into different cliques," Kate continues. "By graduation, you weren't really friends anymore. No one from college would identify you as friends. If your classmates were interviewed, none of them would remember that you two had been close. Because basically only the two of you knew about your relationship, right? You had no public history. Only your private one."

Still no responses. No corrections.

"So fifteen years went by. You"—inclining her head at Julia—"were working at the FBI. Your specialty was investigating cyber crime. Online consumer banking had exploded, going from zero to billions in a couple years, then in another half-decade it was pretty much all the money in the world, transferred via the web. You'd become an expert investigator in this field, at the top of the FBI pecking order. Yes?"

"Yes."

Kate turns to Dexter. "You were working at a bank. You too had become a different type of leading expert, in the same field. Then one day, out of the blue and out in public, you ran into your old friend, your ex-friend. Where did this happen?"

"A bookstore," Dexter answers quietly.

"How quaint. So here in a bookstore, this old friend invited you to a drink, right? Sure, you answered, I'd love to catch up. So you met at some M Street bar, engaged in idle chitchat, then bam, Julia laid out this scheme of hers. She'd

307

figured out a way for your expertise and hers to dovetail into a massive payday. Someday. Yes?"

"Basically."

"Her plan was that if you two could figure out how to hack banking transactions, and you could execute the theft, she could guarantee that you wouldn't get caught. Because she'd be the one doing the chasing. You two would split the booty.

"So you must've danced around each other. Julia, you must've monitored him. *Us*. You discovered that I'd run out of steam in my career. That we had no money. That Dexter, unlike other computer nerds of his generation, had never even come close to making a fortune. He was mildly bitter about this, and he was financially motivated."

Kate stares at the diabolical woman across the table, with her relatively feckless partners on either side of her. "And of course you knew he harbored a deep-seated long-term revenge fantasy against the person who murdered his brother." Still debating whether she's going to let this huge cat out of the bag. Yes or no, no or yes . . .

Kate opens her mouth to add the new twist, the single-word accusation. The word that will change everything for Dexter, again: "Supposedly."

33

Dexter is obviously confused. Bill too. Both men's brows are furrowed.

"What do you mean, *supposedly?*" Dexter asks.

Julia steels her jaw, narrows her eyes. She knows that Kate knows the truth. And she knows that Kate is about to reveal it.

"While you were considering her proposal, Dex"—Kate turns back to her husband—"in the midst of your due diligence, did you receive an update about the Colonel? Something extra-compelling about how evil he was?"

Dexter doesn't shake his head, doesn't nod, doesn't blink, doesn't open his mouth. He stares, thinking, racing to catch up with his wife, to arrive at the conclusion before she says it aloud, to avoid that particular aspect of his humiliation.

Kate gives her husband a grin, a bit of a boast of victory. Bad sportsmanship, admittedly. Even though she's forgiven him, she's still enjoying the look of embarrassed surprise on his face.

"Of course you did, sweetheart." She feels entitled to extract some revenge, which is this, now: revealing that he'd been conned by this person whom he trusted. It will be painful, but it won't last long. Unlike the con itself, which spanned a decade.

Kate can practically hear Dexter's gears churning, smell the smoke, as he figures out that his anonymous Croatian source was bogus, an imposter, another paid actor in the complexly plotted play. Dexter turns to the playwright, Julia.

Here is his aha moment. His mouth actually falls open.

❖ ❖ ❖

"*You* were my source?"

Julia stares at Dexter unapologetically. "Yes."

His eyes are bugged. He's trying to digest the enormity of this revelation, reaching back into his memory for the new beginning of this story. "I told you about Daniel's death," he says, "back in college?"

"Yes."

"And when you first started working at the FBI, you looked into it? That's when you found out that the Colonel was the one who'd killed Daniel?"

Kate sees the childlike expression on Dexter's face. A grown man who's desperately willing reality to bend to his conception. Hoping that if he asserts his idea aloud and with confidence, the world will agree with him.

This is exactly how the children sound and look when they're testing theories about pirates or dinosaurs or space-travel options. "If we let our hair grow long, like birds," Ben explained to her, just this morning, "then we'd be able to fly. Right, Mommy?"

Julia doesn't say anything, reticent to be the one to shatter this last iota of Dexter's naïveté.

He looks into his wineglass. Kate can see that he's peeling back the layers: if there had never been any secret Croatian source, that meant there had never been a State Department official who connected him with the source. Which meant there had never been a report on the brutality of Daniel's death. Which meant . . .

"Colonel Petrovic didn't have anything to do with Daniel's death, did he?"

Kate reaches her hand across the table, takes her husband's, squeezes.

"Wow," Dexter says. His eyebrows have climbed as high as they can up his forehead. He pulls his hand out of Kate's, leans away from the table, retreating into himself, seeking privacy in his humliation. "Wow."

"I'm sorry," Julia says. "Petrovic was still an awful, awful person. He —"

Dexter holds up his hand. "Let me get this straight." He glowers at Julia. "You fabricated the State phone call that alerted me to the fiction that the Colonel killed my brother. You fabricated his death report, and you fabricated an official to give me that report, and to connect me with a fabricated Croatian expat, who over the course of — how long? a decade? — supplied me with fabricated information about the Colonel?"

"In a nutshell," Julia admits.

No one says anything.

"The Croatian word *niko,*" Julia adds, "means *nobody.*"

Dexter lets out a loud, ugly guffaw.

"But I want to clarify," Julia continues, "that most of the information about the Colonel was accurate."

"Just not the parts that had anything to do with Daniel. And thus with me."

Kate glances over at Bill, silent. She's guessing that he too didn't know anything about this aspect of the backstory. But he doesn't particularly care; this sideshow is pure entertainment for him. He has his own fundamental dishonesties to protect.

"You funneled updates to me via so-called Niko," Dexter continues, "getting me further and further on the hook, more and more invested in the story of this illegal arms dealer who'd supposedly butchered my brother. All so that I'd be motivated—I'd be compelled—to help you steal from a rich man. Is that right?"

"Yes."

"So you hatched this plan a dozen years ago?"

"Yes."

"I don't understand," Dexter says, wearing his bewilderment all over his face. "What would you have done if in the meantime the Colonel got killed? Or went broke? Or what if I didn't cooperate? After all that time invested in me?"

"What makes you think," Julia asks, "that you were the only one?"

✦ ✦ ✦

"Monsieur," Julia calls out as the waiter passes. *"Une carafe d'eau, s'il vous plaît."*

Kate notices that Julia's French accent has improved markedly, now that she's no longer pretending to have a bad one.

"What do you mean?" Dexter asks.

"I'm rather thirsty," Julia says to her companions, killing time before their privacy is reinstated. The waiter pours two glasses, for the ladies. Julia takes a long drink, emptying her glass. She refills it, leaving everyone on the hook, bated breath. A strange uncomfortable cloud crosses her face. Then she says, "You weren't my only option."

"I don't understand."

"You and the Colonel weren't the only antagonists I set up."

Now it's Kate's mind that's racing to catch up. But she doesn't get there before Julia starts talking again. "Dexter, you're not the only person in the world who could've pulled off this intrusion. In fact, I'm sorry to tell you that in many ways you're the least qualified. Frankly, I'm surprised it turned out to be you."

"Huh?"

"I spent years—I spent my career—identifying the most clever, most out-of-the-box thinkers in the field of online security. And then I met with all of them. I asked them about their deepest, darkest secrets. Their greatest fears and strongest desires. Their simmering resentments and uncontrollable hatreds. The pressure points at which they could be manipulated."

"How did you manage this?"

"It's pretty easy and completely justifiable to ask anyone anything, when you work for the FBI and you're interviewing job candidates, or conducting an investigation."

At every turn, Kate has become more and more awed.

"In the end, I had a half-dozen of you hackers on the hook."

"If I'm the least qualified, then why'd you choose me?"

"I didn't. I proposed this scheme to all of you. Whoever got there first won."

"And I discovered it first?" Dexter is trying to suppress his pride, mere seconds after digesting a soul-crushing insult.

"Yes. But in the meantime I discovered a bit of a problem." Julia turns to Kate. "Until we set the wheels in motion, I didn't know about you, Kate. I'd done my background on Dexter, of course. But I didn't bother with deep investigations of all my candidates' wives and girlfriends and mothers' ex-boyfriends. But when he showed up with his dual-intrusion gambit, I did."

"And?"

"And I honestly had to consider ditching the whole plan. Or just ditching Dexter, coming up with a reason why it wasn't going to work out with him, pass along his idea to someone else to execute. I also had to consider that maybe I was being set up; a sting. But then I realized that, remarkably, Dexter didn't know about you."

Kate didn't like hearing this bit out loud, here in semi-public. She herself felt entitled to humiliate her duplicitous husband. But she didn't want Julia to be able to do it. He'd already been humiliated enough, by Julia.

"Dexter was too legit," Julia continued. "His life was too verifiable, too above-board. He was nobody's spy, nobody's mole, nobody's rat. He was who he is. And he didn't know that you weren't."

"So what did you do?"

"I told him."

"Why?"

"I had no choice. Dexter was the guy who had the answer. He was the guy who could get the money. It had taken a long time to arrive at that point, and I wasn't confident that any of my other candidates would be able. I would have to go with Dexter and his plan. Or I'd have to extract his whole process from him, then kill him."

Dexter blurts out a laugh, then realizes this wasn't a joke. He frowns.

"But of course killing the spouse of a CIA analyst was ill-advised. So instead I needed to make sure Dexter was extra-careful around you. However secretive he thought he had to be, he had to double it. He had to initiate no contact with me, ever. He had to follow every instruction exactly to the letter. He had to know that however serious he'd thought this was, it was much more serious."

"How did you know he'd believe you?"

"Hey, I'm sitting right here."

"Why did you believe her?" Kate asks.

"Because why would she lie about that?"

"Why couldn't you just tell me?"

It's Julia who answers, with a snort. "C'mon," she says, "tell a CIA officer that we're plotting to hack into banking transactions and steal a fortune?"

"Valid point. So then what?"

"So we—that is, I—set up the whole series of transactions to be traceable to Dexter only. He would be the only person who saw a penny, for a long time. He was the one who'd be guilty of the major crimes and the associated misdemeanors: the falsification of records, the break-ins, the frauds, the American Health theft. Which provided the operational budget, including your family's funds. Which also served as the initial crime that I unearthed—rather easily, obviously—and reported to my superiors, to get myself assigned the case of investigating this new type of problem. This unstoppable form of electronic hijacking. I even had a prime suspect, who I predicted would flee the country. As it turned out, I was right. That cemented that the case was mine. I clearly had a nose for what was going to happen next."

"This whole thing seems to depend on you being the one leading the investigation," Kate says. "Why?"

"Because Dexter can get caught."

"I can?"

"Of course you can. There's a tremendous amount of evidence that incriminates you, Dexter. Records of you opening and closing the accounts—even some photos and videos of you at the banks—through which the stolen money was routed."

Dexter looks confused, again.

"There are records of your relationship with that call girl you hired to commit prostitution, fraud, and theft. There's the girl herself, obviously, and her wildly damaging testimony that you conspired to do exactly what you did, actually, do."

Dexter shakes his head.

"This is convincing evidence. Of serious crimes."

"I don't understand," he says.

But Kate does. "It's her insurance policy, you nitwit." Poor guy.

"Is this true?" He is stunned anew by Julia's duplicity.

"I needed to make sure that you'd live up to your end of the bargain," Julia admits. "I needed to be able to compel you. And in the meantime I also needed to be the one at the Bureau, so I could make sure that no one else discovered what I knew was out there—because I created it—to be discovered."

Kate perks up at the end of this little speech, exactly the type of admission she'd been waiting to hear. "So then me," Kate says, looking to drive some nails into the coffin, as part of her own bargain.

"Yes, you," Julia says. "The wrench in my machine. Well, I had to make sure this CIA wife wouldn't rat out her husband. I didn't think she would; I couldn't imagine that a woman would ruin her own life just because her husband was a thief. After all, he was stealing from someone who he thought was the very worst scum of the earth—the man who murdered his brother. Talk about a justifiable crime. And of course that first million, from the shit-heel mouthpieces of the heartless insurance company, was a no-brainer.

"But I had to be sure, didn't I? Positive. I had to test the wife. Had to lure her inside, make her realize that her husband was guilty. That the FBI was pursuing him, and they were right. Had to let her discover the truth, and see what she did with it."

"I'm flattered you took me so seriously."

"Well, to be honest, I also had another motivation for confronting you."

"Which was what?"

"Which was," Bill pipes up, "me."

✦ ✦ ✦

Kate continues to be impressed with this woman's extraordinary acts of deceit, tucked into her massive web of falsification.

"So the whole time you were in Luxembourg," Kate says to Bill, "you thought you were on a legitimate investigation?"

"I did."

"Hah!" Kate turns to Julia. "Well done, Julia. Absolutely brilliant."

"Thank you."

"So the mission you two were on," Kate says, "totally aboveboard, properly authorized by the FBI: you were investigating that first million that Dexter stole. Julia, you were the lead investigator. This handsome clown was your partner."

Julia nods.

"So you two were *sent*"—air quotes—"to Luxembourg. Posing as a couple. Keeping your eye on my poor husband, seeing what money he was spending, watching his lifestyle. Was this a guy who just stole a million dollars? Was this the guy who had figured out how to steal limitless amounts of money, anytime he wanted?"

Kate shakes her head. "He was living in a modest apartment. He stayed in cramped rooms in midrange hotels, flew coach, went to the office every day. His wife was scrubbing her own toilets. He went to Esch-sur-Alzette to purchase a used Audi. Millionaires don't go to Esch at all, much less to buy secondhand station wagons."

That same secondhand Audi was still their car. They hadn't gotten around to buying anything new. Or perhaps they'd simply decided, without discussing it, that the old Audi was nice enough. It was just a car, after all.

"No, you determined, this guy was not that criminal mastermind, and this family was not rich. Nevertheless, your job was to be positive. Because sooner or later you needed to go back to the J. Edgar Hoover Building, a full report in hand, with your career on the line. So what did you do?"

The waiter comes by with a replacement carafe of water, and Kate waits for him to back away down the Parisian sidewalk, dusk falling, lights coming on. The dinner-hour crowd promenading through the *carrefour* is thick, jostling, merry. Kate feels a rush of well-being, in this pleasant place with these clever people, whom she finally understands fully, and this plot that she finds herself appreciating more every second, as if she's not a participant. The whole thing is goddamn brilliant.

"I give you credit," Kate says. "I love this bit. What you did was you tried to turn the suspect's wife. First, you erected a flimsy cover, one you knew would make me suspicious: Chicago. Then you allowed me to know exactly when I'd have the opportunity to break into Bill's office—you manipulated me into suggesting their midday tennis date, didn't you?"

Julia picks up her wineglass and takes another minuscule sip, savoring the drop of wine. Savoring the story being constructed around her, about her own ingenuity.

"And in this office, I found nothing much to support your cover story. Which would've been easy to fabricate. Yet you did not. Instead, you left a weapon lying around, along with a bunch of condoms. You constructed a fake office that looked exactly like a fake office, for a fake profession. You were from a fake place that I knew would be fake, and you had a fake marriage that looked exactly like a fake marriage. You led me by the hand to all these fakeries. Why?"

"Because I wanted you to find them."

"Yes. But why?"

"So I could control your discoveries. So you would find out who we were, what we were doing. You would discover that your husband was guilty; the one with the money. The one who could be arrested, indicted. I needed you to get invested in being a part of this crime. *His* crime. And I needed you to be able to figure that out for yourself."

Kate grins at the irony.

"Well, not exactly for yourself," Julia admits. "But close enough."

❖ ❖ ❖

Kate feels her eyes drawn to the metal dispenser that holds the sugar cubes where, an hour ago, she discreetly inserted Hayden's transmitter. Her end of the bargain.

"So who was Lester?" Kate asks. "Your fake father not from New Mexico?"

"Les is our boss."

"Why was he here?"

"This was right after the big theft. Les wanted to see our suspect and his wife, for himself. Were these the people who had just stolen fifty million euros? He quizzed the wife about her dining-out habits in foreign capitals. He wanted to know how many stars the hotels posted. The answer: it was pretty unlikely that these were the thieves. Nevertheless, Dexter was still the prime suspect. The only suspect, considering of course that he was guilty. So Lester gave it another month to bring the investigation to a close."

"That's when you decided to confront me."

"Yes. You used to be a patriot, after all." Julia smiles. "And plus we could show you evidence that looked an awful lot like your husband was having an affair with a beautiful young woman in five-star Swiss hotels. You yourself had never slept in a five-star hotel. They don't have those in Nicaragua, do they?"

"No, they don't."

"So we confronted you, to see what you'd do, and bring it to a close."

Kate remembers that early-January day, the three of them sitting on the cold park bench. When Julia said aloud the wrong number — twenty-five million. The look on Bill's face as he tried to figure out what that discrepancy could've meant. The amount of stolen money, he knew, was double that.

Bill looks at Kate now, the same open, unabashed stare that she'd seen before, in the nightclub in Paris, on the Grand Rue in Luxembourg. A look that admits, *You know who I am.* But that also challenges, *What are you going to do about it?*

Kate had underestimated Bill. He'd known the truth well before Julia told him.

Once again, Kate realizes that she'd totally missed a big piece of the puzzle. And this piece? That Bill had been running his own private con. And the person he'd conned was Julia.

34

"You're kidding." Hayden had the tiniest of smiles playing across his lips.

"No," Kate said. "I'm not."

It was nearly six o'clock. After-work tipplers had begun to arrive at the Georges, tourists with early dinner reservations. One of Hayden's colleagues had slipped the maître d' a twenty to buy a perimeter of privacy. But that wouldn't last long.

"What do you imagine you'd *do*?" Hayden asked.

"I'm fluent in Spanish. And now I'm passable in French. I know a bit about Europe. I can make my way around an embassy, or a consulate, or an NGO office. I haven't forgotten how to do the things that need doing."

"Except you don't know anyone. You don't have *any* contacts."

This was exactly why Julia claimed she couldn't be a decorator in Luxembourg. A short-term excuse. A bogus rationalization. "I realize I'd have to start low on the totem pole. And probably stay there, near the bottom. Forever."

Hayden leaned away from the table. "Why would you want to do this?"

It had taken Kate so long to admit that she'd no longer wanted her job, her career. That she'd wanted to be a full-time mother. But over the past two years she'd discovered that she'd been mistaken. This wasn't, after all, what she wanted.

"My kids are in school, my days are . . . they're empty, unless I find ways to fill them. But I need a reason to fill them. A reason better than boredom."

She knew it wouldn't really be her old job. She'd probably never again carry a weapon; she'd never feel the intense rush of mortal danger lurking outside the door of the next asset meeting. So it would be a weak approximation of her old life, her old career, her old adrenaline. But it would be more than nothing.

On the other hand, it would be a more civilized work environment. Plus she now had a lot of money, and lived in Paris, and her increasingly independent children no longer wore diapers, and she had a closer relationship with her husband . . . she had a lot. She wanted just a little more.

"What I don't want," she continued, "is to worry about my children being abducted by some Latin psychopath. I'm more than willing to have a soft, quiet job."

Hayden started. "So that was it?"

"I'm sorry?"

"Torres threatened your family?"

Kate didn't answer. She wasn't going to admit to a cold-blooded, premeditated assassination of a foreign national on American soil. "I'm willing to make compromises," she said, pushing past that old transgression, knowing that Hayden too would allow this large sleeping dog to lie unmolested. "And I'm here to make a deal."

"Okay. What can you offer?"

"The culprit on the stolen fifty million."

"Interesting."

"In return, I get my job back."

He nodded. "De*light*ed."

"Good," she said.

He reached across the table, his hand extended, to shake on it.

"But," she said, "there's a complication."

His smile fell, along with his hand. "Which is . . . ?"

"I need immunity. For me. And my husband."

"Immunity? For putting bullets in Torres? *Please.* No one has ever even thought about investi — "

"That's not it."

"Is it another murder you're talking about?"

"I don't know what you mean by *another*," she said, still refusing to be incriminated in that old mess. "But no, it's not a murder. It's white-collar. Sort of."

He raised his eyebrows.

"So do we have a deal?"

Hayden didn't respond for a few seconds, staring at Kate, waiting for her to say more. Finally resigning himself that she wouldn't.

"I'm sorry, Kate," he said. "No."

Kate was due across the river in an hour, to meet Julia and Bill and Dexter. And she needed to get there early, before the others. Before her husband.

She gazed out over the city, the streets that radiated from the museum, the mishmash of rooftops. Resigning herself that she would, after all, need to tell Hayden the truth. If not the entire truth, at least some more of it.

◆ ◆ ◆

Kate wonders if Hayden himself is in the work van around the corner, listening to this conversation. Or maybe he's across the street, watching. When she left him two and a half hours ago, he was unclear what his involvement would be in the rest of the evening. Hayden was skilled at being unclear.

"Your Hail Mary," Kate says, turning her attention back to Julia, "was confronting me. But this got you nothing. Worse than nothing, because then we cut off all contact with you. You no longer had access to your suspect. Your investigation was now at a permanent-looking impasse. Game over. And suddenly the whole town seemed to be ostracizing you."

"I've been meaning to ask," Julia says. "Who'd you tell, what?"

"I told Amber Mandelbaum, Southern Jewish supermom and gadfly extraordinaire, that Julia—my best friend!—had shoved her tongue down my husband's throat. What a bitch. Obviously, we could no longer be friends."

"Obviously."

"So you left," Kate says. "You didn't have many friends to begin with—you weren't in Luxembourg to make a real life, after all—and it probably came as a relief to you, Bill, to get away from your mistress. I imagine Jane was challenging. Demanding."

Julia bristles.

"But I guess that technically speaking she wasn't a mistress, since you weren't really married to anyone else."

Bill remains unresponsive.

"Anyway, you went back to Washington empty-handed. You were sorry—ashamed—to admit that you'd been mistaken: Dexter Moore was not the thief. Interpol file closed. You were back in the full-time clutches of the Bureau, the old grind. But after you'd invested so much time in such an expensive and spectacularly unsuccessful investigation, your star was glowing a lot less bright. Wasn't it, Julia?"

Julia doesn't answer.

"So it came as no surprise when you quit. Especially since it had become known that while you two were posing as a couple, you'd become an actual couple."

Bill shifts in his seat. Dexter is, once again, confused, and wearing it all over his face. Julia gives him a nod, an admission. He shakes his head in wonder.

"This happens frequently, doesn't it?" Kate continues. "Never happened to me, mind you. But I saw it happen plenty of times. To other operations officers."

Kate stops talking, wonders how much to push the rest of it, whether there's any upside. She knows that one of the most dangerous, self-destructive indulgences is to go around proving how smart you are. It's the type of thing that gets people shot.

But she can't seem to help herself. "So Julia, when did you bring Bill inside?"

"Does it matter?"

"To me it does."

"I told him after I quit," Julia says. "After we quit."

Kate's mind is dragged backward, through the past year and a half in France, back to Luxembourg, to the winter before last, past the night in the restaurant when she and Dexter had playacted for the benefit of the FBI's transmitter, and the previous night when he'd come clean—almost entirely—to Kate.

"You'd been seeing each other how long?"

"A few months."

Kate glances at Bill, who's been silent, letting someone else tell his side of the story. Or rather from his half of the narrative.

"Why'd you tell him?"

"I love him," Julia says. "We're making our lives together." She holds up the ring finger. "We're engaged."

"That's nice," Kate says, a wry half-smile. "Congratulations. But when did you guys first hook up?"

"What do you care?" Bill asks. He's now on alert, his sheath of calm slipping off. Kate suspects he knows exactly where her line of questioning is headed, and why.

"I'm curious. Trying to get the whole story right."

Bill is staring at her, a hard look in his eyes, jaw muscles twitching. Kate knows that he knows that she knows.

"Toward the end," Julia answers. "Right before we left Luxembourg."

Kate's mind alights on that outdoor bench in Kirchberg, when she was confronted by Bill and Julia in the cold.

"So you weren't together over Christmas, in the Alps?"

Julia snickers.

"On New Year's Eve you didn't get drunk and fuck?"

Kate didn't notice when Bill's right hand disappeared under the table, but it did.

"No."

Kate's memory comes to a screeching halt back when Julia said "twenty-five million euros" and Bill looked confused, opening his mouth to say something, to correct Julia that the number was fifty million, but then closing it, letting Julia's slip slide, letting it sit and simmer and stew, checking with the home office in D.C., confirming that the amount that had been stolen from the Colonel was fifty million, double what Julia had alleged to Kate's face, a bizarre discrepancy, too neat and tidy to have been an utterly random case of misremembering, convinced that there must be a logical explanation, puzzling the possible reasons, and finally figuring it out, maybe seeing the whole plot from a bird's-eye view, laid out underneath to be examined at leisure, understanding the immense amount of money at stake, and deciding to use his strengths—his looks and his charm and his ability to keep a giant secret, forever—against her weaknesses—her insecurity and loneliness and desperate desire to have a family, in the stark, unforgiving face of having absolutely no prospects for a husband.

"Maybe," Kate offers, "it was in Amsterdam?" She drops her hands into her lap, plants her palms on her thighs, and leans forward, shifting herself. Then she leans back in a different position, picking her left hand off her thigh and returning it to the table, this whole lean-shift maneuver a flimsy cover for leaving her right hand under the table, sliding into her handbag.

Bill too shifts in his seat, less dramatically than Kate, but accomplishing, she knows, the same thing.

Julia turns to her new beau. But not that new: this happened last January, a year and a half ago. A long time to be with someone you don't love. Or maybe Bill really does love Julia, now. Maybe he grew into it.

"Well," Kate says, "Amsterdam was a romantic place, I guess. What with all the drugs and prostitutes around." But she knows it was after Amsterdam. It was after the bench.

Kate burrows her right hand slowly and quietly past her compact and sunglasses and chewing gum and notebook and pens and key ring and stray pieces of paper, all the way to the bottom of the bag, where the heaviest things rest. One of them under a hard panel, which she opens.

They are now staring at each other, Kate and Bill, eyes locked. They're surrounded by thousands of people in the Carrefour de l'Odeon, dusk in early September, the weather and light and wine and café all picture-perfect. The Europe of everyone's imagination.

Kate closes her fingers around the grip of her Beretta.

Bill's right hand is still under the table.

Kate turns to Julia. An unhappy, lonely woman until this man came along. Now here they are, seemingly happy. Julia's face is glowing, her cheeks a high pink.

But there's this giant deception at the foundation of their relationship, their happiness. This impure motive. There was that small mistake that the woman made, uttering the wrong number. And then the man reconstructed an entire intrigue, a big thick plot — a seduction and affair and relationship and marriage proposal, a whole life — around her error and his notice of it. Taking advantage of her lie.

But does that make their relationship less real? Does that make it impossible that they genuinely love each other?

She turns to Bill, sees hardness, resolve. What will he do to protect his secret?

Kate and Bill are aiming handguns at each other, under the marble-topped table. Is he ready to kill her, now? Will he fire a gun here in the middle of Paris, shoot her in the gut? Will he become a permanent fugitive? Will he give up his whole life — his newly manufactured life — rather than allow Kate to reveal his truth to Julia?

His truth is that he figured out what his partner — and their suspect — were up to, together. But instead of confronting Julia, he got in on the scam. Pretending he didn't know what was going on; pretending to fall for her; pretending it was news when Julia finally told him the truth.

Kate glances back to Julia, this odd woman, so brilliant in so many ways, but so unable — or unwilling — to see something so plainly that's right in front of her eyes.

But who knows? Maybe Julia sees the truth perfectly well. Maybe Julia saw the truth way back before it even became the truth: maybe her slip-up of twenty-five million wasn't an error at all. Maybe she made a fake mistake, leading Bill on so that he would catch her, seduce her, marry her. Maybe she engineered that as well, along with the rest of the intricately manufactured long-play con.

And maybe Dexter hadn't left that yearbook in the living room by mistake.

As Kate's mind drifts, so do her eyes, ping-ponging between the conspirators and the contents of the tabletop, eventually resting on Julia's wineglass. Barely an inch off the top. They've been at this table an hour and a half, on their second bottle. But Julia hasn't had more than a couple of ounces. The woman who used to polish off a bottle at lunch is now guzzling water.

Julia has put on five kilos, maybe ten. Her face is flush, radiant.

"Oh my God," Kate blurts out, "you're pregnant!"

Julia blushes. Despite her claim two years ago that she couldn't bear children. Just another facet of the cover.

Pregnant. That changes everything.

◆ ◆ ◆

Kate and Hayden sat under the glowing sky, puffs of white clouds scattered as if arranged to break up the monotony of blue, lit from beneath by golden rays of low-angle sunlight. A painterly scene, Vermeer light.

Kate had never fully appreciated Northern European painting until she lived in Northern Europe. Until she realized that the artists' skies were not fanciful inventions, not imaginary distortions of reality, but accurate reflections of a unique skyscape. This wasn't what the sky looked like in Bridgeport, CT, or Washington, D.C., or Mexico City, DF, or any of the other places where she'd spent her life, sometimes staring at the sky.

"You need to tell me," Hayden said, "what the immunity would be for."

Their standoff resumed. But Kate knew that her stance was pure bluff, and his wasn't. She'd have to give in. Because she'd finally figured out what she wanted, what she needed, and Hayden could give it to her. But he didn't need a damn thing from her.

Plus she was rushed, and had to wrap this up now, and get back to the Left Bank. "It's for participating in the theft," she said. "Of the fifty million."

Hayden picked up his glass, took a long drink of water, replaced the glass on the table, and resumed staring at Kate.

"Think of it this way," she continued, "this was exactly the sort of operation that the Company would've run. This Colonel was a blight on the planet. Not just a horrible person, but a destabilizing force, an irresponsible maniac whose weaponry would someday — if it hadn't already — end up in the hands of people who wanted to do harm to Americans, maybe in America."

Hayden was unreadable.

"So we — not *me,* mind you, but . . . anyway, this Colonel was taken down. And in the meantime his money didn't end up in the hands of other people just like him. Plus there's a bonus that I think you'll find extra-inducing."

"Yes?"

"The culprit — well, the other culprit — is, if you can imagine it, an FBI agent."

He laughed, a thick meaty chortle, accompanied by an uncharacteristic snort. He thought this was pretty damn funny. "So what about the money?"

"We'll give it back," Kate said. "Well, not back, per se. We'll give it to . . . I don't know . . . you? Also, I have to admit that we don't exactly have all of it . . ."

Hayden looked away, at his colleagues across the rooftop, his minions, on the other side of the restaurant. Then back to Kate.

"So," she said. "Do we have a deal?"

◆ ◆ ◆

"Congratulations," Kate says. "When are you due?"

"I'm just . . . I'm not even four months yet."

"That's great," Kate says. She turns to Bill. "Congratulations."

His hand is still under the table, ready to protect his delicate, elegant wrapping of Julia's bulky package of lies. What's at stake for him is enormous: not just twenty-five million euros, but also a wife, a child. A whole life.

Kate will let this drop. She will keep quiet about his duplicity, forever.

She slides the Beretta back into the compartment at the bottom of her bag. She pulls her hand out, reaches across the table, lays her hand on Julia's, the engagement diamond sharp against the hard skin in her palm, her tennis-grip callus. She gives Julia a caress with her thumb.

Bill nods at Kate, a long blink, an unmistakable thank-you. He too shifts himself, and raises his arm, and wraps his newly empty right hand around his wineglass.

Kate doesn't want this woman to give birth in prison. She doesn't want to be responsible for the compounded horrors of that situation.

She already bears responsibility for something just as horrible.

No: what she did was much more horrible.

✦ ✦ ✦

A TAXI HONKED on Park Avenue; the air brakes of an eighteen-wheeler screamed. Morning light filtered through the sheer drapes behind the thick velvet curtains, dust motes floating in the beams. A room-service tray was littered with uneaten toast, half-eaten eggs, slivers of crisp bacon, chunks of hash-brown potatoes. A silver pot of coffee and a china cup sat on an end table, the aroma filling the room, the pot gleaming in the sunlight.

Torres's blood was spreading in silent pools from his head and chest, soaking the carpet.

The baby cried out again.

A tremendous amount of information ran through Kate's brain in a fraction of a second. She knew about Torres's wife, the one who'd died a few years earlier from complications following routine surgery. That was old information.

Kate didn't have the new information about a new woman or a baby. Kate had done some research: what hotel and room, how many bodyguards, stationed where, when. She'd also done some planning: how to get from D.C. to NYC secretly, how to move between stations and destinations, where to dispose of the weapon, how to exit the hotel.

But she'd been lazy and sloppy and impatient. She hadn't done enough research; she hadn't been exhaustive. She hadn't learned everything there was to learn.

So here was this surprise, this young woman standing in the doorway to the bedroom in the hotel suite at the Waldorf-Astoria, turning her head in the direction of the noise of the crying baby, unable to fight the irrepressible instinct to tend to her child. Unaware that by breaking eye contact with Kate, by severing the human connection created by their gazes, she was allowing Kate to do the worst thing she'd ever done.

This was Kate's fault. It was her failure to plan the mission carefully. This was why she was going to march into her supervisor's office tomorrow, and resign.

In the next room, the baby cried again. Kate pulled the trigger.

✦ ✦ ✦

Kate glances down at the sugar container, considers the microphone hidden there. It was barely two hours ago that she was a mile to the north, across the river, plotting out her deal with Hayden. And now here she is, living it.

It isn't part of her deal to take these two into custody, or even to participate in their arrest. She simply has to get them to admit to everything, which she has nearly accomplished. And tomorrow she has to transfer the twenty-four million euros into a slush fund for covert ops in Europe. Which she herself is going to run.

"Do you need something from Dexter, to access your half of the money?"

Julia nods. But nodding isn't good enough. "What?" Kate asks.

"I need the account number. I have the user IDs and passwords, but I don't know the account number."

Dexter also nods. It's finally time. He reaches into his jacket pocket, withdraws a piece of paper. But Kate grabs his wrist.

He turns to her quizzically. Everyone is confused, unsure of what's going on. Even Kate: she's surprised at the strength of her urge to forgiveness. Impossible to resist. She knows this is because of Julia's pregnancy, turning a beastly villain into a sympathetic heroine, just like that. Kate is now rooting for Julia, not against her. For the most part.

Kate's left hand is wrapped around Dexter's wrist, the small piece of paper folded up in his fist. With her right hand she upends the sugar tray, dumping the contents onto the table. She picks out the transmitter between thumb and forefinger, and holds it up for everyone to see. All eyebrows raise.

Kate drops the transmitter into her wineglass. "You have one minute," she says, "maybe two."

Julia darts her eyes between the transmitter in Kate's glass and the account number in Dexter's hand. Kate carefully topples her glass, spilling the wine and the frizzled device onto the tablecloth. Creating a reason, an excuse, why the thing suddenly stopped functioning.

"You can't have the money." Kate says. The dark red wine has already spread through the cloth, tendrils reaching out through the fibers from the pool. That same pattern, again. "But if you move fast, you can have your freedom."

Julia and Bill stand quickly but not panicked, not drawing attention.

"Walk through the hotel lobby," Kate continues, "and downstairs, and out the back entrance to the side street."

Julia is pulling her bag onto her shoulder. She stares at Kate, a hodgepodge of emotion filling her face. Bill grabs her elbow, already taking his first step away from the table, from the Moores, from the money.

"Good luck," Kate says.

Julia turns back to Kate and Dexter. She smiles fleetingly, her eyes crinkled at the corners, her mouth open as if to say something. But she doesn't. Then she turns again.

Kate watches them merge into the flow of the dense crowd, all the streetlights and lamplights ignited in the Carrefour de l'Odéon, a little red Fiat beeping at a bright green Vespa that's weaving in the traffic, the policeman oblivious while he continues to flirt with the pretty girl, cigarette smoke wafting from tables filled with wineglasses and tumblers and carafes and bottles, plates of ham and slabs of foie-gras terrine and napkin-lined baskets of crusty sliced baguette, women wearing scarves knotted at the neck and men in plaid sport jackets, peals of laughter and playful smirks, hand-shaking and cheek-kissing, saying hello and waving good-bye, in the thick lively humanity of early night in the City of Light, where a pair of expats is quickly but quietly disappearing.

ACKNOWLEDGMENTS

Thanks to the heroic readers of earlier, crappier versions: Adam Sachs, Amy Scheibe, Jamaica Kincaid, Jane Friesen, and Sonny Mehta.

To agent David Gernert, and his colleagues Rebecca Gardner and Sarah Burnes.

To Crown publishers Molly Stern and Maya Mavjee, editor Zachary Wagman, production editor Terry Deal, and all the other people in New York who helped transform a manuscript into a published book.

To editor Angus Cargill at Faber and Faber in London, as well as publishing director Hannah Griffiths and publisher Stephen Page.

To Michael Rudell and Jeffrey Dupler for legal guidance; to Sylvie Rabineau for film guidance; to Layla Demay for French guidance; and to Amy Williams for writing guidance.

To the ladies of Luxembourg: Becky Neal, Binda Haines, Christina Kampe, Cora Demeneix, Cristina Bjorn, Jules Brown, and Mandip Sumby.

To Kevin Mitnick, author of the fascinating *The Art of Intrusion,* my primary background about hacking. But note that the cyber-theft in *The Expats* is of a completely fictional nature, whose particulars are entirely make-believe. As are the logistics I've described of working in and resigning from the Central Intelligence Agency.

To the staffs at Soho House in New York and Coffee Lounge in Luxembourg, who were nice to me while I sat around writing this book.

And to my beautiful wife, Madeline McIntosh, the smartest person I know.